Murder
in
County Tyrone

The Irish Mysteries – Book One

PADRAIG O'HANNON

DEDICATION

To Miss McLeod

ACKNOWLEDGMENTS

Thank you to all the wonderful people who helped bring this book to fruition. To those that have treated me unkindly over the years, through harsh words, actions, or indifference — thank you. You've helped me write better villains. And to my friends and family who have, through the years, shown support and kindness even when it hasn't been deserved — thank you. You've helped remind me what is best in humanity, and what we can become when we are free to dream.

CHAPTER ONE

"She's a beautiful apple, that's for sure. Lovely to look at; sweet and tasty, no doubt. But the core; the core is poison, Johnny. Poison!"

The words echoed in my head, an endless cycle that miraculously eclipsed the pounding of what would undoubtedly be a memorable hangover. It was not how I expected my day to end, but yesterday had been anything but ordinary...

One day ago...

I had long since come to grips with the fact that I was a disappointment. A hack, to be precise; a well-off hack, but a hack nevertheless having long since settled on the notion that good enough was, in fact, exactly that. It wasn't, of course, but I'd stopped giving it much real thought.

Grandiose notions of changing the world and righting wrongs accented my youthful days. Law was not my first love, or really my love at all. Other choices would have been much more to my liking but I convinced myself that having food and shelter was ultimately more desirable. The result was abundance in all areas except happiness. Perhaps my choice of career was at fault, but harsh reality told me the problem stared back at me from the mirror.

Oh, it had started nobly! I eventually became one of a bevy of Assistant District Attorneys, most of us hell-bent on saving the world. Years of plea bargains and watching the guilty walk free removed most of the surviving luster. Eventually, I opened my own practice as a defense attorney but was equally miserable albeit with much better compensation for my troubles; ridiculously so, in fact. A few dozen lucrative cases, a significant inheritance, and some wise investments made for a fat bank account. The fact that I spent precious little kept it that way.

I called off for the day. My current gig was at a local company doing fraud investigation and light legal work. It sounded more exciting than it really was and rarely, if ever, required my best effort. Hell, it rarely required my third best but it was, as they say, something to do.

Days would dawn with notions of grandiose projects and ideas, none of which ever came to fruition. Instead, my time would be pissed away pointlessly on my computer or halfheartedly pursuing the hobby du-jour. Add the inane futility of social media and it would be bedtime before I had accomplished anything. Today wasn't shaping up to be any different. The morning had evaporated before I realized it; only the growling of my stomach interrupted my pointlessness.

Fish and chips at O'Brien's would be the perfect lunch to inspire an afternoon of greatness! I took my normal shortcut, forming an undeniably witty diatribe about parking lot design as I drove. Time to contemplate the finer points of my wording was in abundance as I meandered carefully through the well-manicured obstacle course. Oh, how the world of social media would undoubtedly be agog at my latest revelation!

When I finally emerged onto the street, the flashing blue lights in my rear-view mirror derailed my thoughts. The cop chirped his siren.

Dammit. Not only was this interfering with my lunch plans but also interrupted the music playing in my car. "The Peeler's Jacket," a traditional Irish tune, would have to wait.

In the mirror, I watched the cop talking; first on his radio, then on a cell phone. Odd! My relationship with the police force had waxed and waned over the years but never to the point of having my time intentionally wasted. After a brief delay, he donned his hat and exited his vehicle, looking mildly bewildered as he approached my window.

"License and Registration, please."

I handed him the paperwork, saying nothing. He glanced at them only fleetingly before returning them to me.

"Mister Costa? John Costa, the attorney?" he said, hesitantly.

I looked at him, pausing briefly to frown before nodding my head.

He adjusted his hat, nervously. "Sir, this is a little bit out of the ordinary, but my Captain would like to talk to you; now, if at all possible."

He was right. It was not only out of the ordinary, but damned improper. I noted his name and badge number.

"Who is your Captain, officer Sellig?"

"Captain O'Neil, sir. I believe you know him."

Know him? He was the first to accuse me of embracing evil when I left the D.A.'s office. It was hollow, though. I had won a hard-fought acquittal for his cousin, a police officer brought up on charges stemming from a shooting. It was the last case that I felt good about. Unlike many of the people for whom I had earned freedom, his cousin was actually innocent.

I decided to push back gently to see how serious O'Neil might be. "I have a phone, officer, and he's more than welcome to call me there. I'll even write my number down to save him the trouble, but I need to get going if there isn't anything else."

"Sir, he thought you might react that way, so he told me to tell you that it is in regard to Angela Grady."

Dammit. Why her? Of all the names the young policeman could have mentioned, hers was the least expected. Discordant thoughts raced through my head while butterflies mercilessly teased my heart. Yes, butterflies: the foolish, adolescent reaction that should not exist in a man whose prime had likely arrived and passed without flourish. Yet they lingered, faithfully appearing at the slightest thought or mention of her name.

3

The first time I saw her was indelibly etched in my memory. She walked through my department on her way to a meeting, but for me, the entire universe stopped. The shapely, slender blonde was achingly beautiful; to me, unparalleled. As we mingled through the normal course of work, I found her to be a delightful conversationalist, friendly, warm, and kind. The pedestal upon which Angela Grady stood soared to implausible heights. Infatuation had never known such a warm and welcoming home!

It was then that the notions, the foolish notions, germinated. Talking with her, even briefly, unfailingly lifted my spirits; a kindred energy flowed. Perhaps we shared a common swatch in the fabric of life; we could be friends; or more.

It was a sad day when she told me that she had given her notice to our employer. Outwardly, I forced smiles and positive words, all while secretly brooding. My motives were, of course, totally selfish. I knew all too well that time, any time, with Angela would soon become a precious commodity; and I was right.

I endeavored to stay in touch after her final day. Much to my pleasure, she occasionally replied although frequent periods of silence dominated our electronic conversations. On those rare occasions when we met for lunch, her vibrant conversation unfailingly rekindled the foolish ideas that refused to be banished. But whenever our friendship seemed on the verge of taking root, she would vanish, leaving me grasping for ephemeral threads of hope.

I was, at best, in her far periphery. In truth, she served as a bittersweet reminder of the hollow shell that my existence had become: an empty life, pursued vicariously through the warped, electronic looking glass of social media. To this, she stood in discordant opposition; her life, what glimpses of it I got, seemed full, joyous, and free. Perhaps it was best that I remain in a distant orbit around her star. I had nothing to offer that could improve upon her current situation. Still, in spite of my numerous shortcomings, the dream that was Angela Grady refused to be exorcised. It lingered, rising and falling with her whims. No wonder I drank too much and slept poorly.

"Sir?"

My heart sank as a troubling thought arrived. "Oh my God, is she okay? Did something happen to her?" I blurted.

4

"Nothing has happened, sir. There is a police matter regarding her that the Captain can explain in more detail. Honestly sir that is the limit of my knowledge on it. Whatever is going on, he's been pretty tight-lipped about it."

"A police matter?" My voice dripped with incredulity.

I couldn't think of anyone less likely to garner interest from the police unless perhaps young Officer Sellig was looking for a date. I was the wrong guy to facilitate that, and sadly, the lovely Angela was already involved with a tall, chiseled, and thoroughly superficial man she met at work. I didn't know him well but loathed him simply out of principle. I forced a laugh, to which he did not respond. My eyes narrowed. "You're serious, aren't you?"

He nodded, his expression unchanged.

The smile, such as it was, left my face. "I think, officer, this conversation has reached a conclusion. Am I free to go?"

"Of course you are. The Captain figured you'd react this way, so he told me to tell you one thing before you go."

"And that is?" as I reached impatiently for my keys.

"The Captain says to tell you, *please.*"

Dammit. Why did he have to say please? He didn't say it often, reserving the word for only the most serious situations. My lips briefly wrinkled in annoyance, as my eyes closed. "Okay. I guess I didn't really need lunch today, anyway."

"Thank you. He's waiting for you at the township police station."

"Do I get an escort, complete with siren?"

Sellig cast a dry, humorless smile in my direction, shaking his head as he returned to his car.

So much for excitement! I found a convenient location to turn around and headed toward the police station. Dammit. I hate surprises.

* * *

5

George O'Neil hadn't changed much; perhaps a bit heavier and grayer. Stress and time had long since etched his face, making his real age difficult to determine. His green eyes peered over the thick rim of his reading glasses. They had lost none of their life or intensity.

"Using your officers as a messenger service, are we? I'm not sure the taxpayers would approve!"

"Costa, you snarky bastard!" he growled, trying to sound angry. "Sorry about the fire drill. I would have called you, but I wasn't sure I'd get your attention."

I smirked, but he was right; my voice mail queue didn't always earn a rapid reply. It wasn't disinterest, but after leaving my former world, nothing that happened to me was ever urgent. "Well, you've got my curiosity piqued. By the way, you owe me lunch!"

We shook hands, his dwarfing mine. He was a large and powerful man, both mentally and physically. "Good luck collecting on that!" He took his time as he returned to his desk, taking a moment to stare at me before speaking. "We need to talk about your girlfriend, Angela Grady."

His choice of words caught me off guard. "My girlfriend?" I said, nearly coughing. "I'd hardly call her that; friends, perhaps, with a generous application of the term. Acquaintances might be more accurate." I hated saying it, but it sadly rang true. "Truth is, most times she can barely be bothered with me. In the last few months, we've had lunch a couple of times, and I've sent a handful of emails; sometimes she replies; usually doesn't. And that, my friend, is the hard, cold truth of the matter. I guess at my age, in spite of my obvious good looks, I should be happy to get any attention at all!" I sighed, shifting in my chair. "But what I get, George, is precious little and certainly nothing even remotely romantic."

He ignored my attempt at self-deprecating humor, offering not a hint of a smile. "You may find yourself glad that's the case," he said, removing his glasses. The wrinkles on his face seemed to be amplified whenever O'Neil was serious. They were screaming, but I was still stubbornly deaf to their protestations.

My brow wrinkled as mischievous thoughts danced. "I'm having trouble finding the downside here, George. Smart, friendly, beautiful, sexy as hell; yeah, I definitely want to be spared from *her!*" My face was probably wearing that stupid, dreamy expression that it would get when I thought about Angela. "I appreciate your interest in my non-existent love life, but exactly what is this all about?"

O'Neil remained stone-faced, speaking in an emotionless deadpan. "I'm so glad you're not a sarcastic son of a bitch. Whether you realize it or not, I'm trying to help you. John; how much do you know about her? I mean *really* know?"

He had that look about him — the look that all good cops have perfected: The look of a man who knew more than he was telling.

I softened my scowl, sighing. "Not a tremendous amount, to be honest." In our conversations, Angela had shared only snippets of her past, and then only relatively recent events.

"And your feelings for her, John?" he asked, his green eyes searing the recesses of my soul. Whatever O'Neil was interested in, he wasn't being subtle in his line of questions. Perhaps it was the imperceptible hesitation in my voice before answering or maybe my face flushed involuntarily. Either way, O'Neil, the consummate cop, had his answer before a single word left my lips. His voice sank. "That's what I was afraid of."

He stared at me, silently, for a disconcertingly long time. "I've got someone that you need to meet today," he said, glancing at something on his desk. "He's been in town for a while and is eager to talk to you. And don't give me any of that bullshit about being busy. We both know you're not going to accomplish anything world-shattering today, don't we?"

He had smacked the lonely, sad truth that was my life squarely on the head. I mumbled a few meaningless protestations in reply.

"You'll like this guy although you might not care much for what he has to say. He's a long-time Belfast cop dating back to the days of Royal Ulster Constabulary. He even knows all those silly old Irish songs like you do."

I always felt George O'Neil and I might have been switched at birth, at least in name. He had the perfect name for an archetypal Irish policeman but had no interest whatsoever in his ancestry. My Italian last name, a gift from my father, gave no clue to my deep Celtic roots. I interrupted before he could say whatever was going to follow. "Belfast? As in Ireland?"

"Technically the United Kingdom, but yes. You do know Miss Grady was born there, right?"

I nodded hesitantly. "Exactly what the hell is going on here, George?"

He flipped through some pages in a slender file. "Born in Belfast, or so we believe. Came here for college about twelve years ago, earned her United States citizenship, and has a spotless record." His voice trailed off, impatiently. "Look, John, meet with this guy. The drinks will be going on his expense report, so the worst that will come of it is you'll get free booze."

Booze? That sounded alright, but expense report? "His trip is of an official nature, then?"

O'Neil grunted, offering me only a brief nod.

"Well, don't be so forthcoming with the facts, George."

"This whole thing is a bit unusual and I'm not really at liberty to say any more. But I will tell you this much. The guy I want you to meet is legitimate, and that comes from multiple places including his direct supervisor." O'Neil hadn't cracked a smile since shaking my hand.

"Damn," I sighed. "Should I be taking my lawyer with me?"

O'Neil laughed. "No, but in case you've forgotten, you are a lawyer, dumb ass."

"You've never heard that the person that represents themselves has a fool for a client?" I was trying to coax more information by adding levity but O'Neil wasn't budging.

"Look," he said, with an air of minor exasperation, "tonight is more about listening and learning; I know - you're not good at either, but it would be good for you to pretend, at least for an evening. He'll be at your watering hole around five tonight. Be there, will you?"

"This guy got a name? How will I know him?"

"He'll know you, and for Christ's sake take a cab! He likes his scotch and beer every bit as much as you do, and I'm not going to bail your stupid ass out of jail if you don't take my advice."

"I actually prefer Irish whiskey, to be honest."

"Oh, you know what the hell I mean," he growled. "Just be there, dammit. I wouldn't ask if it wasn't important."

* * *

You may find yourself glad that's the case…

Over and over, O'Neil's voice replayed in my mind, warring with my long-held desire for precisely the opposite. His words were a harsh and personal rebuke of Angela Grady. Even worse, they came from a man I fundamentally trusted which made their bite abysmally painful. I struggled to view the situation with rationality, if for no reason other than to quell my mind's relentless raging. What had Angela gotten into?

I fought to convince myself: whatever it is, she *has* to be unwittingly involved.

She was a witness and doesn't realize what she saw…

She's the victim of extortion…

Forced to be a drug mule…

Family members in trouble…

The list roared on and on, providing no satisfaction until…

The damned boyfriend has involved her in something! The bastard!

It provided a short-term shunt for my obsession, but proved unsatisfactory. Somehow, my gut knew it wasn't the case.

My hand hesitantly reached for the power button on my computer, but veered away. Not only was I unskilled at searching, a small portion of me dreaded what I might find.

Driven more by nervous energy than purpose, I scanned a week's worth of newspapers. The results were fruitless and brought no satisfaction. Mentally exhausted, I settled on denial, repeating a mantra until a false smile nervously crossed my face.

They've got the wrong person.

They've got the wrong person.

My gut didn't like that answer, either, but it quieted my mind enough to think of other things. Perhaps I could will it to be the truth. Clock watching gave way to pacing until finally, the appointed time arrived. I dialed the number for a cab.

* * *

My pub seemed abnormally crowded given the time of day. It turned out to be an illusion, though. The nice weather had made the outdoor tables popular; the interior was exactly as I liked it: quiet.

I was immediately greeted by the wide, pleasant smile of Laura, an attractive young woman with gently curled brown hair, an intoxicating smile, and eyes that danced with the fire of a powerful intellect. A graduate student working her way through college, she seemed destined for success.

"Good evening, Mister C!" My suspicion was that her smile was as much in anticipation of my generous tips as it was in her delight to see me. "A gentleman is expecting you."

I lowered my voice, turning my head so that only she could hear. "I've never met him. What is he like?"

"He seems nice enough; was polite to me, at least, and what a beautiful accent! I've seated him in a quiet spot around the corner so you two could talk." She flashed a mischievous smile in my direction. "I've been hoping you'd bring a date here, but this isn't quite what I expected." Her eyes twinkled from behind her wire-frame glasses.

I gave her a sly wink. "You keep turning me down so I had to look elsewhere! You're always telling me to live a little, so a blind date seemed the thing to do."

She smiled, returning my wink. It was a long-running joke between us, and she could enjoy briefly having the upper hand. She disappeared behind the bar and into the kitchen. She, like Angela, made me wish I were younger.

The corner booth awaited, and with it some answers. Hopefully.

CHAPTER TWO

"Jim Finnegan," he said, offering me his hand. He looked distinguished; his dark hair and beard were both interspersed with hints of gray. I guessed that he was ten years my senior; more perhaps. There was timelessness to him; one of those men that would likely remain unchanged until old. No sooner had I completed shaking the man's hand than a pint of Guinness appeared before me.

"Thought we'd get things off to a proper start," he said in an unmistakable brogue.

"Thank you. Slainte!"

"Slainte, and thank *you*," as he joined me in a drink. "I appreciate you being willing to meet me, especially last minute and all. Hungry?"

Small talk and food occupied the better part of the next hour. Neither of us seemed willing to broach the subject that loomed over us. Instead, we talked about music, songs, all with bits of philosophy intermingled. A strange commonality punctuated parts of our conversation, paying no heed to the thousands of miles that separated us, both in terms of distance and culture.

As much as I enjoyed our conversation, I knew not to underestimate the man. Next to him in the booth was a leather flap-over case showing the unmistakable signs of aging. The pattern of wear denoted heavy use, and its seams strained to hold its contents. The open cover revealed files of various ages, all desperately competing for the limited space within.

A lull in the conversation and the arrival of another round signaled the inevitable change in our conversation. "As you no doubt have heard, I'm here to discuss your girlfriend."

Finnegan used the same puzzling description as O'Neil. I certainly didn't mind the idea, but it rang painfully hollow. "Like I told O'Neil, I wouldn't exactly use that term. In fact, the whole idea is patently ridiculous," I said, laughing, but silently sagging from my own words.

His mouth curled into a sardonic smile. "Well, perhaps you could enlighten me a bit, then, about your relationship with Miss Grady."

"Relationship? Hardly the word I'd use, sadly. We've exchanged a handful of e-mails, had lunch once or twice and that, as they say, is that. Any notion to the contrary is a foolish lark in my mind. She's much younger than I am, not to mention the fact that she's seeing someone; fairly seriously, from what I can gather. But at the heart of the issue, women like her — the nice, smart, pretty ones — aren't interested in men like me. So, I guess you could say she's my Brigid Flynn, to refer to the song."

Perhaps the lovely dark brew had loosened my tongue to excess; I was blabbering on to a nearly complete stranger.

"So," I continued, "call her what you like, but there simply isn't anything there and barring a miracle there's scant chance there ever will be." I drank deeply from my pint glass. "So there. Now you know that in addition to being an incurable romantic I'm also an old fool."

He smiled, but he had that same knowing look that O'Neil had shown earlier. Dammit, I needed to learn how to do that. Unerringly, he quietly recited my song reference.

Now there's little Brigid Flynn,
Sure it's her I'd love to win,
But she never has an eye for me...

He followed it with a sip. "For starters," he said, returning his glass to the table, "when you stop being a romantic and appreciating lovely ladies, you might as well be dead. So live happy with that."

"Appreciation," I said, peering at him over the rim of my pint glass, "is not a suitable substitute for an occasional tumble in the heather now, is it?"

Finnegan laughed. "No, it isn't but I argue that you can't have one without the other."

I smiled politely, trying to stave off the sweeping sadness that lurked within. "Arguably true, but irrelevant to the situation at hand. All of the appreciation in the world doesn't change the fact that she's frolicking elsewhere."

His eyes narrowed, his focus becoming momentarily distant. "Think what you will, but you might be interested to know that she's unattached at the moment. The party you referred to has vacated the scene. Packed up; gone."

I raised a single, inquisitive eyebrow while sipping my drink and using every ounce of available energy to control my expression. Inside, however, I was fluttering like a teenager and not the least bit disappointed by the news. "That is surprising. They seemed to get along well from all indications. Not that I'm privy to specifics, mind you, but simple deduction and observation."

"Seems that he thought better of continuing the relationship; rather suddenly, too. Right around the time I chatted with him, I think, in surroundings not too dissimilar from this." He paused to survey the room, his expression darkening. "Funny what people do in the interest of self-preservation."

Self-Preservation? What in the hell did he mean by that? And exactly what could be said in a barroom conversation that would end a long and serious relationship virtually on the spot? Finnegan knew the answer. He knew, dammit, and was toying with me.

My face must have revealed my internal turmoil because he quickly changed his demeanor. "You don't give yourself enough credit, my friend. You've made quite an impression with her; enough so that your name comes up rather frequently between her and her friends — more so recently, which is one of the reasons that I'm so keen to talk to you. Whatever you guys talked about the last time you had lunch seemed to pique her interest."

How the hell did he know this stuff? My eyes narrowed as I returned my drink to the table. Whatever Finnegan was working on was something serious. A theory entered my mind, and my heart ached with guilt that I had even thought of it: *Angela Grady's a con artist looking for a victim.*

Sadly, it all made sense. It also explained the rapid exodus of her current lover, especially if compelling evidence was available. Even O'Neil's cryptic words fell into place as the notion unfolded in my mind. Gullibility, it would seem, could be added to my lengthy list of character flaws.

Before I could speak he continued, as if reading my thoughts. "In case you're wondering, from what we can tell she hasn't a clue about your financial status. I think it will likely come as a pleasant surprise, but it isn't what has piqued her interest." He watched me twist on the end of the rope for a bit before adding, "The Patriot Act is a wonderful thing for law enforcement, don't you think?"

Patriot Act? What the hell is she involved in? My silence apparently answered his question.

"You've probably guessed that I didn't come all this way to play some sort of half-assed matchmaker. Not that I'd mind seeing you with a fine Irish lady, Johnny, you seem to be a decent man, but we're not talking about a fine Irish lady here." His voice darkened noticeably as he reached for his case.

My brow wrinkled as I regained my focus. "Now just a minute! Angela is one of the finest people I've ever met; not a hint of malice or impropriety from her. You've not gotten to your point yet, but you're intimating something different from everything I've seen from her; and frankly, it is a bit upsetting; a damn bit, to be honest!" The volume of my voice raised enough for Laura to glance my direction, concern flooding her face.

I regretted my outburst almost immediately. Perhaps it was the beer or perhaps I was merely guilty of letting the wrong head do the thinking. Obviously, whatever waited within his briefcase was enough to earn him a trip here. More than that, it had obviously held sufficient merit to authorize surveillance. The smoke, vague as it was, seemed to have some fire with it.

"Take a drink, John," he said his tone calming. "If nothing else, hear me out. Worst that happens is we drink, agree to disagree, and things with you and Miss Grady take whatever course they might. On the other hand, I could be saving you from a world of pain."

I took a few deep breaths. If George O'Neil believed things were serious enough to arrange this meeting, I owed it to him to hear Finnegan out. "Sorry. Didn't mean to over-react there."

"An apology isn't necessary. You reacted like a man defending the honor of his lady. It seems," he sighed, "that the winsome Miss Grady has hooked your heart a little deeper than you are willing to admit. You're probably not going to like much of what I have to say from here on."

Finnegan was developing an annoying habit of being right about me. He had undoubtedly done his homework well. I motioned for him to continue.

"I take it you've heard of Strabane," abruptly changing the subject.

"Sure. A town in County Tyrone, right along the west border of Northern Ireland. Why?"

"In 1998, a bomb exploded there — you may recall it from the news. Thirty-two people were killed making it the worst during *The Troubles*." He pulled some files from his case, pausing to select what appeared to be the oldest and most weathered folder. He dried the table with a napkin and then slid a large color photograph to me. "This is the aftermath."

The picture showed a desperate, chaotic scene with burned cars, police, and ambulances everywhere. Other pictures, taken by citizens, were even more graphic. "It was intended to kill," I muttered as I studied the horrible picture.

"That was our conclusion, too. The positioning of the car ensured casualties. Property was an afterthought." He paused, sipping his beer. "It bore the hallmarks of an IRA car bomb. The explosive was

Semtex, likely purchased through Libya, but we've never been able to trace it. Oddly, though, no claim of responsibility was ever made, nor was a warning given. The only good news, if there is such a thing, is that it went off when it did. An hour later and we'd be talking about a hundred casualties or more."

"Why were so many people in the area that day?"

"It was a market day. The car with the bomb had a vendor placard so nobody gave it a second look. The locals would park early then go off to get a bite to eat before the market opened. The fact that the car sat unattended for a while was not so unusual."

Shaking my head was the only response offered. "I remember bits and pieces of this from the news, but I thought that the responsible parties had been captured and convicted."

Finnegan's expression grew briefly distant. "Nothing like this is ever done alone. It requires knowledge and skill, but it also requires connections - people to get things that aren't widely available. Somewhere in the network, there's always a weak link and that's where we make our discoveries. The car used, a Vauxhall, was nicked from a widow in Mullingar six months prior. To show you how much she drove the thing, it took her nearly two months to realize it was missing! Her entire family was thoroughly investigated, of course, but we came up empty. See this?" He slid me another picture.

"What am I looking at?"

"This is the only bit of the car that told us much of anything, other than the vehicle ID, of course. The car had been repainted."

I nodded. A curved section of metal had shed a single fleck of blue paint, no bigger than a fingernail. The underlying tan color, the car's original hue, was revealed.

"The paint gave us the first real break in the case. We wore out a fair bit of shoe leather tracking it down, but we found the young fella that painted the car. I think he should be considered victim thirty-three, to be honest." A note of sadness tinged Finnegan's voice.

"What happened to him?"

Finnegan sighed, and took a long drink. "I don't think he was the sharpest knife in the set, John, and didn't really understand the severity of what he was facing. He was worried about his painting license being suspended. License? Hell, the fool was looking at a life sentence. Once that finally dawned on him, it didn't take much to get him to finger his friend. I'm betting you've heard the name Donny Cassidy?"

"Vaguely familiar, but I can't recall any specifics." My glass seemed to be emptying itself at an alarming rate, a condition which Laura efficiently remedied.

"When the painter talked, we thought we would be done with this case in six months. But Donny Cassidy didn't crack; he's a hard man, that one. I'd say he was silent out of fear. Hard to think of Donny being scared of anyone, but something surely kept him quiet. Fourteen years and a life sentence later, he's still not said a word."

"All this time and he's not had second thoughts?"

"If he has, it has been between him and God. We pop around to interview him from time to time, and he always gives us the same stone-faced treatment. He's declined to be interviewed for television, authors, you name it. One group tried to get him a new trial, and he wouldn't even speak to them. Whatever he was afraid of in 1998, he is still afraid of today."

"And the painter?"

Finnegan cast his eyes downward. "He never made it to trial. A fight broke out in the jail where he was being held, and he ended up with a knife in his heart."

"The weak link," I muttered. "He had to be silenced."

"We know that now, but at the time we had no idea how big this would become."

"Big? It seems to me that you have all the key players. Go home and sleep well."

"Cassidy pinched the car, of that we're certain, and likely transported the explosives, but he's hardly capable of building a bomb. He's a thug. And one thing is doubly certain: he didn't drive the car to Strabane and set the timer. He was in jail the entire weekend; one hundred kilometers away! And Cassidy didn't get the vendor permit to park the car; that was done by a woman."

My heart sank with these words. I had visions of a younger, impressionable Angela being tricked or coerced into purchasing a permit. "And you think Angela is that woman?" I asked, somewhat fearful of his answer.

"I do not. The permit was purchased by Mary Delane. It was only through some good fortune that we found her. We had a few fingerprints from the permit application form that we had never been able to match. Mary was arrested on a minor drug charge a few months later, and the computers flagged her prints as a likely match. Another piece of the puzzle had fallen in to place or so we thought. Exactly like Cassidy, she refused to talk; offered no defense, and silently took the maximum sentence."

I could see wistfulness enter Finnegan's face. "Go on."

"She was played, and horribly, too. A few months before the bombing, she learned that she had cancer — an aggressive form, and likely terminal. I can't even imagine what was going through her mind, but somehow they were able to convince her that she'd be doing something meaningful — helping to free Ireland or something like that, I suppose. Damn reprehensible."

I couldn't disagree with him. "Donny Cassidy and the painter don't seem the type that would be able to engineer something with that level of subtlety. I'm guessing there are others."

He nodded, raising an eyebrow. "She's a sad case, truly. I don't think she ever expected the bomb to go off in a public area like it did. She was told the target was a police station, and the car with the permit was a distraction. To me, she's truly victim thirty-four."

"Understandable. Did she finally talk?"

Finnegan paused briefly, seemingly to collect himself. "The prison system gave her the best care they could, but it became obvious that her fate was sealed. The priest at the prison was finally able to get through to her; convinced her to set things as right as she could before meeting the almighty."

"A deathbed confession isn't firm legal footing," I said, peering at him with one raised eyebrow. "Especially if she was on pain medication or sedated."

His voice sank. "I know it, but she did shed some light on the few details she knew, and we were able to verify everything she said. The most important detail, however, was the name of the person behind the bombing; the person that drove the car, arranged the details, and set the timer. The real terrorist and the name that has haunted me for a dozen years." He grabbed a napkin, wrote on it, folded it, and then handed it to me.

My heart was thumping, and a sick feeling rose in the pit of my stomach. I hesitated for a moment before opening it.

Siobhan O'Connor.

My spirits lifted, and my lips curled into a small smile upon seeing the name. "Siobhan O'Connor? The way you've been building this up, I expected to see Angela's name," setting the napkin down, noticeably relieved.

He looked at me with cold, unflinching eyes. "Might as well have been." It wasn't what I wanted to hear, and he knew it. He reached into a file, handing a single paper to me. "Mary helped us with a sketch of the woman she knew as Siobhan." I was devastated; the resemblance to Angela unmistakable.

"Several witnesses also remembered seeing a blonde woman leaving the area of the market that morning. They were too far away to provide positive identification, but you have to admit that a pattern is forming."

"Sure, but it is all circumstantial evidence, at best, Finnegan, and thin. You'll be lucky to even get it to trial with what you've got; and a conviction? You simply haven't got the coffin nails, my friend. With what you've shared, I'd destroy you in court — and I'm not even all that good." Hearing my own words calmed my agitated stomach.

He smiled that knowing smile again. "I see the solicitor has made an appearance! What if I told you that I can place Angela Grady, definitively, within twenty kilometers of Strabane on the previous night?"

"What of it? I can place forty thousand people there — likely a few of them are blonde women, too"

He continued, undeterred. "She was visiting a friend who neatly vouched for her, of course. It didn't sit well with me then, and it doesn't now. I tried to break the story or the alibi, dammit, I tried. I investigated Angela, her family, her friends for over a year. Questioned them all several times. Nothing. All of them had strong alibis. Somehow, the answer was there in front of me," he said, gesturing to his stack of files, "but I've never been able to get that coffin nail, as you put it."

I frowned at him. "You've been on this case for fourteen years?"

"From the beginning. There hasn't been a day pass where I haven't given it some thought." Finnegan sighed, motioning for another round of Guinness. He handed me a picture of a young police officer. "That fine young man was my brother, Johnny. He was assigned to the market that day. He was near the car when the bomb went off."

"I'm sorry, Jim, I didn't know. I feel bad to say this, but that fact weakens your standing. Makes it even easier for some scumbag like me to tear apart your case."

He nodded. "All the more reason for me to be incredibly patient and thorough. I knew I was going in the right direction, but your lady friend went off to the United States, and there wasn't a damn thing I could do about it; we had no cause to hold her, just that nagging voice in my head. I ran at least two dozen other leads in the interim, but none of them went anywhere. So I was dead in the water."

He took another deep drink from his beer. "Until last year."

My eyes narrowed as he opened a thin, fresh file. He passed me a picture of a camera. I returned a puzzled look. By now, I figured confusion was becoming a permanently implanted expression.

"An old fellow living right across the street from the market had a few pictures left on his roll of film. He decided to take a walk that morning and used up the rest of it along the way. He tossed the camera in a drawer when he got home." He handed me several pictures and continued talking.

"He made the unfortunate, and fatal, decision to attend the market shortly thereafter. In all the confusion, the camera was simply neglected. It surfaced again last year when a nephew found it going through the old man's things. On a lark, he thought it would be fun to have the pictures developed. Once he figured out what he had, he brought it all to us. The lab has confirmed the age and authenticity of the photographs. You're looking at Strabane shortly before the explosion."

Finnegan continued talking, but my world had stopped when I reached the third picture. It was blurry and grainy, but it contained the unmistakable image of a slender, blonde woman in the immediate vicinity of the car. Her face was turned slightly away from the camera and partially shaded by her hat. Although I couldn't be certain if it was shadow, or merely a detail lost in the blur, her right hand appeared to be resting lightly on the door as if having recently closed it.

The picture answered so many questions. It was a dangerous bit of evidence, even though it was less than conclusive. Given the right circumstances, it could earn an indictment; a skilled prosecutor might be able to ride it to a conviction if Angela's alibi or defense was weak. The specter of modern photographic enhancement technology only made the prognosis worse.

He stopped talking abruptly as my attention was obviously diverted. I handed the pictures back to him, attempting to look indifferent. I must have done a poor job of it, because he cast me a knowing, slightly sorrowful look.

"Not a coffin nail as it stands, but the hammer is in my hand. The lab is working on enhancing it, and from there, the facial recognition specialists will get their say."

He passed me a picture of a younger Angela, looking as lovely as ever. "There she is from about 1998. Now you see why the trail seems to always lead back to her."

My head sunk deeply into my hands, my fingers desperately trying to pry away the headache that was building at my temples. Between the beer and Finnegan's relentless indictment of Angela Grady, I had little viable defense.

He turned serious, his voice deepening. "The results of the

analysis are due any time now. If it is positive, I don't need to tell you what's going to happen. My government is prepared to initiate extradition procedures, and things are likely to get damn ugly on both sides of the pond."

"You'll get to strut around proud as a peacock," I said, sarcastically. "You'll be the hero, Finnegan."

He smiled. "I'd be lying if I tried to tell you it won't be damn satisfying to finally arrest her, but I won't truly rest well until a guilty verdict is read and that heavy prison door slams shut. For good."

"And what if she's innocent? Are you so convinced of her guilt that you'll stop at nothing to get the verdict you want?"

"You've really got it bad, don't you?"

"Why are you telling me all this? Seems a bit, well, improper."

"In all my time, I've never shared details of an active case, and it was difficult to convince my superiors, but they eventually agreed."

"Why now, and why me?"

"It is mostly as a favor to O'Neil. Death surrounds Angela Grady, and he doesn't want to see you become the next victim. My reasons are less altruistic. You're one of the few people with the financial wherewithal and connections to help her escape. You're smitten, my friend, and you might not think rationally if she turns to you for help. Not only do I have no desire to chase her around the world, I don't want to see you destroy yourself for a false hope. Take my advice."

"And that is?" I interrupted.

"Stay well away from her. If that proves to be impossible, however, do everyone a favor and tell her to stay put and hire a good attorney. As much as I want to close this case, it will be a hollow victory without an airtight verdict against a stout defense. Or a tell-all confession — that would work, but I don't see that happening."

I raised my eyebrows, nodding halfheartedly. "This is unbelievable; it's all so utterly out of character."

"It *is* out of character for the Angela Grady that you've seen; the one that has been meticulously created. You've fallen for an illusion, my friend, and you've placed that illusion so far up on a pedestal that you're not thinking straight. For your own sake, stay the hell out of it. All that money of yours can't change the past, and it can't change who she really is."

"I can't wrap my head around this whole thing. I understand what you're saying to me; I really do. I even understand, on some level, that you think you're helping me. Perhaps you are and I'm too drunk or stupid to realize it. But I've looked into her eyes, those lovely, sparkling eyes, and I see kindness and warmth; not a hint of the evil you say hides there. I see beauty — unmarred and genuine!"

"She's a beautiful apple, that's for sure. Lovely to look at; sweet and tasty, no doubt. But the core; the core is poison, Johnny. Poison!"

CHAPTER THREE

My pounding headache would have to take a back seat to my curiosity, although its protests were duly noted. It was already nearing noon, so I called my employer and took the rest of the week off. My boss didn't seem too happy with the late notice, but I didn't care. My eyes reluctantly focused on the computer screen. Coffee and painkillers would be my close friend for the next few hours.

The Strabane bombing was as painful to research as it had been to hear the previous evening. The tales of the survivors, many of whom had lost loved ones, were especially difficult to read. There had been no closure. Cassidy's silence, the death of Mary Delane, and the government's dubious stance on Siobhan O'Connor had left them feeling empty-handed — and rightfully so. She was officially declared to be imaginary; attributed, conveniently, as an IRA pseudonym. Even to my untrained eye it looked like official spin.

I finally summoned the nerve to search the Internet for Angela Grady. Hours later I had learned nothing new. I drifted back to a social networking site where we were connected and stared at pictures of Angela, smiling and happy. The dark, beautiful eyes that looked back at me from the screen could not possibly hold the malice and wickedness Finnegan claimed.

If, as Finnegan professed, extradition was imminent there *had* to be more to the case than a blurry picture and fourteen years of a detective's obsession. I didn't know, nor could I imagine, what it might be. The little voice in my head told me to stay out of it. The damn churning in my gut wouldn't let me.

* * *

My headache was finally easing as I dialed Jerry Keynes, a master information broker. Our paths had crossed many years earlier while working on a case I was otherwise destined to lose. He had a unique collection of friends and contacts that, for a fee, could learn things. It was always best not to ask how; simply pay and enjoy the benefits. This time, though, I feared my request was going to be a stretch even for Jerry's formidable talents, but I didn't have many options.

"Jerry," I said as he answered the phone, "Jack Costa." Jerry had always called me Jack for reasons he never explained. I went along with it.

"Long time, man," he replied. I could almost smell the scent of his cigarette through the phone. He smoked almost continuously.

"I know it; how are things?"

"Things? Things are things, my brother. Still kicking, so I guess that is a good thing."

"It is. I've got a challenge for you if you're in the mood."

"Ha!" he said, gruffly, "I knew you weren't calling to discuss the weather. What has it been? Three, four years?"

I realized that there could be a blizzard going outside. I'd not so much as peeked out the window the entire day. "Hey - nothing stopping you from calling me."

"True that," he growled, "I guess I don't like you enough to call! Does your challenge come with the appropriate funding to make it happen?"

"Of course! This is a tough one, so it comes with a bit extra if you can pull it off."

He grunted something unintelligible. He hadn't hung up the phone, though.

"And I'm in a bit of a hurry."

"Everyone is always in such a goddamned hurry these days," coughing mildly. "No wonder we're all going to get cancer." I held my tongue. He'd heard plenty from me and damn near everyone else about his smoking. "Okay. What do you need, Jack?"

"Hopefully you know someone that can poke around the State Department a bit for me." My comment was met with silence on the other end of the line.

"State?" I could almost see him suddenly sitting up in his chair, likely working on a thousand reasons why he couldn't do it. All of which would raise the price. "You're not asking for much, are you?" coughing.

"Maybe less than you think. I don't need anything specific or secret, but it would be nice to know if the UK, Northern Ireland, in particular, has made any overtures regarding extraditing a US citizen recently. You know — if there's been any water cooler chatter or the like."

"This citizen of yours got a name?" I viewed the fact that we were still conversing as a positive sign.

"Angela Grady, a friend of mine. A Belfast detective believes she's mixed up in a 1998 bombing; even claims to have been close to arresting her back in the day. He's quite a skilled operator, though, so I don't know how much of his story is factual. If State is getting rumblings, though, I'll know."

"State plays things like that pretty close to the vest depending on which way the political winds are blowing. Assuming I know someone, which I'm not saying I do, it isn't going to come cheaply."

"Don't break any laws but the price is not an object here; speed is." I probably sounded desperate and it was going to be expensive, but I didn't care.

"Damn. I've never heard you say that before, Jack. This gal must be really important to you," he rasped.

"She is, I think. And Jerry, if you happen to stumble across anything else about her that you think I should know, don't hold it back thinking you're helping me. I need to know everything — the good and

27

the bad."

"You do realize, of course," his voice brusque with cigarette smoke, "that I would not hesitate to kick you when you're down. If what you're telling me pans out and State is truly involved, you might want to stay the hell out of it. At best, it is a good way to have your name on some lists you really don't want to be on."

"You're the third person that has told me that."

"Are you going to be smart enough to listen to any of us?" he asked, coughing.

"Depends on what you find."

"In other words, probably not."

* * *

I had slept poorly, unable to quiet my thoughts. Even Irish whiskey had failed to work its usual restful magic. The morning brought no clarity to my mind. Breakfast hadn't sat well, either. All made for one hell of a fine day.

My heart won the battle that raged within. Fighting trembling hands, I sent Angela a text message:

```
It's Costa.
The police are asking about you.
Do not text me. Call me ASAP!
Please. This is not a joke.
```

I took a deep breath and hit send. I tossed my phone on my desk and stared off into space. My expectations were low; Angela had not been good at corresponding so I could easily foresee her ignoring my message.

Several hours passed with no response. Part of me wanted to turn off my phone and get drunk. If she didn't want my help, she could deal with Jim Finnegan on her own. But that stupid little part of me, the part that fervently clung to unrealistic hopes, wouldn't let me. I tried one more time.

```
Please call.
```

The cop was named Finnegan.

I tried to focus on other things, but I found myself staring at the phone, occasionally hitting its button to verify it was still on. I must have jumped a foot in the air when it finally rang!

"Angela," I said, "don't say anything. My text message was not in jest, and this isn't some stupid prank. Please agree that I am your legal counsel and this conversation is covered under attorney-client privilege." Maybe it would hold up in court, but against terrorism-focused surveillance, it seemed almost pointless.

"Sure," she said, quietly, in the gentle tone that had forever imprinted itself in my memory. Her voice seemed weaker than the last time I heard it, and I thought I detected a slight quiver in its tone. Perhaps the inclusion of Finnegan's name had shaken her. Hell, it should. He had shaken me up, and I wasn't even the subject of his obsession.

"We need to meet. I don't want to say much over the phone. Attorney-Client privilege or not, I'd rather be careful. Please, can we meet?"

I was met with silence, although I could hear that we were still connected. I made one final appeal. "Look, I'm not drunk, I'm not going crazy, and this isn't a damn joke. Jim Finnegan seems to be the real deal, and he's not saying things about you that are pleasant to hear."

I wasn't sure if I heard crying on the other end of the line, or whether it was one of the many random noises phones pick up. Either way, her voice immediately betrayed her feelings. It was distinctly shaking as she quietly asked, "Where do you want to meet?"

I directed her to the nearest mall. "Leave your phone in the car when you get there," I said. "Is an hour enough time?"

"It is."

* * *

My heart raced to improbable levels when Angela Grady first came into my view. She looked every bit as lovely as the first day I'd seen her although her face bore a far more serious expression than I'd ever noticed. It looked to me like she'd spent a bit of time getting ready — I

29

was fully prepared for a ponytail and sweat pants. Instead, her hair was neatly arranged, gently waved, and flowing over her shoulders; she wore a stylish gray dress that flattered her figure. Hell, anything flattered *her* figure.

As she approached, her look of concern eased into a smile as she saw me. It wasn't the biggest smile I'd ever seen from her, but given the circumstances, I was glad to be greeted with anything other than a scowl. I extended my right hand, but she moved right past it into a brief, but firm hug.

"You look tired," she said, sitting down across from me at the table.

"I've had more than a bit of trouble sleeping recently," I said. "I'd like to go elsewhere if that's alright. I want to get us somewhere out in the open where eavesdropping isn't as easy. You're going to have to trust me."

She still looked mildly bewildered but agreed. As we walked together to the nearest exit, I looked around nervously. Suddenly, everyone looked suspicious and interested in us. I convinced myself that it was merely my imagination running in its highest gear.

* * *

We arrived at a nearby park via a circuitous route. It didn't seem that we were followed, but I lacked the experience to truly know. The day was pleasant; were it not for the onerous subject of our impending conversation, I might have actually enjoyed it. We took a short walk to a shaded picnic table.

"I've always liked this park," she said, her eyes glancing around. "It reminds me of one that I enjoyed while growing up."

I smiled. It had always invoked similar childhood memories for me. "I grew up near a park like this, too. It had a giant sliding board. Today, it would be deemed far too dangerous, of course. But at the time we didn't know any better, so we just had fun. It took me a while to get up the nerve to climb all the way to the top."

The truth was that as a kid, I was an absolute and total chicken. Perhaps some part of that had never left me. I struggled to move on to

30

the inevitably unpleasant subject. I would have been perfectly happy to stare into her eyes forever.

She seemed equally disinclined to broach the subject, but finally the smile left her face. "You met Jim Finnegan, I take it?"

"Yes," I said, reluctantly. "I was on my way home from lunch when one of the local cops pulled me over. I know his captain fairly well, a man named O'Neil, and that's how I ended up with Jim Finnegan. I had no idea what I was getting into."

She stared off into space as she nervously ran her right hand through her hair, fluffing it. "I thought the nightmare was over," a tear quietly ran down her cheek.

"I'm so sorry, but I don't think you're going to care for what I have to say. He caught me totally off guard."

Unpleasant recognition crossed her face. "That's his way. "It's Strabane, isn't it?"

I nodded.

She shook her head. "I went through this a dozen years ago, John. Nothing has changed."

The words stumbled from my lips; it felt surreal, like I was slightly detached and that another person was speaking. "He has new evidence, Angela. A photograph from the morning of the explosion has surfaced. Finnegan claims that you're in the picture. They are running enhancement and analysis on it to determine if a warrant for your arrest will be issued."

She put her elbows on the table, resting her head in her hands, her expression pained. "This cannot be happening," she muttered, her fingers probing her temples as her gaze eventually turned skyward.

I found myself desperately lacking the right words. "I can't say it enough — I'm deeply sorry to have to be the one to tell you this." I felt sick.

With her head still in her hands, she quietly spoke. "I need to know, John. In your heart, do you believe him?"

It was an easy question to answer. "Meeting him was the intellectual equivalent of a sucker punch. When I left the bar the other night, I honestly didn't know what to believe. When I saw you this morning, though, I knew the truth. No — I don't believe him." The words felt right; for the first time since meeting Finnegan, the world seemed somehow in order.

Angela looked at me with teary eyes and smiled. She reached across the table, clasping her hands around mine, firmly. "Thank you," she said. "You have no idea how much that means to me."

I held her hands silently while she composed herself, finally easing my hands away so she could dry her tears.

"Finnegan was a nightmare for us. My only crime was having blonde hair and picking that particular weekend to visit my best friend from school. We had a delightful time together, short as it was, and I drove home. Nothing more. Once Finnegan found me, he never looked elsewhere. He investigated my entire family, questioned all of us, repeatedly. We eventually had to hire a solicitor and threaten to bring him up on harassment claims. It was the only thing that would break his obsession with me. Coming to the States was something I had long planned to do. Finnegan delayed it several months; it almost cost me my scholarship."

"His behavior does seem a bit obsessive to me, no doubt. I also find it odd that he neglected to mention the harassment issue."

"It doesn't surprise me. Knowing him, his meeting with you was completely one-sided."

I nodded, smiling. "Yes; totally his show."

"Initially, we gave him some latitude; the poor man having lost his brother and all. That turned out to be a big mistake; only seemed to add fuel his fire. And now he's at it again." Her voice drifted off, wistfully.

"That does appear to be the case. And with terrorism legislation the way it is, there may be less we can do to control him. I'm sorry to say I think this is fairly serious."

"I can't believe this." She stared at the sky as a cloud drifted silently past the sun, shaking her head. Gradually, composure returned,

32

her voice carrying an air of quiet resignation. "What do you recommend?"

"Well, first off, it sounds like you need someone digging into the case that is actually looking to prove your innocence. You also need a good extradition lawyer. I've got a couple of names I can give you; people I've worked with and can vouch for, but hopefully, it won't come to that."

"That means a lot to me, John, but I want you to represent me if it comes to the point that I need a lawyer."

It was not what I expected to hear. "I can certainly help with the investigation side of things. As to the legal side, I'm flattered, I really am, but I don't feel like I'm your best choice. I've never argued an extradition case in my life, and honestly, I'm not that good."

"Yes, you are. I believe in you. More than that, I want someone that knows and believes in me."

After several rounds of pointless debate, I reluctantly agreed; There was no convincing her otherwise. Perhaps the stress of the day had depleted her to the point where she was no longer thinking rationally. I could try again another day, but I wasn't optimistic. I had seen that look from her while we worked together and I lacked the mettle to resist.

We drove back to her car in awkward silence. She was deep in thought, and I found myself awkwardly lacking words. It was a rare condition for me to suffer, seemingly never lacking a clever turn of phrase or humorous analogy. I just couldn't find one suitable for the situation.

She directed me to her car. "Thank you." The look in her eyes broke my heart.

"Are you going to be okay?"

"I'll be alright; I'm meeting several of my friends this afternoon, and the rest of the week is fairly busy, too. That should help take my mind off of all this for a while."

"Good. I'm going to get things set up on my end to work on this. We'll start by going through the details and your recollections. It won't be fun to dredge it up, but until we know exactly what we're up against, if anything, this is our best course of action. It is going to be a fair amount of work; you'll probably be good and sick of me by the time this is all sorted out."

"I doubt that," she said, gently touching my arm. "Call me when you're ready to start."

We looked at each other in silence for a moment. I took her hand, spontaneously kissing it gently. "We'll get through this," I said, giving it a squeeze. "I promise."

She nodded, squeezing my hand before returning to her car.

I wasn't entirely sure I could keep my promise.

CHAPTER FOUR

Angela's scent lingered in my car, tantalizing my every breath as I drove home. I needed to focus on the task at hand and not on the thoughts that danced through my imagination.

Dammit. I should have listened to George O'Neil and the chorus of voices telling me to stay away! I was already in over my head and I knew it. I needed help; I needed the best damn researcher and technical expert I'd ever met: Jillian MacDonald — or, as I called her, Mack.

Her voice sounded strong and energetic as she answered the phone. "Hi John!"

"Mack, I've got this case; well, it is a bit of a long story, actually. Could turn out to be a false alarm, but between us, I don't think so. We need to dredge up details on a case that is almost fifteen years old."

Her voice twinkled with interest. "You have a case? It sounds interesting, but are you sure this is something you want to do?" Mack was half my age but she understood my demons better than anyone. An old soul, wise beyond her years, she was undoubtedly my best friend.

"I don't really have a lot of choice. It has sort of fallen in my lap, and now a friend is counting on me."

"You'll do wonderfully," she said. "How can I help?"

"Mack, you're the one person I can count on. Thank you."

"I haven't said yes yet," she reminded me. "I need to hear the important details."

"And I thought I could count on the goodness of your heart," I said, trying to sound surprised.

"You can," she said tartly, "I answered the phone, didn't I?"

"This thing is likely to keep us busy for quite a while. Nothing official has happened yet, but I want to get out in front of it as best we can and as quickly as possible. Mack, I don't think I can do this without you." I probably sounded desperate.

She paused before speaking, her voice becoming serious. "This must really be important to you."

"It is. Are you interested?"

"Interested enough to talk further, at least. I've got a few things I'm working on that I'll need to wrap up. That'll take me a few days if you can wait that long."

"No worries. My place is a mess and will easily take a couple days to get ready."

* * *

Cleaning and organizing proved to be both cathartic and exhausting, mercifully leaving my mind largely devoid of the energy necessary to churn on the enigma that was Angela Grady. A call signaled Mack's impending arrival and launched a flurry of last-minute preparations.

"I've cleared off a second work area in my office," I said gesturing toward what had originally been intended as a dining room.

She sat down at the desk, habitually fluffing her long red hair in her hand as she surveyed the area. "This will work, but I'll probably need more filing space. I'm kinda old school that way."

Old school! It always amused me when someone born long after I had graduated from college used that term. "Here is some light reading," I said, pointing to an article on my computer's screen. "Read through it while I take a quick shower. We'll discuss it over lunch."

* * *

"I'm going to try to meet with Angela tomorrow if she's feeling up to it. She was pretty shaken to learn all this, as might be expected."

"Understandable," she said, nibbling on her food.

"I'm a bit worried about her, to be honest. Not only the case, but how she's going to be able to handle all of this."

"Of course you are. Worrying is your true talent in life; you've said so yourself. She's a big girl, John, and this isn't the first time she's had to deal with this. Give her a bit more credit."

I gave her a frustrated look, refusing to acknowledge that, as usual, she was absolutely right. Perhaps I was secretly guilty of wanting to be Angela's knight in shining armor. One wasn't needed; she had done a fine job at living life for over thirty years without my help. Worse, I felt more like a Quixotic caricature, complete with a sad mule and rusted spear. Mack was a damn sight smarter than Sancho Panza, though, and a hell of a lot better looking.

"I like her, Mack; a damn lot; never had the nerve or the opportunity to let her know." I surprised myself a bit by blurting it aloud with such little provocation.

If she reacted to my earth-shattering news, it was not noticeable. "I know it."

The stupid, dreamy expression left my face. "You do? How?"

"It's quite obvious…"

"That didn't answer the question," I said, peering over the top of my water glass, trying to look annoyed.

"I know because I'm a woman and I'm smarter than you." She was right on both counts. "Have you seriously considered telling her how you feel?"

"I've played it over and over in my head countless times. It all sounds good until I look in the mirror and see an old fool staring back."

Mack looked at me, shaking her head. "Has it occurred to you that she may already know?"

I blushed involuntarily, coughing on the small sip of water I had taken.

She laughed. "I knew before you said anything. What makes you think she's any less perceptive than I am?"

I collected myself, my face still flushed. "Well, for starters, you know me a lot better than she does. Secondly, I've been careful in what I've said and how I've acted in those precious few times when Angela and I have been together. At the end of the day, I keep convincing myself to be satisfied as a casual acquaintance and fleeting glimpses would be all I'd ever know of her."

Her expression remained unconvinced. "It would seem, though, that fate has changed that."

"So it does. We're going to get to know each other fairly well, but without a drop of romance. That's my life, Mack."

"I only have one more question for you, John. What if we get into this and find out that the Belfast cop is right? I'm sorry, but I've got to ask the question. With your feelings for her, it would be heartbreaking; what are you going to do?"

Mack's penchant for brutal honesty delivered at key moments was one of the reasons I loved her so damn much. My eyes drifted, unfocused, into the distance. "I really haven't gotten that far." The answer was desperately truthful. "I'd like to think it will never come to that."

My response was hollow and she knew it. "You still haven't answered my question." Her face betrayed amused annoyance at my continued efforts to circumvent her question.

"I'm going to give it everything I've got." I tried to make the words ring true, and perhaps they were. The possibility that Jim Finnegan could be right was not something I allowed myself to dwell on, although I suspected the realization would be devastating.

"And hope you can live with yourself," she said, looking at me with a knowing smile.

I swirled my water glass, my eyes blankly following its motion. "And hope I can live with myself."

"I feel a bit sorry for her. You too, for that matter."

"Why is that?"

"You've got her so far up on a pedestal, the poor girl doesn't have anywhere to go but down. You'll end up hurt by the realization that she's human."

I had no witty reply. Mercifully, Mack allowed me to steer the conversation back to my meeting with Finnegan.

* * *

We finished lunch and consumed the afternoon with an unpleasantly expensive shopping trip for office supplies and equipment. Mack seemed to draw pleasure from my endless flow of miserly protestations, threatening a bevy of additional, frivolous purchases in response. She departed as the afternoon ceded to the calm of a pleasant evening.

I poured a small glass of whiskey and sat in front of the computer, staring aimlessly at a map of Strabane. I replayed my meeting with Angela in my head analyzing every detail of my recollection, struggling to find any reaction that seemed false or out of place.

The ringing of my phone startled me. The number wasn't familiar to me, and I briefly debated allowing it to fall to voice mail. Curiosity compelled me to answer.

"Costa," I answered, my mind still elsewhere.

A familiar voice replied. "Hi, John; Jim Finnegan."

He hardly needed to introduce himself. I had placed his voice on the first syllable, and it snapped my focus sharply back to reality. "Good evening, Jim."

"Have you broken the bad news to your lady friend yet."

He was fishing for information, but he wasn't the only one would could play the game. "I expect that you already know the answer to that if your surveillance is anywhere near as good as you claim it to be."

Finnegan laughed heartily. "I hope the both of you had a lovely time in the park the other day. I have to say, you make a cute couple, all things considered, although she seemed a bit upset toward the end."

Jim Finnegan was still playing from a position of power and was enjoying every minute of it. "Impressive," I said, trying to sound indifferent. "Our conversation was private. I hope you had the decency to respect that."

"Of course."

"That's good to hear, especially since I'm currently Miss Grady's legal counsel, and our conversations are subject to attorney-client privilege. It would be unfortunate for your case were I to reveal violations of such an important and fundamental confidence."

There was a brief delay before he responded. I expected he was as surprised with the news as I was. "Well, can't say that I'm happy to hear this, counselor, but congratulations, I guess. Remember what I said about people that get too close to that thorny rose." His voice to trailed off.

"I'd hate to think that you're attempting to engage in intimidation."

"Far from it; I merely want you going in with your eyes open and your back well-watched. If you happen to find yourself with a spare moment this evening, take the time to look up Maggie Albin. To help you out a bit, she was from Drumquin, a wee spot not too far from Omagh. Not all that far from Strabane, either."

"Still sounds like a veiled threat..." I wrote down the name, anyway.

"Not at all. Besides, it is all moot at the moment since she's not been charged with anything. Yet. Just a conversation between friends." His voice darkened, turning serious. "You'll get all this as part of the discovery process, anyway, either over here or there. Think of it as a preview of coming attractions."

There was an air of inevitability in his tone, especially whenever the notion of a trial entered the conversation. "If you're so eager to be helpful, why not send over the entire case file?"

"I'll talk to my superiors and see what else they're willing to share with you. I know you think I'm obsessed. Maybe I am, but the obsession is in finding the truth, not hanging Angela Grady. I'm doing the only thing I know how to do; follow the evidence and listen to my gut instincts along the way. Sorry for you that the road always leads to the same place."

"They say," I added, "that insanity is defined as repeating the same action and expecting different results."

Finnegan chuckled. "That might be true. I guarantee if you ask her about me, she will question my sanity; stay around her long enough and you might, too. She's a master of manipulation, my friend. Everything about her is the result of careful, precise, and deliberate planning. Think about it; can you name anything about her that isn't meticulously crafted?"

"Everyone is image-conscious these days," I replied, "doubly so for women given all the unrealistic standards that movies and television set for them."

"You didn't answer my question."

"Have a good evening, Jim. I'm enjoying a fine bit of whiskey at the moment. Perhaps you should consider doing the same."

I heard a gentle laugh from the other end of the line. "Look up that name, will you?"

"What am I going to find?"

"More questions. If there were answers, Angela would be living out her days in Hydebank Wood Prison. But the questions need answers. The truth has to mean something to someone or we're all lost. It means a fair bit to you, I'd say; something to not lose sight of. Be well, Johnny."

* * *

Finnegan had a way of pulling my strings and it was damned

annoying. After nearly an hour of fruitless searching I found the subject of his call. Maggie Albin of Drumquin was killed when her car veered off the road and crashed violently. The newspaper article, hastily scanned, showed the image of a mangled car; below it was her senior picture from the Garrett academy in Belfast.

I studied the location of the wreck. The road was typical of many that snaked through the western part of county Tyrone; scenic and picturesque, but narrow, curved, and certainly not designed with speed in mind. Maggie's fatal crash happened at a curve that looked to be deceptively sharp. Inexperience; inebriation; speed; all deadly. To me it seemed like an unfortunate but clear-cut case of a young person making a poor decision; one that proved to be fatal.

It was a poignant story, but the connection to the case remained elusive. I stared at it for several more minutes before something finally caught my eye. The name of the school listed in the article seemed familiar but I couldn't place it. Another search finally revealed the answer: Angela and Maggie attended the same school. This was Finnegan's way of telling me who Angela had visited on that fateful weekend.

My phone chirped, signaling the arrival of a text message. Somehow, I knew that it would be Jim Finnegan, a step ahead of me as always.

```
Maggie was allergic to alcohol.
Gave her hives and anaphylaxis. She never
drank.
No hives on her body when they pulled her
from the wreck.
```

A second chirp beckoned me to my phone.

```
She  had  no  friends  or  family  in  the
immediate area.
Why was she there?
Was a long way from help.
Victim 35.
```

CHAPTER FIVE

Mack arrived well before I was ready to acknowledge that a new day had dawned. I was able to summon little more than monosyllabic grunts to a flurry of questions that she unleashed. She looked at me with an irritated expression to which I could respond with only a shrug. Groggily, I wrote *Maggie Albin* on a scrap of paper and staggered back to bed.

I wasn't sure how much time had passed, but the next time I woke up, the sun was quite bright. Mack was nowhere to be found, so I devoted my attention to preparing coffee and breakfast. The effort produced burned toast and a slightly-underdone egg, but at least the coffee was tolerable. A shower helped complete an unsatisfying morning ritual. The terrifying prospect of Angela's impending arrival was the only reason I had gotten up at all.

A file covered my keyboard. An attached note read, "Going to the library." I hated libraries. Mack, on the other hand, could squeeze a library for all it was worth; she knew all the tricks, both in terms of research and dealing with ill-humored librarians. It also meant that she was on the trail of something that was likely both germane and interesting.

She also uncovered a few more details pertaining to the death of Maggie Albin that reinforced the notion that her death had never been satisfactorily explained. The official finding was vague and disturbingly incomplete, mentioning intoxication but completely ignoring her allergy. In spite of this, it was officially declared an accident and closed accordingly.

* * *

I invited her in trying not to appear nervous, although inside I was in shambles. Angela Grady was standing in my foyer; imagine the odds!

"Good Morning," I said, hugging her. "How have things been going?"

"Well enough," she said. "My friends know something is wrong, but I didn't elaborate. My mother knows all of it, though. She called early this morning and could tell right away just from the sound of my voice that something was wrong. I hope it is okay that I told her; I've never been able to lie to her without her knowing."

"Oh, it's fine. I understand completely. My mother always had a way of knowing, too. Are you ready to start?"

"I am," she said, sounding much stronger than when last we spoke.

"First," I said, offering her a chair in my office, "I need to explain to you what is going on from a legal perspective and what the steps are. Now, that said, all of this might be a giant ruse from our Irish friend. Keep that in mind at all times."

"What do you mean?"

"He could be trying to goad you into behavior that he can interpret as questionable or risky. For example, I do not recommend any significant travel. He could twist a perfectly innocent trip into deeming you a flight risk."

"So you're telling me that I'm sort of under arrest already?"

"I suppose you can look at it that way, unfortunately. Technically, you're as free as anyone. I recommend that you manage impressions and appearances carefully, though."

"I understand. I just don't care for it."

I nodded. "It is merely advice, not a dictum. And, truthfully, nothing happens from a legal perspective until the UK makes a formal request to our State Department. I've got someone nosing around to see if any of those conversations are going on. I don't know if we'll get anything from that, but it is worth a few bucks to try."

"So nothing official has happened yet that you know of?"

"Not that I know of, but we'll need to be ready in case that changes. Have you reconsidered your choice of attorney? I still have those names."

"I haven't. I simply can't afford it, to be honest." Her expression grew distant as she peered into space. "I'm not going to ask my family for any more help with this. It tore us up emotionally the last time and I know it set us back financially."

"Money is unimportant, Angela; it is your *life* we're talking about here." I tried hard to emphasize my point. It didn't seem to be working.

"I just don't want to do that to my ma. She's worried enough already — I don't want to burden her with the financial thing."

"I'm sorry — don't mean to be nosy, but I always had the impression you were rather well off."

"I was doing well enough, but was a tad careless with my money, I admit it. I thought that my relationship was going in a certain direction, but all that has abruptly changed. The new job didn't work out so I've been using my savings to keep afloat. I'll probably have to move, and now damn Finnegan is trying to put me in prison for something I had nothing to do with. I know you've always thought of me as unfailingly positive, but it has been a bit tough lately."

"Understandable. I need you to be sharply focused on what we're doing. If finances become a distraction, let me know."

"Got it," she said, forcing an unconvincing smile.

I launched into a lengthy explanation of the entire extradition process and the various possibilities that might unfold. An alarming number of scenarios ended with her going to prison.

"You know," she mused, looking off into space, "a couple of days ago I was thinking about things like paying my rent and looking for a job. They suddenly don't seem quite as important."

"I can," I said, "be brutally honest at times. I want you to know what we're up against and to make a wise decision regarding your representation."

Her eyes returned to meet mine. "I *have* made a wise decision."

My gut fluttered, and suddenly I wanted to kiss her. It was a stupid and hopelessly improper notion, but there it was, nevertheless. The sound of a key turning in the door interrupted any thoughts or ambitions that I had. Probably for the best.

"I'm back," Mack announced, loudly. Angela gave me a look of surprise.

"That's Mack," I said. "Er... Um... I mean... Jillian MacDonald; the best damn researcher I've ever met. I've hired her to help us."

Angela smiled, nodding at me, her expression easing.

"Mack! Angela and I are in the office starting to go over the case details."

"Nice to meet you," she said to Angela. "You two go ahead with whatever you were doing, I'll take notes if that's alright."

Go ahead with whatever we were doing; an interesting choice of words, Mack! Between that and her boisterous greeting, it was almost like she had expected actions akin to the thoughts vividly dancing in my imagination. "I just finished going over the extradition process with Angela."

"Good," said Mack. "Let's walk through your recollections of the weekend."

"Let's start with the basics, Angela," I said, "and then we'll ask questions. You're likely not to care for some of what we ask about. We may press you on things, challenge you, and ask you the same thing multiple times. It isn't because we don't believe you; it is because we have to think like prosecutors to plan our investigation and ultimately build your defense. Deal?"

"Deal," she said, quietly.

I knew that she had likely been through this with Jim Finnegan a dozen years ago, but that didn't make me feel any better about it. "Please share your recollections."

Angela took a deep breath and exhaled slowly before starting to speak. "At the time, I was working as a paid intern for an advertising firm. They typically only had enough work to keep me Monday through Wednesday and then I'd have the next few days off. I was still living at home, trying to figure out what I wanted to do with my life. I used the money mostly to pay for clothes and petrol. It was a fun time up until the weekend of the Strabane incident. I had been working out plans to visit my friend..."

"Maggie Albin?" interrupted Mack.

Angela nodded, visibly sagging. "I was supposed to leave on Wednesday, but as it happened they needed me an extra day that week, so I left Thursday after work and drove to Omagh. From there, it was a short jaunt to Maggie's house. I arrived a bit after eight in the evening. It was getting toward dark, so we had a bit of food and stayed in for the evening."

"You didn't go anywhere?" Mack asked.

"We didn't. I was tired so we talked for a while, caught up on things, and went to sleep. Friday was more eventful. We took care of a few chores in the morning then went horseback riding in the afternoon. Maggie and I drove into Omagh around six. We had dinner, listened to some music, danced a bit, and then went home."

"I assume you were seen throughout all of these," I interjected.

"Maggie's mum was with us the entire morning. Maggie's neighbor let us use two of his horses. He was there when we picked them up and when we returned them."

"How long would you say you were riding?"

"A bit under four hours. It was a slow, easy pace; it was so good to get out of the city and see the countryside."

"And when you went into Omagh" I added, "were you seen?"

"I'm sure we were, and I'm sure Finnegan verified that whole bit," she said. "I used a bank card for dinner, I believe."

"How much did you drink while you were out on the town? Finnegan could claim that your memory was distorted from alcohol."

Her response was quick and emphatic. "Not a drop. I never drank around Maggie. She had a serious alcohol allergy. I never wanted her to feel pressured to fit in with the crowd."

"And you left the next morning, right?" She nodded at me, maintaining consistent eye contact. If she was lying, it was a polished and impeccable performance.

"Why did you leave so early? It doesn't seem that you two got much time together."

"We were happy for what we had. Maggie had volunteered to help prepare meals at her church that morning, and my father needed the car for business so there was no choice but to leave when I did. Strange, had one or two things worked out differently, I would have been helping Maggie at her church when all this happened, and Jim Finnegan would be meaningless to me."

"That is often how things work out," I said, nodding in empathy. "Tell us about the drive home."

"I left Maggie's house and took Gillygooley Road to where it meets up with the A5 a bit north of Omagh. I made it a bit south of town when the motor stopped running. I was fortunate enough to be near a house. The lady that lived there happened to be outside working on her garden and she helped me."

"What happened, exactly?"

"I was going to call my father, but a short time later her husband arrived. He was quite handy with cars and discovered that I was simply out of petrol. I learned later the gauge was broken. He gave me enough fuel to make it down the road to a station where I filled the car. Then I drove home. Nothing else. My father took the car on business and had a new gauge fitted at some point later."

"And how does this establish your alibi?" Mack asked.

"When I stopped, the lady popped inside to check the time because I was worried about waking my parents. I was at her house when the bomb exploded in Strabane."

"How far..." I started to ask, but she anticipated my question.

"A good twenty miles away, thirty-five minutes or so."

"And you were also seen at the station?"

"Sure I was. The young man at the till was as interested in flirting as he was in collecting payment. He seemed eager to help with everything, including dispensing the petrol."

I smiled. It was likely a condition she was used to. "And you paid for the fuel how? Cash?"

"I did."

I knew Finnegan was a good detective, but it smacked of improbability to think that he could find one young woman from a single, cash transaction. "And how did Finnegan find you, then, if you paid cash?"

"The young man remembered my name and offered up a pretty good description. I had originally handed him my card to pay, but they were having issues with their terminals. I took it back and paid cash, instead."

"I would expect that the station had security cameras. A quick check of those should have cleared this right up. I can't imagine that it wasn't part of their investigation."

"As far as I know, there were no recordings available."

"And the rest of the trip?"

"Like I said, it was thoroughly uneventful. The only thing even remotely unusual was an increase in police around the Belfast area. I didn't add it up at the time, but the news of the Strabane incident had them in a heightened state. I was just listening to music, driving along."

"And when did you learn about the Strabane Bombing?" Mack asked, stealing my next question.

"As soon as I got home. My ma had it on the telly."

"And how did it make you feel when you saw it on the news?"

The question caused Angela to pause, almost beyond perception. She refocused almost instantly. "I didn't quite know what to feel at first, I think. A combination of shock, sick to my stomach, you know; and then a bit of anger. It probably isn't smart for me to say it, but since we're being honest here, I did feel a bit angry." Her eyes left us, briefly, before returning.

"What about it made you angry?"

"I think it was a bit of the helplessness and wanting to be able to do something. I think a lot of people over here felt the same thing when the planes hit the twin towers. We were making progress toward peace; it hurt to see it happen." Her eyes remained in direct contact with mine the entire time.

"Did you go anywhere or do anything the rest of the day on Saturday? I ask because the people with you might be able to vouch for your mental state."

"I stayed in with my ma. I'm sure she can tell you that I was no different upon returning than when I left. We were rather restrained in what we did that evening, given the news."

Mack and I spent the next hour needling her about the timing of the events that morning — it seemed clear that her alibi hinged on it. No matter how we twisted and turned her story, it always came around to the same thing: *She could not have set the bomb in Strabane and been out of gas south of Omagh at the same time.* Her answers stayed simple, consistent, and focused. I decided to try a different tactic.

"Why does Finnegan think you did it?" He had provided me almost nothing to go on regarding means and motive, and this continued to gnaw at me. "Sure, you were in the area, but there were another forty-thousand with arguably better opportunity than you."

She sighed heavily as her eyes turned downward. "I have been asking myself that for almost fifteen years. Up until you mentioned his name the other day, I had almost completely rid him from my memory. Honestly, I don't think he is entirely sane. How he has stayed a policeman all these years is beyond me."

Finnegan had accurately predicted this response, but it hardly required exceptional psychological insight to do so. In Angela's shoes, I might have come to the same conclusion. "I understand why you feel that way, but has he ever shared with you anything beyond the fact that you were in the area? Like I said, lots of people were in the area. There has to be more; what motivated you to do it? How did you do it? In his mind, of course."

"He never got to the point where he totally verbalized his theory, at least not to me. He asked a fair number of questions about my academic records. I did well in school, including chemistry and science. To him, I expect that made me able to build a bomb. But John, it was just the stuff everyone over here learns in your High School classes; certainly not a class in explosives!"

I laughed, reflecting on my own efforts in high school chemistry class. "Yeah," I sighed, "I did well in chemistry, too, but have forgotten most of it, of course."

She smiled at me, "same here. I remember some of the terms, but I couldn't answer even the simplest question."

"And your motive?"

"He spent a lot of time asking political questions. I was twenty and wanted to see the world, come to America, and attend University. What did I care about politics? But that wasn't what Jim Finnegan wanted to hear. He was relentless, and when he found out that my grandfather fancied himself a rebel back in the day, it got even worse. That is when he started seriously investigating my entire family. It eventually got so intrusive that we had to hire a solicitor."

"He fancied himself a rebel?"

She laughed quietly. "He did, but nobody took him seriously, of course. He'd tell the same stories over and over again, often mixing up the details along the way. Most of them were taken directly from various songs he'd sing. Spinning the tales, even though we'd all heard them dozens of times, seemed to make him happy."

"Would you say you had a close relationship with him?"

Her face brightened. "I would; we were close. He had many grandchildren, but he always told me I was his favorite. I suspect he told the others the same, but that didn't keep me from believing him. Ever since I was little, I always looked forward to visits with him. He lived in Mullingar, so we didn't get to see him as often as we'd like. At least once or twice in the summer, though, we'd either go to see him or he would drive up and see us." The smile drifted from her face. "He moved in with us when his health started to fail; he passed when I was sixteen."

I glanced over at Mack; she returned a subtle nod. The Mullingar connection was likely coincidental, but interesting enough to pursue. I had more questions, but Angela's phone rang before I could continue.

"I need to take this," she said, looking worried as she walked into the hallway.

Mack and I busied ourselves, but it was difficult not to overhear certain words pop up in the conversation. The word *payment* was the most notable.

"I'm sorry," she said, looking distracted as she returned. "I have a few things I really need to take care of today. Can we continue tomorrow?"

"Of course," I said, standing up. "I'll walk you to your car."

Mack cast a wry smile in my direction. "Nice to meet you, Angela," she said, warmly. "See you tomorrow."

Angela smiled and waved. "Nice to meet you, too, Jillian."

As we walked quietly toward Angela's car, I finally broached the subject. "I couldn't help but overhear a few words of what you were saying. Not trying to stick my nose in where it doesn't belong, but if there is anything I can help with, please don't hesitate to speak up. If all this is unfolding with the speed and severity that Finnegan keeps intimating, we're going to need you one-hundred-percent focused on your case."

"That is sweet of you, but I can't ask you to do that. I wouldn't want you to put yourself out financially on my behalf, and given my current situation, I have no idea when I might be able to pay you back."

"I'm not the least bit worried about that, Angela. Pay me back when you can, absolutely no rush."

Her brown eyes studied my face. "Are you sure?"

"I am."

Her lips curved into a warm smile. "Okay. If you can help with my car, I should be fine on all my other bills, at least for a while. If Finnegan has his way, I won't have to worry about any of it, though, will I?"

"I don't think you would find the accommodations he has in mind the least bit suitable."

It turned out that her situation bore more urgency than she originally implied, but I was able to forestall the impending repossession of her vehicle. It had been several months since she had made a payment, and the bank's patience had grown thin. The records showed neither partial payments nor explanations. A terse lecture from the banker, a slender, middle-aged woman with short, auburn hair, followed. It was met with quiet contrition that seemed authentic to me. The banker appeared less convinced, her eyes casting me an unexpectedly disconcerting look as I silently handed her a cashier's check. It felt as if she expected to see me again. She wouldn't; I'd paid the entire balance.

Angela, for her part, thanked me repeatedly but offered little in the way of a tangible explanation for the issue. It was as if she expected her willpower or her hopefulness to solve the problem. Perhaps it had worked with me serving as the unwitting catalyst.

* * *

Angela had plans for the evening, the details of which she did not share, so she dropped me off and went on her way. Pleasant daydreams occupied my thoughts as I walked to my door. Mack was still hard at work, offering little acknowledgment of my arrival. Mild sarcasm decorated my voice as I responded to the snub. "And good afternoon to you, too, Mack!"

She peered up over the top of her monitor. "Did you ride in and save the day, Sir Galahad?"

"You smart-ass! Remind me again why I hired you?"

Mack stuck her tongue out, crossing her eyes in the process.

"Thanks, Mack. That's the best you've looked in days. But seriously, what do you think of her?"

She stopped whatever she was doing to answer. "She seems nice enough from what I've seen so far. No glaring red flags, but there is something about her that bothers me. I just get the feeling that there is more than she's telling us. It could be that all this is overwhelming to her; it could be as simple as being uncomfortable with me around. I'll need some girl-time with her to know for sure. And when I know, I'll tell you exactly as I see it."

She would. That, I could count on.

CHAPTER SIX

The gravelly voice of Jack Keynes crackled from the speaker of my cell phone.

"Make sure you read your newspaper this morning, Jack. Real interesting article from a man named Brown. You can't miss it."

I wanted to ask him more, but he had already hung up the phone. Still wearing sleeping pants and a t-shirt that had seen better weather, I opened my front door. Normally, fetching the newspaper required a trip to the driveway. Today, it was sitting proudly on my front porch.

I grabbed the thicker-than-average bag, dragging it unceremoniously into my house. Stuffed into the middle section was a simple flip-phone. It looked like something I might have used ten years prior. Pinched between its halves was a single sheet of paper.

```
Call Mister Brown. If he can answer, he
will.
     Do not leave a message.
     He will return your call as soon as
possible.
```

The phone's memory only contained one number and no name had been assigned to it. The area code, however, was Washington, D.C. I walked out on my front porch and dialed the number. A man's voice answered.

"Yes?"

"I was told to call Mister Brown."

"Ah! The lawyer. I'll tell you what I can, friend," the voice said. "A preliminary inquiry concerning Miss Grady came in to State a few weeks ago. Didn't make much of a buzz around here though, so I don't think there is much to worry about right now."

"That's good, I guess."

"I looked in to it a bit, and from what I know at this time, a provisional warrant doesn't seem to be likely. State has its hands full with some other events and isn't going to be too keen on locking up an American citizen without a pretty solid case behind it. The PR wouldn't go over real well, and we need all the help we can get in that area at the moment. Not to mention the fact that the Brits are being a bit stubborn on a somewhat similar matter. It might turn out to benefit your lady and keep her out of jail a bit longer."

"The fact that she's innocent doesn't seem to be entering the equation."

Brown laughed. "It isn't the first and foremost thing that is considered, and that really isn't up to us to decide. Besides, there's always more at stake here than people realize. Your gal's problem is just one of hundreds that come through here every day. It isn't that we don't care."

"Sounds like reasonably good news, all things considered."

"Good news for now," Brown said, emphasizing the final word, ominously. "The bad news is that the Brits are serious enough to bother with an inquiry at all. It doesn't get that far without some real cause. It may go nowhere, but that isn't usually the way these things go. More likely, they'll regroup and try again. And when they do, it will be impossible to ignore for long."

"Will you know if that happens?"

"Certainly, and yes, I'll let you know. Not that it will do you much good. Your woman is already on a few lists that nobody wants to be on; she's not going anywhere. We'll talk again when I know more. For now,

I have two pieces of advice for you. The first you've already heard from a few people and ignored. The second is this: it isn't too early to start assembling your overseas team. Choose wisely — you're going to need a good one."

Lists? At every step, the seriousness of Angela's situation reared its head. "This is probably a ridiculous question, but I'm not entirely sure what I'm up against here. Any chance I could get my hands on some case files?"

There was a disconcerting pause before Brown spoke again. "You don't ask much, do you?"

"Hey, cut me a break here. You said it yourself — State can't afford bad PR right now. On the other hand, standing up for a productive, law-abiding citizen in the face of a questionable witch-hunt could look pretty good in the eyes of the public. Worst case, she ends up going to trial, and I make it a point to put State in a good light to the press. Not much down side."

"I can see why your reputation is as it is. I'll see what I can do, but no promises."

"That's all I can ask. How should I reach you?"

"I'll contact you."

* * *

It was a beautiful day, enough so that I had spent the majority of it working from my back porch. The weather report was equally promising for the near future. I wrote Angela a quick e-mail:

```
Good morning,

    I think Mack and I have enough to keep us
busy for the next few days. The weather
outlook looks lovely, too, so if you've got
fun stuff that you'd like to do, it looks like
a good opportunity. I'll call if anything
urgent surfaces.

    Enjoy!
```

Not surprisingly, I received no reply.

* * *

I was not looking forward to calling Angela's mother, sure that the subject of our conversation would bring back unpleasant memories. Reluctantly, I dialed her number.

"Hello, may I speak to Shanagh Grady, please?"

"Speaking."

"Mrs. Grady, my name is John Costa from the United States."

"Oh yes! Of course! It is so wonderful to hear from you. Angela has spoken so warmly of you. I can't begin to say how much I appreciate the help you're giving her."

"I haven't done much yet, to be honest, but I appreciate your kind words."

"You may not think you've done much, but Angela's voice brightens whenever she speaks of you; always has."

Always has? The comment was perplexing. "Shanagh, has she brought you up to speed on what is going on over here?"

I could hear the enthusiasm drain from her voice. "That bastard Finnegan; all of his questions were answered, several times over, the last time we went through this. Someone should be investigating *him* instead of us."

"Actually, that is part of our plan. Investigating a police officer is never an easy matter, but we'll do what we can."

"I'll give you the name of the solicitor we hired to deal with Jim Finnegan. He can tell you all about him." Her voice oozed with animosity.

"Thank you. I expect it would be helpful if I could talk to him."

"There were nasty rumors about the Royal Ulster Constabulary. After that first day with Finnegan, I understood where they came from."

"If you don't mind, can you tell me what happened?"

"It was like something from a movie! They brought cars, three at least, maybe more and parked one of those drab-colored land rovers at the end of our street so nobody could get in or out. Some of them had guns; they came in with a search warrant and went through our whole house. It was terrifying. After they seemed satisfied that we didn't have any bombs or guns, Finnegan made his grand entrance. They kept us all separated, asking questions about the Strabane bombing. Where were we? What were we doing? Did anyone see us? Over and over, the same thing."

"Angela mentioned she was questioned, but she neglected to mention these details."

"I don't blame her. He spent most of his time with her, and after about thirty minutes, they hauled her away. She was crying, scared out of her wits. They wouldn't tell us where they were taking her or when she'd be back. They say the worst thing for a parent is to lose a child; this felt awfully close to how I imagine that would feel. I don't think Sean was ever the same. I certainly wasn't."

"Sean?"

"My husband; Angela's father. He died a few years after all this happened. The doctors said he had a weak heart, but he had never had a bit of a problem until Jim Finnegan entered our lives."

"I'm sorry. Angela has spoken about you frequently, but never her father. I wasn't sure of the situation."

"He died after she left for the States. When his health turned, she rushed home but it wasn't in time. It really broke her heart."

"I know the feeling." My father had never approved of my career choice and it fractured our relationship for many years. Only in the immediate years before his death did the chasm close. He ran out of time before I ran out of words of reparation I wanted to say to him.

"The police brought Angela back in the wee hours of the morning. She was shaken up pretty badly and wouldn't talk about it for days. We didn't hear anything for a few weeks and foolishly started thinking it might be over. They questioned all of us at least two more times; Angela at least double that."

"At some point, I take it, you decided to get a solicitor to defend you?"

"We did, and that is how we got the complaint filed and the questioning stopped. I must've answered the same set of questions dozens of times. No wonder the cops never smile, the lot of them. I'd get tired hearing the same answer to the same question over and over, too. I left there sick every time I was dragged in."

"It is a technique they use to detect lies, Mrs. Grady. The truth is unchanged when it is told over and over. Lies tend to morph and change, evolve. I forgot to ask you, what did Sean do for a living?"

"He was educated as an engineer, but he ended up doing more work with computers than anything else. For most of the nineties and up until he died, he was working on systems for several big grocery store chains. That's why he had to travel a fair bit. I guess it runs in the Grady blood or something. Angela loves to travel; her father loved it, as did her grandfather."

"Angela mentioned something about her grandfather fancying himself a rebel."

She laughed gently. "Oh, her Granda Connor! He did."

"Can you elaborate? Angela seemed to think that this had something to do with Finnegan's interest."

"Sure, it probably did. Connor Grady was Angela's grandfather on Sean's side. His mind had been slipping for about five years and everybody knew it. Sad to watch, really. He'd tell stories about how he lit up the Black and Tans as a young rebel, but he was mixing up song lyrics with reality. The Black and Tans were disbanded when he was only a few years old."

"That must have been hard to watch. How did Angela deal with it?"

"It got worse and worse for Connor. He started to confuse Sean for his brother George, call me Meryl at times; but he never forgot Angela. He always seemed to perk up when she visited, had a better grasp on things. We were able to move him in with us for the final few years of his life. I think it helped them both deal with things."

"Do you think there was any truth in any of his stories?"

"Oh, I seriously doubt it. If you ask me, the peak of his rebellious activities involved getting together with his old friends playing music and singing songs."

"I would have loved to hear that. I've always wanted to find myself at a pub in Ireland listening to traditional tunes. Perhaps someday. Is it alright if I call you again if I have more questions, and do you have any questions for me, Mrs. Grady?"

"You may call anytime, and I'll answer any question no matter how unpleasant. This latest kerfuffle has my stomach churning and my nerves are on edge. I've not been sleeping well ever since she told me what is going on. John, be honest with me. What do you think is going to happen?"

"It's difficult to say since I don't know exactly what we're up against. I don't want this to sound alarming or negative, but between us, I'm gearing up a full defense. Not just an extradition defense, but to be fully ready in case we have to go to trial in a Crown Court. I'm going to assemble the best team I can find. I pray that we don't need it."

"I know you'll do well and Angela will be fine. I need to take care of myself or I'm going to end up sick! I'll e-mail you that name as soon as I find it."

* * *

As difficult as it was to find the motivation to leave the comfort of my porch, I rose and returned to the drab confines of my house. Mack's eyes followed me as I grudgingly made my way to the desk.

"I cut Angela loose for a bit to enjoy the weather while we work on a few things. How did your library visit go?"

"Too early to tell, impatient one. I'm working on the Maggie Albin situation. The Internet had a foothold when all this happened, but it wasn't anywhere near what it is today. A lot of the records, news stories, and the like are public, but not digitized. Doubly so for smaller, more rural areas, so I'm going to have to do this the old fashioned way and you're just going to have to wait."

I nodded, raising my eyebrows at her appreciatively. "I've had a couple of interesting conversations this morning, Mack, and there's a few things we need to look in to as a result. I talked to Jerry when all this stuff started and someone from the State Department actually contacted me this morning. I knew Jerry was well connected, but damn!"

Mack looked at me, both surprised and impressed. "That *was* quick. You think his contact is legit?"

I knew more about Jerry than I had ever told, and I probably didn't know the half of what he had really done. His sources were eerily impeccable. "Yes, Mack, I do. I knew it the minute Jerry didn't hang up on me when I asked. We've got good news and bad coming out of Washington at the moment. The bad news is that the UK has made some overtures to State."

"So the whole extradition thing could really happen? It isn't a figment of Finnegan's imagination?" Mack reclined in her chair, a look of concern crossing her face.

"According to my source, it is *likely* to happen. The good news is that we've got a bit more time than Finnegan claims. The political winds are blowing in our favor right now. My guess is that Finnegan is trying to goad Angela into running."

She sat up, looking irritated. "That's a bit underhanded. He used you to deliver his message, didn't he?"

"He sure did, at least that is how I see it. My source told me that Angela's name is already on a few lists. I'd say they have her pretty well boxed-in, and I'm betting Finnegan knows it. He was figuring on me delivering the message and Angela ignoring my advice and running. If she did that, the UK would ask for, and probably get, a provisional warrant. Fighting it would be impossible after that, and it would likely work against her at trial."

I paused long enough to get a bottle of water from the kitchen. "My conversation with Angela's mother was quite interesting, too. They hired a solicitor and filed a complaint about Finnegan; she's going to send me the name. I think it might be worth a bit of our time to investigate our long-suffering policeman. He was in the Royal Ulster Constabulary, and all this unfolded during a time when they were under heavy pressure and scrutiny for all sorts of bad things. It was only a few years later that they were disbanded in favor of the Police Service."

Mack's blue eyes twinkled at the prospect. "As soon as I get the name from Shanagh, you're free to have at it."

Mack raised her eyebrows. "Investigating a cop can be tricky business. It is likely to get back to him."

"I don't really care. He's dancing a bit of a fine line as it is. Besides, I'd go so far as to say he expects us to give him a look."

"Well, if that is the case, I don't plan on disappointing him. He's rattled your cage quite a bit recently, seems only fair to give his a bit of a shake."

It was obvious that Mack was enjoying the prospect — perhaps a little too much. "A gentle shake, only. I don't want to reveal all your capabilities on something that is likely tangential. Use your best judgment, of course."

"Always!"

"There are a couple of family connections that we should look into. Sean Grady, Angela's father, was an engineer of some sort, although he worked in the computer field. We'll need to find out all we can on his background; specifically, could he design and build a bomb?"

"And *would* he?"

I nodded. It would be hard to quantify the intent of a man who had been dead for over ten years. "The second name doesn't concern me as much, but give it a quick look. Connor Grady was Angela's grandfather — the one from Mullingar. He probably had Alzheimer's or something similar toward the end, so I'm not expecting anything to come of it. I expect, though, that Finnegan looked into him, so we will, too."

Mack cast a briefly confused look before glancing at her computer screen. "Angela never mentioned anything about her grandfather having memory issues — the opposite actually."

"Shanagh did mention that Connor never failed to remember Angela, so perhaps she was unaware of the true degradation of his state. Either way, it is worth looking in to; see what you can find."

"This gives me more than enough to get started looking in to the

Grady family. We should probably give Shanagh's family a look as well, don't you think?"

"Probably; and Mack, run a full check on Angela. She signed all the release forms when she was here, so have at it."

Mack looked at me sheepishly. "I already started it."

"And?"

"How many times do I have to tell you to be patient?"

I retreated to the safety of the porch.

CHAPTER SEVEN

A cool breeze from the northwest ended a streak of beautiful weather. Clouds built, eventually culminating in a persistent rain that spent the afternoon challenging my resolve. The constant sound of dripping water when combined with the ceaseless clicking of Mack's keyboard cast a dismal, hypnotic pall that even strong coffee couldn't challenge. Energy, overall, was in short supply.

Finally, Mack's keyboard went silent, and she slowly rose from her chair. She looked at me with exhausted eyes, yawned, and muttered something about getting some sleep. I nodded.

"Get some rest, Mack. Sleep in if you need to."

I could tell by her face that she might, for once, actually listen to me. My designs were on a simple dinner; frozen pizza, perhaps. I rolled my eyes as my phone rang, and, uncertain of my ability or desire to carry on a conversation, contemplated letting it ring. Habitually, I glanced over, pleasantly surprised to see Angela's name on the screen.

As I reached for the phone, I realized that it was the first time that she had ever initiated contact. All of our previous conversations, even our rare meetings for lunch, had been my doing. I answered, desperately hoping that my voice didn't betray my foolish, adolescent eagerness.

"Hi John! I was wondering if you're busy tonight."

"I'm not doing a thing. Was trying to decide between frozen pizza varieties when you called. What's up?"

She paused briefly before continuing. "I was wondering if I could pop over for a bit. I can pick up some dinner if you're heart isn't set on frozen pizza."

"Sure, of course you can come over." I tried to suppress the elation that darted through me.

"I don't mean to put you out. I just want to sit and chat, like we did at lunch before all this stuff happened. Not a word about the case, I promise!"

"I promise, too — no legal stuff!"

Her voice sounded relieved. "Thanks a million. I'll see you in a bit."

"When you get here, come on in; I'll make sure the door is unlocked."

She sounded like someone who needed a friend. It was a puzzling situation since by all indications she had myriads of friends, all of which were younger, better looking, and far more active than I. But I wasn't going to spend too much time questioning my good fortune. The evening would unfold into whatever Angela had in mind.

* * *

A gentle knock on the front door was followed by the sound of it slowly opening.

"It took a bit longer than expected," Angela said. "I stopped to get a pizza for us. I think, though, you'll find it preferable to the frozen option."

"Excellent," I laughed, enjoying the humor in her choice of food. "Put it on the counter, I'll be right in."

Angela turned to me and smiled warmly. We hugged; her arms pulled me closer, holding tighter and longer than on any previous embrace. My mind raced, desperately attempting to preserve every detail of the moment; the soft, gentle scent of her perfume, the feeling of her hands against my shoulder blades. We'd hugged before, but this one carried a different energy. I dismissed the feeling as the work of my overly active imagination and nothing else, but for the moment, brief as it was, it felt wonderful.

The pizza proved to be a good decision, and dinner was dominated with lighter conversation. It was nice to laugh, but it was truly joyous to see Angela smiling and laughing. For the first time since meeting Jim Finnegan, the magic she cast on my heart had returned.

"Come on," I said, rising and motioning for her to follow. "Bring your drink with you." I led her toward the door to my music room. "I've been meaning to show you this for a while, but we've been so busy with other things I didn't want it to become a distraction."

I turned on the light switch and led her down the stairs. She stopped abruptly at the bottom of the stairs as the scope of my one indulgence came into perspective.

"My guilty pleasure," I explained. "I lack the motivation to use it to its full capabilities. I mostly come down here to blow off steam. Recording, effects, processing," I said, showing off in the most modest way possible, "everything I need to accomplish something. Everything except ambition and that creative spark. It was there many years ago, and from time to time, I still feel it. It has been such a long time since I connected with it," I said, wistfully.

"You still have it," she said, confidently. "Believing in yourself will go a long way. May I?" She pointed to a guitar that hung on the wall.

"Of course," I said, gesturing toward the instruments, "please, help yourself."

"It has been a while," she said as quiet tones slipped from the guitar's strings. "This is a tune Granda Connor taught me. Miss McLeod's reel — I don't imagine you know it, do you?"

"Actually, I do." My answer seemed to be a pleasant surprise. Her playing was rusty, but it didn't matter — she was smiling and having fun. I picked up a violin and played along. It was a mistake-filled performance that meant more to me than any that had come prior. Several more tunes followed, each every bit as inaccurate as the prior, yet joyous.

"Here," I said, turning on my rarely-used home theater, "I bet you'll enjoy this."

I showed her the cover of a concert video from a group that was a mutual favorite. She nodded eagerly in approval. "Can I get you a refill?" pointing to her now-empty wine glass.

"Please."

The introductory sounds of the concert video could be heard as I trotted up the stairs. Eagerly, I filled her wine glass and grabbed another beer before heading downstairs. Angela had taken off her shoes and was sitting cross-legged near the center of the love-seat that faced the television. I handed her the glass and sat down to her left. Her position on the narrow sofa left little opportunity to avoid sitting close. She offered no objection, and the reciprocal certainly held true.

The video ended well into the early hours of the morning. The passage of time had been unseen, during which she ended up stretched out on the sofa, her feet on my lap. At some point, I had instinctively started massaging them; no objections had been lodged so I continued, even beyond the end of the video.

I switched off the television, turning my head to look at her. Her eyes met mine, a distant expression crossing her face. "I'm scared, you know."

"I know," squeezing her feet tightly, trying my best to give a reassuring look.

"We weren't going to talk about it, I know, but I'm scared; really scared. If I keep myself busy, I can get through. Today was dreary, which didn't help, either, and things got to be a bit much."

"Any problem is amplified on a rainy day, I think. You know you're welcome to come over any time you want. I don't really have much of a life."

She swung her feet off my lap, causing me to momentarily panic that, perhaps, I had inadvertently said too much. My fears were quickly banished as she moved directly beside me, wrapping her arms around my chest, her head resting gently against my right shoulder. My right arm reflexively wrapped around her shoulder. She squeezed and I did likewise.

We stayed there silently for a long time before she whispered, "I'm tired, Johnny, so very tired." She looked up at me with her soft brown eyes, beautiful as always, but dulled with exhaustion. She had masked it well, but it was now painfully obvious that quality rest had been eluding her for many days.

I kissed the top of her head gently, "I can't really imagine what you're going through, but I'll help in any way I can."

Gradually, her grip on my chest eased slightly as I realized that she was falling asleep. From the look in her eyes earlier, I could tell it was badly needed. It was only a short time later that she jolted herself awake.

"I'm so sorry!" she said, realizing that she had drifted off. "I didn't mean to do that."

"No worries," I whispered, "I don't want you trying to drive home like this. I've got a guest room if you want to crash or I can drive you home."

"If it isn't too much trouble, I'll crash here."

* * *

The guest room was rarely used, but I kept it ready for an unlikely situation such as this. Angela sat on the side of the bed while I pointed out where she could find light switches and the like. I wasn't really sure she heard any of it, because before I could finish she had tucked herself, still fully dressed, under the top blanket. Sleep was quickly overtaking her.

"Good night," I whispered, reaching to turn off the lamp.

"Don't you leave me, Johnny…"

I hesitated, uncertain as to what she was asking. "I can sit with you a while if that will help."

She tapped the bed with her hand. "Here. I want you nearby."

I sat on the edge next to her. "How's this?"

She slid away from me. "Get under the cover with me," her voice barely winning over the fatigue.

"Okay," I said after a slightly awkward pause. I removed my shoes and hesitantly slid under the top cover. "I promise, I'll behave myself," I said, wishing instantly that I had said nothing. Embarrassed, I turned on my side, facing away from her. Either my clumsy attempt at humor hadn't been heard or it didn't bother her, because as soon as I settled into my position, she pressed close to me, putting her arm over my shoulder. She muttered something before sleep overtook her, but it was not intelligible. Her warm breath rhythmically teased the back of my neck as the bedeviling nature of my own ironic fortune kept me awake for a few moments longer. Dreamless sleep followed.

* * *

The morning found me alone in bed, still dressed and desperately wanting a shower. I never cared for the feeling after sleeping fully-clothed, but if the previous night had helped Angela rest and regain her resolve it was well worth it. Still not fully awake, I lumbered into the kitchen where I found Angela sipping on a cup of tea and eating fruit. She looked a bit unkempt, but her eyes looked refreshed and full of life.

"Good morning, John."

I started a pot of coffee then flopped down in the nearest chair. Sleep was still tenuously clinging to me; hopefully the coffee would banish it quickly. "Did you sleep well?"

"For the first time in ages, wonderfully, although it looks like you didn't. I'm sorry if I made you uncomfortable or kept you awake."

"You didn't; not in the least. Mornings following a late evening are rarely kind to me these days; I'll be back to my old self once I've gotten some coffee and a shower."

She rose, rinsing her cup and putting her plate in the dishwasher. "Speaking of which, I need to run home and do the same. I can be back after lunch if you need me today."

"Sure, that sounds good."

My attention had briefly drifted elsewhere, when her right hand gently cupped against my rough, unshaven cheek. Mildly startled, I looked up at her. She leaned over and kissed my forehead gently before silently leaving.

* * *

It was only moments after Angela's departure that Mack arrived, leaving me little time to deal with the thoughts swirling in my head. Perhaps it was the inevitable and imaginary byproduct of my foolish notions about Angela Grady, but in that brief moment as our eyes met and her lips graced my forehead, I felt a hint of reciprocity in the feelings I held for her. In the swirling maze that my mind had built, it had never considered the possibility that interest could be mutual, dismissing it as too improbable. The resulting limbo left me momentarily disoriented, albeit in a pleasurable way.

Mack gave me a strange look, somewhere between surprise, pleasure, and confusion; perhaps even a bit of anger twinged her face — I couldn't be sure.

"I just passed Angela on her way home," Mack said, suggestively. "She seemed to have a bit more spring in her step than you do." She sat in the chair that Angela had occupied only moments before, her eyes intently studying my expressions. "You're not going to tell me, are you?"

"Tell you what?" attempting to appear disinterested.

"Okay, a few short days ago you're pouring your heart out to me about this woman, and now I find her leaving your house in the morning and you look exhausted. You can't tell me your curiosity wouldn't be equally piqued."

"Well, if it means that much to you, Mack," I drawled, elongating each word to prolong her misery, "Angela brought over some dinner and ended up spending the night." Her look of shock was priceless. "And yes, since you seem to believe it to be your business, we slept together."

She remained unable to offer a coherent reply. I waited, fighting valiantly to suppress the laughter that was waiting to burst forth.

"I, uh, well, I guess I didn't know you had it in you to move so quickly," Mack said, obviously struggling to find the right words.

She was still searching for a reply when I could no longer contain my laughter. "Sorry Mack," I said, responding to fury that was building in her face, "it isn't how it sounds. She had a rough day and needed some company, nothing more. We ended up crashing in the guest room, but fully clothed, which is why I look like I do. Last night was my life in a microcosm, my friend, but at least I've gotten to the point where I can have a good laugh about it."

She glowered at me before stomping into the office.

* * *

The initial set of background reports on Angela had arrived. The more in-depth searches were still in progress, but at least we had something to start with. They confirmed my initial impressions: Angela had maintained a flawless record since arriving in the United States.

Her credit history wasn't quite as stellar, revealing a handful of late payments most of which looked like common, youthful mistakes. After correcting them, she had enjoyed a rather lengthy period of consistent finances. Recently, however, the report looked worse. The problems all seemed to roughly correspond with her departure from our one-time mutual employer.

Mack had seen this correlation and had probed a bit further.

"I used one of your shell companies," Mack said, proudly. "I called her last two employers looking for a reference and verification of employment. Told them she had applied for a position within our organization and we were doing some screening."

"And?"

"She left your company to go to a private advertising agency. She only lasted a bit over a month there, John, and they wouldn't give me any details around her departure; only verification of her time there. You know what that usually means, right?"

"Usually means they parted on less than amicable terms."

"That is the diplomatic way to phrase it. I pressed the man I talked to a bit, told him we were thinking of offering her a significant salary and an important, global role. I emphasized what an unforgiving task-master of a boss I have. How he would think nothing of firing me..."

"Mack!"

"Oh, alright. Off the record, he referred to her as unreliable and unresponsive. She did well in her interviews, looked great on paper, but delivered absolutely nothing. Her projects went nowhere, attendance issues, e-mails went unanswered — sound familiar? Your current employer would only verify that she worked there, and the woman I talked to was terse about the whole thing."

"Interesting, especially since Angela told me that she was leaving for a better opportunity. I never gave it a second thought. I can get some specifics on it the next time I bother showing up for work. At this point, we need to know the truth. I guess I'll have to remind Angela of that again."

Mack handed me another stack of papers. "Some good news here, John. Her tax and bank records are all consistent. If she's got some hidden source of income, it isn't showing up on paper. Looks like Mom helped her out a couple of times, but everything is nicely accounted for. Bad news is at the current rate, she's going to be broke in a month or two."

"Yes, she mentioned that to me, Mack."

"For at least the last five months it looks like she's been paying all the rent. Combine that with no income and you can see why she's going to have to find somewhere cheaper to live. Or get a job."

"I'll probably have to help out a bit financially. She doesn't need to be distracted with a job search; she needs to be helping us keep her out of jail."

"If you don't have a slew of things on your list to ask her, how about I get some girl-time with her this afternoon? I still have that nagging feeling about her. I know you think the world of her, John, but I just can't shake it."

"That sounds like a plan, Mack. I'll swing by work and get some of those questions answered. I'll probably give them my notice anyway. It isn't fair for me to be gone all the time, and I've got the feeling that this is going to occupy all of our time. And when I'm done there, I'm going to play golf if the ground is dry enough. Don't know when the next opportunity will show up."

"Golf? When was the last time you played?"

"It has been a few years. It is likely to be brutal, but I need a diversion."

"Good for you! See you later!"

CHAPTER EIGHT

My employer was neither surprised nor particularly disappointed by my decision to resign. My visit, more importantly, produced a few answers about Angela's departure, most of which I did not like. She had not earned widespread accolades during her time there. I had apparently been her staunchest, if not sole, professional ally. The fact that this detail had been noticed by more than several people caused me to question how subtle I had actually been in disguising my feelings. Fortunately, nobody hinted at the truth — or at least if they knew it wasn't mentioned to me.

Several themes arose when discussing her work. Reliability, honesty, work-ethic, and timeliness were regularly mentioned. The other common point of feedback was all too familiar: she was not good at answering e-mail. Ultimately, her departure had been voluntary, although likely in response to an obvious inevitability looming on the horizon. Beyond that, few details were offered.

* * *

My golf outing, much like my life, was a frustrating comedy of errors. It served, however, to clear my mind; enough so that I must have been elsewhere on my drive home. A fellow driver's displeasure was signaled by flashing headlights, horn-honking, and an aggressive pass that nearly sent me off the road.

I returned to an empty house. It was just as well as I was already feeling the consequences of my spontaneous golf outing. Undoubtedly, there would be hell to pay the next morning. My lone waiting message was an e-mail from Shanagh containing contact information for the solicitor that had helped them with Jim Finnegan years ago. A quick glance at the clock told me that it was likely too late to call so I forwarded the information to Mack.

Mack and Angela arrived some time later after what, by all appearances, was an enjoyable afternoon. Likely expensive, too; both of them were carrying several bags.

"I hope at least one of those bags has some food in it."

"Sorry," Mack said, "you two are on your own. I've got a date!"

"Mack, you've been holding out on me!"

"Not really a date, I guess. I'm watching my little nephew so her parents can go to the movies." She departed quickly. A brief moment of awkward silence was quickly broken as both of us simultaneously blurted out something about dinner. Laughing, I motioned for her to speak first.

"I was hoping we could have dinner tonight if you've not got other plans," Angela said.

"It's generally a safe assumption that I'm not doing anything. What did you have in mind?"

"There is a benefit concert at a park not too far from here. I bought two tickets when I was still with Sam. Three local bands are playing and the food is provided by local restaurants. The money all goes to a good cause. Several of my friends will be there, and they're dying to meet you. We can eat, chat, dance a bit — what do you think?"

I hadn't been to a concert for years. The thought of dancing and the high probability of looking foolish, not to mention my already-protesting muscles, caused me to pause. The prospect of meeting Angela's friends, however, was sufficiently intriguing to sway my answer. Using the ticket once intended for the loathsome Sam Thomas was icing on the cake. Before sanity got the best of me I found myself blurting, "Sure! Sounds fun!"

* * *

The event, much to my pleasure, was not overflowing with people. In spite of the good weather, attendance was manageable resulting in relatively short wait times for food and drink. Our arrival had been fashionably late, but Angela's friends had thoughtfully saved us a spot at their table. They proved to be a friendly, talkative bunch, and quite accepting of my presence.

The notion that Angela's friends could shed some light on her enigmatic behavior was quickly dismissed. Angela's childhood friend, a petite dark-haired woman named Karen Boyle, consumed nearly every free moment of my time with questions that fell only slightly short of interrogation. From the handful of queries I was able to interject, I discovered that Karen's arrival in the United States preceded Angela's by slightly over a year. It was Karen's idea, or so she claimed, to attend University over here. They both liked it and stayed.

During my ongoing interrogation, Angela flitted around, smiling, chatting, and mingling. Occasionally, people would glance in my direction in response to whatever conversation was going on. I was too busy sweating under Karen's relentless spotlight to notice any reactions to my presence.

Finally, as the evening's third band took the stage, Angela rescued me. The daunting prospect of dancing was suddenly welcome. The music, although not my style, was fun, energetic, and conducive to dancing. I felt clumsy and out of place, doubly so when contrasted with Angela's effortlessly flawless and beguiling movements. If my two left feet bothered her, she never let on; her smile dominated the evening.

What proved to be the band's penultimate song was the requisite slow ballad, likely at the behest of the event's organizers. It chased most of the younger couples off the dance floor in favor of the older and likely wealthier couples. I briefly watched the changeover and started to make my way to the sidelines. The hand of Angela Grady lightly touching my shoulder stopped me.

"May I have this dance?" She slipped her arm around me leaving little doubt as to the correct response.

"Of course."

Our danced started with formality and spacing. As the song progressed the distance between us unerringly shrank, our form reduced to little more than a hug gently swaying to the breeze of the music. The dance, as much as I willed it to last forever, passed in the blink of an eye, and before its last note faded, the band launched into their final, spirited song. And with it she was gone, off dancing merrily with her friends, smiling as widely as I'd ever seen.

* * *

"Thanks a million for tonight. I hope you had a good time."

I was tired, but my spirit was lighter than it had been in recent memory. "I had a wonderful time, Angela. This was a great idea - thank you for inviting me. I'm going to sleep well tonight, that's for sure!"

Angela laughed. "Not quite ready for rock climbing?"

"Not quite. Something a bit tamer, I think."

"I'll keep that in mind. See you first thing in the morning, then?"

I nodded, uncertain how my muscles would respond to an early morning. Nevertheless, we had work to do and questions that needed answers.

She sighed, staring into the distance with a slight smile on her face. "I guess running away is out of the question, isn't it?"

"That is rhetorical, I hope."

The smile drifted from her face. "It is, of course. Many times I've thought that if I could somehow do that weekend over again, I would have just stayed home."

"I think it is safe to say that we all have our share of regrets from the past."

"I don't regret tonight, not one bit." She smiled warmly at me. "Goodnight, Johnny."

"Neither do I." I returned her smile. "See you tomorrow."

* * *

The morning brought with it the anticipated soreness from underutilized muscles, a strong reminder that I was no longer young. A quick walk around the block, something I had not done in years, followed by a warm shower helped.

A quick glance showed that I had a message waiting. It turned out to be a cryptic text message from Angela sent several hours after she left my house:

My friends approve of you.

My mind was still contemplating what the text message might mean when Mack arrived, offering me a wry smile as she walked through the door.

"Good to see you, too, Mack."

"Did you two have fun last night?"

I couldn't tell if Mack was being serious or condescending. "We went to a benefit concert, danced a bit, and then said goodnight. Why?"

"Please tell me that someone got you dancing on video," said Mack, trying to repress laughter. "I'm surprised you went. Happy, but surprised."

"You knew?"

"Angela mentioned it to me when we were out. She was hoping you'd go. Did you get to meet her friends?"

"I did, and apparently they approve of me, whatever that means." I showed her the message on my phone. She handed the phone back to me, staring at me with a coy smile. "What exactly did you tell her, Mack?"

"Nothing that she didn't already know." She was getting great pleasure watching me squirm. "John, you're not fourteen and neither is she. Just tell her how you feel!"

I sighed. "It isn't that easy. Perhaps if the situation was different, but I've got the entire professional ethics thing to worry about now. It has always had a good chance of ending badly. Now it has a chance to end *really* badly."

"Suit yourself. If you must know, I told her that you're the best lawyer I've ever met and an even better friend. She's lucky to have you on her team and is right to believe in you. There. Now you know."

I felt like a first-class idiot, but at least I was an idiot blessed with a wonderful friend. What was it about Angela Grady that always left me fumbling over life's simplest matters? I had more questions for Mack, but they would have to wait — Angela had arrived.

* * *

Our day started with another review of the fateful trip to Drumquin. We pressed on every detail, trying to twist and distort her answers. Again, it was to no avail. Her answers remained consistent and calm. I decided to try a different approach, abruptly changing the subject.

"Tell me about when the Constabulary first came around to your house."

"The first time wasn't really that big of a deal. They had tracked me down from the attendant's statement. I told them where I was and what I was doing that weekend and they seemed satisfied. They recorded our basic information, took my picture and left."

"I take it the experience got worse from there. Can you tell me about it?"

She seemed briefly upset by the question, but collected herself quickly. "I don't like talking about it. Is this really something you need to know?"

"I'm trying to lock in on what caused Finnegan to get so fixated on you as a suspect. Perhaps from there, I can figure out what he thinks he has other than a fuzzy picture."

She held a deep breath momentarily before releasing it. "To this day, I still have an occasional nightmare over it. It happened a few weeks later after a few people saw the picture they took. We had finished eating dinner, and I was looking through catalogs and literature from various colleges here in the States. Karen had sent me quite a few, and I was trying to finalize my decision, get my applications underway and all that. I heard a bit of commotion downstairs. Naturally, I opened the door to see what was happening. A policeman was waiting for me, though he looked more like a soldier. Another one joined him, and they just started searching everywhere. They wouldn't tell me what they were looking for. They made me stand there with my hands on my head while they made a mess. One had his gun pointed at me the entire time."

"Jesus. That must've been terrifying."

"It was awful, but it got worse. They finally allowed me to sit down and told me to wait. I could hear some raised voices downstairs, but couldn't make much of what they were saying. It eventually grew quiet and that was when he came upstairs to talk to me."

"Jim Finnegan?"

"Finnegan. It all started calmly enough with him asking me a few questions, my name, where I worked, basic stuff. He seemed to take great interest in my mail from the States, asking why there was so much of it, what my plans were. On and on. Then he got around to where I had been on that Saturday. I didn't see any harm in telling him. The next thing I know, they're putting me into a tiny, dark cage in the back of a police truck."

"What happened next?"

"We drove for what felt like an hour, and when we finally stopped, I didn't know where we were — a police station, obviously, but no idea of which one. They hustled me into a holding cell and left me there alone for quite a while. I must have looked quite the sight by the time they finally got around to asking more questions. I'd been crying nearly continuously since leaving my house."

"Do you remember what they asked you?"

"It started out with the same stuff over and over again. Where was I? Why was I there? Who saw me? When did I leave? We did that for a while. I guess after answering the same question the same way fifty times they were happy because then it switched to asking me about my father."

"Your father? What were they asking?"

"They kept telling me that they knew that the both of us were involved and how I could make things go easier if I told them the truth. They kept asking about circuits and timers — I understand now what they were getting at, but back then I had no idea. It eventually got so bad that I couldn't answer questions because I was sobbing so much. They took me back to the cell for a while and tried again a bit later, but I just didn't have anything more to give them. It was two or three in the morning before they took me home. As they were taking me out to a waiting car, I remember seeing Finnegan in a room having a heated conversation with someone. I'm sure he wasn't too happy that they were letting me go. You know how you can read someone solely from their gestures? His were unmistakable."

"I'm sorry to have to bring all these memories back, but this is important. They questioned you again, didn't they?"

"At least three more times. It stopped when they finally located Julia Rohnan and got her statement."

"And what about the solicitor?"

"We thought it was over, and then Finnegan came up with that damned sketch. It was months later, and I was making my final arrangements for University, travel, and so forth. It all started again, the heavy questioning, inferences, accusations. More questions about my father, too. After a few rounds of it, though, we finally hired the solicitor and he put a quick stop to it."

"Sounds like they were fishing for motive in an attempt to implicate you and your father. Do you know if they questioned him?"

"I know they did on several occasions. He never talked about it much, but I'm sure it was because he knew he needed to be strong for all of us. It was a difficult time."

"And your mother? Were they interested in her? How did she deal with all of it?"

Angela paused, sighing deeply. "Sure, they questioned her a few times. Nothing like what my father and I went through, though if you ask her it was, maybe ten times worse!"

"Why do you think she acted that way?" interjected Mack.

"Hard to say. Maybe it was her way of coping with things. I tried to stay positive and work through it."

I would approach the subject of Shanagh later. "Why do you think they were so interested in your father?"

Angela's posture eased. "That's an easy question to answer. They thought that he had the knowledge to build a detonator."

"That is not surprising, looking at it from the perspective of the policeman's mind. They had a lead that matched a description, all the better that her father was capable of being involved. Your alibi proved inconvenient, no doubt."

A bigger question, one that Angela would likely be unable to answer, was why Jim Finnegan persisted in the face of a seemingly airtight alibi. The surface of the iceberg was obvious; what lay beneath the waves still taunted me.

* * *

Lunchtime arrived, and with it the departure of Mack. She had received a call from the library and would be occupied for the remainder of the afternoon. I pressed for more details on Sean Grady, learning only a few tantalizing tidbits beyond what Shanagh had already told me. Sean, it seemed, had served in the military. Angela did not know any details beyond that, claiming that he rarely talked about it. Nevertheless, it would be something that Mack would be able to research.

Although Angela seemed perfectly contented with continuing the interview in my office, the afternoon was far too nice to be stuck inside. The prospect of continuing at a nearby park, however, seemed to pique her interest. We chatted casually on the way there and for the first part of our walk to an awaiting pavilion.

"Let's talk about your job and such."

The smile left her face. "Are you always going to take me to a park for difficult conversations, John?"

"I didn't think of it that way, just wanted to get out of the house for a bit. You have a point, though."

"Sorry. I'm not sure what this has to do with my case, though."

"I want to make sure your mind is in a good place or at least the best place possible. We ran your finances, Angela, and the good news is that you don't seem to fall into the *no visible means of support* category. The bad news is it looks like you're going broke. That said it could work against us indirectly in a couple of ways. First, if your head isn't in the game your defense could suffer as a result. Secondly, it could be used to show a pattern of reckless behavior. A good prosecutor can twist things, suggest things, and sway a jury. I know; I've done it."

"You think the extradition thing is going to happen, don't you?" Her face looked deeply troubled.

"I think the chances are over fifty percent right now. I know it isn't what you want to hear, but that is where my thinking is at the moment."

She stared into space, expressionless. "I left work because I knew my time there was ending anyway. My annual job review hadn't gone well, and the signs all pointed to me being the next to go. I took a job that wasn't a good match for me. In retrospect, I would have been better off waiting for something better."

"You weren't there long."

"I wasn't. They let me go after a month. In my mind, it wasn't entirely justified, but I didn't really have any recourse."

"And that gets us to where we are now."

"Not entirely. It was about this time that things with Sam changed. I still don't know everything that was going through his mind, but he clearly started drifting away. He was mad when I quit. He was mad when I didn't find a job right away after getting sacked. Then he couldn't come up with his half of the rent, or so he said, not once but twice. Then things got worse. A couple of months ago, he went out for what was supposed to be one evening and was gone for a couple of days. When he finally showed up, it was with a truck and a couple of friends to move his stuff out."

"I take it this was quite unexpected."

"At the time it was; less so in retrospect. I'll never forget the look

84

he gave me right before he left — like I repulsed him. I tried to talk to him for about a week after, but he wouldn't speak to me. He broke every connection he had with me, and I've not heard a word from him since, so I still don't really know all his reasons. All this after nearly three years…"

"I'm sorry. I really am. You've had quite an unpleasant few months."

"So there you have it," forcing a smile. "And as you've discovered, I'm going to be out in the cold after this month, next at the latest."

I looked her squarely in the eye. "No, you're not. I'm not going to let that happen."

"Your friendship has helped me through this, more than you know. But financially, you've done too much already. As things stand, it is going to be forever before I can pay you back for the car, not to mention any legal bills. I don't want you going bankrupt on my account."

"If I promise you that won't happen, will you promise me that you won't worry about it again?"

She looked at me with a briefly confused look, but my expression remained serious and unchanging. "Are you saying that because it is true or just to make me feel better?"

"Because it is true. Honestly. I've saved a bit for a rainy day, and when it's raining on a friend, it is raining on me."

"Then I promise. I just feel like such a failure right now."

"I'd be hard pressed to agree with that, Angela," I said, frowning at her. "You traveled thousands of miles to a different country, did well in college — I've seen some of the records — and built a decent career. That isn't the work of a failure. That is the work of a strong, independent, and free woman. I'm not saying it's going to be easy, but I know you have it in you to get through this."

She stared at me silently, her brown eyes studying me intently. She rose, walking around the picnic table to sit beside me, facing the opposite direction. She leaned back, her elbows resting on the surface of the table. "Thanks a million, Johnny. I needed to hear that."

"That's what friends are for." I took her hand, giving it a gentle squeeze.

She leaned forward, gently kissing my right cheek before rising. I hoped she hadn't noticed the trembling that rolled through me as a result. "Ask anything you want, no matter how unpleasant. We can do this."

Fear prevented me from asking the one question that I desperately wanted her to answer. "Tell me about your Granda Connor, Angela."

Her face brightened at the mention of his name. "What do you want to know?"

"I talked to your mother the other day. She hinted that he was slipping mentally toward the end. When we first interviewed you, though, you pointed out that he was sharp and with it up until the end."

She frowned at my words. "I don't know why my ma insists on saying that. Granda Connor was as sharp the last time I saw him as he was from my earliest memories."

"Is it possible that his mind somehow remembered you and not others?"

"I don't see how. He knew everything that was going on in my life. He always asked me about my classes, my grades, and my friends; always remembered exactly where our last conversation left off."

"That doesn't sound like someone with Dementia or Alzheimer's. Was his demeanor the same?"

"Absolutely. He was my Granda. Nothing changed, except he physically got weaker. He couldn't get around as well, simple things tired him out. His body failed him, not his mind."

"I'm sorry to belabor the point, but I don't understand why your mother insisted that his mind had issues."

"I've heard her say that before, and we've actually argued about it. She usually dismisses my memories as fantasies, but I was a teenager when he died, not a confused child. Whatever the reason, we've mutually steered clear of this and a few other subjects over the past few years, and it has helped us get a bit closer."

"So what did you and Granda Connor talk about and do together?"

"He taught me how to play the guitar and tin whistle, tried to get me to play the flute — which I tried, without much success. He taught me a bunch of traditional songs."

"Rebel songs?"

"You could say that, I suppose. They're mostly thought of as traditional now, though. Otherwise, the normal stuff. How was I doing in school? What classes did I like? How were my friends?

"Did you believe his rebel stories?"

"No and neither did anyone else. He told them as much because people reacted to them, correcting his mix-ups. Those were intentional, by the way. He was a funny old guy; I think you would have liked him."

"I take it he was quite the musician. I would have enjoyed playing a music session with his boys, I expect."

She laughed. "Granda tried, to be sure, but as a group they were awful! You'd think that for as much as they played together, they'd improve a bit but I don't recall much change over the years! I think it was more of a social thing for them as much as anything. They'd play a few tunes, talk for a while, play a few more."

"What did they talk about?"

"Oh, I don't really know. There were usually a few cousins visiting as well, and we'd be off on our own in another room gabbing away."

"Did you ever meet any of the people he played with?"

"Sure I did. I heard them play many times. They'd even let me play along for a song or two on occasion."

"Do you remember any of them?"

"I do, at least a few of them. Granda Connor played the flute and whistle, sometimes guitar if they needed him to. Mister O'Hegerty played the box and Mister Brennan the fiddle. Mister Dillon played the guitar, I think. Sometimes another fellow would join in on the violin, but

I was never really introduced to him. They all called him Seamus, but I have no idea what his last name was. Others would come and go, but those are the ones I remember. My ma would likely remember more. I can ask her to write them up and send them to you."

"That would be good. Did they play at a pub or something?"

"No. They played at Mrs. O'Sullivan's house. She was a widow, and I think they all kept an eye on her, help her with repairs and such — neighborly stuff. I always thought Granda liked her a bit, though. They seemed to get along fairly well."

"I'm surprised your grandmother let him out of the house if that was the case..."

"Oh, my grandma Grady died long before I was born. Grammy Flanagan is still around, though. Eighty-three years old now and going strong. She's a spry little white-haired lady." Laughing. "Ma says I get my energy from her, and I think she might be right. I hope I'm doing as well when I get to be her age!"

"I'm sure you will, likely even better!" I would never see it. Living into my mid-nineties was neither expected nor particularly desired. My grandfather's final years, lingering but not living, seemed grossly unfair in comparison to his energetic life.

"What?"

"Sorry. I was thinking about my grandparents."

"Tell me, Johnny" returning to the table, sitting down next to me.

"My mother was born in Cork, but came over here with her parents when she was wee little. Ended up marrying a third-generation Italian. I don't know much about my Dad's family; I take after my mom's side of the family anyway."

"She was Irish? That explains a few things."

"Oh, like what?"

"Like why we get on so well and how you know all those traditional tunes. You really would have enjoyed meeting my Granda Connor."

"I'm sure I would have. I think you would have appreciated my Grandfather O'Brien, too. He was so full of zest — he really loved life."

"And your mom taught you the songs and culture?"

"She did, as did my grandparents. Music was always an important part of my life growing up."

"Was your dad musical? You don't talk much about him, do you?"

"He was one hell of a piano player, classically trained but he never did anything with it. We started growing apart when I was a teenager. My career choice really drove a wedge between us. We reconciled a bit toward the end, but not as much as I'd like. I know that you can't change the past, but it doesn't stop me from sometimes wishing I could. More so on those dreary days, you know."

"I understand — all too well." She had slipped her hand into mine, unnoticed until I felt her squeeze as our eyes met.

"Thanks," returning the squeeze.

Our conversation had run at a leisurely pace. Not only had we lost track of time, but the skies had clouded unexpectedly. Rain arrived with little warning and an accompanying gentle wind sent us scurrying to the center of the pavilion for shelter.

"Well, I didn't see this coming," I said.

She laughed, gently. "This is just a normal day back home. Want to wait it out or make a run for it?"

"I don't want my notes to get all soaked and ruined, so if you don't mind waiting a bit…"

She sat down, straddling the bench. Her eyes studied the rain falling outside. "The weather was so lovely those days that I was with Maggie - warm by Ireland's standards, sunny with only a few clouds. We had such a fun time together, short as it was. It rained the Sunday after, came up all sudden like this and stayed for a while. My Dad said that God was crying for Strabane. That was the only time I heard him speak of it."

"Was he a religious man?"

"Spiritual more than religious. The violence around Belfast upset him; that, I know. We were fortunate that his job allowed us to live in an area that was peaceful, but it was always lingering there in the background; news stories, television, radio; it was hard to escape. I think he wanted to move us south into the Republic, but his job demanded him to stay. That and my ma had so many friends and relatives in the area. She can probably tell you more about that than I can."

"How did you and Maggie meet?"

"We struck up a friendship at school. By all rights, we should have never gotten along. She was from the country, I was from the city. But there she was, like the sister I never had."

"She was from a long way away. Was it common for people to come that far to go to school?"

"The Academy was well regarded, so there were students from all over. Her parents scrimped and saved so she could go, although I don't think they liked the fact that it was in Belfast, given the troubles and all. After she graduated, I always went to visit her, never the other way around."

"You know Finnegan has insinuated that you are somehow involved in her death."

"I know it and strange as it may sound, I think that bothers me as much, if not more, than the whole Strabane accusation. Maggie was a wonderful person and a dear friend, John. I'd not do a thing in this world to hurt her. I hope you're planning on talking to her parents as part of all this. They're still around, living in the same place so you'll have no trouble finding them. Ask them what they think of Finnegan and his various theories."

"I'll do that."

"There is one, and likely only one, point where Jim Finnegan and I agree. There is no way that Maggie's death was an accident the way the official report gives it. She was too smart and too careful for that to happen."

"It is certainly something I plan on looking in to..."

Angela interrupted me, abruptly. "They never found her pen,

John. She always carried an EpiPen just in case. The initial report stated she left it at home, but her parents pointed out that she had two — one for home and one she carried with her. They came up with some nonsense that it was tossed from the car and amended the report accordingly. Of course, it was never found."

"And your thoughts are?"

"She kept it in a special spot in the glove box. Maggie was a closer. She closed doors that were open, always zipped her purse, and always closed the glove box. She didn't have her pen sitting on the dashboard or on the seat, or between the cushions, and it didn't get tossed from the car!" I had never heard Angela's voice quite so strong and forceful. "Regardless of what happens to me, promise that you'll investigate what happened to Maggie. Promise me."

"I promise."

Her eyes watered. "You spoke earlier of changing the past. I talk about wanting to change that weekend because I know Maggie was murdered because I was there. I don't know how or why, but I know it in my heart. Had I chosen another weekend to visit, she might still be alive. I can bear that burden most of the time, but on lonely, dreary evenings it occasionally gets to be weighty." I nodded, sadly. "If it wouldn't be an imposition," she said, hesitantly, "would your guest room be too much to ask?"

"You're more than welcome any time."

We sat together silently watching the rain.

CHAPTER NINE

Our afternoon conversation had taken longer than expected, delayed even more by the unexpected rain. A quick visit to Angela's apartment followed, from which she emerged carrying a small suitcase. Dinner, quick and simple as it was, made us even later. The house was dark upon our return. Not surprisingly, Mack had already departed. Tomorrow's agenda, however, was quickly obvious. Several thick file-folders were stacked on her desk. A note on the top read simply, "Maggie Albin."

I offered several suggestions for activities, but Angela vetoed all of them preferring to stay in. Fatigue overtook her after an hour of light conversation and halfhearted television watching. I retreated to my office to catch up on e-mail and case reading. My phone rang shortly thereafter.

"Hello Jim, I was beginning to think you didn't care anymore."

Finnegan chuckled quietly. "You two are getting quite chummy these days. Was getting caught in the rain intentional or a happy coincidence?"

"Purely unintentional, although I feel the need to remind you of the protected nature of any conversations Miss Grady and I engaged in."

"Of course, but we're keeping a close eye on her whereabouts. Is she warm and comfortable in your bed, Johnny?"

"That would be alone and safe in my guest room, Jim, but I imagine she is warm and comfortable as well. Thank you for asking."

"I bet that nags at you something awful, doesn't it. So close, yet so far — now there's a feeling I know all too well."

"The whiskey must be working overtime. What's really on your mind?"

"I received the go-ahead from my superiors to release some information on poor Maggie. Some you might be able to get on your own, but there's quite a few goodies that you might find helpful."

"Helpful with what?"

Finnegan laughed. "Helpful to learn what you've got sleeping under your roof for one thing. My superiors don't believe Maggie is germane to our case, and since you've got a bit more time on your hands than we expected, poor Maggie deserves a second look. Might as well come from you."

"More time?"

"More time — sad but true. Seems that things aren't moving as quickly as I had hoped. But the result will be the same nonetheless. No doubt there. But don't wait too long to notch your belt — it is easy to lose track of time."

* * *

Mack arrived uncharacteristically early, but I had long since showered and eaten. I had not heard a sound from the guest room since Angela retired the previous evening, so I opted to review the morning newspaper in my office.

"You're up and about awfully early. Couldn't help notice Angela's car in the driveway again." She looked around, suggestively.

"She used the guest room last night. We had a long talk about Maggie yesterday, and I think it weighed heavily on her. I'll fill you in sometime when we're alone."

"Well, it seems like Maggie is going to be our subject for a while."

"I couldn't help but notice the pile of stuff on your desk. Do you think it is promising, or is it a red herring?"

"Why do you ask?"

"Finnegan called me last night promising to send some files to us — specifically about Maggie Albin. I wouldn't put it beyond him to try to get us sniffing up the wrong tree."

"I suppose anything is possible. I won't go crazy on it, I promise, but if it starts yielding gold, I'm going to run with it. Call it my intuition, but I think it is all interconnected."

"Then we're all in agreement. That is Angela's theory as well. I trust your judgment, Mack. Run with it as you see fit."

* * *

I met Angela in the kitchen. She arrived looking well rested and unusually alluring. I couldn't identify what it was, but I could hardly take my eyes off her.

"What?" she said, obviously noticing my leering.

"I'm sorry, it's just that, well, you look nice this morning. Not to say that you normally look otherwise. Oh, you know what I mean!" Damn me and my awkwardness!

"Thanks, Johnny." She smiled warmly, apparently not upset by my fumbling. "I slept well last night. Good morning, Mack."

"Morning," said Mack, grabbing a bottle of water before returning to the office.

"Have you eaten?"

"I have, but feel free to go ahead." I opened the refrigerator. "Fully stocked!"

"Wonderful!" Angela selected a yogurt. "I chatted with my ma a bit this morning, and she came up with an idea. I'm not sure how you're going to react to this, but I promised I'd bring it up."

"Okay — what is it?"

"I know you're willing to help me financially, and you say it isn't going to put you out, which I believe, but how would you feel about renting me your guest room? I can help out around here to earn my keep. When I'm back on my feet, I can start paying whatever rent is still due."

The butterflies, dormant for quite some time, made a triumphant return. It was all I could do to speak calmly. "It actually makes a lot of sense, come to think of it." I tried desperately to not sound overtly eager.

She smiled, seeming relieved by my answer. "I promise not to take up too much space or be a burden."

"I've got a couple of concerns, though. Firstly — I'm not exciting and I don't want to cramp your style. A bigger concern is more hypothetical." She raised an eyebrow. "Well, what if a line of questioning upsets you? We've still got lots to cover and it could happen quite easily. If you get upset with me, you've nowhere to go to be rid of me for a while."

She flicked her hair back over her shoulder. "I'm not going to let that happen. If I give in to that, Finnegan wins."

I raised my eyebrows, appreciatively.

"There's one more question…" Angela appeared hesitant, but I motioned for her to continue. "When I was with Sam, we used to get together with my friends and have dinner from time to time…" Her voice started to trail off.

"Of course, your friends are welcome. Between the kitchen and the living room, you should have plenty of space for dinner and socializing. I'll get you a key made if you're serious about staying here. No hard feelings if you change your mind."

"Deal. I've got to let the rental company know that I won't be renewing for another month. My friends and I are going to meet for a late lunch today, so if I'm not needed I'll go get things started. Do you think you could help me move my things?"

"Sure. I can get a truck and scare up a few friends to help. Do you think you're going to need to rent a storage unit?"

"No. Between your car and mine we should be set. Is this evening okay?"

I wrinkled my eyebrow in confusion. "I guess so."

She reached out, touching my arm gently. "I'll call you later — you'll understand when you get to my place."

* * *

Mack peered at me around her monitor, muttering something about keeping your enemies closer. "Are you sure you know what you're doing?"

"No, not really. It just kind of happened."

"Does it worry you that things are going a bit *too* well?"

Mack had a point. A few short months ago, Angela Grady was little more than an unattainable enigma. "You think she's using me? Did she say something that gives you that idea?"

Her forehead wrinkled. "No. I know you think I don't like her. Honestly, I'm still undecided. I just can't shake that feeling about her — that there is something important she isn't telling us."

"Or is it the improbability that someone like *her* would take an interest in *me*?"

Her lips pursed with annoyance. "Not at all. It seems quick and convenient. That's all. I'll be happy if it works out for you. Like I've said before, neither of you are fourteen. If you don't think she has a pretty good idea how you feel about her, well, you're only fooling yourself. I just don't want to see you get hurt."

I smiled, giving her a wink of approval.

She paused, eventually sighing deeply. "Do you want to hear about Maggie Albin?" she said, raising her eyebrows. I motioned for her to continue. "Maggie was a good student - solid grades, flawless attendance, and zero disciplinary records. Her coursework followed a similar track as an American college preparatory curriculum although I've found no evidence of college applications. I even talked to a few of her teachers, all of whom spoke well of her. It was a casual mention

96

during one such interview that led me to the discovery of the reporter."

"Reporter?" I leaned forward, intrigued.

"He was a young reporter with aspirations to be an investigative journalist." She was positively beaming at her discovery. "Of course, he was at the bottom of the pecking-order and got served a steady diet of uninspiring stories to write. One of his assignments was to write a piece on drunk driving incidents among young people. It was forming up to be a run-of-the-mill story of bad decisions leading to bad outcomes until he started looking in to a certain accident..."

My eyes widened. "Maggie Albin? Please tell me it was Maggie Albin."

"Maggie Albin," Mack said, proudly. "And it gets even better from there. He dug into it a bit, conducted a few interviews, and quickly realized that the official findings were shaky. It was enough to convince the editor to let him write it."

"How come I wasn't able to find it on-line anywhere?"

"The newspaper folded many years back. Most of it hasn't been digitized, so it isn't widely available. But you can think of it as another reminder of why you hired me."

"Duly noted." I rolled my eyes, but Mack was too engrossed to notice.

"Anyway, this reporter wrote his article about Maggie's case. It got enough feedback that the paper hired a private investigator to do some more digging. They managed to get a second article published before getting stonewalled."

"What do you mean?"

"Official sources all went quiet, people stopped talking — all except one." Mack stopped, her eyes studying my face. I returned an inquisitive look. "You're not going to like it."

"Mack!"

"Okay. Don't say I didn't warn you. A source told the PI that he had seen Maggie in the company of someone shortly before the bombing in Strabane. And do you know who that might be?"

"Mack!!"

"Siobhan O'Connor, John. He claims he saw Maggie with Siobhan O'Connor."

Dammit. I sank back in my chair.

"It gets worse…" I motioned halfheartedly for her to continue. "He danced with a woman in Omagh the Friday before the explosion; a blonde woman who was there with Maggie and told him her name was Siobhan O'Connor."

It was an emotional punch in the stomach. "Dammit. That's not good news. Over here, it might be hearsay. Over there, all bets are off. This witness got a name?"

"Still working on it, but the investigator and the reporter share the same opinion that we do — Strabane and Maggie Albin are somehow connected. I reached out to both of them — they're willing to talk to us about both."

That sick feeling was creeping back into my gut. "Set it up. Circumstantial or not, it is another dangerous piece of evidence, especially if he's willing to testify under oath."

* * *

It took Joe Quinlan several hours to return our call, but he seemed eager to talk about Maggie Albin. The stories had been his first real and meaningful foray into investigative reporting, eventually catching the eye of a Dublin-based news service. In spite of the passage of time, the story was fresh in his mind. The hollowness of the official explanation and the eventual stonewall made it difficult for him to forget.

"I'm glad you're giving this another look, to be sure," Quinlan said, his speech fast but clear. "Miss MacDonald told me a little bit about what you're working on. Sounds like you've got quite a challenge in front of you."

"That I do. My client was a person of interest in the Strabane bombing during the initial investigation, but her alibi forced them to look elsewhere."

"Angela Grady?"

"Yes. Angela Grady."

"I'd not heard of her until Miss MacDonald brought her up in our first conversation. I even double checked my notes from the stories I did at the time; there was never a mention of her name in anything I found. I checked with some contacts I've got in the Belfast area, and there's not a peep coming from the Police Service about any of this."

It was the day's first encouraging bit of news. "I'd prefer to keep it that way, Joe. We're early in the process, enough so that I might be able to end any talk of warrants and extradition before they start. I'm interested in Maggie because she was Miss Grady's best friend in school."

"I was new to the business, sent out to write a formulaic story on the evils of drunk driving. Life in that area was tough for a lot of people back then, and a fair number of them drowned their sorrows in the juice of the barley, so to speak. Including Maggie's case in the story was an easy decision. She had a lot going for her, and her life ended way too soon. The story could damn near write itself on that alone."

"What convinced you that things weren't as they seemed?"

"The first interview with her parents. I expected the normal grieving parents. Sure, there was plenty of sadness, but more frustration — even anger, I'd say — with the official findings. They picked it apart."

"Such as?"

"The report characterized Maggie as young and careless. They pointed out to me in no uncertain terms that she was anything but. It didn't take much convincing for me to agree with them. Seeing her room was the clincher. Everything was organized, labeled, neatly done. Not a sign of carelessness to be found. And then there was the whole alcohol thing."

"The allergy?"

"And how it never factored into the official verdict. According to the report, Maggie likely consumed the alcohol at a nearby party. Of course, they never located such a party but they simply wrote that off as an unwillingness of the folks involved to speak up. They said the combination of intoxication and high speed led to a fatal driving mistake."

"Possible, I suppose, but usually at least one participant in such parties feels guilty and talks."

"True. But there is more. The report doesn't give a specific location, instead claiming that it was common to use available barns, sheds, or even suitably isolated fields. It had rained heavily the day before. Any fields or off-road parking would have left Maggie's tires muddy."

"Let me guess, no mud."

"Correct. So I started searching — maybe they had their party at a nearby house. Nobody in the area had kids the right age, a connection to Maggie, or any of her friends. The timing is problematic, too. From the ingestion of alcohol in any appreciable quantity to the onset of her allergic reaction was fifteen minutes, at the most. Now, for sake of argument, let's say the report is accurate. She would have consumed a tremendous amount of alcohol in a short time and departed immediately thereafter — ostensibly to seek help. But she went in completely the wrong direction and without any help from her friends, all of whom knew about her allergy and looked after her. And none of whom admit to going to any party." Quinlan's voice built, growing even faster as he rattled off one conundrum after another.

"Fishy."

"And then there's the matter of the EpiPen, or rather, the missing EpiPen."

Joe's account matched Angela's nearly verbatim. "Nobody ever found it?"

"They did not. I spent hours out there searching for it. Maggie's parents joined me on several occasions. She always kept it in the glove box. The glove box stayed shut during the accident, with the driver's side taking the worst of it."

"If it stayed shut, where the hell did the EpiPen go?"

"Well, it either vanished into thin air, was pinched by one of the attendants who arrived, or was never there in the first place."

"Or it was not included in the findings intentionally."

"Possibly, but I don't think they understood its significance until after the report was released."

"What ended up being the official cause of death?"

"Massive blunt force trauma and a broken neck. But it didn't really matter. If the curve hadn't gotten her, the reaction to the alcohol would have. Poor Maggie was a dead girl either way."

"How do you know she didn't use the EpiPen and toss it out the window?"

"Part of the Coroner's examination was to check for needle marks to rule out drug use. Nothing was found. Besides, Maggie was not the type to throw things out the window. Neat and organized, remember?"

"And you published all of this?"

"I published an initial article that contained some of the information that didn't jibe. It got enough attention to warrant more investigation. Tully Smith even went so far as to respond, standing by the original findings. He said my story was nothing more than the fanciful imagination of a young and enthusiastic reporter."

"Tully Smith?"

"The coroner. When he responded, my editor knew we were on to something and hired Charlie Hannon."

"The PI?"

"The same. He discovered the problem with the EpiPen and made some of the strange Strabane connections before we got shut down."

"Before we get into that, Joe, does anyone know why Maggie was out that evening at all? Was it common for her?"

"Unheard of! Her parents were out when Maggie left, so nobody knows for certain the reason she was out. I subscribe to the theory that she left in a hurry, though."

"Why is that?"

"A drawer in her desk was left partially open, like she had grabbed something in haste and neglected to close it."

"My understanding was that Maggie was closure-oriented, almost to a compulsion. For her to rush off and leave something open like that..."

Quinlan finished my thought for me. "Great haste and importance. You're right about her in that regard. I'd go so far as to say she felt it was a matter of life and death."

"Sadly, it turned out to be. Anyone know if anything was missing from the desk?"

"A small notebook was missing. According to her parents, she carried it with her everywhere."

"I'm going to go out on a limb and bet it was never found."

"Never found."

"Quinlan, if you were to wager on what happened..."

"I'd wager Maggie was murdered, to be sure, and that it was covered up but I have no idea why. Charlie Hannon will likely be able to tell you more, especially since you're up to your neck in the Strabane unpleasantness. I've already told him to expect to hear from you or Miss MacDonald. One word of advice: have your checkbook ready. Charlie won't tie his shoelaces unless he's getting paid to do it, but it will be money well spent."

"Thanks, Joe."

"Good luck to you. And if you ever get over here, see if you can talk Miss MacDonald into joining you on the trip. I'd love to meet her — she sounds delightful."

"She is — I'll see what I can do, Joe. Thanks again."

Mack had earned her pay and then some. She beamed at me with an odd combination of pride and concern. "Mack, I think this warrants a bonus. Do you want it now, or as a lump sum when we're all done?"

Whatever hint of a smile had been on her face faded quickly with my words. "Honestly, now would be good. There are too many bodies piling up around your girlfriend. Even if she's not to blame for it, the chances of all this being coincidence are dropping pretty quickly. And now, she's living under your roof."

"Mack, do you really believe she's capable of all that?"

"Perhaps. Has it occurred to you that some of the people involved in the original bombing are likely still out there? I know you like her, John, and it pains me to say this, but she's involved. I'm not saying she's guilty or innocent, *but she's involved.* Somehow."

"I'll write you that check now, Mack…"

* * *

A call summoned me to Angela's apartment, where I was greeted with a smile and a hug. A quick glance around her apartment explained so much. Apart from an aging television on a rickety stand and a futon, the main living area was barren. A few knick-knacks survived on a largely-empty built-in shelf. Several boxes held her more important keepsakes.

A quick glance into the bedroom confirmed another suspicion. She had been sleeping, likely poorly, on the futon since Sam's departure. It also bore evidence to a strong candidate for some of her monetary dalliances. The closets would prove to be a daunting challenge and undoubtedly lead to a sore back the next day.

"Sorry. I sold a decent amount of it," she said, sheepishly. It was good fortune that my guest room had an ample closet and a dresser. Both would be challenged by Angela's collection. "I'm not going to take any of the larger stuff. The building super said he would get rid of it for me. If he's able to sell any of it, he'll add that to the amount returned with my security deposit."

I looked around, skeptically. She'd be lucky if he didn't deduct the cost of disposal from her security deposit. "I wish you would have said something. I could have helped."

She lowered her eyes briefly. "Remember the last time we met for lunch, before all of the Strabane stuff happened?"

I nodded. Of course I remembered. It had been a gold-star day for me.

"I just wanted to have a fun conversation, laugh a bit, toss ideas about and so forth. The last thing I wanted you to think was I met you only to ask for money."

"I wouldn't have thought that, Angela. Not in a million years."

"I've never told you this, but you really lifted my spirits that day, Johnny. You believed in me and encouraged me; the fact that you had no idea what was going on made it all the more genuine."

"I enjoyed chatting that day, too. You've never failed to brighten my day. I wish we'd had more time to explore and develop our friendship before this situation started."

She took my left hand, holding it between hers. "Friendships aren't defined by situations. Quite the opposite, really."

I added my right hand atop hers. "And right, you are! Let's get you moved."

CHAPTER TEN

Charlie Hannon proved to be every bit the challenge that Quinlan predicted. Although only a few years my senior, he was already developing curmudgeonly habits. The prospect of money, however, quickly chased them away; more money and he became downright friendly. Most importantly, Charlie believed with uncompromising certainty that Maggie Albin was murdered. His voice raged with confidence as he spoke.

"The official report was pure and unadulterated bullshit. Anyone who thinks otherwise is cracked in the head. Went to a party, but nobody ever admitted to having one. Parked in a rain-soaked field, not a spot of mud on her tires or her car. The girl who carefully checked the ingredients in her mouthwash to make sure she wasn't getting alcohol drank an entire quart of Vodka? Bullshit! Assuming for a minute that she did go drinking, where the hell was her pen? She sure as hell didn't leave it at home. God damned thing has never been found. Did you ever see the autopsy photographs?"

"No. I wasn't aware that they were ever released."

"They weren't, but I've got them nevertheless. You probably shouldn't let your client see them, seeing as how she was friends with Maggie. They're not a pretty sight."

"If there's nothing to see, I don't really need them, I guess."

"The hell you say! The tech that leaked the pictures to me took a couple of shots of her left wrist. The pictures never made it into the report and only a passing mention of the bruises. No way those happened in a car accident. Bruise on her jaw looks suspicious to me, too, but they insisted she hit the steering wheel."

"Ligature marks on her wrist?"

"You ask me, some big bloke grabbed her wrist with one hand and probably belted her in the jaw with the other."

"And thus the bruise."

"Of course, nobody wants to hear from me on this these days. You're the first that has inquired in the longest time."

"What do you think really happened, Charlie?"

"I'd offer that someone lured her out of her car. Not sure exactly where or how. When she figured out she was in trouble, the big son of a bitch grabbed her and belted her. I'd guess she was in no position to resist him pouring alcohol down her throat."

"Between you and Quinlan, you've definitely got me interested. But why? Why was she killed?"

"That's nagged at me, Solicitor. Why was she on that road? Why was she out at all?"

"If she had stayed on the road, where would she have ended up?"

"Strabane! It was that little detail that got me digging. Who did she know there? Why was she going? Sure, she had a couple of friends there, but they were off at University. So I expanded my search a bit — all of her friends, associates, what she did. That's how I've heard of your client. Her parents mentioned her. Spoke well of her. It never went beyond that, at least for me it didn't."

"What do you mean?"

"There was no connection to anything with Angela Grady. But a couple of folks remembered Maggie with a young lady called Siobhan O'Connor. That got my attention, especially when the Strabane stuff came to light. One young fella even claims he danced with Siobhan the night before the bombing, right in Omagh, too."

"That statement is of particular interest to me, Charlie. You see, my client was in Omagh that night with Maggie Albin. Credit receipts prove it, and she makes no claim to the contrary."

"That might make things tricky, Solicitor."

"I know it. That is why I'm so eager to talk to the guy that supposedly danced with her."

"Well, the man's name is Fergus Clarke. I've not had any contact with him in recent years, but I can try to turn him up if you're willing to pay me for my efforts."

"I am. I pay well and on time, but I also expect results. If this works for you, consider yourself hired to work on the case again. Maggie, Siobhan, Strabane, anything along those lines you can turn up will be good. You mentioned others?"

"At least one of Fergus' mates made the same claim, but I honestly don't know if he heard it from the gal first hand or from Fergus. Can't talk to him, though. He died on the job a few years ago. A lineman - hit a live circuit. Didn't stand a chance."

"Anything fishy about it?"

"If there was, Tully Smith never let it out. He got better at being a corrupt gobshite after the whole Maggie Albin mess. He died a few years back. Was out walking his dog and fell over dead. Catastrophic heart failure, they said. A lot of records went missing on his watch. The lady they've got in office now seems sincere enough, but she's not got a lot to go on for old case files."

"I almost hate to ask this, but is there any suspicious circumstances around Tully's death? There does seem to be a theme forming here…"

"Nothing ever made it into the papers, but I know there were a lot of rumblings at the time."

"Seems strange that no investigation ever took place, especially in the face of obvious corruption."

"I'll ask and let you know what I find. Who is leading the investigation you're working on?"

"Jim Finnegan."

"Shit. You're really up against it."

"Why do you say that?"

"According to rumor, he's never lost a case that's gone to trial."

"Well, if it gets that far, Charlie, something's got to give. I've never had a defendant convicted, either."

* * *

"I don't care for Charlie Hannon," said Mack, her nose wrinkled. "He's crude and boorish."

"He's not exactly polished; I'll give you that. Crudeness aside, he's got one important advantage over anyone else we might hire: a head start."

Mack nodded in quiet acknowledgment. "On the other hand," the twinkle returned to her eyes, "I have some preliminary information on our friend, Jim Finnegan."

"Oh?"

"It seems that he's got quite a reputation. In spite of that, he survived the transition from the Constabulary to the Police Service as did most of his core group of investigators. It does seem that he has mellowed extensively in recent years."

"Do tell…"

"The solicitor Sean Grady hired was helpful. Finnegan was a bit of a strong-arm in his younger days. Some accusations of excessive force, none of which led to anything more than a slap on the wrist. There was one where he got a bit carried away. Beat the stuffing out of some punk, this after dragging the kid in for questioning half a dozen times. Problem was, the kid was innocent, and the whole bit eventually came out. Finnegan damn near lost his job over that one."

"There's a disconcerting similarity here…"

"And that is part of what eventually became a successful effort by Sean Grady's solicitor to quell Finnegan's zest. It seems after the incident, he was more inclined to use subtler, mental means to coerce his confessions."

"Like dragging someone out of their home at gunpoint and belaboring accusations in the face of direct evidence to the contrary?"

"That was more or less the solicitor's angle. He argued that Finnegan was, essentially, reliving the same case. True or not, the threat worked, and the higher-ups forced him to back down and look elsewhere."

"So what about Charlie's claim that Finnegan has never lost?"

"Not entirely fictional." Concern flashed across her face. "A fair majority of the cases where I've been able to find records never went to trial. A significant portion involved confessions, but he's an effective case-builder, no doubt. No losses, so to speak, although several ended in mistrial with the prosecutor opting not to continue. But here's an interesting little tidbit that I turned up on my own: Finnegan has had two cases where he actively disproved his own theory. Charges were dropped on the spot."

"That is good news. It sounds like he's honest when it counts, albeit given to obsession."

"True, and in spite of significant corruption rumored within the Constabulary, Finnegan's name was never associated with anything remotely related to financial or political wrongdoing. As much as I hate to admit it, he's either damn good at not getting caught being a dirty cop or he's fundamentally honest."

"He's honest, but with some issues. I've met some dirty cops in my day, and I've always gotten a vibe that something isn't quite right. Finnegan is still an enigma to me but I've never read him as dirty. Manipulative as all hell but not crooked."

"On another note, I've found a bit about Finnegan's brother."

"Oh?"

"Yes. Gregory Finnegan, the brother that died in the Strabane explosion. He was five years younger than Jim and joined at his brother's urging, against the wishes of his parents."

"God, no wonder Finnegan is so obsessed. The poor bastard feels some responsibility for his death."

"He started through the normal cycle of police training, basic patrol duty and so forth. But the interesting part is how in the world he ended up in Strabane rather than Belfast."

"I never gave it much thought. I figured he went wherever they sent him."

"That is true, to a point, but the real reason was much more interesting. Gregory Finnegan scored at the absolute top of his class in every regard. He had his choice of any assignment he wanted. Do you want to take a guess at what he picked?"

"Basket weaving? I've no idea."

"He was part of a team that investigated rogue republican activity throughout Northern Ireland."

"Interesting… I assume he was there working on something related?"

"Nobody knows. Whatever he was working hasn't come out yet. I'm still looking into it."

"Strange."

"What is?"

"Well, nobody has ever taken responsibility for the bombing. At least two of the high-profile republican groups specifically denounced it and vehemently denied involvement. Yet there he was, an officer specifically chartered for such things."

"Some have theorized that it was a rogue loyalist group that did it, specifically to implicate the republican factions. That angle has never borne any fruit either. But you're right. He was there and likely with a purpose."

"Keep working on this angle. If he was a regular cop, I'd write it off as unfortunate coincidence, but it sounds like he was anything but."

* * *

As a much-needed diversion, I purchased tickets to see the local sports team. They were a lovable bunch that tried hard but lacked the talent to achieve more than an occasional playoff appearance. Nevertheless, their arena was usually well-attended and lively. Angela protested mildly, feigning a desire to stay in for the evening, but I was undeterred. We needed a change of scenery, and an evening of entertainment was precisely what the doctor ordered.

It took at least half of the first period before Angela finally relaxed and got into the spirit of the proceedings. When she did, though, it was joyous. Smiling, clapping, rising and falling with the emotions of the game. The end result, surprisingly a win, made little difference. She was thoroughly lively and exuberant in her celebration.

We joined the happy throng making its way out of the arena. The surrounding eating and drinking establishments were overflowing with patrons, some already severely inebriated. "Angela, do you want to get a drink or something?"

"Sure, but these places are too loud and crowded for me. Can we try to find someplace a bit quieter?"

"Well, if you fancy an Irish pub, my favorite place isn't far once we get out of the traffic. I've not been there for a while now. I'm surprised they haven't sent out a search party."

"That sounds fun!"

* * *

My pub had a fair number of patrons, above average for the hour, but thankfully restrained and quiet. Angela studied the decor and design, nodding in approval.

"Reasonably authentic look — not bad at all," she said. "How is the food?"

"I've not been disappointed. The chef is a young man from Galway — bright and talented. Most selections are fairly authentic; other bits are Americanized, but all good."

Laura spotted me immediately as we walked through the door. "Good evening, Mister C! We were beginning to think you didn't love us anymore."

"Sorry, Laura, I've been rather busy with work lately. This is my friend Angela. Angela, Laura."

Laura whispered into my ear, "that's more like it!" She winked as she zipped into the kitchen to retrieve an order.

We found a quiet corner booth where a Guinness appeared in front of me almost immediately upon being seated. Angela opted for white wine. Conversation erupted shortly thereafter and flowed ceaselessly until Laura politely reminded us that it was past closing time. My pint had survived the evening, the last mouthful only briefly preceding our departure. Laura cast me an odd, but appreciative look as I handed her cash significantly in excess of our bill.

"I've been negligent in my visitation, Laura. You always take good care of me when I'm here. This is a little something extra to show my appreciation for all you do."

"Thanks, Mister C! Have a good evening, and it was nice to meet you, Angela. Don't let this guy give you any trouble!"

My car sat alone in the parking lot, illuminated by a lonely street lamp. Angela started to walk around to the passenger side, but my hand caught her. I pulled her back to me. Ignoring the look of surprise on her face and my own trembling nerves, I leaned in, gently kissing her lips.

I tried to pull away, my fears raging, but Angela's lips followed mine refusing my attempted exodus. Any thoughts of escape were quickly vanquished as I felt her hand caress the back of my head, pulling me closer. A long, passionate kiss followed. Electricity pulsed through my body as rational thought utterly failed me.

"Johnny!" she whispered, smiling as our lips separated. "What a wonderful surprise!"

In a few years, I would reach the half-century mark, and here I was as nervous as a teenager! Hopefully, she didn't notice. "I've got to confess, Angela, I've wanted to do that for quite some time."

"I'm glad you did."

"But now I'm thinking maybe I shouldn't have."

"Why? I certainly didn't object. Didn't you like it?"

"Oh god yes, I enjoyed it. I enjoyed it a lot! But it comes down to professional ethics and client relationships. So I'll completely understand if you want different representation. And god, I hope I didn't ruin our friendship."

The smile that had momentarily faded returned, and with it, my confidence. "You really *do* worry a lot, don't you?"

"Mack tells me it is my one true gift in life."

"Well, I have no interest in looking elsewhere, legal or otherwise. Let's take it slow and easy and see where the universe takes us, but I like the general direction."

"You've got a deal, Miss Grady!"

She pulled me in for another long kiss then a tight embrace. My thoughts were racing so quickly I was barely able to drive home.

* * *

A full slate of activities, all coordinated by Karen, awaited Angela starting early the next day. I retired to the office to enjoy a small nightcap and review anything that might need my attention. Concentration proved to be elusive as thoughts of Angela dominated. I finally dismissed all notions of achievement and allowed a myriad of fantasies to dance unfettered through my mind.

All was right with the universe until the inevitable happened: Jim Finnegan called.

"Finally getting brave are we, Johnny? She didn't seem to mind, though. I expect you're happy right now."

"Jim, are you sure you're not just a lonely voyeur at heart?"

"Hardly. Like I said, I'd love to see you with a fine Irish lady. What you've now, though… you know my thoughts on the matter. And living under your own roof at that! Downright brave!"

"I surprise myself sometimes. I assume you're calling to throw a wet blanket on my otherwise enjoyable evening."

"Do you know what Sean Grady did in the army?"

"I do not."

"He was a demolitions engineer. He was more than capable of building every bit of that car bomb. I guess you could call it keeping terrorism in the family. Dad builds it, daughter sets it off. What a sordid affair!"

"It is a long step from being able to build a bomb to actually doing it. Do you have records of Sean Grady buying parts for the timer circuit? And where on earth did he get the explosives? You said it was Semtex smuggled in from Libya. That's no simple fertilizer bomb and you know it. And so will the judge, if it even gets that far, which I doubt."

"Spoken like a man blinded by love. Angela Grady will be arrested before the year is over, mark my words. I hope you're smart enough to get out before things get too dangerous for you."

"Dangerous? What the hell do you mean by that?"

"You're dating the wrong Grady if you're serious about that question. Shanagh is more your speed — you two could live out your days in blissful denial. Death surrounds Angela Grady. Can't you see it? This case is a hornet's nest. Watch yourself — there's only so much George and I can do to protect you."

"Did your brother disturb the same nest? You neglected to share with me the nature of his particular assignment."

"I see your little researcher has been doing her job well."

"Mack's exceptional, isn't she? Avoiding the question, or was it just a bit too close to home?"

Finnegan sighed. "Maybe it was, maybe it was at that."

"You don't know either, do you?"

Finnegan's voice grew quieter. "I don't. What I do know is that he was working on *something*. He'd always give it away unknowingly talking to our mother. He had a certain lilt in his voice that wasn't there when he was working on something ordinary."

"Which gets back to my original question, Jim. Do you think he was disturbing the same hornet's nest?"

"Off the record, Johnny, and I've nothing to back this up, but that would be my suspicion. It's a deadly game to be playing. You should be watching over your shoulder, my friend. I sure as hell am."

"That's a hell of an implication, Finnegan."

"I warned you not to get involved."

CHAPTER ELEVEN

Mack looked at me, expectantly. "Well, you certainly look like the cat that swallowed the canary, John. Spill it."

"I kissed her, Mack."

"Oh, that explains why the sun rose this morning! I thought you had some real news."

"I thought you'd be happy for me."

"Don't get me wrong, I'm delighted. I simply don't understand why you've made this such a big deal. If I were in her shoes, I would have probably asked you why it took you so damn long to get around to it. I might have even lost interest waiting for you, but she's more patient that I am. Speaking of which, where is she this morning?"

"Out and about with Karen and crew."

"So I take it she didn't object to your wayward lips?"

"Surprisingly, no, not at all. Between you and Jim Finnegan, I swear I have my own personal rain-cloud following me around. He called me last night to tell me that Sean Grady was a demolitions engineer in the Army."

"That isn't good news; it gives him an avenue to create a method by which Angela could have obtained the bomb. Bastard! One of these times when he calls, you should let me talk to him. I hate the way he's constantly jerking your chain," she growled.

"Well, I turned the tables on him a bit when I started asking about his brother. I don't think he expected you to get as far with that as you have — certainly not as quickly. He did confirm my suspicions, though: Greg Finnegan was working on a something important when the bomb went off. Problem is nobody knows what."

"It might be something that your PI can dig in to. Strikes me as a bit beyond coincidence."

"I agree. I'll turn Charlie loose on it. Between us, I've also reached out to a couple of associates that can help me get our Belfast legal team together."

"You think we're going to need it, don't you?" her face darkened.

"I've got to be realistic. Finnegan, love him or hate him, is one hell of an investigator and he didn't come here to leave empty handed. He was sent to bring Angela Grady back for trial. Things are merely taking longer than he thought, so he's occupying his time toying with me. Strange thing, though, is that I think he means well. He really thinks I'm in some sort of danger."

She sighed. "The next bit of news probably isn't going to brighten your day, then…"

Connor Grady, Angela's beloved Granda, had been difficult to find until Mack discovered that we didn't know his real name. He was born in Belfast and christened Connla O'Grady.

Young Connla, it seemed, had earned a bit of a reputation and even a few arrests — all for rebel activity. Nothing was serious enough, however, to prevent him from volunteering to serve in the Second World War. He ended up spending most of his time fighting in North Africa, eventually leaving in late 1944.

"So, the old boy *was* a bit of a rebel after all," I said, superficially looking through Mack's research. "Doesn't sound like anything too remarkable or all that uncommon, though. Sounds more like youthful misbehavior than anything else."

"He either outgrew it or got better at not getting caught after leaving the army. He ended up working for a construction business in Mullingar for most of his career. He seems to have done alright for himself."

"Please don't tell me he did *too* well."

"No. There's nothing to indicate an invisible means of support. I'm still working on it, of course, but I've not turned up anything to suggest his lifestyle, spending, or anything else was out of the ordinary. He had four kids with his wife, Meryl, one of which died in infancy. Gerald, Jane, and Sean survived into adulthood, all taking Grady as their surname."

"Are you..."

"Yes, I'm going to look in to all of them as well. Gerald and Jane are alive and well, as far as I can tell. Jane married a carpenter; they moved to Canada in the early sixties. I've not found much on Gerald yet."

"I don't see much here to get worried about."

"You haven't heard all of it yet. I've not told you about Meryl."

Mack's expression drove the smile, brief as it was, from my face. "Connla's wife? What about her?"

"She died in 1972, but that isn't what worries me. It is how she died. She was in the wrong place at the wrong time, a victim of a loyalist reprisal for Bloody Friday. As far as I can tell, she was there visiting friends. Connla was back in Mullingar at the time."

"Not the best news I've heard all day..."

"Connla took it pretty hard. The local paper referred to him as *angry and vindictive* in an article about Meryl's death. Hard to blame him, they'd been together for over thirty years."

"I wonder if Finnegan believes that Connla radicalized Angela when she was young. Is there any indication that he took action as a result of his anger?"

"Nothing that I've been able to find."

"I'm still curious as to the difference in accounts at the end of his life. Angela insists that he was in command of his facilities, while Shanagh says the opposite. Any word on that?"

"I've not found anything definitive. I'm still trying to track down Gerald and Jane; perhaps they can offer an unbiased account."

* * *

An unintended siesta was interrupted by a courier's knock on my door. True to his word, Jim Finnegan had sent me copies of his case files on Maggie Albin. The binder, stuffed to nearly six inches of thickness, promised to tantalize me well into the early morning hours. I made a large pot of coffee and started my review. Mack would undoubtedly do a better job combing them for details, but at least I could do something in preparation.

The first page set the tone for the rest. A photocopy of the original newspaper report of Maggie's death showed Finnegan's handwritten notes, likely taken shortly after publication. Maggie's name was underlined and an arrow pointed off to a single word, written, re-written, and circled many times: *Suspicious.*

Dinnertime slipped by entirely unnoticed as I read Finnegan's scathing review of the Coroner's report. Notes in the margin were consistent with Charlie Hannon's assessment of Tully Smith. Impropriety flourished under his time as Coroner, and Maggie Albin's tragic death was an egregious example.

Finnegan's critique started with an extensive analysis of the accident itself. He had painstakingly computed speeds, stopping distances, and the pattern of skidding recorded at the accident. All were tantalizingly inconsistent with Tully Smith's final report. Completely ignored throughout the woefully inadequate investigation was the presence of a partial, muddy boot print on the car's rear bumper. Finnegan's notes tagged it as a man's work boot, size twelve. He had even listed a handful of possible brands based on the tread pattern.

The notes lacked the missing injury photographs that Charlie Hannon had supposedly seen, but Finnegan had carefully noted their absence. His theory scrawled into the margin and spanning several pages, followed precisely what Charlie had conveyed: the photographs showed inconsistencies with the prepared narrative of an alcohol-induced crash.

The notes took on a more disturbing countenance toward the last few pages. Finnegan had made the same connection as Charlie Hannon, backtracking Maggie's friends and associates. One particular note caught my attention:

```
Omagh Witness Fergus Clarke.
Danced with woman who gave her name as
Siobhan O'Connor.
Has positively identified Angela Grady from
picture.
```

The final line was underlined repeatedly and angrily.

<u>Will Testify</u>.

* * *

Angela had not returned by the time I had gone to bed, and a quick glance out my front window revealed that she had spent the night elsewhere. With the pressure of financial hardship and roofless nights removed, the enigmatic free spirit had returned — or at least was showing its presence.

Charlie Hannon was my first e-mail of the day. Our association was rapidly turning profitable — for him. Fergus Clarke was added to his investigative list; I needed to know how much of a threat he presented. I also added a cryptic line onto the end of the message: *Find out his shoe size.*

Finnegan's notes on Tully Smith awaited me. Smith died from a massive heart attack while walking his dogs, something he did several times each day. From all accounts, he had been fairly health-conscious making the death unexpected. But, almost predictably, his cause of death was ruled natural causes.

The binder contained a complete copy of a handwritten ledger. Several of the entries had been circled, presumably by Finnegan, but their purpose was not clear to me. I'd need Mack to decipher what might fit between the lines. Failing that, Jerry knew a forensic accountant that might be able to shed some light on what I was looking at.

Angela's absence provided an opportunity for what might otherwise be a bit awkward. I wasn't looking forward to talking to Maggie Albin's parents, knowing that our conversation would inevitably open old and painful wounds. Her mother answered my call, her voice light and lilting. Angela had told them to expect my call and within a few words she successfully surmised my identity.

My call turned out to be more welcome than I could have imagined. Margery Albin had never given up on the dream of having her daughter's death investigated and explained. She ripped the official findings mercilessly, offering a scathing indictment of Tully Smith.

"They had the answer decided before they ever started," she seethed. "I wouldn't be surprised if one of Tully's boys wasn't directly involved."

"Tully's boys?"

"Oh, he had a crew that he was seen with regularly. Nary a one of them was worth a damn!"

Dammit. More questions for Charlie and undoubtedly more payments! "Tell me about the notebook. I understand it was the only thing to come up missing."

"That and her EpiPen. Maggie was a neat girl, always closing doors, tidying up, folding her clothes. She took after her father in that regard: good with the details. I knew something was wrong the minute I saw it!"

"The notebook?"

"No. Her desk. The upper right drawer was left open, like she grabbed something and left in a hurry, so much so that she forgot to close it. The problem is that Maggie never forgot to close anything. She had a bit of a compulsion in that regard."

"Was there anything else in the house missing or out of order?"

"Not that we know. We were never as neat and organized as Maggie, even at our best efforts. She'd try, organizing our bills, receipts, statements and so on, but it would always drift away until the next time she sorted everything for us."

"This might sound like an odd question, but are you sure it was Maggie and not someone else in the house?"

"There was nothing to indicate someone broke in. The door lock was intact, no windows broken, nothing like that. And with only one drawer left slightly out of place, it was hard to think it was anyone else."

"Wait. She was in so much of a hurry that she forgot to shut her desk drawer, but she had the time to lock the door on her way out?

"The door always locks unless we specifically set it not to. There was a time when we never locked it but when some neighbors had some problems with young people getting out of hand and pinching a few things, we started locking the door. It became a habit, and honestly, I think it made Maggie feel a bit better."

"Was it like her to go out without leaving you a note?"

"It was not. To be sure, it was not."

"Do you know what she spent the day doing?"

"She was with her father most of the day. They were tending to a variety of chores around our sheep farm and likely a run into town. It was an ordinary morning, Mister Costa."

I pressed Margery Albin a bit more on the events of the day, but nothing remarkable stood out. She also had no insight as to the contents of Maggie's notebook, but did mention that it was something that Maggie carried frequently.

"She kept it with her quite a bit. I don't know what all she used it for, but it was common to see her with it. She'd jot notes from time to time, but I never pressed her as to what she was doing."

"Tell me about her reaction to the Constabulary's original investigation into Angela."

"Her reaction was similar to mine: utter disbelief mixed with frustration. Not only did we know Angela's whereabouts that morning, we knew that she was utterly incapable of being involved. That detective's insinuations were ridiculous from the outset and got worse as time went on. Angela and Maggie would talk on the phone fairly regularly; I know the pressure from the Constabulary was a common topic for them. The whole thing upset Maggie terribly."

"You know, I've promised Angela, regardless of the outcome of her current situation, that I will look in to Maggie's death. I fully intend to keep that promise to her."

"We want you to know that we support you and Angela fully. Perhaps if she can prove that once and for all, she will stop blaming herself for Maggie's death. We certainly don't hold her responsible."

"Have you told her that, Margery?"

"Countless times. We keep doing it in the hopes that someday she'll let go of that weight. Angela brought so much joy into Maggie's life. Without fail, if Maggie needed a friend, Angela was there; in many ways, she was like a second daughter to us. That's how much she meant to Maggie. She doesn't belong in prison. She had nothing to do with Strabane and nothing to do with Maggie's murder. I'd bet my life on it. If there's anything you need, give us a call. And if you ever fancy a visit to County Tyrone, don't you dare think of staying elsewhere."

CHAPTER TWELVE

I spent the remainder of the morning at my gym swimming laps. I had been a member for a few years, but rarely went. My use of the pool was more of a diversion than exercise.

Lunchtime arrived without any word from Angela, so Mack and I took a break from research to enjoy a well-earned respite at a nice restaurant. As much as we tried, the conversation inevitably drifted back to our work. She was picking at her salad, selecting the various leaves seemingly at random. "I'm sorry if my reaction this morning was less than enthusiastic. If it hurt you, I didn't mean it that way."

I hadn't really thought about it, having written it off to her normal, indifferent facade. "Honestly, it hadn't crossed my mind until you mentioned it just now. No, you didn't hurt me."

"Good. You've worried me quite a bit these last few years, skulking around at home and drinking so much. I want you to know that I love you. You're a dear friend, albeit a bit neurotic and goofy at times, but you get the idea. And I want you to be happy, more than anything."

"You're not dying or something, are you, Mack?"

"No, but you might want to kill me when you hear what I have to say." she had that look: the look of someone who knew more than they were telling. Dammit. I really needed to learn how to do that!

"Mack!"

"Okay, Okay." Her face twisted, painfully. "The bad news comes in two parts. Must I?"

"Mack!!"

"I've talked to some of her past boyfriends, and there's a bit of a pattern emerging. She's quick to move in, and financially, well, it isn't pretty. Her money goes to clothes, shoes, parties, and trips. The man is left holding the bag for everything else. Another thing in common from talking to them was that they all felt that her commitment was, well, less than genuine. She had lots of friends, male and female, and couldn't be counted on for much of anything. Plans? What plans? Not to mention a pattern of borderline honesty. Sound familiar?"

"It does. Go on."

"Sam was the only one who even remotely held her feet to the fire, so to speak, when it came to things like rent and car payments. The others were so happy to have her hanging off their arm from time to time that they simply overlooked the rest."

"You talked to Sam Thomas?"

"Yes, John. I talked to Sam. I'll know more when I meet him. We have a date next week."

This surprised me, and with it, a tinge of anger spread through me. I still held Sam, rightly or wrongly, in low esteem. "Mack, I would never ask you to do something you're not comfortable with. Don't do anything on my account. Besides, that is providing aid and comfort to the enemy."

"It would seem that you've vanquished that enemy. I did a bit of digging on him and he seems a genuinely decent guy. It's just lunch; nothing to worry about, sir frets-a-lot! Speaking of which… It was a lunch you had with Angela that was the tipping point in their relationship. What on earth did you two talk about? Or did you do more than talk?"

"Funny, but Finnegan hinted at the same thing when we met at my pub. He said that my name kept coming up between her and her friends afterwards. We were catching up, you know; a friendly conversation; it really wasn't anything earth-shattering. And yes, oh nosy one, it was only talking. I enjoyed her company, to be sure — I always do. But seriously, I can't imagine that our conversation triggered anything. Hell, I didn't even hear from Angela for several months after."

"Something changed and Sam sure as hell noticed it. He was tiring of her prior, but that set him on his way out of the relationship; then Finnegan came along and removed any lingering doubts. He is completely over her. And all right around the time she got together with you. Awfully convenient; one man gives her the boot and another one is waiting in the wings, eager and willing to spend money on her. Don't fool yourself too much, sir sneaky, I suspect she's known your feelings for a while now."

"Honestly, Mack, I don't care if she wants to bleed me a bit financially; I'm well-protected in that regard. And I enjoy the hell out of her company. It isn't the first time I've gone ass-over-tea-kettle nuts over a gal, either. Something similar happened to me before I knew you. Big difference was I was too damn scared to say or do anything about it; and just like you said this morning, she got tired of waiting for me and went off and met someone. She's married with three or four kids now. I'm happy for her, I really am, but there are times when I can't help but wonder what her reaction might have been had I spoken up; or did what I did last night with Angela. I'll never know. With Angela, I do, at least to some degree."

"Do you know? I mean, at all?"

The smile vanished from my face. "You've got a point, of course. No, probably not. Maybe I don't want to know; hell, I might not even care anymore."

She wrinkled her nose, totally unconvinced. "Oh, you care. You can tell yourself that all you want, but you care. And there are a lot of ways that this can end badly. And you know that, too."

Dammit, Jillian MacDonald. Why do you have to be right so much of the time? "Yeah. Yeah."

Mack sipped her water, nervously. "Well, in that spirit, this is the second bit of bad news, and far worse. Finnegan showed Sam the picture and the sketch from Mary Delane without giving him any background. He identified both of them as Angela without hesitation."

"I can see that, Mack. My stomach got all twisted into knots when I saw them, too. The resemblance is there, no doubt."

"Sam didn't say resemblance; he said it was her. Definitive on his answers, enough to be a good prosecution witness. He might do it, too, if asked. He's not the least bit happy with her, you know."

"The picture is a tough bit of evidence, but I think we can beat it. I really do."

Mack plunked her water glass on the table, strongly enough for a bit to spill out of the top. "Finnegan's got more than the picture, John."

I interrupted before Mack could finish. "Yeah, I know. He's got the guy from the club that claims to have danced with Siobhan O'Connor that will testify that it was Angela."

Mack started to cry, her talking interrupted by ebbs and flows of sobbing. "No. He has her fingerprints, John; he has her fingerprints on something related to the car! My god, I am so sorry to have to tell you this. The thing is, I want to like her, and I want her to be innocent for your sake. And I'm so damn happy that you're finally getting to spend time with her because I know how you feel. But every time I find something new, things look worse for her. I'm supposed to be helping you defend her!"

Mack's blubbering was loud enough that several patrons looked over at us. A few gave me a look of disdain. They earned a scornful look in return for failing to mind their own damn business.

"Mack," I whispered as I moved to where I could hug her, "It's alright and I'm glad you told me. Always keep one thing in mind: Finnegan is a master at what he does. He could be telling the truth, lying outright, or somewhere in between — whatever it takes to swing things in his direction. I think if they truly had such a damning piece of evidence, she'd already be in handcuffs. Besides, fingerprints can be beaten, witnesses can be discredited, and we have an adamant eyewitness working in our favor. You keep following the evidence wherever it leads."

She collected herself, somewhat. "It was easier doing this when the people were just names and clients. With Angela living there and your feelings for her the way they are, it suddenly made it all so real. What is really driving me crazy is that nothing is definitive. I'm sorry, John. I'm tired, frustrated, and damn hormonal right now, if you follow me."

I nodded, holding Mack while she regained her composure. "You're right. Right now, our entire defense hinges on an eyewitness that I've never met. I don't know anything about her, really."

Mack's face suddenly brightened and she quickly sat up straight. "Oh my god! I almost forgot! I do have a bit of good news for a change. The name of Angela's alibi is Julia Rohnan, and do you know what she did for a living before she retired?"

I shook my head.

"Guess!"

"Mack!!"

"You really need to learn to be more fun, sometimes. She was a police sketch artist... which means..."

"Please tell me she was a sworn police officer!"

She nodded, beaming ear to ear.

I started smiling widely as well. "No wonder her statement has carried so much weight all these years! And you said you never had good news!"

Mack and I hugged in celebration. The waiter and several nearby patrons started applauding, and before I realized what was happening, Champagne appeared at our table. We exchanged looks of bewilderment and amusement before I decided to give in to mischief.

"Champagne for everyone! My treat!"

I winked at Mack who was bright red from trying to contain her laughter. "You were saying something about learning to be more fun?" I whispered. It was all she could do to avoid spitting out her drink.

* * *

128

Angela's car occupied its usual spot outside my house but was joined by a second, unfamiliar one parked nearby. We found Angela and Karen, both looking decidedly bedraggled, sprawled on the couch, sleeping. Mack and I quickly curtailed our conversation, but it was too late. We had awakened Angela.

"Sorry," I whispered, "we'll be in the office, so you two should be able to continue resting undisturbed."

"I hope you don't mind that I invited Karen and a couple more friends over for dinner this evening. You met all of them at the benefit."

"Sure, they're more than welcome. I'll hide in the music room."

"Don't hide; please join us." She hugged me briefly before returning to the sofa. Given their appearance, I was fully expecting her to reek of alcohol. Instead, her perfume seemed to be fighting a losing battle with perspiration.

It was several hours before they were up and about. Angela, with Karen lurking in the periphery, popped into the office. "Well, you two look better! When are the others coming over?"

"A couple of hours if it's still alright," answered Angela.

"Of course. Do you need me to help get anything ready?"

"It's my turn to handle dinner. Karen's going to help, but we're both so worn out another helper wouldn't hurt."

"Sure, I'd be glad to, what did you have in mind?"

Angela hesitated, a sheepish look appearing on her face. "I had planned on going to the seafood market for fresh crab legs, but I lost track of time and they're closed now."

Karen leaned her head into the room. "She's not the best at planning in case you hadn't noticed." Angela blushed as Karen continued. "But, I'm going to cut her a little slack this time around. She worked hard helping us."

My curiosity had gotten the best of me. "I don't mean to pry, but what were you two up to?"

Karen laughed. "Oh, the normal stuff yesterday: breakfast with a couple of old classmates, shopping, then afternoon drinks and dinner. The evening, though, turned into more work than we expected. My father's organization held their big food drive yesterday, so we were out collecting donations of canned goods. A lot of the volunteers didn't show up, so a handful of us ended up having to sort and stock."

Angela took over the narrative. "That took us into the wee hours of the morning, then a couple hours later we were up cooking and serving breakfast."

Karen handed me a business card. I recognized the charity, having anonymously donated to them on several occasions. They collected canned goods and ran several places where the homeless could eat. "This is your father's organization, Karen?"

She nodded. "He came over to the United States a few years after I did to lead the charity."

"I've heard of them, but I never made the connection to your father. They do a good thing; I'm sure you're quite proud of his work. You know, since you two were basically up all night, the least I can do is take care of dinner tonight. How many people are coming?"

* * *

A little bit of good fortune and a few beneficial contacts helped me orchestrate a successful dinner for Angela and friends. My attempts to vanish into the scenery, however, were less fortunate. I smiled and nodded politely for several hours, finally slipping quietly into my office. The conversation, prodigious alcohol consumption, and the laughter, replete with unknown names and events, continued well past midnight.

Karen lingered past the departure of the other guests, making the welcome offer to help clean up. We retreated to the kitchen while Angela remained in the living room.

"Angela told me Sergeant Finnegan is back in the picture," she said while filling the dishwasher. "I find the whole thing utterly unbelievable and have since the beginning."

I tossed a dish towel over my shoulder. "Yes, it caught me by surprise to say the least. You were there for part of her first go-around with this, weren't you?"

"That I was." She stopped what she was doing, lowering her voice. "The first Constabulary visit was nothing. Ange told them about her trip to see Maggie and they were done with her. We joked about it a bit. Must've brought bad luck because a few months later, all hell broke loose. I had already made my arrangements to come here for University. I felt bad leaving her, but she insisted that she'd be okay."

"I do have to say, she is a delightfully optimistic person. I really like that about her."

"It can get her in a bit of trouble at times. She always means well, though."

I laughed quietly. "I've seen a bit of that in action, I think."

Karen leaned toward me, speaking quietly. "Like with dinner tonight, she means well but doesn't always do the best job of following through. If you want something to happen, probably best to set it up yourself — then be ready for it to change. But like I said, things with her have a way of working out in the end."

"From your lips to God's ears!"

She smiled, nodding gently. We finished our chores in silence before she departed for the evening.

* * *

Angela intercepted me on the way to my bedroom, waving me into the living room. It bore no evidence of the evening's merrymaking and, in fact, looked better than it had started the evening. She motioned for me to sit with her on the sofa.

"Wow! Thank you! You didn't have to go to all that trouble, but it looks great."

"After all you've done for me today, Johnny, it seemed the least I could do. My friends appreciated your hospitality tonight, and so do I. Thanks a million."

"My pleasure. It was nice to hear the sounds of people having a good time. I guess I didn't realize how annoyingly quiet this place had become. Happiness has an energy that lingers, doesn't it? I'm sounding corny, aren't I?"

"Not at all — I understand completely. Speaking of energy, what's the weather supposed to be like tomorrow?"

"I think it is supposed to be nice, why?"

"How would you feel about taking a bike ride? My bike and carrier are over at Karen's house — I'll need to go pick them up."

"I've not been on my bike in five years. What kind of ride are you talking about?"

"Oh, nothing too extreme — mostly paved, some trail. I'll go gently on you."

"Sure, why not? I've got to die of something, right?" First dancing, now a bike ride. What the hell was I thinking?

She laughed. "Old age, preferably."

"I suppose a little exercise wouldn't hurt, but I'll warn you — I'm terribly out of shape, so I don't expect to be able to keep up. It turns out that it takes more than *having* a gym membership to get in shape; something about actually having to go."

"You have a gym membership?"

"Yeah. I go swimming every so often, not much else. You're more than welcome to come along any time you want."

Her face brightened. "I love swimming! Bikes tomorrow, then swimming the following day — how does that sound?"

"Painful!"

* * *

The blinking message light on my cell phone had gone unnoticed. Without thinking, I opened the awaiting message. I should have surmised the source, but it still managed to catch me off guard. Damn you, Jim Finnegan!

A dozen lifetimes of penance and good deeds will not make up for what she has done.

Another message awaited in the queue. Obediently, I read it.

You're probably wondering about the fingerprint. Is it real, or was I toying with you and poor Sam?

I could make you wait for discovery but I won't make you suffer any more than you already have.

It is real.

Drink up, Johnny.

CHAPTER THIRTEEN

Mack found me in the garage pumping air into the tires of my bike, dirty and undoubtedly red-faced. She looked at me, her lips curled into the hint of a smile. "What on earth are you doing?"

"Angela wants to go on a bike ride."

"I didn't know you even knew how to ride a bike, let alone owned one."

"Jillian MacDonald! Believe it or not, I was a kid once."

"Oh, I know that. I just wasn't aware that the wheel had been invented at the time."

I pretended to glare at her. "Don't you have some work to do or something?"

"Oh, sure I do. But I'm not doing it right now and this is more fun. Have you tested it to make sure the wheels aren't going to fall off?"

"Relax, Mack, you're in my will. I'm leaving you my coin collection."

"You don't collect coins."

"Exactly!"

She glared, stomping back into the house only to reappear a moment later with a large bottle of pain medicine in her hand. "Good luck finding this when you get back!"

She waved goodbye to me as she closed the door.

* * *

Angela returned, her bike secured to the carrier on the back of her car. I added mine and climbed into the passenger seat of her car.

Her eyes studied me, briefly. "Where's your helmet and water bottle?"

"I don't have a helmet. I've never done any riding that was intense enough to warrant one. I was hoping we could stop somewhere and grab a sports drink or two."

"Okay. I'll let the helmet thing slide today since we're going on an easy ride, but make plans to get one."

We drove a few miles out of town, turning onto a narrow access road that led to a small parking lot. A marker and an attached map charted the course of the trails, the variants marked with different colors. I was hoping for the green trail, the shortest loop on the map. Somehow, though, I knew my fate and impending cardiac arrest was on one of the other, longer, loops. At least the surrounding countryside looked flat for the most part.

Angela was dressed like she knew what she was doing, complete with helmet and proper riding attire. The outfit, while covering her nearly completely, complemented her toned and shapely figure leaving little to the imagination — not that my imagination hadn't labored overtime in that area already. I, on the other hand, was dressed to conceal.

"Let's get going," she said, snapping the straps from her helmet into place.

"I'll be lucky to have enough breath left to speak after we've gone a hundred yards, Angela. I'm not kidding — it has been a long time since I've done this and I'm really out of shape."

"You've got to push a little bit or you'll never increase your fitness level. But I promise to go gentle." She threw her leg over her bike, ready to start riding. "At least a little bit. Follow me!"

What had I gotten myself into?

* * *

The soreness had already started, making each step an uncomfortable proposition. "Jesus, Mack, that damn near killed me."

"Well, sometimes you should be careful what you wish for. Are you going to make it through the afternoon?"

I stretched, pacing the office in an attempt to stay loose. "I think so, as long as I keep moving. I'm beginning to see the futility in all of this."

Her face grew suddenly troubled. "Our case?"

"Oh no, sorry, I didn't mean that. I mean the foolish idea that things could work out between Angela and I. She keeps telling me that age is just a number, but I've got to be realistic. I'm wiped out from short ride and she's out for a run. There's no way I could keep her happy, if you know what I mean. I'm such an idiot, Mack."

"All this after one bike ride? Something you haven't done for, what, five years? Give it time."

I smiled and nodded, mostly to allow the subject to drop gracefully. "Anything new or interesting?"

"You really should learn to develop an appreciation for libraries. I've never quite understood why you avoid them with such zeal."

It was because librarians, from my youngest recollections, hated me. I could never understand their enthusiasm for card catalogs, sorting, and relentless organization. But worse was the condescending look they would give me, peering over the counter, inspecting every book choice I made, rolling their eyes if something didn't meet their standards. And I could never find anything — my mind simply didn't categorize things the way librarians did. Things hadn't improved much for me with the advent of the Internet and search engines, but at least computers didn't belittle me when my attempts failed. "Call it childhood trauma. What do you have?"

"If you ever get to Mullingar, there's a delightful librarian there that you should thank. We've been chatting for several days now, her name is..."

"Mack!"

"Alright, already! I started investigating Connla O'Grady a bit more and got stuck pretty quickly until my new friend suggested trying the traditional spelling, O'Gradhaig. Once I did that, things became a bit clearer to me. Connla was born in Cork in 1919, right in the middle of the Irish War of Independence. When things went crazy in 1920, Connla's mother took him and the other children to Mullingar to live with her parents. It was good timing, too. They got out before the Black and Tans went nuts and burned a chunk of the city. The interesting part in all this was that the dad was hardly around."

"Why not?"

"He was a proud member of the IRA, right in the center of some of the biggest conflicts almost up until the treaty was signed. The British captured him and held him in the north in 1923. He escaped and made his way back to Mullingar. The stress of it all likely shortened his life. Between disease from his captivity and war injuries, he ended up dying when Connla was a teenager."

"So Connla's stories about his rebel days were probably bits of his own mixed with stories from his father."

"Likely. What I've not been able to reconcile is Angela's and Shanagh's divergent opinion of Connla's mental state late in life. I'm still working on that. But you have to admit that there is a pattern emerging in the O'Gradhaig clan."

"It would certainly seem that republican tendencies run deep on her father's side of the tree. I can see the foundation of Finnegan's circumstantial case, at least part of it. Have you had any time to work on Shanagh's family yet?"

"Not much. I reached out to her, but she's not returned my calls."

My brow wrinkled. "Really? She's always been fairly reliable at getting back with me. I'll send her a note asking for her to call you. Now will you please tell me where you hid my aspirin?"

* * *

Angela burst through the front door, quickly closing it behind her. Something in the sound caught my attention, so I ventured out to the foyer. I found her, sweaty and breathless, hands on her knees. "Did you have a good run?"

She looked worried. "I don't know if all this has me paranoid or if you've got a creeper in the neighborhood." Her words flowed irregularly as she caught her breath.

My face curled into an angry frown. "What do you mean?"

"I saw the same man three or four times. It didn't register at first, but then it started to get creepy. As I came around the corner, the last turn onto your street, he was standing there, watching me. I made one heck of a sprint toward the door! What are you doing!?"

I opened the front door, my eyes scanning the street beyond. A man, likely a few years older than Angela, walked toward my house. My appearance at the door caused him to abruptly change course and quickly walk away. I closed the door and secured the dead bolt.

In spite of rarely interacting with my neighbors beyond cordial greetings, I knew all of them by sight, many by name, even into surrounding blocks. "I don't recognize him, Angela. Has that happened to you in this neighborhood before?"

"It hasn't; I've not seen this man before."

"Well, you're definitely not paranoid. He changed direction in a hurry when he saw me."

"A policeman, perhaps? You said I was under surveillance."

"Unlikely, unless he is the worst undercover cop that has ever lived. I don't know what his game was, but I agree with your intuition. I'll get you added to my membership when we're at the gym tomorrow. Until we can figure out who he is and what he was doing here, you'll be much safer there than running around the neighborhood."

"How are you going to find his name?"

"My security cameras probably captured a good image of him."

"You have cameras? Why?"

"I do. I've dealt with some unsavory characters in my time, a fair number of which aren't too happy with me. The system seemed like a wise investment."

She pulled close to me, her arms wrapped around my shoulders. "Thanks. That guy had me rattled." We hugged, tightly. "I'm going to get a quick shower," she whispered as we separated. "I have a lunch date with Mack."

"Okay. Keep your eyes open and if you see that guy following you or something, call the cops!"

* * *

Jerry's friend had set up my original security system and had returned on several occasions to keep it up to date. The most recent update had come at a fortuitous time; the images it captured were startlingly good compared to its predecessor. I found numerous views of the unknown man's face, saved a handful of the best, and called Jerry.

"Jack! Good to hear from you. Rumor has it that you've gotten yourself a pretty roommate these days."

"Why does it seem that everyone knows my business these days? I've got a bit of an urgent matter…"

"Always in a hurry!" Coughing. "What can I do for you?"

"I'm going to send you some pictures of a man that was lurking around the neighborhood while Angela was out for a run. I've never seen him before, so he's not one of my long-lost friends, so to speak. See if you can find out who he is."

I was met with a brief period of silence, interrupted only be Jerry's occasional coughing in the background.

"I've got them. He looks foreign."

"How the hell can you tell that from a picture? How does a
139

foreign person look different, exactly?"

"For being so damn smart, you can be mighty dumb at times. I know a guy that might be able to help. I'll get back to you on these."

CHAPTER FOURTEEN

The young lady working in the gym's membership department was pleasant but frustrating. I wanted to add Angela to my membership and get busy swimming before my loudly protesting muscles got the upper hand. She felt it necessary to endlessly review membership options, training plans, personal trainers, diet plans and, of course, the myriad of classes they offered.

We finally got through the process and Angela had her membership card. "You were getting a bit frustrated with her, weren't you?"

"She's only doing her job but yes, my muscles started to complain while we were sitting there. It was more of an ongoing argument with them, really. Some unsavory character spent the morning yesterday subjecting me to untold forms of torture that are, in civilized parts of the world, banned. It was only through great cunning and personal resolve that I was able to escape at all!"

She smiled. "I'll be sure to defend you from any unsavory characters that might attempt to abduct you this morning. I promise!" She winked as she entered the women's locker room.

It was my favorite time of day to visit the pool. The early morning before-work swimmers were long gone, leaving several hours before the swim-at-lunch crowd would arrive. The majority of the pool was left to more casual, less hurried members. Today's population was as hoped; a few people swam laps; others waited on chairs, poolside, swimming whenever the spirit moved them, insatiably on their phone or reading during their long respites. I recognized a few of them but had never made any effort to get acquainted.

Angela emerged from the locker room a short time later. It was all I could do to avoid staring at her. Her two-piece suit was more modest and athletic than a string bikini, but not by much. It teased my imagination even more than her riding outfit.

"This is a great pool! Thanks a million for bringing me!" she said, placing her towel and a small bag on the seat next to mine. "Come on!"

I normally entered the pool judiciously, even though it was heated, but I followed Angela's lead, diving in to the deep end. Her swimming, much like her riding, was effortless and graceful. I fared a bit better, though, staying with her on our first swim to the pool's shallow end.

"Not bad, Johnny! I knew you had it in you."

"Well, that was only one lap. But unlike bike riding, I've actually done this a bit recently."

She slipped gracefully under the water, popping up directly in front of me. A quick kiss followed. "Just so that the ladies here know not to have their eye on you!"

She zipped back under the water, starting another lap. Many followed, as I did my best to keep up. She looked so flawlessly beautiful that it was difficult to avoid leering. Several times, I caught myself being an observer rather than a participant.

Out of breath and energy sagging, I offered feeble protestation to another lap. "I'm going to take a short break to catch my breath and check for messages. I've got a friend of mine researching the identity of our stranger yesterday. Perhaps he has some news."

"Okay, I'm going to swim a few more laps and then I'll join you."

A quick check of my phone revealed no awaiting messages. It was optimistic on my part, but I didn't want to miss any urgent messages. My eyes returned, as if beckoned by the Siren's call, to the sleek motion of Angela as she slid through the water. It was as she climbed the ladder that I first noticed the scar; then the second smaller blemish to its right. At first, I dismissed it as lighting, then as birthmarks. As she neared, however, their irregular, jagged shape removed all doubts. The scars had healed with a slightly different coloration, redder, that the surrounding skin. A subtle downward shift in the waistline of her bottoms exposed them, ever so slightly. Otherwise, I would not have noticed. I quickly glanced back at my phone, not wanting to get caught staring. She had apparently not noticed, or so I hoped.

"Any word?"

I glanced up at her, smiling. "Nothing yet. Wishful thinking, I expect."

She shrugged her shoulders, tossing a towel onto her head. "Nothing wrong with that!"

* * *

As much as I wanted to spend the afternoon disengaged, work beckoned. Mack and I brought Angela up to speed on our recent progress. The existence of the supposed fingerprint, although we never mentioned how we learned about it, summoned an immediate and passionate reaction from Angela.

"Impossible," she said, her voice resolute and strong. "It simply can't be."

"All we know at this point is that it was found on something related to the car and they needed to use a new technology to find it. While I find it troubling, we don't know enough about it yet to truly react to it."

"Well, I can react to it." Angela's voice was as loud as I'd ever heard it. "It is total crap. I wouldn't put it beyond Jim Finnegan to plant it there to get a conviction."

Mack and I exchanged glances, her face wrinkled with concern.

"Honestly, Angela, based on what we've found investigating him, it wouldn't be in character for him to do that. Hauling you into the police station for questioning, attempting to coerce a confession, that's his style. Planting evidence isn't. But that does bring up an interesting point, and something I'm going to tread a little bit delicately asking. Can you think of anyone who would benefit from your conviction? Anyone who has a grudge. Anything?"

Angela's face paled. "You think that I'm being framed?"

"I don't know, but I'm leaving it open as a possibility."

"I thought Finnegan might be trying to exact revenge for his brother. Beyond that, I've not given it much thought. But I just can't imagine why anyone would do that to me."

"I can't either, but I've seen it happen before. It is often someone close, someone unexpected."

She nodded, silently staring into the distance.

* * *

A trip to a local coffee shop helped restore our focus. Mack briefed Angela on the progress of our family research to-date. Revelations about Connla's background seemed to both intrigue and confuse her.

"So some of his stories might have been a wee bit true after all," Angela said, smiling gently. "He *was* a bit of a rebel, but his father was a real one. What I don't understand," the smile departed from her face, "is why my mother, never told me any of this. She kept insisting that his mind was slipping."

I shook my head. The differences in their recollections had been troublesome and sent my mind spinning off into different directions. The conversation between Mack and Angela faded into the background while thoughts raced through my head; disconcerting thoughts that I wasn't ready to share with anyone yet. The sharp noise of Mack clearing her throat drew me back into the present.

The conversation had shifted all the way back to Connla's parents. The O'Grady family's move from Cork to Mullingar was facilitated by their longstanding friendship with the Brennan family. Young Connla and David A. Brennan became fast friends. David eventually took over the family construction business, immediately hiring Connla to be a site boss."

"Mack, is this the same Brennan that was a participant in her

Granda Connor's musical group?"

"One and the same. Seems that their friendship was lifelong. The families were close knit, John. Connla married David's sister, Meryl."

A quick look through Mack's research showed that Brennan's construction company was quite successful, gaining strong profits from bidding various construction jobs throughout Ireland — both in the Republic and the North. Their breakthrough, however, came in the lucrative contracts awarded for post World War II reconstruction, specifically in North Africa.

"North Africa includes Libya, Mack..."

"That is does. Connla served in that theater of the war — maybe he made some valuable connections when he was there. Now I can't say for certain if the North African jobs were his idea or not, but I can with absolute certainty say that he served as the contractor for a lot of them."

Finnegan's establishment of method was looking better by the minute. Angela knew it, too; her face was troubled.

"Any idea how long Connla's trips into North Africa continued?"

Mack looked at her laptop, clicking vigorously. "Into the early 1990's with certainty. Of course, by that time travel to certain countries — Libya in particular — was closely monitored. I've not turned up anything even slightly out of the ordinary or remotely improper about his dealings."

"I remember that occasionally he would go on business trips," interjected Angela, "but I had no idea where he was going."

"Assuming for a minute that Finnegan is, at least partially, on the right track, Connla would know that his trips would be watched and monitored closely. I'm betting he would stay high-profile and squeaky clean while letting others do the dirty work. And take the risk..."

"John, there were a veritable alphabet soup of associates that tagged along for his various trips and jobs. Not to mention the local companies in North Africa that supplied labor, materials, you name it."

"Yeah. The real activity would be happening behind the scenes, anyway. If we're somehow on the right track, it is way beyond our capabilities. It would take an entire task force years of research and investigation to shake out the details. And Connla's been gone for almost twenty years. When did David A. Brennan die?"

"He died in 2000 leaving the company to two of his sons. They've done alright, mild growth moving with the ups and downs of the economy, but nothing like the success David and Connla were able to achieve for the firm."

"And nothing out of the ordinary for Connla's finances, right?"

Mack sighed. "Fortunately, no. I've looked at it every way I can. If he had a secret stash of money, none of his kids or grandkids got any of it. Inheritances were as expected, as was his lifestyle."

Angela nodded, her expressing easing. "I'm going to get a refill. Can I get anyone anything while I'm up?"

We shook our heads. "And what about Brennan's company, Mack?"

"Still working on it. They're privately held, so they don't have to release as much data. I may have to engage Charlie to look into them a bit more. Good thing you're not paying by the curse. You'd be bankrupt already."

CHAPTER FIFTEEN

While Mack and Angela had disappeared early, ostensibly to visit the library to do some family tree research, I took the opportunity to call Shanagh. Our conversation was cordial but uncharacteristically sparse as we discussed recent developments. It took an entirely unexpected turn, however, when I mentioned the scars.

"Shanagh, Angela and I went swimming recently, and I couldn't help but notice several scars. If it isn't any of my business, tell me and I'll drop it. She's not said anything about them, so I don't expect it is relevant."

There was a pause, long enough for me to be uncertain if Shanagh was still on the line. "Hello? Shanagh?"

"Sorry, John, I'm surprised that she's not mentioned them to you, especially now, you two being a couple and all."

Couple? A brief flit of butterflies reminded me that some things hadn't changed. I'd let it go. "I'm not trying to stick my nose in where it doesn't belong."

"This is something you need to know." Shanagh's voice had dropped, in both pitch and volume. Her words arrived deliberately, almost hesitantly. "She should have told you right away. They are the result of something that happened when she was twelve — almost thirteen. What a hell of a birthday present. Those scars are from shrapnel. Angie was seriously injured by an explosion in Belfast, ironically only a few blocks from where Meryl died. It was touch and go for a while, but she's strong and pulled through it."

"Jesus."

"There's more." Shanagh's voice stumbled, breaking slightly. "Sorry. I'll get with it, here."

"We don't have to do this now…"

"No." Her voice strengthened. "You need to know, and Angela should have told you. She's not able to have children, John, the injuries were too extensive. That isn't the most important part, though, unless, of course, you had your heart set on a family."

Stunned, I blurted out the first remotely rational comment I could muster. "No, we've not really discussed that."

"She was, expectedly, deeply hurt by it. The emotional scars took a long time to heal; perhaps some of them never have entirely. There was a period of time when she was discouraged, angry, and bitter. I'd not seen that part of her, and thankfully with time and therapy, it passed."

"I can't begin to imagine what she went through. I think it is best to drop the subject, though, and let her share it when and if she's ready."

"I've not gotten to the part that you need to know, yet. When the Constabulary searched our house, they took her diary from that time period. Apparently, she had written something in there that piqued their interest. Finnegan focused on it a lot when he questioned me."

"What on earth did she write?"

"You'll have to ask her that question, and I'm betting she isn't going to like it when you do. The Constabulary intimated that what was in there might hurt her case. Our solicitor told me, privately, that it was fortunate that she had a strong alibi. Whatever was written had him rattled a bit, I think. I don't see how you can possibly defend her without knowing the contents."

"I'm afraid you're right. I'm not looking forward to the discussion."

* * *

I spent the majority of the morning and early afternoon dreading the upcoming conversation. I rehearsed various ways I could broach the subject delicately. None of them seemed to be any good. It was an exercise in futility. Shanagh, it seemed, had inadvertently disclosed our conversation.

Mack was first through the door, casting me a sorrowful look. She offered no explanation, making a silent bee-line for the office. Angela followed, looking visibly upset. She closed the door, solidly, glaring at me. "I would appreciate you minding your own business. And worse, you couldn't even ask me about it! You went skulking to my mother!"

"I shouldn't have needed to ask at all! If the Constabulary found it germane to their investigation, I need to know. It's that simple."

"It is anything but simple! Believe it or not, there are parts of my life that aren't any of your business. My mother should have kept her mouth shut, and trust me, she's already heard about it."

"I'm sorry, but when I talked to you about your financial situation, I thought I made it clear that I'm not a fan of surprises. I'm trying to respect your privacy, but at the same time, I'm also trying to save your life in case you've forgotten."

A few more heated exchanges, each covering the same ground, followed. The conversation had spiraled downward to what was its inevitable conclusion.

"You know what? I think we're done here. I'm leaving. Figure out what I owe you and send me a bill. I have no idea how I'll pay it, but I'll think of something eventually."

As quickly and implausibly as Angela's arrival into my life had unfolded, it seemed to be collapsing. Perhaps it was inevitable, anyway. "Okay, if that is what you want." I started to feel shock and sadness give way to frustration, then to twinges of anger. "If you're not going to be honest with me, there is no point in continuing. I'm just wasting my time!"

"Well, waste no more of it on my account!"

She stormed into the guest room, emerging with a hastily packed bag. She didn't even make eye contact with me as she left.

I found myself standing in the foyer, both dumbfounded and angry. I lingered there for what felt like an hour trying to rationalize what had occurred, but I could not summon enough energy from which to draw either theories or optimism. I poured some whiskey and retreated into the sanctity of the office.

"Mack, we're done with this case. I'll pay you per our agreement, of course, but if you want to start looking for other gigs, have at it. I'll call Charlie in the morning, but tonight I'm going to get good and drunk; then I'm going to go to my bar and get more drunk. Care to join me for a drink or three?"

She shook her head, looking at me with an annoyed expression.

"Why the look?"

"Are you really going to drink that, John?"

"I am, and why not? The woman of my dreams just walked out of my front door, likely forever and probably straight into a life sentence. The woman that I was trying to save demonstrated the kind of temper that could make her guilty. Don't you think I deserve to get fall-down, slobbering, hammered?"

She took the glass out of my hand, placing it on her desk well out of my reach.

"Drink it if you want, but hear me out before you do."

I put my feet up on my desk, motioning for her to proceed. My gesture, unnecessarily grandiose, was poorly received.

"You can get mad at me for this later, but I watched that entire exchange. You're wrong, John."

"Enlighten me, Mack…"

"Well, first off, you're wrong about her temper. Totally wrong. That wasn't anger, not the way you're thinking of it. It's overload. Most men don't understand or appreciate it, but that's what it is. Think about it; in the span of a few short months she's lost her job, her relationship, her place to live, and almost her car. On top of this, she's got the prospect of extradition, a trial, and the possibility of spending the rest of her life in prison hanging over her every day."

I tried to say something, but Mack's hand quickly and definitively signaled otherwise. I stopped, accordingly.

"And then you had to go and be so damned likable; now she's got those feelings to deal with, too."

"You heard her; we're done. She's gone."

"She didn't give back her key, did she?"

"No. I figure she'll give it back to me when she comes to get her stuff. Frankly, I'm not sure I care. How can I trust her? First she promised no more secrets; then she promised to handle whatever questions I asked, no matter how tough. She's not kept either."

"You'll have to decide that for yourself, but if you want my advice it is to give her the time and space she needs. She didn't make those promises expecting to break them; they were made without understanding how quickly they would be tested or how truly difficult they would be to keep. Do what you want, of course. Take that drink, push her away, whatever. But you've been a better person since she came into your life, difficult circumstances or not. Think about it. I'm going home."

Mack had an annoying habit of being right more often than not. I carefully returned the whiskey to its bottle, its appeal gone. Equally gone was my appetite — dinner was more for decoration than anything. I picked at the previous day's leftovers, eating only a few bites. Sleep proved equally elusive as the same nightmare repeated every time I closed my eyes.

* * *

My thoughts continually drifted back to Angela, making focus nearly impossible. Swimming helped. Lazy, halfhearted laps gave way to angry, powerful swims that left me exhausted. I was heeding Mack's advice, although I found it increasingly difficult to do so. Perhaps that is how, deep within, I knew it was the right thing to do. It still didn't make it any easier.

Finally, a few agonizing days later, a text message from Karen awaited me after a particularly torturous swim. In no condition to read it, regardless of its contents, I tossed the phone aside, allowing the hot tub's jets to do their magic. A light lunch and the crisp hints of autumn in the air finally brought some clarity. It was into the early afternoon hours before I got around to the message.

```
She's okay, John.
Just needs time.
Call me this afternoon.
```

Taking a deep breath, holding, and exhaling quickly, I dialed the phone.

"Hi John. How are you holding up?" Karen's voice was quiet but steady.

"Ups and downs, I guess. Mack told me to give her time, so I'm doing it, but it isn't easy."

Karen laughed gently. "Men always want to solve things, fix things. Remember, this isn't a leaking pipe that can be mended."

"I guess I threw too much at her all at once. I didn't mean to."

"Well, Shanagh didn't exactly help. I'm furious with her, to be honest."

"Now that you mention it, you're right. Looking back on my conversation with her, I was expecting to be able to gently broach the subject at my own pace. Shanagh took that option off the table."

"I'm not sure what she hoped to accomplish by doing that. Sometimes that woman boggles my mind! The good news is that Angela isn't speaking to her at the moment, so she can't do any more damage. I know it isn't easy, but you're doing the right thing. I do have a suggestion that might speed things up a bit."

"Yes?"

"She loves yellow roses. Tomorrow or the day after would probably be good, if you're so inclined. She's out with some college friends and things are likely to run well into the early morning hours. I'll text you my address."

"Speaking of your address, a man followed Angela the other day when she was going for a run. I'm going to send it over to you in the off chance that you see him around. If you spot him hanging around, call the police."

* * *

I returned to find Mack hard at work, as focused as ever. If there were any doubts about the future of our case, they didn't dwell within her. She glanced at me; then looked again. "What happened? You seem to be feeling a bit better."

"I talked with Karen. She basically confirmed what you told me. So it seems like, shockingly, you are going to be right, for once!"

"You mean as usual... modesty is one of my many better qualities." I found myself genuinely laughing for the first time since Angela's acerbic departure. "She's not the goddess you had on your pedestal but she deserves a fair chance to prove her innocence. The job has fallen to us and that means you've got to be at your best even when things look bleak. I can't do this by myself; I need your best every day!"

Mack's words had stoked a fire, long since dismissed as extinguished, that still smoldered deep within. The feeling, familiar but distant, was good and I wanted more. "You've got it, Mack."

CHAPTER SIXTEEN

Mack had spent the better part of the morning deep in thought, sufficiently so that I thought it best not to interrupt. Whatever she was working on involved several computer monitors, a laptop, and a collection of papers spread across her desk and a folding card-table. I turned my attention to my e-mail. It had gone woefully untended for days:

```
Costa,

Made a bit of progress on poor Maggie.
Nothing definitive yet, but expect to have
something to report soon.

    CH
```

```
Costa,

Things are getting interesting. Pretty sure
Tully Smith met his end due to foul play.
Turns out, he had more than his fair share of
questionable dealings over the years. Had his
house built, too, for damn near nothing. He
paid for it, all legal and clean to be sure,
but nowhere near what it is actually worth.
```

Even when property values started to sag a couple of years ago, his widow pocketed a tidy sum when she sold it.

Good call on the shoes, too. Fergus Clarke wears size twelve. But then again, so do a lot of others, but I have to admit it's damned interesting.

CH

John,

I've really muddled things up. I was only trying to clear the air, but now Angie isn't talking to me. She completely misunderstood what I was trying to share with you. Sorry. I'm such a mess right now.

All the best,

Shanagh

Costa,

Started to look into that construction company that MacDonald sent me. The company is fairly large, several subsidiary companies operating here and in the Republic. Will take a bit to sort out. Bastards who set it all up didn't make it easy to follow.

CH

John,

And it appears I can add you to the list of folks angry with me. Angie, then Karen, and

now you, too. I expect Angela is looking for a
new attorney. Such a shame - I really thought
you were her best option. I'm going to call
the doctor and see if he can give me something
to help me sleep.

Shanagh

Strange. If Angela was looking for a new lawyer, word had not
reached me. I quickly, but carefully, crafted a reply making sure to blind-
copy Karen in the process. Lesson learned!

Shanagh,

While I wish the situation would have
happened differently, what has been done
cannot be undone. I am giving Angela the time
and space she needs. Until told otherwise, my
team and I are unequivocally committed to
building a stout defense against all charges
that might be brought against her.

With that goal in mind, we will reach out
to you periodically if we require your insight
or have questions that you might be able to
help us answer. If you would like an update on
any pending charges or legal developments,
please feel free to contact me.

I hope you are feeling better soon.

Respectfully,

J. A. Costa, Esquire

A text message from Karen arrived moments later:

Well said. That made both of us smile.

Mack was still too focused to interrupt, but she had left me a list of things to review. Mack had tracked down some of the Connla's fellow musicians. I could not begin to match her speed or efficiency, but she had given me an outstanding starting point.

Accordion player Patrick O'Hegerty was born in 1940 and worked for David A. Brennan's construction company. He died in a work-related accident late in 1997. The incident, which killed O'Hegerty instantly, involved a forklift and a mobile crane on a construction site at the Port of Cork. Heavily investigated, the findings focused on poor and missed maintenance of the crane which ultimately led to its collapse. Brennan's company was fully exonerated from any liability or wrongdoing, fault settling on the maintenance company responsible for the cranes. A significant settlement went primarily to his widow with an additional amount spread among several children. Mack had circled Brian, the name of O'Hegerty's eldest son, but had not elaborated within her notes as to why.

Brian O'Hegerty was the majority owner of a home-building business based in Derry, a venture that started before his father's untimely death. It was hard to assess the current health of the company, although their web site boasted that they had built homes in Counties Antrim, Londonderry, and Tyrone. An inquiry as a prospective property buyer confirmed that the business seemed to be doing well, in spite of years of declining property values. They quoted a six-month backlog of jobs, citing speculative property investment as the driving force in their workload.

Next on Mack's list was guitarist Gerald Dillon, born in 1944 and recently retired. Dillon had worked as an independent electrician before starting his own company in the late 1960's. The company, which apparently flourished, was sold to the Brennan interests at the time of his retirement. The terms of the sale, not revealed but likely lucrative given the size of the company, allowed Dillon to pursue world travel. Mack had traced him to the Far East as of a few months ago, but had no record of him beyond that.

I had become so engrossed in my work that I failed to notice that Mack's gaze was focused on me. A gentle clearing of her throat finally caught my attention. I started speaking before she could say anything.

"Brennan construction is much bigger than I realized. David A. Brennan did alright, to say the least. Too bad we can't contact Gerald Dillon — he'd be able to offer us an unbiased account of Connla's mental state in the final few years of his life."

"I've not been able to track down the man named Seamus. There are several possibilities within the Brennan organization. I'm still looking in to it. But that isn't why I wanted to talk to you."

"I'm sorry, I was engrossed in what I was doing. Please..." I motioned for her to continue.

"It is actually nice to see you focused again, so I'll let it go this time. I've found some interesting things on the ledger Finnegan included. I've not made all the connections yet, but I've been able to decipher a fair amount. And when I say decipher, I really mean that."

"Really? I've seen books obfuscated, but you're telling me that Tully Smith, the coroner, actually encrypted his entries?"

"I'm telling you exactly that. Once I figured out what was going on it was just a matter of breaking the cipher."

"Just..." Mack had a special way of making complex subjects sound trivial.

"He used something that he could decode quickly and accurately in his head if absolutely necessary. Simple but clever. I can explain it in more detail if you'd like." I stared at her, silently. She rolled her eyes before continuing. "Some of the entries are encrypted, others are not. The really clever part is that the ledger adds perfectly as it is. However, when the code is applied, it shows a different picture. Take a look. I've recreated the pages as they really were."

She slid several large printed pages in front of me. She had color-coded some of the entries to help clarify the meaning of her discovery. I carefully went through the results, amazed, yet again, by her prowess.

"He was up to some naughty things, Mack! The pattern looks a lot like money laundering, but these entries are inconsistent." I tapped my finger on several red entries.

"Correct. From what I can tell he was laundering money, but taking payments as well. Here; take a look at these."

On the third page, three red entries were circled. "These three are all payments from the same source, and all within days of Maggie Albin's death. The previous incoming payment was two months prior, the one that follows is a full three months later. Finnegan had worked out some of it, but I don't know how far he got with it."

"Mack. Are you saying what I think you're saying?"

"I thought it was a long shot, likely coincidence, until I found this one…"

She turned to the last page. A large, single entry was circled aggressively.

"Mack! This is a week before the official coroner's verdict came out. Okay, I'm officially impressed and convinced."

"Problem is that I've not been able to link the entries to anything else yet. I don't know who paid him or who he was laundering money for."

"We discover that, and we'll find who killed Maggie."

* * *

I sent flowers, but they were met with only a fleeting supportive comment from Karen. My spirits were beginning to flag. Mack, however, proceeded unfailingly and it was in her confidence that I continued to draw inspiration. Still, my evenings felt empty. Plunging myself into work helped as did regular trips to the gym for aggressive exercise.

Shortly into a call, I hit the mute button on my phone, excitedly calling to Mack. "Charlie has earned his pay on this one! You need to hear this."

"It was a damn fine bit of work on my part, Solicitor, with a touch of luck along the way. I tracked down one of Gregory Finnegan's Constabulary buddies. No bullshit, either, I found the man he was working with at Strabane."

Mack and I stared at each other, wide-eyed. She clicked her mouse furiously, her hands on the keyboard, poised. Charlie was rough, unconventional, and thoroughly uncouth, but he was a damn fine detective.

"This fellow, Greg's partner, left the Constabulary as it gave way to the Police Service. He's been working private security since, not by choice, either, so keep that in mind."

"Do you think that makes what he's saying less than reliable, Charlie?"

"No, but I suspect if you tried to call him to the stand, the prosecution might have a bit of fun with his past."

"I'll keep that in mind. Go on."

"Gregory Finnegan was sent to County Tyrone to investigate reports of politically motivated corruption. Specifically, republican-leaning corruption, favoritism, and the like. Allegedly, bids were being altered, contracts were being granted to firms sympathetic to the cause. According to his partner, it was fairly rampant. In the course of working on this, Gregory started to turn up some disturbing connections. Nothing solid, at first, of course, mostly annoying coincidences, rumors, and speculation. He kept at it, though, and that is what eventually took them to Strabane."

"What kind of stuff are we talking about?"

"At first, they thought they might be dealing with some sort of business syndicate. You know, the type that extorts, pressures, gets sweetheart deals, but as they kept digging, it became obvious that it was something different."

"How so?"

"They turned up hints of a republican group operating in the area."

"Something like the Provisional IRA?"

"Along those lines, but independent, not associated with anyone."

"So they think this group might have been related to the corruption they were originally sent to investigate?"

"That's the theory that they were working with, Solicitor. But that is all it was — a theory. They were never able to get it beyond that, and once the bombing happened, the focus shifted to finding the people responsible. Gregory Finnegan's theory mostly died with him that day."

"Where was his partner when all this happened?"

"In Omagh, meeting with an informant to talk about the awarding of a bridge-building contract. But get this, Solicitor; Gregory called his partner on Friday night, the night before the explosion, to tell him that he'd found a solid lead for them to work on Monday."

"Any idea what the lead might have been?"

"Sadly, no. I'll send over what I've got so far. Along with my bill."

"Thanks. And Charlie, I've said it before, but be careful. I don't think this is entirely over."

"No shit, Solicitor. You're goddamned right I'm watching my back over here."

I stared at my notes, then at Mack, my eyes eventually returning to my tablet. "That is enough to get someone killed." My voice was barely above a whisper.

"Are you saying that Gregory Finnegan might have been the intended target of the bomb?"

"I'm saying we should consider the possibility. Theorize with me for a second, Mack. If a cop starts nosing around and the cop dies, what happens?"

"The cops will think he was killed because he was looking in the right place. They'll send more cops; investigate aggressively and relentlessly until they find the killer."

"Correct. But an explosion that looks to be another horrible part of the Troubles…"

"I see where you're going with this. There could be a thousand reasons for the bomb, and Gregory Finnegan being there would probably look to be an unfortunate coincidence, especially since he was working under cover. That makes the person that set the bomb…"

"Brilliant and utterly reprehensible, killing all those people to get their real target. But, it wouldn't be the first time something like that has happened."

"It is an interesting theory but since Gregory Finnegan took most of his secrets with him to the hereafter, I don't know how we'll ever prove it."

CHAPTER SEVENTEEN

The gravelly voice of Jerry Keynes greeted me as I answered the phone.

"Jack! How are things?"

"Things are things, Jerry."

He laughed, his rough voice distorted by my speakerphone. "You're starting to lead an interesting life, my friend."

"Why do you say that?"

"I found the man that was following your girlfriend. Not exactly your typical neighborhood creeper. I've sent the details over to MacDonald. I figure she's not going to lose it or accidentally delete all my hard work."

"You're never going to let me live that down, are you, Jerry?"

"The man's name is Declan Clarke."

"Declan? I'm guessing..."

"From Colerain, County Londonderry, last official address was in Belfast, though. He's the kind of man who has a knack of being around when there's trouble. No record, though; a few charges, all dropped for lack of evidence. He's always conveniently gone or has an alibi if the police some sniffing around." Coughing. "Your girl was right to high-tail it back to your place. I don't think he was there to reminisce about the view from Galway Bay."

"What does this guy do for a living — at least ostensibly?"

"He works for an international shipping company. Conveniently, most of his travel is related to business. He's trouble all the way. 1992, a man that owned a chain of gas stations in the Dublin area went missing. Found him dead a few weeks later with a couple of bullets in his heart. No charges were ever filed in the case, but Clarke was a man of interest for a while." Jerry stopped, hacking violently and cursing. "He was in town for some sort of business; had a nice alibi for his entire time there, all thanks to his work buddies. Police tried to chalk it up to drug violence, but my sources say otherwise. Rumor has it the owner was supplying diesel to one of the republican groups. I doubt it was used to power farm equipment, either."

"Doubtful."

"In 1994 one of the top men in a violent loyalist group was found floating in Lough Foyle. 1996, an Egyptian businessman, thought to be involved in smuggling explosives into Northern Ireland, died when his car exploded. 1997… Jack, are you seeing a pattern here?"

"Point taken. Where was this guy in 1998? Or more specifically, where was he during the timetable that I'm interested in?"

"For better or worse, he was nowhere to be found. Not a peep until three years later when some shit happened in London. Same old story, though — person of interest, briefly, but no evidence. I hope you don't mind, Jack, but I took the liberty of asking a couple friends of mine to keep an eye on your girl and her pals when she's not with you."

"Thanks, Jerry, I was about to ask you to do exactly that."

"Clarke might have already bugged out, especially since you saw him, but better safe than sorry. I'll let you know if anything changes."

* * *

The weather had snapped unexpectedly cold for autumn causing the furnace to come on for its first serious run of the season. Another lonely evening was staring me in the face, my frozen dinner offering only minor appeal. A quiet knock at the door pulled me out of the impending doldrums. I stared through the peephole, rapidly opening the door. Angela, woefully unprepared for the cold, stood shivering on my porch. I motioned for her to come in, which she did, silently. We stared at each other in silence for a moment before she walked over to me, embracing me tightly.

"Can we talk?" she whispered.

"Of course. Would you like something hot to drink?"

"Tea would be lovely. I also wanted to thank you for the flowers. They meant a lot to me; I hope you don't think it was rude of me to not respond sooner, but I wanted to say it in person."

An awkward silence followed as I prepared her drink. It continued as we sat in the living room, regarding each other.

"This isn't going to be easy for me," she said, sipping her drink and obviously still suffering the effects of the cold. Her opening sentence sent my spirits tumbling as I dreaded what would follow. My heart had been broken so many times previously by similar words that the outcome seemed inevitable.

"I was thirteen years old, healthy, happy, enjoying time with my friends. It was such a lovely day, Johnny; the sun was shining, and it was warm. My friends and I were walking from one house to another. We were talking, laughing, just being girls. For some reason, I don't remember why, I ran to the corner, wanting to get there first. I turned a bit to look back at my friends, and then, suddenly, I was looking up at the sky. My eyes were having trouble focusing and my ears were ringing terribly — so badly that I couldn't hear my friends talking to me. They ran to me and looked worried. I thought maybe I had merely tripped but then I felt the burning, like my stomach was on fire. And it wouldn't stop. I tried to get up but couldn't. Then everything went black."

I moved next to her, holding her trembling hands in mine. I was ashamed of myself; this was not about me.

"The next thing I remember, I woke up in the hospital. My parents were there, several other relatives, too. I didn't understand why they looked the way they did — exhausted, worried, pale. I don't think my dad had slept the entire time. His brother hadn't, either, from the look of things. They made quite a sight!" A short, tearful laugh followed. "It was some time later that I learned that my life hung in the balance for several days. If I had turned slightly differently or kept going after reaching the corner that I wouldn't have survived. Strange how fate deals her hands sometimes."

I nodded, silently.

"The next few days were mostly a haze for me. I was in an awful lot of pain following the surgery and they had me on some pretty strong medication to keep it tolerable. It was a few weeks before I really knew all the details of what had gone on. The surgery had saved my life, but the two largest pieces of shrapnel had left my uterus so damaged that a viable pregnancy is all but impossible. Those are the scars you saw, John."

I offered no comment, other than to tighten my grip on her hands. She forced a tearful smile, briefly, before continuing.

"The news was devastating. I had matured earlier than most of my friends, if you know what I mean, so my mind was all about guys, family, and children. And all of it was gone, just like that. I was so angry; angry with everyone, angry with nobody. Truth is, I didn't even know who to be angry with. I've never felt that way, before or since. It took a long time to learn to deal with it. Lots of trips to the therapist, different medicines that were supposed to help, the whole lot.

And this brings us round to the Constabulary and my diary. Writing helped. I didn't believe my therapist at first when she suggested it, but she was right. Usually, I'd write something and throw it away, but a few made it in to my diary. I had no idea that the police would read them. They were the words of an emotional, hurt teenager trying to deal with her issues; nothing more." She bit her lip, gently, fighting back tears. She hung her head. "In one of the entries, I wrote that I'd like to blow up the people on both sides responsible for the Troubles. A few years later came the explosion and I was right there in the area when it happened."

And suddenly I understood Jim Finnegan's obsession. And his confidence. I started to say something, but she didn't let me.

"Christ, I wish I had burned that damned diary! I never imagined my words would come back to haunt me like they have. The photograph, the fingerprints; they place me there, and my own damn words will convict me. Her voice was barely audible, eyes cast downward. "You probably don't trust half of what is coming out of my mouth after all this and I don't blame you. I've always been fond of you, but when all this started I saw you more as a way out of my problems than as a friend. I knew you had feelings for me and I played to them. I'm so ashamed of myself, but that's the truth. I used you, Johnny."

She nervously took a drink from the mug of tea, now likely lukewarm. "But something happened along the way, and I found myself genuinely and deeply caring about you. That made all of it worse. I was afraid that the truth would disappoint you, so I hid it even after I promised not to. I'm so very sorry. I'm damaged goods — you deserve better. You deserve someone you can trust, someone who can give you a family. I've ruined the first and can't do the second. I expect you want to be rid of me, and I absolutely deserve it. I need to get my coat and a few things before I go."

She rose, but I refused to release her hand from mine. "I want you to stay, Angela, and I pray that you do. I truly mean that. And I don't care about the money or anything else like that. I offered it freely and without condition. The truth is, being with you makes me happy and, according to Mack, I'm a better person with you in my life." She managed a feeble smile as I continued. "I thought about what she said a lot, and she's absolutely right. I was drinking too much, doing nothing, going nowhere; Sure, I had you up on a pedestal that was unrealistic, and I'm sorry because I'm sure that didn't make things easier for you. But you know what? I like the Angela that is here with me right now more than I ever liked the girl on the pedestal. Human? Sure. Damaged goods? Hardly."

"Karen said that you were good for me, too."

"Then stay, and let's find out where the universe takes us."

"Okay," she said tearfully, crawling onto my lap, her head on my chest. "I want you to know that when I said that, it was true, and it is true now."

"I mean it, too."

Our embrace tightened as her lips found mine, and the night that followed was free of inhibitions.

* * *

We were enjoying an uncharacteristically large and fat-laden breakfast. Mack's face was bright and expectant as she walked through the door. Quickly, she walked over, hugging Angela tightly.

"I'm so glad you're back, Angie."

"So am I."

"Mack, you're welcome to have some breakfast. Be warned, though — it is slightly high on the caloric scale. Enough so that we're going to the gym this morning."

Mack's nose wrinkled. "I think I'll pass on both, but thank you for asking. And you two will have to go later; we have work to do."

I glanced at Angela, who had already started toward the office. I joined the procession out of the kitchen. "Okay, Mack... What's on your mind?"

"We've been researching and investigating everything except the one person we should be. It is so obvious that none of us thought of it, including me."

"I'm all ears, Mack."

"We need to find the girl in the picture." Mack's words were like a solid right to the jaw: simple, effective, and deadly accurate. I couldn't get a word out before she launched into more conversation. "We're missing the fact that *someone* is in that picture. Eyewitnesses saw *someone* matching that description leaving the scene. We've been so fixated proving that it *isn't* Angela that we've neglected to figure out who it really is. I know it is a bit of a needle in a haystack, but I got a phone call last night that has gotten me thinking."

"Okay, I'll bite. What's going through your mind?"

"Perhaps the name of the caller is more interesting than the actual subject…"

"Mack!"

"Angela, now do you see what I have to put up with?"

"Mack!!"

"Alright, already! Jim Finnegan called me, completely out of the blue. He's a bit strange. Not creepy or anything, just different."

"What on earth did he want?"

"He shared a few details about our friend Declan Clarke. I don't think he truly understands the depth of our sources and connections, either that or he was fishing. I wasn't biting, though. I was born in the day, not yesterday, though."

"He's damn good at that, isn't he?"

"He sure is, but he let one additional piece of information slip while we were talking about stuff."

"He never lets anything slip. If he told us something, it is because he felt we needed to know it. Likely because it makes Angela seem guilty."

"Not this one. At least not the guilt part. The fingerprint, Angela's for certain, was found with the car, but it wasn't found *on* the car."

Angela looked puzzled, even more so as she could see my interest building. "I don't quite understand what just happened," she said, tentatively.

"Something important, Ange," I said. "There is a huge difference between finding your prints *with* the car and *on* the car. The wording means everything. Your prints somewhere on the car, or parts affixed inside the car, put you in contact with the vehicle and would be tough to explain. We could impugn the chain of custody, the analysis techniques, but it would be a bit of a struggle."

"And Finnegan said *with* several times. He chose his words
169

carefully."

"Mack, he didn't happen to mention…"

"They think it was a hat. The analysis pulled Angela's prints from several surviving bits of leather."

Angela looked deeply troubled. "I lost a hat a couple of months before all this happened. We never did find it. When I went riding with Maggie on Friday, I remember wishing I had that darn hat!"

"Any idea when or where it might have gotten misplaced?" interjected Mack.

Angela shook her head. "It was just one of those things. I thought it would turn up. When it didn't, I figured I left it somewhere. I was zipping around quite a bit between work, music lessons, shopping, and friends. It wouldn't have been totally out of character for me, but most of the places I went knew me, or I went with friends. If I had left the hat at one of my common haunts, I expect someone would have pointed it out or returned it."

I stretched, beginning to regret the large, weighty breakfast sitting like a rock in my stomach. "If Finnegan has your hat, it is entirely logical for your fingerprints to be on it. I've got an idea. Hang on a second."

I grabbed my phone and sent a text message to Jim Finnegan.

```
The fingerprints were on a hat.  What color
was it?
```

I winked at Mack. "Playing a bit of a gambit. And now we're back to the original question of the morning. Exactly who was the gal in the picture, and was her similarity in appearance intentional or, for her, a happy accident?"

"Angela," Mack interjected, "who knew that you were going to Strabane that weekend?"

"I guess a fair number, now that you mention it. Maggie and I had been trying to get it worked out for over a month. Work knew; friends knew. The tricky part was finding a weekend when the car was available."

"Were there any friends or co-workers that resembled you? Similar build, height, things like that? Even casual acquaintances?

"Not really. There was a girl at work who was about my height, similar physique. But by the time of Strabane, she was noticeably pregnant."

"Oh well. Was worth a shot. Cousins, relatives, anyone?"

"I can't think of anyone. I'm sorry."

"Mack, it looks like we've got our work cut out for us, but you're absolutely right. Finding the girl in the picture will end all of this unpleasantness once and for all."

* * *

It was well into the evening before my phone chirped with an awaiting text message.

```
It was a blue plaid hat, or rather, the
remains thereof.
```

I replied, with Angela watching over my shoulder.

```
You win the prize. Thank you!
```

Angela gave me a puzzled look. I smiled, wryly. It was a while before the next message arrived.

```
That's good, I guess. What do I win?
```

```
The conviction of the real bomber.
```

```
You are the eternal optimist, Johnny.
```

```
I'm well on my way to a conviction of the
real bomber. Enhancements and analysis will
only confirm what I already know.
```

```
Then your gal gets some lovely steel
bracelets, compliments of Her Majesty.
```

```
You'll be putting the wrong person on
trial, Jim.
```

Then find me the right person, Solicitor.

But all roads lead back to Angela Grady as you shall see.

"That has got to be my blue hat! What I can't figure out, for the life of me, is how it got there. I lost it somewhere around Belfast, to be sure."

"I think when we discover how your hat traveled ninety miles across Northern Ireland without your head in it we'll have a lot of our answers."

CHAPTER EIGHTEEN

The layers of the stinky onion that was Tully Smith were slowly being pulled away. Even Angela, revitalized, dove in. Her computer savvy was a pleasant surprise, yielding results almost immediately.

Perhaps it was the fact that we were looking at things in retrospective, but Tully was overtly and obviously corrupt. From before his election through to his death, he was surrounded by a cloud of malfeasance.

Smith surrounded himself with a cadre of local business owners, all of whom skirted a variety of legal fine-lines. One or two were borderline scofflaws, successful enough to be largely untouched, and all were well-off. It smacked of favoritism at best, racketeering at worst. But what really caught our collective eye was the ever-present muscle that appeared in every picture of Tully Smith.

The business owners were easy to locate and track. The muscle was not. However, a couple of tips from Joe Quinlan quickly sent Mack in the right direction, relentlessly.

One of the strong-men was Tully's cousin, Larry. In and out of trouble as a youth, he worked a variety of odd-jobs until returning to County Tyrone. Rounding out the veritable rogue's gallery was Padraig Bannion and an unnamed, but strangely familiar man that graced only a handful of photographs of Tully Smith.

It was Angela who finally came up with our first major breakthrough. Her eyes wouldn't leave the photograph until finally her expression changed, her face paling noticeably. "Johnny!" nearly breathlessly, "that is the man that followed me. I'm sure of it!"

I quickly printed the best of my surveillance pictures. "You're right. Damn. Good job! That's Declan Clarke and he's bad news." I directed her to our rapidly growing dossier on the uninvited stalker. "Long and short of it is that bodies tend to show up around him. But he's always conveniently got an alibi or vanishes before anyone can connect him to anything."

"Christ," Angela said, her color still hiding, "do you think he was here to kill me?"

"I don't know, but I'm guessing he wasn't here to discuss the real estate market in Ulster."

"Why on earth would he want to kill me?"

"I don't really know, but the most obvious reason is that your death would stop our investigation. That reason alone has me thinking that we're looking in the right places. Beyond that, I'm damn short on ideas."

"Oh no!" She sat up in her chair, turning sharply toward me. "I went stomping out of here without even thinking about him. You don't think he would hurt Karen or my friends, do you?"

"I warned Karen about him before I knew his identity. She has his picture and will call the police if he shows up. I've also got a friend that knows a few people. Well… Suffice it to say that they're keeping an eye on your friends, just in case. They'll be safe. Once we figure out if he's still in the country, we can plan on how to deal with him."

Color slowly returned to Angela's face. "Thanks a million. I can't imagine going through losing a dear friend again."

Mack's voice was strong and insistent. "Guys!"

"Yes, Mack?"

"You wouldn't happen to know if Declan Clarke is somehow related to Fergus?"

It was a great question. In the heat of things, the commonality of the name had eluded me.

Angela turned to Mack. "Who is Fergus?"

Mack was about to answer, but I interceded.

"Fergus Clarke is the man that claims to have danced with Siobhan O'Connor in Omagh the night before the explosion. Finnegan's notes say that he positively identified you as the girl he danced with."

"Maggie and I danced for several hours that night. I remember dancing with three or four guys. Nothing serious, just for fun. And no conversation; the music was too loud for much of anything."

"Finnegan claims that Fergus is prepared to testify that you gave your name as Siobhan O'Connor."

"It was loud. Anyone wanting to get names and phone numbers would have to write it down and I'm sure I didn't. Do you happen to have his picture? I could at least take a look and see if I remember him."

"We don't have his picture yet. Charlie is working on finding him. And Mack, I don't know if they are related. Sorry — it *is* a common name."

Mack shrugged her shoulders. "Was worth a try."

"Mack, find out what shoe size Declan Clarke wears."

Angela gave me a puzzled look. "Shoe size?"

"There was a partial muddy shoe print on the bumper of the car Maggie was driving. None of this made it into the official findings, all thanks to Tully Smith. A man's size twelve, likely a work boot of some sort."

"Why on earth would he leave that out of the report?"

"That's one of many things we're trying to figure out. The boot print, the EpiPen, and the notebook. All left out of the official report."

"Maggie's little notebook?" Angela looked surprised. "She carried it everywhere. It was a bit of an obsession, but it helped her deal with other things."

"How so?"

"Maggie had some issues. She was anxious and had obsessive-compulsive traits, to be sure. Perhaps that was one of the things that caused us to be such good friends. I understood, from my own struggles, how difficult such things can be and how important it was to have friends who listened, understood, and accepted. The notebook helped her with the anxiety. If she had bills, papers, anything important, she would fold them up and shove them into the notebook. If she wanted to remember something, she wrote it in there. It was one less thing for her to worry about."

"It has never been found. She left in such a hurry that she left her desk drawer partially open and the book was gone."

"She would have had it with her; No doubt."

"We don't know what happened to it or why she was out driving in the first place. The fact that one of Tully's former associates showed up on my street tells me that we're definitely looking in the right places."

"It also tells me that we should all be damn careful," added Mack, her voice quiet and serious.

* * *

The various business owners with which Tully associated enjoyed varying degrees of success after his unexpected death. Most survived, although enjoying significantly less prosperity; a few foundered.

"According to these records, Tully Smith paid well below market value for his house and land," Mack said. "Let's just say that what he paid for his house and land was less than the value of the land by itself."

I stopped what I was working on, peering up at her. "Did he get a sweetheart deal from a relative or the in-laws?"

"Hardly. He bought the land from a business associate."

"What about the house?"

"Still working on that one. The company of record is A&C Construction, but they're long gone. It isn't beyond the realm of possibility that they were created by a holding company or a venture capitalist and then vanished when the markets soured. Regardless of who or what that company was, he paid less than one-third the assessed value of the home. If my numbers are even remotely close, he paid below cost for it."

I laughed, sardonically. "Deals like that usually come with a price tag that doesn't show up on the type of books you report to the authorities."

"Perhaps Tully didn't keep up his end of the bargain."

"Why do you say that?"

"Charlie dug up a couple of interesting things, including this. Probably shouldn't ask who or how…"

The documents were clearly photocopies, likely hasty given the poor alignment of the page. They were medical records. "Mack, um…"

"Like I said, don't ask. But look at the date — about a week before he died of a massive heart attack. Turn to the second page. You'll see some test results."

My face curled into a perplexed frown. "Am I reading this correctly? Because if so, this is a cardiac stress test that he passed with flying colors. And if that is the case, then it makes it highly unlikely that his death was truly of natural causes, doesn't it?"

Mack nodded.

I put the papers down, looking off into space. "And this was never really investigated, was it?"

"Not really," answered Mack. "The fellow that did the autopsy was, ready for this, the same old fellow that prepared the report on Maggie. Or at least it was his name and signature on the form. This was basically his last official autopsy prior to retiring."

"Let me guess, he died shortly thereafter."

"No. He died earlier this year at the ripe old age of ninety six." Mack started to say something else, but her attention was briefly drawn to her computer screen. "Oh my god!"

"Mack, what is it?"

"Did you see the note from Charlie?"

I shook my head, looking at Angela in confusion.

"He talked to Gregory Finnegan's partner again. The partner confirmed one of the people they were there to investigate. Guess who!"

"Mack!"

"I bet Angela has a guess; you're no damn fun sometimes, John."

"Mack!!"

"Okay, already! Tully Smith. They were investigating Tully Smith! And he's even going to send us some information..."

I stood up, stretching, and breathing a deep sigh of relief. Angela looked puzzled, but seemed to sense my mood. "You look happy," she said, "although I'm not entirely sure why."

"I am happy. We're not there yet, but this could be what we need to formulate our own version of the events in Strabane. You know," I said, finally acknowledging that the pangs of hunger were tugging at me, "we worked straight through lunch and nobody noticed. I'm in such a good mood tonight that I'm going to take you both out for dinner. There is a new place in town that has the best steaks..."

"You two are on your own," said Mack. "I've got a date!"

"Suit yourself. Angela, have you tried South Avenue yet?"

"I've heard wonderful things about it, but there's no way we can get in. The list is months long!"

"Get ready. We'll get in, I promise."

"He's not kidding," interjected Mack, putting on her coat. "He knows the chef or something."

* * *

"I know the general manager," I said, carefully reviewing the wine list. "I helped him out with some legal issues a while back, and he owes me few favors."

We were guilty of being mildly overdressed for the occasion, but Angela seemed to be having fun and looked absolutely stunning. I wasn't used to dining with the most beautiful woman in the room. Hell, I still wasn't used to dining with anyone, but this was something I could definitely get used to.

"This list is impressive," she said, quietly, "but some of these are really expensive," her voice dropping to nearly a whisper.

"I read an article about this place shortly after it opened. They hired experts to select and review all the beverages so that everything on the lists will result in a good experience. Or so they say — I'm not savvy enough to really know."

Her finger pointed to an entry on the list. "I've read about this but have never been anywhere that actually has it. I've heard it is amazing, but a bottle of it is more than I've ever earned in an entire month. Maybe someday! These other wines are quite good, too."

"You know about wine?"

"Mostly from reading and a few tastings. My friends and I enjoy it when we're together, but we're limited to more modest selections. Let's try this one. It's far more reasonably priced and well reviewed." Her finger rested on a modestly-priced bottle of white wine.

Our waiter came around to fill our water glasses and take our drink order.

"We'd like this," I said, my finger pointing to an entry on the wine list. He nodded, expressionless, before disappearing into the back.

Angela's attention had turned to the dinner selections as the general manager subtly entered my view. He raised an eyebrow at me, inquisitively. I returned a wink and a nod to which he smiled before quietly fading into the background. A short time later, he reappeared, carefully cradling our wine bottle. I nodded in response to reviewing its label.

"The lady knows far more about wine than I do," I said in response to being offered the cork. "Please allow her to review it."

She looked at it quickly, placing it to the side. "The only true test is to smell and taste the wine."

"It's your show, Angela!"

The manager dutifully poured her a small sample which she, in turn, swirled, sniffed, and regarded carefully. "Do I look like I know what I'm doing?" she said, jokingly. The first taste quickly drew her face into a serious, but happy, expression. Her eyes closed and her lips curled into a gentle smile.

"I take it you approve?"

She nodded, eyes still closed. It took a moment for it to dawn on her what she was drinking. A wide-eyed glance at the label confirmed her suspicions.

"Johnny! Oh my God!" her voice was an excited whisper. "Why? How? You can't possibly afford this!"

"There are a few details about me I've not shared. You've been brave enough to share some difficult secrets with me; it seems only fair that you know a bit more about me." I took a drink, my first of anything so expensive and highly regarded. Dammit. It really *was* good. I could learn to like this kind of evening. "The truth is I'm rather well off. I don't really let anyone know apart from a handful of close friends that I trust."

"I appreciate your trust."

"To be completely honest, when Jim Finnegan first approached me, the notion popped into my head that he might be chasing an international con artist. My heart knew it wasn't true, but it crossed my mind. After all, why else would someone as young, pretty, and alive want to have anything to do with a sour old goat like me?"

She laughed quietly. "You don't give yourself enough credit."

I smiled. "Not too long ago, someone else told me the same thing. In this case, I wasn't giving you enough credit, either."

"I can't blame you for being careful, especially given my lack of prowess with money in recent times." She shook her head, smiling gently. "I really had no idea that you had money. You do a good job of hiding it."

"I actually go to great lengths to do so. I don't want wealth to define me, and I certainly don't want it defining my friendships. I've spent many hours, especially in recent years, drinking, glued to social media watching other people live. It is an easy trap to fall into: believing a vicarious existence is a suitable substitute for living. My life was hollow; I didn't realize it until I met you. So there's my dirty little secret. That and the fact that I worry too much, drink excessively on occasion, have had my heart broken more times than I care to remember, will spend every penny to my name to defend you if that's what it takes, and really, really don't like asparagus."

A tear ran down her face. "I knew everything I needed to know about you the first time you kissed me, Johnny."

CHAPTER NINETEEN

The first snow of the year arrived earlier than expected and the days, growing ever shorter, were consistently dreary. To add to the malaise, our investigation had entered the doldrums. Charlie had dutifully filed reports, but his progress had equally stalled. He persisted nevertheless, regularly noting that most complicated investigations have an irregular cadence. Mack, equally tenacious, faced similar frustrating results.

Our gym visits increased as outdoor activities became infeasible. Although my conditioning was steadily and noticeably improving, I still couldn't challenge Angela at anything except weight-lifting. Even there, I couldn't begin to match her endurance. It was a humbling and steady reminder of the difference in our age.

Concerts and shows of any and every genre filled many evenings, but quiet time together, often spent lazily in the music room conversing or playing, was even more precious. Even Jim Finnegan seemed to be in a lull; uncharacteristically, at least two weeks had elapsed since his last missive. That streak was finally broken in the midst of a dreary and snowy afternoon.

"Good afternoon, John."

"It's been a while, Jim. I was beginning to think you didn't care anymore."

"Officially, this call is to warn you about Declan Clarke. I'm sure you and MacDonald have long since figured out that he's here. We are prepared to offer Miss Grady protective custody if she wants it."

"I'm sure you are, but we'll pass."

"Not surprising. Look, Clarke's presence here makes no sense. We don't know what type of backlash bringing charges against her will cause. There are old wounds about to be reopened, quite unpleasantly, but none of them involve Declan Clarke. He ties up loose ends, silences flapping tongues; he's not about revenge. Someone is afraid of what Angela Grady is going to say. I expect it is her accomplices trying to save their hides fearing that she's not willing to hang alone. But I have to tell you, I'm fully aware of other implications to his presence."

"Like the fact that our investigation might expose the real terrorist?"

"As loath as I am to admit it, yes, that possibility occurred to me."

"You sing a good tune but I've done my homework on you, my friend. You'd not sleep at night if you convicted the wrong person."

"Your wee Jillian certainly earns her pay, doesn't she? I've got to admit, you two are a powerful team. You really should be working on our side."

"If my theory is right, we are."

I could hear him sigh, perhaps with an air of resignation. "What is it you need?"

"Tully Smith. Anything and everything. Somehow, he holds the key."

There was a long pause before Finnegan spoke again. I was taking a chance, gambling on the man's principles, but we needed progress.

"He was an interesting sort. Mixed up with poor Maggie's case to be sure. I'm curious why you're focused on him, though."

"He died of a heart attack, you know. But did you know that only a matter of days earlier he passed his physical with flying colors, including a cardiac stress test! His heart was probably in better shape when he died than mine is today, and I've been swimming almost daily. He had a good racket going. Nice house, lots of land, both of which he owned outright. It doesn't take a rocket scientist to connect the dots: the man was on the take, and that is why your brother was investigating him. Somewhere along the line, Tully screwed up or became unnecessary and had to be silenced; just like Gregory for whatever he was exploring."

It was a hell of a risk, but in some odd and inexplicable way, I knew I could trust him to do the right thing. Bluster and bravado aside, Finnegan's heart was in the right place. Well, maybe, with a bit of nudging, which I was unafraid to do. "You might have enough circumstantial evidence to get a conviction. I know that, but you've said yourself it will be hollow unless it is airtight. Help me out with Tully and his boys. Anything you can. Please."

Finnegan exhaled again, even more noticeably, before speaking one final sentence. "I still think I'm right about Angela Grady, but I'll see what I can do and John, Declan's not a man to be trifled with. Be careful."

* * *

Mack's interview with Julia Rohnan, Angela's alibi, extended well past its allotted time. Her words were emphatic and her recollection of the day's events was flawless down to the minutest detail. It was a powerful testimony, but would it be enough?

Meanwhile, Angela was pursuing an angle for which she was uniquely qualified. Connla's mental state in his final years remained an open, lingering question. For Angela, though, it was a deeply personal enigma that needed to be solved. Starting with Mack's research on the family of Connla O'Grady, Angela expanded it adding distant cousins, even friends and neighbors.

Pretending to be researching the Grady family tree, she sent inquiries and made phone calls. Her gentle voice and native knowledge of Ireland led to numerous conversations. Most went nowhere, but one resulted in a series of phone calls that gave us what would likely be the best and most unbiased answer we could hope for.

"John," Angela said, excitedly, "I was right! Granda Connor was sharp as ever right up until the end."

I immediately stopped what I was doing. "How so?"

"I tracked down one of Granda's friends from the Army, from his days in North Africa! Eighty-eight years old and sharp as a tack, too. I recorded all our conversations…"

Lucas Malone came from Galway. He volunteered to serve shortly after turning eighteen, ending up in North Africa assigned to the same company with Connla O'Grady. Eventually, they were in the same squad and became lifelong friends. Malone deemed Connla as intense, but exceedingly loyal.

More importantly, Connla was, as Malone described it, an *operator:* "Conn was always making deals, trading, selling, you name it. He had connections that could get anything, and he set up a decent business along the way. The boys knew that if they needed something, they could go to him. You didn't want to cross him, though. That was a good way to end up with a black eye!"

Malone laughed. His voice had thinned with age, but Angela was absolutely right: The clarity of his thoughts was unmistakable.

"But that was Conn for you. If you were his friend, you could count on him through thick and thin. Damn, that boy had connections! He'd meet a guy who knew a guy and the next thing you know, old Conn was in business. I ended up with a sweet assignment in France after the war, and I swear he had something to do with it. That's where I met my girl. You know, we've been married for sixty four years now."

Angela allowed Malone to talk about his wife at length before gently steering the conversation back to Connla. I nodded to her in approval. She returned a wink. "Maybe I have a future in this business," she whispered.

"Music? Conn, God bless him, he tried but he was awful. I visited him in Mullingar back in the eighties, met all the boys he worked with and so forth. You'd think all those years later he would have improved!" Malone chuckled, gently. "Of course, they spent more time talking than playing."

"I have Connor passing in 1994. I talked to a woman named Shanagh Grady; she told me his death was due to complications of dementia."

"I think I might have met Shanagh once or twice. Conn's daughter in-law, right?"

"Shanagh Flanagan married Connor's son Sean, but I've not worked on that part of the tree yet. Does that sound right?"

"It does. Sean was a nice boy. I recall meeting him a few times, too. Timid fellow; took after his mum in that regard. Gerry was more like his old man. Shanagh must be confused. Conn didn't have dementia; he died of pancreatic cancer. They found it too late and he opted to allow nature to take its course. I got a letter from him about a month before he passed. I'd share it with you but it's a bit personal, you see. I'll say this much, though. There wasn't a thing wrong with his mind."

* * *

We were in the midst of a healthy debate over Connla and his musical friends when my phone rang. I left the office to answer it, not taking the time to see who was calling.

"Finnegan here."

I could tell by the change in his voice that whatever news he had was serious. "Jim, what's wrong."

"The results are in. Our experts have concluded that there is an eighty percent chance that Angela Grady is the woman in the picture. The United Kingdom will issue a domestic warrant for her arrest soon. A provisional request to your State department will follow."

Dammit. I didn't want it to unfold like this; I wanted to be the one to save the day. It felt like a punch in the stomach.

"John? You still there?"

"Yeah, I'm here."

"The wheels are in motion. You're going to need something compelling, and I mean deadly compelling to stop them now."

"I would have expected your tone to be happier than it seems to be. This is a big win for you."

"I thought it would, too. Perhaps it will sink in later."

"Or perhaps I've got you thinking that you've got the wrong person."

"Perhaps, but that discretion has been taken out of my hands with the analysis. I have to do my job, Solicitor. If the warrant is issued and we extradite, I'll be taking her back to Northern Ireland with me."

An odd amalgam of sadness, frustration, and anger rushed over me. "Thanks for letting me know."

* * *

Mack took one look at me and immediately hugged Angela.

"They're going to do it, aren't they?" Angela's voice was shaking.

I flopped into my chair, hanging my head. "They are. Apparently, eighty percent was their threshold point and the latest round of enhancements and analysis hit that mark. They're preparing a warrant for your arrest in the U.K."

"I'm so sorry, Angela," said Mack, crying.

I pounded my fist into the arm of my chair. "I was hoping to have a bit more time, perhaps convince them to explore our alternate theories before deciding." I paused, collecting myself. "I'll start some conversations with State to see what the political climate is. Perhaps we can buy some more time."

"Not that I'm ever going to be ready for this," Angela said, her voice still unsteady, "but how much time do you think I have?"

"I wish I could give you a solid answer. These things move on unseen wind currents. Political wheels can turn slowly, squeak a lot, and I'm not going to do anything to grease them. Plus we have the holidays coming up, so that might be something that can be made to work in our favor."

"I hope so. I don't want to spend a minute in prison, and I really don't want to spend the holidays there." She sighed, collecting herself. "I guess I need to let my mother know what is going on. We've not spoken for a while now, but she really needs to know this."

187

"Yes, she does. Karen, too."

Angela nodded, her eyes cast downward as she slowly arose from her chair. "I guess I'll go make those calls."

* * *

Angela was in her room for several hours before emerging, her eyes red and puffy. Mack and I could only sit there silently as she worked her way slowly back over to us.

"Karen knows," she said, hesitantly. "We've had a bit of a good cry," a smile briefly crossed her face, vanishing quickly with the words that followed. "I didn't call my ma — just not ready to do it yet. Maybe you or Karen can, at least to let her know."

I nodded, not really sure what to say.

"I'm ready to get back to work if you are. Crying isn't going to beat damned Jim Finnegan." Her voice was gathering strength with each word.

"Are you sure? We can knock it off for today if you'd prefer."

"No. Let's work — it will help keep my mind off of things. I'm going to need to keep busy."

"Works for me. Mack, are you game to get started again?"

She nodded, emphatically.

CHAPTER TWENTY

As outwardly calm as I appeared, it was all an act. When nobody was around, I paced, fretted, and worried over every detail. Dammit. I was doing it again — wearing a hole in the flooring of the kitchen.

A note was stuck to my computer. Written in Mack's distinctive hand, it simply read:

Declan Clarke: UK Size 8.5 (US Size 9.5)

Unless the man was wearing preposterously oversize shoes the night of Maggie's death, the footprint wasn't his.

I hadn't heard from Charlie in several weeks. More importantly, I hadn't received a bill. That would likely change, as a short e-mail arrived from him and with it the promise of progress.

Costa, I've found a reasonably good lead on Fergus Clarke. Need to track it down and see if I can find the bastard. That construction company is a monster. More to follow - will send to MacDonald.

In the mean time, I thought you'd find this interesting...

Attached was a scanned photocopy of a Constabulary document. It predated the explosion and offered no explanation as to what prompted its existence. Charlie's evaluation of the document's importance was, likely intentionally, grossly understated: It was an assessment of Sean Grady.

Sean Thomas Grady, born 16 September, 1945, resident of Belfast.

Father: Connla (Connor) (O')Grady (1918 – 1994) (52-0192*, 55-0372*, 59-2123*, 62-0821*, 66-0620*, 68-1029*, 71-0201*, 73-0732*, 74-0102*, 74-0227*, 76-0319*, 77-0077*, 78-0117*, 80-0362*, 81-0201*, 84-0083*, 89-0091*, 93-0181*, 94-0166)

Mother: Meryl Brennan O'Grady (1920 - 1972) (72-1062)

Spouse: Shanagh Elaine Flanagan

Married: 14 October, 1977

Military Service: 1965 - 1972

Occupation: Engineer (Demolition Specialty)

Civilian Occupation: Engineering (Network Connectivity and Point-of-Sale)

Employer: [REDACTED]

Assessment:

The subject, in spite of strong republican parental influence, has served Her Majesty with loyalty and distinction. His service records are consistent and commendable. No disciplinary records; promoted on or before schedule. No evidence of republican activities or affiliations.

Psychological evaluations of the subject indicate that he remains generally loyal to the Crown and a staunch advocate of peaceful solutions. Additional psychological profiling indicates that he has passive tendencies. We do not consider him a threat to engage in violence for either republican or loyalist causes.

Additional Findings:

Wife: Shanagh Elaine Flanagan (born 3 December, 1959). (76-0319*, 77-0077*, 80-0362*, 82-0031*, 88-0111*, 93-0202*, 96-0096*)

Children: Angela (b. 13 June, 1978), a minor attending Garrett Academy in Belfast. (92-0092*, 92-0184, 96-0096*)

Family Assessment:

[REDACTED]

The remaining three paragraphs, redacted were tantalizing. Dammit! I stared at it, reading it repeatedly, trying to make sense of it.

"Mack, I printed a document that Charlie found. Ange, I want you to look at this, too. It is some sort of Constabulary profile of your father."

Mack had only looked at the document for a moment before speaking. "Angela, what do you remember from 1996?"

I spoke before she could answer. "Why do you ask, Mack?"

"Because I think these numbers cross-reference to something else, likely by year."

I nodded — her thoughts mirrored mine.

"That was the year I graduated. That was probably the biggest thing that happened. I inquired to a few Universities, both here and there. Beyond that, nothing much." Angela sat down, studying the document closely. "I think Mack is probably right, though; the explosion injured me in 1992 and there are two entries that start with ninety-two."

"And Meryl died in 1972, and that matches, too." I settled back into my chair, folding my arms behind my head. "That explains a few of the entries, but not the rest. What the hell do the asterisks mean? Unfortunately, the only person that I know that would be able to explain this file in its entirety and maybe even pull some of the cross-references, if that is what they really are, is the person sent to arrest you, Angela."

"Finnegan," Angela said, her tone smacking of disgust. "That's a dead end, then."

A few months ago, even weeks, I would have agreed with her. Now I wasn't as sure. Finnegan's demeanor, at least over the phone, had subtly changed. Perhaps it was a well-crafted act, but that wasn't my reading of the situation.

* * *

"Costa, Brown here." The call was inevitable but that didn't make it any easier. "We had nothing but silence for many months, but now the UK is evaluating our willingness to issue a provisional warrant for Miss Grady."

"How is the political climate looking in the State Department these days?"

"We might have some latitude to push back, at least for a while. Even with your money in the picture, we don't consider her a flight risk. Hell, you've known about this for months and haven't made a single questionable move. Problem is the seriousness of the crime and the label attached to it."

"Understood. Would it help if I brought you up to speed on our working theory? Provided you keep it top secret, of course."

"It would give the Secretary something to think about, that's for damn sure. They claim they've got enough evidence to place her there."

"They've got electronic wizardry that, after massaging, hit their arbitrary threshold, and they've got a fingerprint, but it wasn't on the car. It was on a hat that she lost months prior to the event. Their method and motive claims are equally dubious."

"I've got to say, I'm damn impressed with your little team. Send me something. I'll get it in front of the Secretary so he's ready when their request comes in."

"It would really be appreciated if the Secretary could be deliberate in his review. Ideally after the holidays; preferably *well* after the holidays, if you catch my drift. "

"The Secretary loves to ski, you know. Makes a great diversion around the holidays."

"We're getting into prime season for that right now. I might know someone who has a lovely, private cabin not too far from some of Colorado's best slopes…"

"Now you're talking, Costa! This thing is going to get interesting for all of us. No need to rush into it, is there?"

* * *

Our efforts immediately turned to Brown's request. Mack started assembling an outline of our evidence and theories. I spent my time and a painfully large sum of money securing the use of a suitable cabin.

"We have a lot of smoke but we're still painfully short on fire," Mack said, sending me the latest draft of her document.

"Remember, we don't need to prove the case, only convince them to drag their feet, and force the U.K. to draft a formal extradition request. If we can buy some time, there's still a chance we can turn up evidence that will cause them to quash their warrant."

"Well, if confusion counts, we've probably bought Angela a few more years of freedom. I don't know how much better we can do with what we've got now."

I read through it. "This is good, Mack. You didn't play all our cards, but you hinted that they're there. I don't see any point in waiting any more. I'm going to send it along with the information on that damned cabin…"

* * *

In spite of our frenetic pace, time passed painfully quickly. Mack became a fixture, routinely sleeping on the couch after long workdays. Even Charlie Hannon redoubled his efforts, hiring, at my expense of course, an assistant to work on the case. He produced results nearly immediately.

"Mack, you look confused."

"Charlie's new investigator started looking into the various Mullingar connections. Something turned up when she was investigating the widow."

"Mrs. O'Sullivan?" interjected Angela, looking interested.

"No. The other one. The unwitting supplier of the car."

Mack spun one of her computer monitors around so we could see. A double house occupied the screen. It looked pleasant, although strangely asymmetric thanks to dissimilar paint on each side.

"Looks cozy," I said, "is this where she lived?"

"The left side was hers."

Angela was staring at the screen, intently. She offered a quiet but loudly disconcerting comment. "I've been there, Johnny. I don't remember why, but this house is familiar. Sure, it was painted differently, but I remember it."

I frowned. "Dear God, I hope nobody asks you that question under oath unless we can explain why you were there."

194

"I'm sure it was during a visit to see Granda. I remember the wall and the gate. Beyond that, it is just a hazy childhood recollection."

"Well, it is better to know than not. At least we can start working on it. Mack, what else do you have?"

"It took a bit of digging, but Charlie's associate was able to find the rightful owner of the property. The widow rented through a property management company, which in turn was owned by a holding company. The holding company was nothing more than a front. Two more well-obscured layers and you get to the real player, sufficiently isolated as to have nearly unlimited plausible deniability. And all of it ties back to none other than David A. Brennan!"

"It could be coincidence. Any idea how many properties in County Westmeath the holding company managed?"

"No, they dissolved a few years ago. When Brennan died, it looks like the sons did a fair amount of consolidation and reorganization from what we've been able to piece together."

"They could have owned and rented dozens of properties in the area. Do you happen to know if the property management company owned both sides of the property?"

"They did. Why do you ask?"

"I want to know who rented the other side."

"In 1998, it was rented by a man named Seamus Milligan. We've not looked in to him."

"Probably should, if for no other reason than to learn a bit about our widow and her car. I expect that the police would have interviewed him at some point."

"I'll have Charlie take a look."

Angela's eyes had not left the screen for some time. Finally, she spoke. "Which side did the widow rent?"

"The left side when facing the property. Why?"

"For what it matters," Angela said, her eyes still focused on the screen, "I think we went to the right side, but I could easily be wrong. It has been a while."

"Mack, I think it is probably worth a look to see if the other renter has any sort of connection."

She nodded in agreement, returning to whatever she was working on.

"Angela, I've been putting this off, but I'm going to call your mother and let her know what's going on. Do you want to participate, listen in, or stay in here?"

She sighed. "I suppose I should at least listen to what she has to say."

* * *

The phone rang quite a few times, enough so that I had almost hung up the phone before Shanagh finally answered.

"Hello, Shanagh," I said, hesitantly, "John Costa here."

"Solicitor. What can I do for you?"

Her words were short, abrupt, and edgy. Angela leaned over to me and whispered, "that's the voice she uses when she expects an apology for something *she's* done..."

I nodded. Perhaps it would be expedient to fall on my sword in the interest of all parties involved. I'd see where the conversation took us first, though.

"I want to bring you up to speed on the recent developments in Angela's case."

"I wasn't aware that there were any developments, Mister Costa. Nobody, including you, sees fit to call me these days."

"I'm calling you now, like I promised to do if anything came up. The news I have is important. You might want to be sitting down." I got no response, although I could tell we were still connected. The gentle din of the television in the background continued uninterrupted. "I'm sorry to have to tell you this, but the facial recognition software has reached the threshold necessary for the United Kingdom to start the process of issuing an arrest warrant in Northern Ireland. From there, the extradition proceedings start."

"I understand. When do you think, well, when will she...?"

"We don't know how the timing is going to work out. There are a lot of politics involved and we're continuing to actively search for exculpatory evidence. My hope is that we can turn up enough to quash the warrant before it evolves into anything else."

"And how is that going?"

"We are making progress, albeit slower than I'd like."

"Thank you for the update, solicitor. If there isn't anything else, I have a hair appointment to get to."

"Shanagh," my voice turned stronger and more insistent, "I feel bad about what transpired, and I'm sorry for setting it in motion, but she's going to need you. Stay as upset with me as you want, but please, be there for Angela."

There was a pause, followed by several sighs. "I suppose I've not reacted the best possible way. But put yourself in my shoes for a moment, and perhaps you'll understand the stress that I'm dealing with right now."

Her level of stress? I shot Angela a look of incredulity. "I'm sure it is quite a stressful time for you. I really didn't mean to make it worse."

"Don't give it a second thought. And I'm sure it wasn't quite the reaction you expected from someone who might be your mother-in-law one of these days. Hopefully soon, right? I really need to keep my anxiety under control."

Mother-in-law? Where the hell was she getting this stuff? I looked over at Angela who was bright red and obviously angry. I quickly motioned for her not to talk, grinning mildly. "I don't think either of us wants to burden you with any more right now. We should probably focus on Angela's case before we plan other things, don't you think?"

"Oh. Yes. Good point."

"While I've got you on the line, on your trips to Mullingar to see Granda Connor, do you recall ever visiting a house in the Auburn Road area or thereabouts?"

Angela leaned forward on her chair. She whispered to me, excitedly. "She'll remember the house, I'm sure. I clearly remember her along the time we visited there. She didn't want me climbing on one of the walls that ran along by the street — made quite a fuss about it, truly."

"Auburn Road? I don't think so. Why?"

"It was something that came up in some notes, and I was curious if you might happen to remember it. I'm sure it isn't important."

"Connor lived northwest of town. I don't think he would have had much cause to go to that part of town. He might have taken Angela to the park when she was young, I suppose. Maybe he knew someone over there."

I had to aggressively motion to Angela, who was fuming, not to speak. "Like I said, an address showed up on a couple of case notes. I didn't really expect it to amount to anything, but I also didn't want to ignore it and risk a surprise by Finnegan later on. Thanks for trying, though."

* * *

Angela waved her hands in the air in exasperation. "Why did she say that?"

"I'm honestly not sure." The differences in their recollections were growing increasingly disconcerting. Small things I could understand, but this was the second potentially salient point upon which they fundamentally disagreed.

"Look, I don't remember everything about the visit and it has been a while, but it wasn't a trip to the damned park. My mother and Granda Connor went to visit somebody and I waited outside. They were in there briefly and we left. I'm not going crazy!"

"It confuses me, too. Perhaps she has forgotten."

"Possible…" Angela sounded less than convinced.

"Do you think she's in denial? Perhaps she's remembering what she wants to remember."

"I honestly don't know. Every so often, she really puzzles me. We have an interesting relationship, plenty of ups and downs. We were doing pretty well until Jim Finnegan re-appeared. Actually, we were doing pretty well until he appeared the first time."

"Sounds like she doesn't deal with serious stress well."

"That would be an understatement! You'd think *she* was the one that was facing life in prison; some of the things she's said!"

"Speaking of which…"

Angela immediately reddened, again.

CHAPTER TWENTY-ONE

Mack's voice positively sparkled. "Finish the sentence, John! Most days I'm damn good, but on other days I'm…"

"Incredibly annoying?"

She rolled her eyes in feigned exasperation. "No! The correct word was *amazing*. No prize for you."

"I didn't realize that there was a prize. I might have actually tried had I known."

Angela looked at us with an amused expression. "In this case, she's right. You need to hear this."

"Okay Mack, what do you have?"

"A deeply bruised ego."

"Mack!"

"Alright, already! See what you're getting yourself into, Angela?"

Angela smiled, blushing slightly.

"So, I don't think I broke many laws to get this. I used your name, so if Interpol comes looking for you, you'll know why."

"Gee, thanks. Now, about what you found…"

"Do you have any idea how many people named Clarke there are in Ireland? It is a ridiculously common name."

"Sadly, that's true. I think I've got a few relatives with that name as well, and spelled a couple of different ways, too."

"But, I, your truly amazing researcher, managed to sort through layers of deception and subterfuge. And guess what? Declan and Fergus Clarke are first cousins!"

I sat down, heavily. "Oh, Mack…"

"Yes — I know. Amazing doesn't quite seem to be a sufficiently lofty description." She turned quickly serious. "It was hidden in plain sight mostly thanks to multiple marriages and name confusion with Declan's mother. Well, that and a little bit of intentional obfuscation of records. Nevertheless, they're cousins. Declan is eight years older, but they seem to run in the same crowd. Fergus had a few minor dust-ups with the law as a young man, all of which stopped quite suddenly. Right when he took a job working for one of County Tyrone's beverage distributors. The same one that was in bed with Tully Smith, and the same one in this picture."

She pointed to a picture on her monitor. Tully was with some of his business associates with Declan lurking menacingly in the background.

"I don't think for a god damned minute that it is coincidence," I growled, "that Fergus Clarke is willing to testify that Angela is Siobhan O'Connor. The problem is we don't know why. Angela, I'm sorry to ask this, but is there any possibility that Maggie somehow got mixed up with the wrong people?"

"Absolutely not!"

"Would she have told you?"

"She would have, and she probably would have written it down."

"In her book?"

"Among other places."

"I'm sorry to bring this up but that is something we're going to have to investigate. At least enough to rule it out. If she inadvertently saw something, knew someone, dated the wrong person, her habit of writing things down might have gotten her killed."

Angela looked pained, but nodded, nevertheless. "I understand. They killed her, didn't they?"

I sighed. "I think it is a distinct possibility, but it doesn't really help us unless we know exactly who and why. Mack — how did they hide something as obvious as being related?"

"There's no doubt that it was intentional and well planned. Whoever they had working on it was damn good, and the whole thing reeks of some pretty serious corruption in a few key areas."

I raised my eyebrows, appreciatively. "No doubt Gregory Finnegan, had he lived, would have had a field day ripping through Tully Smith's little empire."

"And there's another possible motive for wanting Greg Finnegan out of the picture," said Mack, fidgeting with her long, red hair. "It might not have anything to do with republican activities; maybe it was all about good old money and power."

"I wouldn't put it beyond the realm of possibility."

"Maybe Maggie stumbled on something and they had to eliminate her."

Angela stood up, stretching. "I don't think so. She would have told someone. If not me, then her parents. It was almost impossible for her to keep a secret. Her death has something to do with me. I've known it in my heart for a long time."

* * *

I had purchased tickets to the opening night of a Broadway show that was visiting our city. Knowing that such events would likely be impossible in the near future, I took the opportunity to get a little bit extravagant with my plans, including a limousine, dinner, and the best seats.

Angela vanished to the guest room well before I needed to get ready, leaving me the opportunity to talk to Mack in private.

"Mack, I sense there is something you're eager to talk about."

"Yeah, but I didn't want to do it in front of Angela."

"Sure — what's on your mind?"

"Is there any possibility that the woman in the picture is Maggie? I've only seen pictures of her face, so I don't know the answer."

"I don't think so. Maggie was quite a bit shorter than Angela and, well, a bit wider, too. Don't get me wrong, she wasn't fat, but her physique was different. Even with a wig and a disguise, I don't think they could be mistaken for one another and definitely not to eighty percent certainty."

"I didn't think so, but I had to ask."

"That gives me an idea, Mack. I have a friend that is a professional photographer for a modeling agency — I'm going to give her a call. See if you can figure out the software that the Police Service is using to perform their facial recognition. Our defendant should have the opportunity to cross-examine her accuser."

Mack smiled. "I see where you're going with this, and I like it. I know a camera expert who can probably help with the specifics of the film and development process."

"There's another thing I want you to do, and please, *please* keep it between us."

"Of course. What do you need?"

I handed her a small scrap of notepaper with two names written on it. She glanced at it, staring at me with a heavy, confused frown. "I want you to turn up anything and everything you can on these people. If you need me to hire someone else to help you, I can. We're racing the clock here and I don't want to lose the momentum we have in other areas, especially since I'm playing a hunch." Her expression remained unchanged. "Yes. Both, and prioritize it in the order I've given it to you."

She sighed, raising her eyebrows. "I understand why you want this to be between us. Are you sure about this?"

"No. It's just a hunch — one that I hope to God is wrong in both cases."

"Are you paying overtime on this, because if so, I'll stay and get started tonight?"

"Sure, I'll pay, but don't put your social life on hold."

"No offense, but I planned for no social life the minute I agreed to work with you. But fear not, oh worried one, you'll get my bill."

* * *

Our evening out was a lovely diversion, enough so that I let my guard down. That quickly changed during intermission when I caught a glimpse of a man that looked eerily like Declan Clarke. Angela, however, had gotten a better look and quickly abandoned her trip to the ladies' room.

"He's here," she whispered, her face pale and concerned. I nodded, trying to find him, but he had long since vanished behind the crowd working its way back into the auditorium. "What should we do?"

I peered over the railing, looking down to the first floor and the multiple doors that made up the main entrance. I quickly pulled back, hoping that Clarke hadn't seen me. "He's watching the main entrance, and he's doing something on his phone."

I risked a second peek, this time making a better effort to avoid detection. Two other men joined Clarke and after a brief conversation, his compatriots left in opposite directions, but neither exited.

"Dammit. He's not alone. We're going to have to find another exit."

I frantically tried to contact the limousine company. The driver couldn't make it back in less than fifteen minutes. I was about to make another call when Angela tugged at me sleeve. A man, betrayed by his shadow, was slowly climbing the main stairs. I didn't wait for him to come into view.

"Come on!" I whispered.

We darted up a gently curved staircase, one of several that led to the theater's loge level. The show had resumed, so the doors were closed. Our only choices were to try to sneak back down via a different staircase or risk entering the theater.

"This way!" We slowly worked our way down a descending staircase that took us in the opposite direction of the main entrance. "I don't remember exactly where this ends up, but this building has many exits and he can't watch all of them." At least I hoped that was true.

"Look!" Angela said, pointing to a sign.

The exit, at the end of a descending corridor, hardly looked inviting or heavily used. I opened the door carefully, only enough to see. It led to a narrow walkway that ran parallel with the side of the theater, leading back in the direction of the main entrance.

"This isn't good," I whispered. I started to say something about the walkway having only one point of egress, but Angela interrupted me.

"No choice!" she said, alerting me to approaching footsteps. They hastened immediately as we slipped out the exit. Dammit. It was cold and our coats were still back in the theater! It became irrelevant, though, as we started a quick walk toward the main street. The sound of the door opening behind us triggered a full-on sprint.

We reached the main street, turning quickly left and away from the theater's entrance. A quick glance revealed Declan Clarke exiting. He gave chase immediately upon seeing us.

We reached the corner. I wanted to turn right toward a more active area of the downtown but traffic, oblivious to our desperate situation, prevented it. We veered left, sprinting toward a nearby parking garage.

The nearly daily visits to the gym, at Angela's insistence, were suddenly showing their value. A few months ago, I would have been breathless before reaching the main street. "Maybe we can lose them in here!"

Another sharp left took us into the parking garage. We rapidly climbed the steps to the second floor before darting into the middle, hiding behind several large Sport-Utility vehicles.

I took a moment to text George O'Neil. Hopefully he would be able to send help. We did not wait for a reply — the sound of the elevator arriving on our floor drew our attention. Two men, silhouetted, emerged. They looked around, but the lighting and arrangement of cars was in our favor. I knew it wouldn't last if they opted to search the floor closely. They didn't, opting instead to return to the elevator. We watched as it climbed to one of the floors above.

"Should we make a run for it?" Angela whispered.

"There are at least three of them, perhaps more, and we only know where two of them are. My guess is they've got someone watching the exit and they're going to work their way from the top down."

"Herding us right to the slaughter."

"Something like that," I whispered. With our options rapidly evaporating, I worked my way to the edge of the garage, careful to remain in the shadows at all times. Peering down over the edge produced the expected results: there was nowhere to go.

The sound of an approaching car caused us to scamper back to our hiding spot. It rolled slowly through the garage, its headlights casting macabre shadows as it navigated the turns and ramps. It slowed as it neared but proceeded ponderously onward, seemingly oblivious to our presence. We listened as it quietly climbed from floor to floor.

"Do you think that was the third man?"

"I don't know, but we're sitting ducks if we stay here much longer. I guess George didn't get my message."

I looked around, surveying the garage one final time. "We've got two exit signs, one the way we came in and one on the opposite side. Any preference which one we try for?"

"Back the way we came?"

"I'm game. Move quietly, but be ready to run like hell if someone shows up."

We crept to the stairwell, opening the door and quietly closing it behind us. We descended, every step slow, measured, and above all, quiet. The green door to the ground floor was heavy and windowless.

"There's no way to open this and not be seen," I whispered, my lips nearly touching her ear. "When we go through the door, turn right and run back toward the theater. It has been long enough that our driver should be waiting for us out front. I hope. Ready?"

She nodded.

I pushed the door open, hesitating slightly to see if anyone was waiting. Then we ran, all out, the cold evening air rushing at us. From behind us, I heard footsteps followed by a sharp snapping sound, then a second followed nearly immediately by a brief spray of cement shards just to our right. As we rounded the corner, a third round rang sharply against a metal railing. It only served to propel our feet faster than we ever imagined possible.

As we turned the corner, the limo driver was, as promised, waiting. We dove into the back of the vehicle, ducking immediately to the floor.

"Lock the god damn doors and drive! Now!" I bellowed. The startled driver hit the gas and sped off into the night.

"Are you okay?"

"I think so," she said, clearly shaken. "You?"

"The same."

"What the hell just happened?"

"Something we've discovered lately has turned into a hornet's nest — only the hornets that came at us tonight were made of lead."

"Do you think it is safe to go home?"

"Yeah. I've not gotten any alerts from the security system. Seems to be quiet. I better call Mack to make sure she's okay."

* * *

Two police cars awaited us.

"O'Neil sent us to keep an eye on things, Mister Costa. The only thing that happened was your assistant leaving about an hour ago. It's been quiet since."

"It's unusual that I've not been able to reach her. Did O'Neil send someone with her?"

"Yes. They drove by her place and all was quiet. We're sending extra cars through the neighborhood to keep an eye on things as best we can. Would you like us to clear your house, Counselor?"

"No. Honestly, I'm more worried about Mack and I'm going to go check on her. Ange — do you want to wait here or come with me?"

"I'm going with you."

"Counselor, the Captain said we're supposed to keep an eye on you."

"Then you better stay close to my back bumper!"

* * *

Mack's townhouse was dark, and knocking on the door didn't change anything. I tried peeking through the front window, but her curtains obscured what was beyond. Repeated calls also produced no response. A brief debate between the officer and me about entering the property was interrupted by an elderly woman from the adjacent townhouse.

"Are you investigating the noise?"

The officer and I looked at each other, wide-eyed and troubled.

"What noise, Ma'am?"

"Sounded like she was moving furniture around or something. I don't mind her doing it, but not this late."

"Now you've got your exigent circumstances, officer, and that's coming from one of the biggest scumbags in the city. Either you break the damn door down or I will!"

The front room showed no signs of anything out of the ordinary, but the kitchen and dining room told another story. Furniture was out of place, several pieces were damaged.

"Costa!" The cop was quickly on his radio, his voice sounding urgent. "We need an ambulance…"

Mack had put up a hell of a struggle, but had taken quite a beating for her trouble. The police, their numbers increasing quickly, shooed us away from what was now a crime scene. All we could do was watch helplessly as they wheeled Mack out, connected to a variety of machines and IVs. She was still unconscious and the paramedics looked concerned.

"Where are they taking her?"

"Conley East," answered the officer. "We're going to need to get a statement…"

"I'm going to be with Mack. Tell O'Neil where to find me. He can get his damned statement there."

* * *

The wait in the Emergency Room felt eternal. O'Neil's officers came for our statement and left, mostly empty-handed. I was intentionally short on details. Another hour passed and George O'Neil himself showed up, another police officer in tow.

"You two have had quite a night," he said, his massive left hand cupping my shoulder. "All in one piece, I see."

"We are, but Mack isn't, George. I've not heard anything for over an hour."

"Not much to go on downtown, unfortunately. Nobody recalls seeing much of anything — you know the story."

I sighed. "Yeah, I do. I really don't think you're going to find much — a couple of bullet strikes, but I'd be surprised if they revealed much of anything."

"Your statement from earlier has them firing three times."

"Yeah, the first one didn't hit anything, but I sure as hell felt it fly by."

"John. A word in private? This officer will stay with Miss Grady and will let you know if there are any developments with Miss MacDonald."

We found our way to a small vending area with a few tables. A man lounged lazily in the corner, oblivious to our presence.

"You stirred up one hell of a shitstorm, Costa. Guess my advice fell on deaf ears."

"Nice way of saying *I told you so*, George. I appreciate the support, but there's no way in hell I'm letting this go, especially not now. As far as I know Mack's in there dying. I'm going to find the people responsible for this, and when I do there will be hell to pay." I could feel the veins in my forehead pulsing.

"I hear both sides of your heritage talking there. Keep it in the fairway, my friend. I might be able to turn my back on a few shots that drift into the rough, but not off into the woods. Do you follow me?"

"Perfectly."

"What the hell are you guys into? If you're over your head, let us give you a hand."

"I was in over my head the first time I laid eyes on Angela Grady. While I appreciate the offer, you're still playing for the team that's trying to put her in prison. There's more to this that even Jim Finnegan realizes and tonight was confirmation. If you want to help, keep an eye on Mack while she's here."

* * *

Several more hours passed before we got word that Mack was conscious and asking for us. They were going to admit her soon, so our visit would have to be brief. A weak smile greeted our arrival. She looked rough. Her left arm was heavily bandaged and in a sling; other bandages covered parts of her hands, face and head. Bruising was fairly noticeable, and likely to look worse before looking better.

"How is she?"

The physician looked over at Mack who nodded.

"We were worried that she might have some internal bleeding, but it looks like everything inside is okay. A couple of bruised ribs that will hurt for a while. Her left elbow will probably need surgery but we need to let the swelling go down before we'll know for sure. Surprisingly, no evidence of a concussion, so that's definitely good."

"I also broke a nail," Mack said, weakly.

The physician smiled. "She fought back pretty hard. The police should be able to get some DNA from what was under her fingernails."

"His nose is probably embedded in my elbow, too." Her voice was barely above a whisper, but had lost none of its spunk.

"Mack, I'm sorry. This is my fault; I should've seen this coming and hired someone to keep an eye on you."

She looked over at Angela who returned an equally apologetic expression. "I'll remind you of that every day. And you neglected to share tomorrow's winning lottery numbers, oh prescient one!" She started to laugh, but pain cut it short.

"What the hell happened?"

"He was waiting for me. The moment I got into the kitchen, all hell broke loose."

"Do you have any idea what he wanted, who he was?"

"He was foreign for sure, had an accent. Similar to Charlie's overall, but different. I wish one of the two of you had heard him. I'm not as attuned to those things as you are."

"That's okay. Anything else you can remember?"

"If you'd let me finish, Sir Interrupts-a-lot..."

"Sorry."

"He told me to tell you that Siobhan sends her best wishes. And that next time, he'd kill me."

"That's not going to happen. We're going to find the bastards, all of them. No matter how long it takes." My blood was boiling.

"It may not take as long as you think," said Mack, offering a feeble smile. "The other thing he was there for was my laptop."

"Oh no... And our files..."

"I think the painkillers are kicking in. Damn. This is some good stuff!"

The physician leaned in. "This is why I said a short visit. She needs to rest."

"Mack! What about the laptop?"

"The joke's on them! They've got the wrong laptop... Oh! This is kind of fun! When are you guys getting married, Angie?"

It seemed to be catching, and now Mack was infected! I looked over at Angela who was, again, beet red and speechless.

* * *

I stomped out of the hospital, mostly mad at myself — I should have known better. I dialed, angrily.

"Dammit Costa, do you have any idea what time it is?" Jerry's voice growled more angrily than I'd ever heard, and I didn't care.

"I know perfectly well what time it is."

A long profanity-laced tirade followed. I let it run for a while, ending it with a single sentence. "Mack's in the hospital, Jerry. Someone was waiting for her when she got home — sent us a warning that we're getting too close by beating the hell out of her."

He coughed violently. "How is she doing?"

"Could have been worse, I guess. She's got injured ribs, elbow problems, and lots of bruises everywhere."

"No wonder you sound so god damned pissed off. What do you need?"

"Muscle, and not the kind that work as night security guards at a warehouse, either. I want the scary kind. I don't care how much it costs, but I want Mack and Angela protected."

"I'm on it."

CHAPTER TWENTY-TWO

Mack looked worse the next day, which only served to infuriate me more. I wanted to find the coward that attacked her and personally pay him back — with interest. She tried to explain what she had done with the laptop, but the painkillers had other ideas. She'd manage a lucid sentence occasionally, but most of what she talked about was incoherent babbling. It would have been funny had I not been so damned angry.

There was nothing funny whatsoever about the people Jerry sent. They were the spooky black-ops types that wouldn't take any crap from anyone. Even the cops guarding the room seemed intimidated when they showed up. O'Neil told me the city police had found the bullet strikes, but, predictably, had little else to go on. Perhaps it was a forty-five, likely subsonic, but they couldn't be certain. It made sense, but certainly wasn't concrete evidence.

A call arrived from Jim Finnegan.

"Sorry to hear about Miss MacDonald, John, but I can't say I didn't warn you."

"Has anyone ever told you that you can be quite the wanker, Jim?"

"I've heard it a few times. Always makes me smile, too. For a change, my news is good for you."

"Let's hear it."

213

"Angela's cell phone was off the entire evening; dropped off the tower about an hour before the show started and stayed off through the entire ordeal. In fact, she's barely used it in days. I know you think I'm obsessed, but I had to be reasonably certain that she didn't order the attack."

"I could've told you that. You weren't there; those bullets barely missed us and they weren't blanks. I figured you'd be spending your time trying to pin one more thing on Angela rather than looking for the real culprit. Thanks for wasting my time."

I almost hung up the phone, but he started speaking so quickly I hesitated. It was a good thing that I did.

"Now you're not giving me enough credit. I've made the recommendation to my superiors to delay issuing the warrant and the extradition request at least until this business with MacDonald gets sorted. I can't promise anything, of course, but there you have it."

Dammit. Now I owed Jim Finnegan an apology. He continued before I could offer my contrition.

"At least for the moment, we're all interested in finding who attacked Miss MacDonald, and it's almost a foregone conclusion that this is all somehow related. If you and those goons you've hired find him first, make damn certain that there's enough left for us to question."

"As much as I would like to hand what's left of him to you in a baggie, we need him alive and intact, too. And Jim, sorry."

"Don't give it a second thought. At least for the moment we're playing for the same team, Solicitor."

* * *

The DNA recovered from Mack's fingernails returned a name unfamiliar to any of us. The man, from County Armagh, had a lengthy list of offenses on record with the Police Service dating back almost ten years although none of them violent in nature. Another anomaly was the lack of any records showing his entry into the country. The prevailing theory was that he arrived illegally via Canada, but there was no evidence to substantiate that claim.

I seemed more troubled by this news than either Finnegan or

O'Neil. Perhaps it was my paranoia showing through, but I saw the workings of a large, well-funded endeavor operating behind the scenes. My suspicions were confirmed when some good old-fashioned police-work turned up the assailant's hotel room.

The police found the room unoccupied and likely unused for several days. A small case containing a large sum of cash, several credit cards, and multiple passports was the main evidence. They were counterfeit but of the highest quality, good enough to require extensive examination to detect.

"George, you're going to find a body," I said, insistently. "He either failed his assignment or was expendable from the beginning. Did you dust it for prints?"

"Of course we did, but there are a thousand and we would have to exclude the whole damn hotel staff. Knowing the place, we'd have to exclude the last twenty guests and several dozen hookers, too."

"All that money and those cards and he decided to stay in a dive. What does that tell you?"

"It tells me that he lacked taste. Seriously, though, it is simple — he went to a place on par with what he's used to. Plus he's going to blend in. A two-bit Irish thug in an upscale hotel might garner some unwanted attention."

"Perhaps, but it also tells me that he was trying to make his money last. I'm betting they promised him a pile of cash if he'd kindly do one little job for them. Maybe if it worked out they'd let him disappear, but I doubt it — doubly so when Mack put up a struggle and took a chunk or two out of him. He's a loose end. If we don't find him first, he's a dead man."

"We're looking for him, but it is a big city."

"Did you find any blood in his room?"

"No blood."

"Dammit! That's what I was afraid you'd say…"

I knew that our chances of finding the man alive were nil. He'd gone to his compatriots for help, likely never adding up the fact that he was the disposable element in their plan. Dammit! We needed him alive to have a real chance to forestall the warrant.

* * *

Jerry had his own sources, many of which were willing to talk to us rather than the police. If the massive bodyguards that shadowed my every move were intimidating, it quickly faded when I produced cash for information. Most of what my money bought was rumor, but we came out with a few tidbits that warranted additional exploration.

A chain of informants finally produced a truly promising lead taking us to a seedy motel on the east side of the city. Situated on what was once a main thoroughfare, it had long since lost what little luster it might have held. The manager was exceedingly uncooperative until I produced a stack of hundred-dollar bills. Strangely, they held more appeal than the broken arm one of Jerry's men offered.

The room, laughingly registered to "Mr. Smith", faced away from the main road. The parking area was abandoned except for one lone car occupying a spot several doors down from the room in question. I stopped a few feet from the door.

"That could be blood," I said, pointing to several small spots on the ground. One of the bodyguards grunted in agreement. The trail was faint but certain, and led back to the car. A small smear on the car's door handle confirmed my suspicions.

"We should call O'Neil. They'll need the lab to take a look at this."

"We can do that after we're done," said one of Jerry's men, knocking on the room's door. There was no answer. A louder knock also received no attention from within.

"Let's take a look inside," said the taller bodyguard, putting on a pair of thin gloves. I started to mildly protest, but by the time I had formulated what I was going to say, he'd already defeated the lock.

"We saw blood and the room was unlocked," he grunted indifferently, returning the tools to his pocket. "He might need our help."

It took only a glance to convince me that we had found the right place. The bathroom wastebasket was stuffed with blood-soaked tissues and bandage wrappers. A shirt and several towels were wadded in the shower.

"Looks like your friend did quite a number on him. He probably came directly here, stopped the worst of the bleeding, and then went out for some bandages. Good for her!"

I nodded. "She's pretty damn special." I started to say something else when I was interrupted by the tall bodyguard.

"Costa," he grunted from the main room. "Check this out." A small piece of paper, its corner stained with a bloody fingerprint, had drifted partially underneath the bed. He quickly snapped several pictures of it before announcing, "time to go."

"I've got to let O'Neil know about this place."

The bodyguard handed me a phone. "Text him from this phone."

I followed his instructions after which he removed the phone's SIM card, twisting it violently until it broke into several pieces which he tossed out of the window. "You owe me a phone, Costa," he grunted.

"Where are we going?"

"Cityview Drive, to the address listed on the paper."

* * *

I had never heard of Cityview Drive and for good reason. In spite of its auspicious-sounding name, it was anything but. The road, near the airport, had not been finished, never connecting to its intended destination. Instead, a hastily constructed cul-de-sac marked its ending. Several small one-story buildings, somewhere between warehouses and offices, lined the side of the road. A few still had cars parked outside, the others looked unused. Our target was of the latter variety.

We got out, trying to make the best use of the fading light. There was no sign of activity, and a knock on the door produced no answer.

"Back door was open," said one of Jerry's men, emerging from around the corner. "I don't think our boy ever made it here. There's a car parked behind this door." He motioned toward the tall garage door. "It's got a suitcase, another ID and passport waiting for him. Quality stuff, too."

"I'm guessing he had a rather sudden and unexpected change of plans. Probably not voluntary since he didn't drive himself here."

A man approaching from the distance interrupted my train of thought, the bodyguards quickly interposing themselves between us.

"You interested in renting? That unit isn't available, but I've got several others that are."

"My friends and I are only interested in this unit." He started to say something about availability, but stopped when I produced money from my pocket.

"I'm primarily interested in contacting the current lessee, and I expect you have that information available." I started slowly peeling hundreds off the roll. "The holidays are coming up, and I'm in the giving spirit right now."

"Well, my kid mentioned something about violin lessons… and my car needs some work…" Each protestation brought with it another bill.

"Now… about that name…"

He wrote the name and contact information on a sheet of tablet paper then handed it to me. I stared at it in stunned disbelief. "Are you sure?"

"I think I'd know who the check comes from every month, pal." He flipped through a filing cabinet, handing me a signed lease agreement.

"Son of a bitch," I muttered, as if dazed. "Merry Christmas, buddy." The bewildered man couldn't manage a reply as I handed him my entire roll of bills.

Even Jerry's men didn't quite know what to say as we walked slowly back to our vehicle. I grabbed my phone. "George O'Neil, please. Yes, I'll hold…"

* * *

I returned in time for the final few minutes of visiting hours. Mack, looking noticeably improved, knew immediately something was wrong; Angela did as well. They immediately stopped their conversation as I entered the room, their faces turning serious.

"Mack, the afternoon before you were attacked, I asked you to do something." She nodded. "Was this what you happened to be working on?"

"No."

"That's what I was hoping you'd say."

I handed the paper to Angela who shrugged her shoulders. "I don't understand."

"We tracked the man who assaulted Mack to a lousy motel on the east side. He was long gone, but I'm certain we had the right place. We found an address over by the airport, so we checked that, too. He had a car, ID, passport, money, all sorts of stuff stashed there. My intuition is that he's not going to need them."

"But how does that have anything to do with this?" Angela held up the paper again, looking more confused.

"I paid the landlord to find out who rented the space. That was what he gave me." Angela gasped, collapsing into the nearest chair.

CHAPTER TWENTY-THREE

"Sure, I've been leasing that property for almost a year now," said Karen, shrugging her shoulders. "That's not a big secret or anything. I don't understand why it is suddenly so important."

"Why are you leasing it?"

"At this point, I'm planning on using it as a tax write-off. My father's charity was thinking about a second location on that side of town and that was available cheap. I could lease it and sublet it to them for free."

I finished her sentence. "And take it as a charitable donation."

She nodded, smiling. "They decided against the alternate location a couple of months ago, so I figured I'd keep it and start a business or something; I could write-off the rent. I've never even been there since signing the lease. Now will you *please* tell me what the big deal is?"

Angela joined the conversation before I could offer a single word of explanation.

"The man that attacked Mack hid his getaway car, supplies, and false ID in your building, Karen."

Any hint of a smile left Karen's face. "Oh no… you don't think that I had anything to do with that. Angie! You of all people should know that I'd never be involved with anything like that!"

"Karen," I said, drinking my third coffee of the morning, "is there anything we should know about? Any financial issues, problems, anything that could be used against you?"

She shrugged her shoulders. "I'm not really all that interesting when it comes right down to it. I work for my father's charity, go out with my friends from time to time. It's all out there on my site. Here — I'll send you a connection request." She pulled out her phone, tapping on the screen feverishly.

We weren't directly connected, but I knew by proxy that she was a prolific participant. The vast majority of the pictures on Angela's site had actually originated from Karen. "You don't owe anybody money you can't pay back? No gambling problem? Medical bills? Drugs? Anything like that?"

She peered up from her phone, the angle and thickness of her glasses made her eyes seem artificially large. "No, nothing like that. What are you getting at?"

My expression softened. "I'm eliminating the possibility that you've been forced into using your property to help these people. None of us found the notion remotely probable, but I had to ask you in person. It wouldn't be the first time something like that has happened."

I was about to say something else when my phone chirped several times. The first was Karen's connection request; the second was an e-mail from Shanagh looking for an update. I'd write a reply when I was at a real keyboard.

I drifted briefly into Karen's site while a conversation continued in the background. It was a veritable photomontage and narrative of her daily activities, most accompanied by her location. "Karen," I said, interrupting whatever conversation was ongoing, "how much of this is open to the public?"

"Almost nothing. Why?"

I turned my phone around, showing an update from ten months ago. It showed a picture of her building, complete with the address and a tag line:

```
Second distribution center? Small business?
I don't know, but I just rented this!
Feeling excited!
Visible to: Friends and Friends of my
friends
```

"Karen," I said, sighing, "somewhere in your network, there's a friend that isn't a friend."

"That could be quite a list," added Angela. "Everyone in her immediate circle that I know of has hundreds of connections."

I glanced over at Mack. "Anything you can help with?"

"See what I have to put up with, ladies? I'm still bruised, sore, and mostly one-handed and he's still cracking the whip!"

That old glint in Mack's eyes had returned. "Mack!"

She winked. "Send me a link request, Karen, and I'll see what I can do when they finally send me home. You probably need to lock-down your site a bit too from the sound of things. You're a case of identity-theft waiting to happen."

My phone rang and I stepped out to answer it. Karen suddenly had bigger problems than identity theft.

O'Neil called with the news and sadly, my intuition proved to be correct. The assailant's body was found, tossed in a local landfill, killed by a single forty-five caliber bullet to the heart. He bore the battle scars from tangling with Mack, but otherwise there was little to identify him. Declan Clarke's reputation for leaving bodies had apparently followed him to our side of the pond. And I didn't think he was done.

All three of them stared at me in disbelief when I shared the latest news.

"They found your attacker in the landfill, Mack; his heart lost an argument with a forty-five slug. It wouldn't be a bad idea for you to get yourself a lawyer, Karen. One of the last calls to the dead man's phone came from your cell phone. In the eyes of the police, that makes you involved."

"Possibly a prime suspect," said Mack.

The already-petite Karen seemed to shrink in front of our eyes. "That isn't possible," she muttered, her eyes growing wide, voice trembling.

"It seems," Angela added, woefully, "that being my friend is a dangerous condition these days. I'm so sorry that you're getting embroiled in my problems."

"I'm going to give you a name and number. Call him and mention my name. If the police want to ask you questions, or in the off chance they arrest you, don't say a damn thing without this guy there. You understand?" She nodded, her expression reminiscent of Angela's the day that Finnegan reappeared in her life. "This guy is the best there is, and I'll cover any legal bills. In the mean time, I expect that the cops will be watching your every move, Karen. Don't give them any reason to go snooping."

"I didn't think I had." She peered at her phone. "This is strange."

She turned her phone around, showing its outgoing call log. "None of these numbers are familiar to me, and they were all made around the same time."

The log showed four calls made within a five-minute span several hours before Mack was assaulted. "Where were you when these calls were made?"

"That would have been right in the middle of our weekly receiving cycle when the local grocery stores send us their donations. We have to catalog and sort all of it, and the reception out in the main part of the warehouse is so bad that phones are pointless. I usually leave my phone at my desk."

She went on to describe the layout of the building. With the chaos and drivers coming and going, it would be a nearly trivial matter for someone to slip in unnoticed and use her phone. Karen promised me access to their surveillance system, but warned that it was primitive. I recorded the numbers in hopes that Jerry could do something with them but didn't hold out much hope; they'd probably trace back to disposable phones, but it was worth a shot.

"Unless you tell me otherwise, I'm going to arrange for some security for you. I underestimated Declan Clarke once; I'll not do it again."

She nodded, weakly. "Should I erase these calls from my phone?"

"I can't advise you to do that. There isn't much point, anyway. If they investigate your cellular call records, it will be a trivial matter for them to see that these calls originated on your phone. That will be hard enough to explain. Call the number I gave you as soon as possible and don't mention a word of this to anyone else."

* * *

Karen spent most of the afternoon and early evening with us, as much to help get Mack settled in to my guest room as for her own protection. She departed after dinner, bodyguards in tow, undoubtedly feeling both bewildered and terrified.

Angela settled in next to me, arm around my waist. "Is she going to be alright?"

"Jerry's men are the best and half the planet is actively looking for Declan Clarke. He's crazy to go after any of us now; he missed the best shot he had at us."

"But why Karen?" Angela's eyes searched my face for answers; answers I didn't have.

"I really don't know. I've a few theories, but hardly anything solid. The one thing I'm certain of, though, is that they want our investigation to stop, and stop quickly. Something we're into is getting close. Problem is, we have so many things going it is hard to know which it is. Hell, we don't know half of what Charlie and crew might be turning up, either."

She leaned closer to me, head on my shoulders. "I had no idea anything like this would happen when I asked you to help me. I hope you know that I never meant to put anyone in harm's way."

I ran my fingers through her hair, reassuringly. "I know it, Ange. One thing I'm a little curious about, though, is how they knew we were going to be at the theater."

"Do you think they could have followed us?"

"I suppose it's possible, but I didn't see anyone from the surveillance recordings. Who knew about it?"

"I'm sorry — I told a few people. I didn't realize that it was a secret."

"You couldn't have known, don't give it a second thought. How many people?"

"No more than a handful. Karen and crew to be sure; Ma, I think, maybe one or two more."

"Oh? You and Shanagh are talking again?"

"We are. Small steps, but we're getting back to where we were."

* * *

It was difficult to get Mack to listen to the doctors. She wanted to get back to work; they wanted her resting. She won, although her pace was noticeably slower than her normal frenetic rate.

"Mack, you said something about them getting the wrong laptop."

"Yeah," she said, smiling at the screen as if in admiration. "All of my real files are stored in the cloud on various providers and encrypted, so even if they got my main computer, I'd not really lose anything except the hardware. What they got is an older model that I keep around for just such an emergency."

"Okay, Mack, you've got one hell of a wicked smile going. Spill it!"

"The laptop has some tracking software installed. In other words, whenever it has an internet connection it phones home and tells me as much as it can about where it is."

I peered over at her screen. Whatever was making her smile so broadly was not immediately obvious to me. "I don't see what you're so excited about."

"Each line represents an IP address. Check this out! Here is a traceroute back to one of my servers, nearby WiFi hotspots, you name it!"

She went on and on with a lengthy and unintelligible technical explanation. Normally, I would have cut her off the moment I stopped comprehending, but I let it run to its conclusion uninterrupted. "So when does it pop up a cool map showing everywhere the laptop has been, like on television?"

She stopped, glaring at me. "There is a reason it is called fiction. This stuff takes time and is a fair amount of work, but we've already gotten quite a few good chunks of data back from it, so now the fun begins!"

"What do you mean?"

"I can tell when the machine comes on-line. The tracking software has a few special features that I can control manually." Her smile returned. "Like turning on the built in camera and taking a picture, recording the audio from whatever room it is in."

"Mack! You are..."

"Say it…"

"Absolutely amazing!"

* * *

"We're in business!" Mack proclaimed, eagerly rotating one of her monitors into a position where all could see it. "I'm going to take a quick picture from the camera."

An image appeared a short time later. It was dark, but clearly showed a man intently focused on the laptop's screen. Two others lingered in the background, but the lighting made identification impossible. "Recognize that guy, Angela?" I said, glancing to my right.

She shook her head. "I do not, sorry."

"I'm going to record what they're talking about," said Mack.

I watched the monitor as one of the men from the background moved closer, saying something to the man operating the laptop. "Declan Clarke," I muttered.

"That's him for certain," said Angela, nodding in agreement.

We watched for a bit longer before Mack gave me a thumbs-up. "I've got it," she said, her voice quivering with excitement. She handed me an address. "It will be in this vicinity."

"Are you sure?" Mack stared at me incredulously. "This is in the same area as Karen's rental. No damn way it's a coincidence."

"What are you saying, John?" Angela looked mildly upset.

"My guess is they picked their place because they somehow knew about Karen's rental. It was likely a happy event for them that she wasn't using it. Made it all that more convenient for them to dump some evidence in there for us to find." It wasn't the only theory I had, but was the only one I was willing to mention aloud.

Angela was about to say something when Mack interrupted. "They shut it off, but do you want to hear what they had to say?"

"Sure, Mack, let's take a listen."

The audio was quiet and choppy. Even after Mack enhanced it, there were sections where parts could not be heard:

Have you found anything yet on that laptop?

Yeah, a few things. They're all over the place. What does she want us to do?

[unintelligible]

Another day or so and I should be done with this computer.

We going to give it another go?

The damn lawyer has more protection than we expected. We can't get close to any of them.

[unintelligible]

I'll ask her the next time we talk. Close that thing. We need to be ready to clear out.

Dammit. It looked like they were getting ready to move and without Mack's laptop tracing their steps, we might not be able to find them again anytime soon. I needed a way to keep them interested for a day or two more so we could refine their location. "Mack, is there someplace that you could put a file where they could see it?"

"Sure. What do you have in mind?"

"I want them to think that we're putting all our efforts into investigating Karen, trying to tie her to Strabane and so forth. Maybe they'll relax a bit." Mack stared back at me, unconvinced. "Sorry. I'm doing the best I can here, Mack, trying to buy some time."

"I suppose I could accidentally forget to encrypt a document and leave it on one of the cloud providers where they can see it. That might work and would be more believable than something randomly showing up on the machine's hard drive."

"Mack, I'm putting my faith in you."

"No pressure, huh? Angela, I'm going to need your help with this.

227

I'll need some details on Karen's past that I can twist into a believable connection."

Angela rose, quickly shooing me from my chair. "Got it."

CHAPTER TWENTY-FOUR

I knew it was going to be a rough day when I had a pre-dawn message from Jim Finnegan awaiting me.

```
The warrant has been issued.
The formal process is starting.
Time for Angela's day of reckoning.
```

A call from Brown confirmed Jim's text — the machinery was in motion. "Your sources are accurate, Costa. Northern Ireland has issued a warrant for Miss Grady's arrest. We expect that an extradition request will follow."

I sighed, my spirits sinking. "What do you think the Secretary will do, ultimately?"

"Their evidence is strong enough to get a warrant issued. Without something compelling enough for the warrant to be withdrawn, I view the chances of State declining extradition to be slim."

"Their case is largely circumstantial. Is there any opportunity to buy more time?"

"We'll approach this with the necessary diligence, of course, so it isn't likely that she'll be arrested until after the holidays. That is about the best I can offer you." I started to speak, but Brown interrupted.

"We've got a treaty in place that can't be ignored. It isn't like she's going to an island nation run by an unstable dictator; she'll get her day in court."

"But…"

"Look, Mister Costa, their prima facie case is compelling. You're going to have a hell of a time disputing probable cause. Like it or not, the facts are simple: your girl has made it to the United Kingdom's most-wanted list. They consider her a fugitive and a terrorist; things aren't going to be pleasant for her any time soon."

"Don't think for a moment, Brown, that I'm going to idly stand by while you throw her in some secret hellhole. I'd rather not play the publicity card, if you follow my drift."

Brown's tone softened. "I didn't mean to imply she's going to Gitmo, but she's not going to Club Fed, either."

"There's a perfectly good minimum security women's facility under an hour away."

"No promises."

Dammit — we needed more time. Brooding followed, but a short missive from Charlie Hannon served to lift my dismal mood somewhat.

Costa,

I was finally able to trace Tully's house, the one he got for next to nothing.

Traced it to Padraig Bannion, but the trail went cold.

We kept digging and discovered that Padraig Bannion's real name is Padraig Brennan. Yes, from the same family. Cost me quite a bit to find this and you'll be getting my bill.

Works at a place that builds houses, among other things, run by Brian O'Hegerty.

```
Best,

CH
```

I showed the missive to Mack. She barely had time to react before one of her computers beeped at her, immediately stealing her attention.

"What is it, Mack?"

"We get to see if I'm a super genius or merely a genius." Angela joined us, peering intently over my shoulder at the monitors in front of us. "The laptop is on-line." A window on one of the monitors opened, revealing dark, jumpy video. Audio crackled from the speaker.

```
Something new here, boss.

What is it?

Looks like a temp file of some sort, big
one, too. Want me to see if I can get in?
```

A figure, mostly shadowed, moved closer to the camera. He mumbled something unintelligible.

```
Look! His researcher forgot to encrypt it.
Probably the pain killers at work. Murph
must've done a number on her.

If Murph would have done his job, we
wouldn't have to be dealing with her at all.
Stupid bastard.
```

The screen went black, but the sound continued. I looked over at Mack who seemed unconcerned as her eyes studied the monitors.

From the look of things, they're spending
all their time working on connecting the Boyle
woman to everything!

Doesn't mean shit. Until she's dead or
locked up forever, nothing's done. Shut that
thing down, god dammit, we've got more to do.

Mack looked at me, a sadness crossing her face. "I guess only a genius," she said quietly.

"No luck?"

"I got what I could. To get the real address, we're going to have to go for a drive."

"What do you mean?"

"We're going to have to drive down there with one of my laptops and a GPS if you want the exact address."

* * *

"Mack, this is likely the craziest thing I've ever let you talk me in to," I whispered as our borrowed truck turned into the bumpy, pothole-ridden street that led to the rows of buildings where our quarry might be hiding.

"Shush," she said, staring at the screen. "We're getting closer; the next row or the one after it, probably."

"Turn here," I whispered to the driver as we neared the corner. Karen's rental was the last unit in the row on our right. Most of the way down the road Mack tapped my arm, excitedly.

"We're close! Can you back into one of the parking spots across the way?"

The driver grunted in agreement. The vehicle eased gently into the parking spot, the driver turning off the engine and lights.

"I'm ninety-nine percent certain my laptop is in the place directly across from us. I'll know for certain if they turn it on."

"Close that damn thing," said the driver. "Someone is coming out!"

I quickly ripped off my coat, tossing it over Mack and her computer to hide the light it was casting in the truck's cabin. We all sank down in our seats hoping the man wouldn't notice us. From my vantage, he seemed oblivious to our presence, far more interested in his cigarette and his phone. He was joined a few minutes later by a man that looked familiar. "Mack," I whispered, "take a quick peek at this guy, would you?"

She silently closed her laptop, peaking up from beneath my coat. "That's the guy that has been working on the laptop. I'm certain of it!"

"That's what I thought, too. We need to get the hell out of here so I can call O'Neil."

"We can leave as soon as they're inside," said the driver, gruffly. "Son of a bitch! Get the hell down you two — one of them is coming over. Not a sound, not a move, you two."

Mack and I quickly ducked onto the floor of the back seat, tossing my coat over us. The lighting where we parked and the layout of the truck's interior worked in our favor, but it wouldn't hold up to close scrutiny or a flashlight.

I heard the window roll down and a man with an Irish accent, from the north undoubtedly, started to speak. "You boys lost?"

"We have a delivery for the brewing company."

"Nobody there, mate; been gone for a couple of hours."

"I know it. This whole thing has been a giant pain. The shipment was delayed at the airport and we're on tap for the entire damn delivery charge if we can't reach the owner; comes out of our damned checks right before the damned holiday, too. You know the guy?"

"Can't help you, friend. A word to the wise, though. The cops troll through here from time to time; might not want to be here when they do. Been a few problems with drugs and whatnot around here — they can get a bit touchy."

"Thanks. Last thing I need is another hassle."

I heard the window roll up and the engine start. We had only rolled a short distance before Mack spoke, excitedly. "Pull over! The laptop is on."

"Why? We have what we need and I've already sent O'Neil the address."

"Don't you want to know what they're up to? Get closer!"

"Mack, I've got to be out of my damn mind for even bringing you here!"

"John!"

"Okay, Mack… you win."

We turned the van into the next street, one away from our previous location. Lights out, we rolled as quietly as possible down the road. Voices could be heard from Mack's laptop:

```
Timmy, change of plans. We're to meet
Declan up north. Close up things here and
tidy-up — you know what to do.

I do.

Where are you with that damned laptop? She
wants to know what we've found.
```

A woman's voice, broken, distorted, and likely on a speaker phone, could be heard briefly in the background, but we couldn't discern any words.

```
Everything is decrypted and organized,
including the new stuff. Fire it up and go.

Good. Give it to me and take care of
business here.
```

The connection died moments later, followed shortly by a quick glimpse of headlights visible through a gap between buildings.

"Dammit, they're moving again. Follow them!"

"You sure about that, Costa?" said the second bodyguard, speaking for the first time.

"Yes. It took us days to find this location; we may not have that luxury next time around."

It wasn't until we neared the main road that we turned on our lights. The vehicle we were following, an innocuous silver sedan, seemed oblivious to our presence. That changed quickly as a row of police cars screamed past us going the opposite direction.

"I don't know if they made us or not," grunted the driver, "but they're definitely being more careful."

I didn't know how he could tell, but I'd take his word for it. "Let them go if you have to. I'd rather keep them guessing on how close we are."

We had to abandon our surveillance a few miles north of the city. As they worked their way onto progressively less-used thoroughfares, the chances of our discovery increased. At least we knew their general area and with any luck, Mack's laptop would pinpoint their new location.

* * *

Angela met us at the door, her face etched with concern. "You had me worried," she said, hugging me tightly. "These guys may provide wonderful protection, but they aren't much when it comes to conversation." She motioned toward the expressionless bodyguards who had been her companions while we were gone.

"We're okay," I said, "a bit chilly, but all in one piece. But as usual, more damn questions than answers."

"I made some hot cocoa," said Angela. "Let's get you all warmed up!"

Mack's hands cradled a mug as she looked off into space, her countenance decidedly discouraged. "I really thought they'd bite on what we fed them, Angie. I feel like I let everyone down."

"You didn't let anyone down," Angela said. "What you did was absolutely amazing."

I put my hand on Mack's shoulder, reassuringly. "She's right." I was about to say something else when my phone rang. I stepped out of the kitchen to take the call.

"Yes, George?"

"Someone tipped us off to an address near the airport."

"Imagine that…"

"It was a good tip, too, not the kind we usually get. You'll see it on the news soon enough, but we've got another body on our hands. We put his picture out and started getting hits right away. Turns out he was from Londonderry. Mean anything to you, John?"

"Oh sure! It means he was Irish…"

"Snarky bastard! He died from a forty-five caliber bullet right through his heart like the guy that attacked Jillian MacDonald. Want to take any wagers on it being fired from the same gun when the ballistic analysis comes back?"

"I'm not a betting man, George, and neither are you. What's on your mind?"

"Don't you think maybe it's time you let us in on what you're working on? Especially now that we've got two murders on our hands, all likely related to your girlfriend. I'd hate to have to drag all of you in on an obstruction charge."

"I'd hate to have to eviscerate you in front of a judge, George."

"Costa, has it occurred to you that you might be in over your damn head?"

"Every day, my friend."

* * *

Mack, angry and focused like I'd never seen her, worked well into the early morning. She pursued the connection between Padraig Brennan and Tully Smith relentlessly, but watched for another signal from her wayward laptop. By the time I reluctantly surrendered to sleep, it hadn't made a peep.

The morning found things unchanged. Mack was still at work, clearly fighting exhaustion but pressing onward. Her work had produced a massive chart filled with boxes, lines, arrows, and notes.

"David A. Brennan's magnum opus," she said to me, her voice quiet, but forceful. "Charlie and I have been working on this for a while now."

"What am I looking at?"

"Holding companies, umbrella corporations, you name it, but it is a monster hidden in plain sight. He got his start with rebuilding contracts after the Second World War. Incredibly lucrative, too. Since then, it has blossomed into this." Her hand pointed out various boxes. "Shipyard construction, renovation, demolition, lumber, steelworks, home construction, imports, exports, cement, and electrical."

"How does the money flow between all these?"

"No idea. Given how this is set up, it would take a battalion of forensic accountants years to dig through it. The brilliance of the whole thing is that each company is precisely the right size. Big enough to bid lucrative jobs, but small enough to avoid a lot of scrutiny."

"Each one could be squeaky clean, huh?"

"Yep, and modest in all regards. But when all this stuff rolls up to the top," her hand hovered over a large rectangle at the top of the chart, "we're talking hundreds of millions, annually."

"Strange..."

"What?"

"Connla O'Grady was right in the middle of building all of this, likely instrumental in getting all the overseas connections worked out. You'd think he'd have more to show for it than what he had. When they settled his estate, he had his house, a couple of modest bank accounts, and a few small investments. You'd think that the man he played music with all the time, one of his oldest friends, would have taken better care of him."

"Same could be said for David A. Brennan, now that you mention it. Maybe they both reinvested so heavily in the company that they didn't have much of their own."

"Or they were investing in something else, Mack; something that isn't going to show up on the books. Either way, we've closed the circle. We just don't know what it means yet."

"Closed the circle?"

"The cover-up of Maggie's death is tied to Tully, who is tied to Padraig Brennan, who is tied to David A. Brennan, who is tied to Connla Grady…"

"Who is tied to Angela," she said, completing my sentence with an air of sadness, "but no solid connection to Strabane."

"Except through George Finnegan, who was investigating Tully, and happened to be there…"

CHAPTER TWENTY-FIVE

A call from the State Department made a bleak midwinter's day even worse. Our best efforts had fallen short. We finally agreed for Angela to surrender to the United States Marshals two days hence. I did my best to prepare her for what would happen but in spite of her regular assurances, I still worried. I had seen the destructive effects of arrest and incarceration; Angela would need every ounce of strength she had.

We made a handful of plans but it was a halfhearted effort at each step. Angela wanted to spend time with me, a sentiment I echoed heartily, but that was not in the cards. A call from the United States Marshals changed everything.

"Counselor, this is Deputy United States Marshall Edward Jones."

"What can I do for you, sir?"

"Are your intentions still for Miss Grady to surrender around midday tomorrow?"

"They are. Is there an issue?"

"Yes there is. Homeland Security has advised that they have been unable to eliminate the threat against Miss Grady's life, likely yours also. They consider it serious enough to recommend we take measures to insure her safety."

"What do you propose?"

"We'll leak it to the press that you're bringing her in tomorrow, but we're going to come to your place after dark tonight and take her into custody. We've got a few other things planned, but I'll discuss those when we're there."

I relayed the news to Angela who could offer little in response but a shrug and a look of reservation. "I'm not sure exactly what one wears to go to prison," she said, her voice distant and melancholy. "This is a first for me, and not something I ever wanted to think of."

* * *

Darkness arrived in what felt like the blink of an eye. Black SUVs rolled into my driveway shortly thereafter followed by a heavy knock on the door. Six Marshals, four men and two women, entered my house. A tall, dark, veteran-looking man introduced himself as Jones.

"Here is the warrant, Counselor. Please take a moment to review it and the attached search warrant. Specifically, it is for Miss Grady's computer and cell phone."

I reviewed it, finding it all properly done.

Jones motioned to another Marshal. One of the women, roughly Angela's height, joined us. "This is trainee Evans. She's volunteered to be a decoy."

The woman removed her cap, revealing blonde hair in a familiar style. "I did the best I could with short notice. Miss Grady, I'd like to borrow one of your tops if I may, preferably one you've worn in public a few times — a jacket, too. It will be returned to your lawyer when I'm done with it."

Angela nodded, motioning toward the guest room. The woman emerged a few minutes later, a passable likeness of Angela, especially on a dark night.

"We're going to take Miss Evans out first. Counselor, we'll need you to play along in order to make this convincing. Walk out with us. Give her a hug, you know what to do."

"Then what happens?"

"We'll take Miss Grady into custody, but she'll be wearing Miss Evans' cap and jacket. She'll be going here." He handed me a note with the name of a federal facility on it. "It is medium security, not quite what you wanted, but it is reasonably close and she'll be away from the general population for the duration of her stay there. As her counsel, you'll have a significant and regular opportunity to see her, especially given the situation of the case. State is being picky on this one — you must've really gotten under their skin."

"Thank you. I'm told I have a way about me for such things." I slipped the note into my pocket. "I'll need to let her family know, a few close friends as well."

"Please wait until we've arrived safely at the prison. I'll call you as soon as we're there. Miss Evans, are you ready to go? Counselor?"

We both nodded. The decoy was handcuffed. Angela's coat, tossed over her shoulders, added to the disguise. I did my best to be convincing although my conversation was decidedly contrived. Apparently it was satisfactory as Miss Evans, now secured in the back of the SUV, nodded to me in approval. I leaned in, quietly thanking her and feigning a kiss.

Jones and I stood there quietly as two massive SUVs roared off into the night accompanied by two local police cars, lights flashing, as they reached the end of my street. The inquisitive neighbors that had been peering through their windows returned to the humdrum of their normal existence.

He slapped me on the shoulder. "Well done. Now for the difficult part."

We returned to the house, my legs heavy with unwillingness.

"Turn the porch lights off along with the lights in the foyer. We're going to hang around for a few minutes, like maybe we're going over some paperwork with you or something. Then we'll take Miss Grady out. You're going to have to say your words of parting here. Following us out will ruin the illusion."

Conversation failed us. Instead, we sat together, Angela on my lap her arms wrapped around me, in silence. I tried to drink in every ounce of her I could, the feel of her hair, her scent, the pace of her breathing, but most importantly her beautiful dark brown eyes and the joyous light that, even in this dark hour, unfailing twinkled within.

When Jones finally spoke, it felt like only seconds had elapsed. The clock, claiming nearly thirty minutes, was a liar.

"Counselor, here is an inventory of her belongings. Miss Grady, please stand up. This Marshal," motioning to the remaining female agent, "is going to search you while I read you your rights."

I had hoped to prevent what followed but given the nature of the crime for which she stood accused, it was inevitable. The Marshals moved with swift precision, their process undoubtedly well practiced. Shackles ratcheted closed around Angela's ankles. They secured a chain firmly around her waist; from a loop at its center, handcuffs collected her wrists. The short chain connecting them afforded her the freedom to do little more than interlace her fingers, almost as if in prayer. It looked decidedly uncomfortable, but she offered no protest nor did her expression change. It all seemed unnecessary — the woman I knew posed no threat. To the Marshals, though, she was merely a name on a warrant.

The Marshals permitted one brief kiss, a gesture I appreciated more than words could express. "Stay strong and I'll see you soon," I whispered as our lips parted. She managed a weak smile and a nod in return.

Jones nodded, his expression betraying what might be a hint of understanding, or so I convinced myself. Deputy Evans' cap and jacket, zipped high enough to hide the chains, completed Angela's disguise.

"You're going to walk with me, ahead of these other agents, Miss Grady. Climb straight into the back seat and stay calm. One of us will buckle you in once the dome light goes off.

Angela spoke quietly, barely above a whisper. "Yes sir."

Marshal Smith continued. "Counselor, keep your phone on. State has requested that I call you with updates as I can."

"Thank you."

The vehicle departed into the night, joined subtly by several nondescript cars. A solitary unmarked, but obvious, police car remained parked halfway down my street.

* * *

My hand instinctively reached for a bottle of whiskey, but I demurred. Retreating to my music room brought no solace. Solitude, an existence I had embraced for the majority of my life, now brought only pain and longing. Television offered no companionship, either. I flipped through the myriad of channels, stopping only when I saw Angela's picture on one of the local stations.

Breaking News...

News Channel Seven has learned that an extradition warrant has been issued for Angela Grady, a local woman allegedly implicated in a 1998 bombing in Northern Ireland. Our reporter was able to obtain a statement from the United States Marshals. We now go live to Colleen Shelton who is downtown at the federal building where Miss Grady will surrender to federal authorities tomorrow.

The scene cut to a local reporter, young, wide-eyed, and excitedly nodding her head. A formulaic and predictable report followed.

Thank you, Krista. That's right, just minutes ago a spokesperson from the United States Marshal's office has confirmed exclusively to News Channel Seven that the State Department has, earlier today, authorized an arrest warrant for Angela Grady, honoring a request from Northern Ireland. This will be the start of extradition proceedings which will determine if a sufficient case exists for Grady to be returned there to face a trial. The spokesperson also confirmed that Grady's attorney, John Costa, has arranged for her voluntary surrender to the United States Marshals tomorrow afternoon.

Now Krista, we know that this is in connection with an explosion that occurred in the town of Strabane in 1998, but few details

beyond that have emerged, including the nature
of Angela Grady's alleged involvement...

Some meaningless banter between the reporter and the news
anchor followed. I took the release of the story as a good sign; events,
ostensibly, seemed to be unfolding as planned. With equal certainty, the
phone in my office started to ring as the press began their inevitable
feeding-frenzy. I couldn't blame them; the story was as compelling as it
was implausible. Ignoring their calls was easy. Ignoring Karen and
Shanagh, though, was not. They needed to know, but for now, it was
more important that the illusion remain.

I continued to watch, the station breaking in periodically with
more meaningless updates. A quick glance at my security system cameras
validated my suspicion. Members of the press were already beginning to
congregate on my street.

Finally, after two hours of waiting, the call arrived.

"Counselor, Jones here. Miss Grady arrived safely and will call you
tomorrow. You'll be sent all of the pertinent details, of course, and the
Unites States Attorney will be in touch."

* * *

Karen scolded me harshly for not answering her calls sooner but
grew quietly contrite as I described the situation. "How can I help?"

"She'll need support from her friends, of course. I've not seen
where she's being held yet, but I doubt that it is the least bit pleasant,
especially given the seriousness of the accusation. Familiar faces will do
her a world of good. I'll send you the details, and you can figure out
when you want to visit."

"What happens next?"

I explained the most likely series of events. Karen could offer little
in response. As devastating as it was to me, I could not begin to imagine
the pain she was feeling for her friend.

"It doesn't look good, does it?"

"I confess that we're looking at an uphill struggle, but I'm not
conceding anything, and I'm certainly not giving up. Neither is Angela.

You know how she is."

"I know, I know, but it doesn't make it any easier to deal with. Of all the people I know, she's the last one I'd expect to be visiting in jail. I thought this nonsense was finally behind her."

"I think Angela did too. What do you remember from those conversations you had?"

"She was in utter disbelief, simply couldn't understand why she'd be suspected of anything so heinous. She's always been one of the good ones, John. No trouble in school, no trouble outside of school; a spotless record over here, too. All this works in her favor, doesn't it?" Karen paused as her voice faltered. "There is one other thing I remember, now that I think back on it. I don't think she ever said it in so many words, but I don't think she got the support she needed from her mother."

"Interesting… Shanagh's got her issues, of course, but she's always seemed supportive, at least from what I've seen."

"That's the result of a more recent bridge-building effort. It warms my heart to see it, honestly, but there was a long rough patch that preceded it. I'm no psychologist, but I think Shanagh blamed Angela for Sean's death. Maybe if she hadn't gone to visit Maggie the Constabulary wouldn't have come calling, and maybe Sean's heart wouldn't have been under so much stress. You know."

"She never shared that with me. That must have been an awfully heavy burden."

"It contributed, no doubt, to her choice to leave Ireland. Part of the reason I pushed her so hard to come here was to get out of the situation. It was getting toxic. I'm glad she listened to me."

"I am, too. Please let me know when you're planning to visit her. Remember, Declan Clarke is still out there somewhere, so be careful when you're out and about."

CHAPTER TWENTY-SIX

Angela's call finally arrived, much to my joy and relief. "I'm set up in the system, and they promised me some books today. I have nothing but the walls to keep me company most of the day. Most of the guards will talk to me a bit, some won't. I'm completely off by myself, constantly guarded."

"I'm sorry we weren't able to stop this," I said quietly. "I'll get your commissary fund stocked as soon as we're off the phone. I should be able to visit the day after tomorrow, or so I've been told."

"I can't wait. I miss you, Johnny."

"I miss you, too. Hang in there; I'll be there before you know it."

* * *

My first visit arrived on schedule and went as planned. Her cell was in an area undergoing renovations, away from the general population as promised. It seemed safe but desperately lonely.

"The food isn't good, but I'll survive." She forced a weak smile. "Getting outside only an hour per day isn't much fun, either. Strange, but I feel more like a caged animal outside than inside. There's nothing but a fenced area between buildings for me to walk around in so I pace the perimeter. It is hard to enjoy the outdoors when there are armed guards ready to put a bullet in me at the slightest provocation. I've resorted to doing yoga in my cell when there's nobody to talk to. There is so much negative energy here, it is difficult to stay positive."

"I can start raising a stink if the conditions are intolerable. I may be able to get a little bit of traction since you've not been convicted of anything yet."

"I can endure for now. If they do something to make it worse, things might change."

"Have you been able to get some books to read at least?"

"Yes. They won't let me go to the library, something to do with security, but I made a list of a few things and they did the best they could. I've met a couple of inmates — trustees, they call them. They bring me books and meals and on occasion stay for a chat. It breaks up the monotony a bit, but is hardly a substitute for companionship. One of the guards mentioned trying to get a television rigged up, but I have no idea if that will actually happen. Christ, it is boring."

"We should have our preliminary hearing early next week. If nothing else, it will be a change of scenery. I'm still going to take a shot at getting bail, too."

"Are they going to let Karen visit me?"

"She should be here tomorrow or the day after. Then I'll be back to review our strategy for the preliminary hearing and bail. I've got a few ideas, and Mack keeps working diligently."

Her face brightened. "Okay. Thank you again. This is just a brief detour in the direction the universe is taking us. I'm sure of it."

I needed to keep telling myself the same thing.

* * *

My first surprise was when Karen, contrary to her promise, did not call me regarding her visit to Angela. I only knew of its happening from glancing surreptitiously at the visitor log. Angela delivered the second, devastating surprise in person. She arrived looking thoroughly forlorn and distant; my mind raced with possible explanations.

"This won't take long," she said to the guard who closed the door behind her.

I lacked words, offering only a confused look in return.

"I've had a lot of time to think, and I've decided to let things take their course. I'm not going to fight extradition. I can't have you risking your life, career, and reputation for me anymore."

I tried to offer a reply, some form of protest, but she stopped me in my tracks before I could utter a single syllable.

"Damned Greg Finnegan was right about me from the beginning. You should have stayed away. Since I have no faith that you'll listen, you're fired. You're not my lawyer any more, and I'm taking you off my visitor list. Goodbye, Johnny. Guard!"

I could offer nothing but silence in response as I watched her walk slowly away, disappearing behind a heavy door. I left, dejectedly turning in my credentials and walking slowly to my car, accompanied by the ever-present and stoic bodyguards.

"Take me to my god damned bar," I grunted.

* * *

Dammit. Someone had gotten to her. Whatever threat they held was potent enough to cause an abrupt strategy change, but not enough to truly break her spirit. Gregory Finnegan, indeed! But appearances had to be kept, and we would have to proceed cautiously.

It wasn't an entirely unexpected contingency, although its strength and severity was disconcerting. Karen held the answer, but I needed to think of the best way to reach her surreptitiously. There was no better place to keep up the illusion than a quiet corner in my bar, all while I appeared to be drinking myself into a coma.

Mack joined me, doubling the count of forlorn countenances at my table. "So that's the word," she asked quietly.

"That's the word. Can you handle Karen, please?" She nodded, taking a sip of Guinness. "I'll let Jerry and Charlie know. Does our esteemed Mister Hannon have what he needs?"

"He does. This is going to slow us down a bit. Are we going to have enough time?"

"God, I hope so. If they're pressing her for a confession it may get tricky. Karen's the key, Mack. We've got to know what she told Angela.

You're sure she's clean, right Mack?"

"After the last screw-up, are you sure you trust me with such a big decision?"

"Of course I do."

"Then I say she's clean."

"Good. I'm going with that. Now — leave here all sad and upset — we don't know who might be watching."

"That isn't going to take an award-winning performance on my part. I'm not exactly brimming with confidence right now."

"Mack, I'll always trust you. Go on; get out of here."

* * *

The evening rolled around, lonely, cold, rainy, and with it a surprise visit from Jim Finnegan. He quietly pulled up a chair opposite me, ironically only a few tables away from where we first met.

"Tough day, Costa?" His voice trailed off.

I motioned to Laura for another round. "Well, you could say that, Jim. You here to rub my nose in it?"

"All these years and things are finally moving in a positive direction. I really expected a bit more elation than I'm experiencing now. Strange how things work."

"Strange indeed."

"There's a lot of speculation going around. Some are intimating that she might even be willing to confess."

"Only she knows for certain what is going through her head. I sure as hell don't. She fired me before I could ask her a damn thing."

"Strange what happens when the handcuffs go on. I've seen all sorts of reactions, including what's happening here. Maintaining an illusion like hers for all these years must have been exhausting. With nothing but prison walls to stare at probably gave her time to think and reflect on the reality of her situation. Maybe having you in the picture was good after all."

"How so?"

"Perhaps she finally cared about someone enough to not leave them along the wayside. Only a theory, of course. But you, John — are you going to be able to let it go? A few months ago she was the woman of your dreams. You're walking away?"

"Sometimes, Jim, wanting is preferable to having." I took a deep quaff from my drink. "Walk away? Yes. Get over it? Not any time soon."

"What are you going to do with yourself?"

"Oh, I'm going to crawl back into my shell, where I probably should've stayed in the first place. Do me a favor, will you?"

"What's that?"

"Let me know when I can stop with all this damn security. No point in paying these guys any longer than necessary; and Jim, one other thing." I slid a paper across the table to him. He glanced at it, raised a single eyebrow, nodded, and departed without saying a word.

* * *

I spent the better part of a week ignoring a torrent of calls from the press desperately looking for interviews. I let them engage in endless conjecture, most of which was strangely amusing to watch. Angela's initial court appearance had gone about as expected, resulting in a continuance so that her hopelessly over-matched public defender could become familiar with the case. I felt sorry for the poor bastard.

I started to return to being a regular fixture at my pub, observing snippets of the case from a-far as they appeared on the bar's television. Angela remained steadfast, though, and eventually got her wish. The judge ruled that the warrant was consistent with existing extradition treaties and that probable cause existed. The remaining roadblock was swept aside as Angela waived her right to a hearing. The final details, likely to take months to sort out, shifted to the logistics of her transport to Belfast. I hated to see her stuck in prison, but it was time that I needed for my plans to unfold.

Social media, predictably, erupted with a torrent of conjecture. Quietly, in the periphery a dismal trend continued: the slow but certain exodus of Angela's connections. Her contacts, once nearing a thousand, dwindled on a daily basis. A glance showed the quantity had fallen to slightly below one hundred.

Some of Angela's true and remaining friends tried a valiant and spirited social defense but were frequently shouted-down by throngs of loud-mouthed, uninformed louts. One voice, however, was conspicuous in its absence. Karen hadn't offered a peep since her first visit to the prison.

Mack had, for several days, worked on the details of a meeting. Karen arrived after dark looking nervous and uncomfortable. My demeanor did little to assuage her fears. "If I had my way, Karen Boyle," I growled, "you would be in handcuffs right now and depending on how the next few minutes unfold, that may be how you leave here." She shrank into the lone chair in the center of the room. "Intimidation, tampering with a federal case, not to mention the entire nefarious bit with Declan Clarke, I expect you'll be looking at some fairly hard time."

Karen started to sob. "No! You've got it all wrong."

"Then talk to me, because George O'Neil is in the next room ready to take you into custody. I've enough experience and influence to make your situation go exactly how I want it to, and right now I'm in the mood to do something you won't like."

"They're going to kill Shanagh," she blubbered. "That is why she never came to any of Angela's court appearances or visited her in prison. Angela told her to stay away; that she was too ashamed to be seen."

"That certainly explains a few things, like why I've not heard from Shanagh. Why were you picked to be the messenger?"

"They told me that they've got a piece of evidence that will implicate me and that if I didn't deliver their message, they'd send it to the police. I'm so sorry; I didn't see an alternative but to do what they asked."

I pulled a chair close, facing her directly. "What exactly did they make you do?"

"I told Angela that if she wanted to see Shanagh alive, she would do whatever was necessary to stop your investigation. I hope you know that it was incredibly difficult and painful for her to do that. Firing you and hinting at a confession seemed like the most direct approach."

"I figured as much. Are you able to contact Declan Clarke?"

She hung her head. "I was given a number to call if you or the police contact me."

"When Mack reached out to you, did you call him?"

"No, I didn't. If he knew I was here or talking to you... Oh my God, I hope what I said didn't get Shanagh killed. I don't know how Angela would ever find a way to forgive me. Hell, I can't forgive myself for what I've already done."

"Karen, Mack has investigated you thoroughly. She's reasonably certain you're not involved in this outside of your friendship with Angela. I'm sorry I had to be heavy-handed, but I needed to satisfy my own lingering doubts. If you want to help your best friend, and I mean truly help her, I need you to do something for me."

"Not at the expense of Shanagh. We don't always get along, but she's my best friend's mum. I can't. I just can't..."

"In case you haven't noticed, the public has already decided Angie's guilty. People who claimed to be her friends are bailing at an alarming rate. We've already lost the public relations battle and with threat to Shanagh, we can't even offer a fight. Worse, I don't have enough to be certain of an acquittal at trial. I've got a plan, though, and I know that it comes with Angela's blessing."

"How do you know?"

"Because of something she said when she fired me. If my plan works, there is a chance we can protect Shanagh and collect the evidence we need to exonerate Angela. All of it depends, however, on Declan Clarke believing that I've given up. If you need to eviscerate me in public for quitting I don't care, but it *has* to be believable. We're all she's got."

Karen looked up at me, her eyes betraying desperation. "What do you need me to do? I'll do anything you ask if it will truly help Angela."

"Tomorrow afternoon, call Declan and tell him I reached out to you. Tell them you just got off the phone with me and immediately called them. The message is that I'm only interested in protecting Jillian MacDonald and myself at this point. Tell him that Angela Grady is on her own and that I'm ending my investigation."

Her eyes searched mine. "I'll try..."

"Trying isn't good enough. It has to be so real that you believe it yourself. Can you do that?"

She drew a deep breath. "I can."

* * *

I left the meeting with Karen under the cover of darkness. My bodyguards faithfully returned home, but I headed to the airport and a private plane chartered by one of my shell corporations. Fueled and on standby, the plane would be airborne within two hours of my arrival.

Mack had arranged everything brilliantly. My clothing, travel necessities, laptop computer, and a satellite phone were all waiting for me. It was now reduced to a waiting game, and all depended on Karen.

The jet was quite comfortable, a far cry from the commercial offerings I had experienced. Dreading the long day ahead, I reclined, closed the windows and dimmed the lights. The engines whined slowly to life then thundered as the plane accelerated down the runway. As it leveled, sleep called but it was not restful. I had too much on my mind.

CHAPTER TWENTY-SEVEN

My first stop after dealing with the various formalities of international travel was the first barbershop I could find. I emerged a short time later with a short, almost military haircut. My Italian heritage worked to my advantage, too; a few more days and I would have a decent beard started and with it, hopefully, a significant reduction in the chances that I'd be recognized.

I left Belfast and headed west along the same route that Angela took to visit Maggie almost fifteen years earlier. The drive passed quickly. I eased my car into the Albin's driveway. Margery, apparently waiting for me, emerged from a side door and motioned me to drive around to the back and into their garage. Frank, Maggie's father, lingered in the doorway.

"You look a bit different than in your picture, Mister Costa," Margery said, extending her hand. "I understand why, though."

Frank, a tall, spindly man of few words, shook my hand firmly as I entered their home. "Thank you for your hospitality," I said.

Margery had tea waiting which proved to be a welcome respite. A brief tour of Maggie's room followed. She had left it painstakingly intact, even to the detail of the unclosed drawer. I was quiet, unable to find any appropriate words.

Frank pulled me aside, speaking quietly. "Do you want to see the

254

accident site? Margery won't go, but I can show and tell you everything I know about it."

"Please." He shrugged, silently motioning me toward his car.

We snaked through a variety of narrow roads, before beginning a long, but gentle, climb. "This road will take you to the A5 if you stay on it long enough," Frank explained, "and from there on to Strabane if you head north. Why Maggie was here we might never know. No family up this way to be sure."

Frank Albin eased his car onto the side of the road. "Down there." He pointed, a pained look crossing his face.

The road was straight, descending slowly at first before briefly leveling. Beyond the short, flat section of road, its downhill slope increased. At the bottom of the grade the road jogged sharply left; a series of road signs offered warning. An old stone wall and several large trees, likely ancient, awaited any motorists who did not negotiate the corner.

The wall marked the periphery of an old but well-maintained church. Frank pulled into their drive, parking the car in the nearest available location.

"Over here," he said, motioning me back toward the wall. "This tree is the one. For a time, you could see where her car took out a chunk of the wall and the tree. They've mended the wall and the tree healed. Wish it worked that way for us."

I had no reply other than to gaze out at the road, studying the surrounding area. Frank continued after a long pause. "They said she was so drunk she didn't see the corner coming. By the time she realized it and turned the wheel, it was too late. The skidding, such as it was, started back there." He pointed to an area where the road flattened slightly. "It wasn't from her brakes, though, it was from the car going sideways. They said it was from her turning the wheel, but I say it was from the bump."

Frank knelt down, lowering his head to a few inches above the ground. I did likewise, and in so doing understood what he was telling me. A bump in the road, obscured by our previous viewing angle, became immediately obvious.

"The car's right front tire caught that bump. I figure it jogged the steering slightly to the left. With nobody to hold the wheel, the forces and speed took over. The car damn near got up on its side. The tree smashed the driver's side pretty completely, including a bit of the roof. My Maggie never had a chance." He stared into space, a strange lifelessness in his eyes. "As I figure it, the car traveled straight down the road at speed, probably from about where we stopped up at the top of the hill."

It was as good of a theory as I had heard, and consistent with the calculations Jim Finnegan had made regarding the crash. My eyes scanned the countryside as Frank spoke.

"I've been out here a hundred times, maybe more. Margery doesn't know, she thinks I'm out working, but I can't let it go. I hope you can find us some answers."

"I hope so, too. I have many pieces, but not much glue holding them together yet. I know Tully Smith covered the whole thing up. His official findings were ludicrous. Somehow, it all ties together but I don't know how. You ever heard of Fergus Clarke?"

"Can't truly say that I have."

"Fergus was about Maggie's age, give or take. I thought maybe she might have mentioned him. He claims to have danced with them on that Friday night when they went into Omagh."

"Well, sadly the place to look to know for sure would be her notebook, but I've not heard that name before."

"What about Declan Clarke?"

"I've not heard that one either. Who is he?"

"He's Fergus' older cousin and one of Tully's boys, but if you ask me his real employer all along was someone else; someone further up the food chain."

"Do you think they were involved in Maggie's death?"

"I think it is possible, even likely. Hopefully we'll have some answers soon." I looked anxiously at the time.

"You keep looking at that phone. You expecting a call?"

"We set a trap for Declan and his boys. Maybe we can get one of them to talk. I'm a bit anxious about the whole thing."

* * *

The Albins had converted a small, normally unused first floor room into my guest room. It was small, but comfortable and ideally suited for what I needed to do. Most importantly, it was private, and I was with people that I knew wouldn't reveal my whereabouts. My job now was to wait — and to stay awake. A nearly continuous flow of tea, courtesy of Margery Albin all but assured my alertness.

The call from Mack that I had been waiting for finally arrived.

"We got him, John, and he's looking to make a deal! The gun they found on him was the one that killed my assailant, so he's looking at a murder charge."

"What about his henchmen?"

"One of them was stupid enough to take a shot at the cops and didn't live to tell about it. The other one is in custody."

"How much time can O'Neil buy me?"

"Homeland security is already interested, but he should be able to get us a day or two."

"God bless him. I owe the bastard a bottle of good whiskey when I get back. What's the weather there?"

"Dreary, a few hints of snow. Snapped cold as hell early this morning."

"Got it. Is your gadget ready?"

"It sure is. How are you feeling?"

"A bit sick in my stomach. I really want to be wrong, Mack…"

* * *

Mack had put together a device, the inner workings of which I could never begin to understand. She assured me that it would make every call I made to it appear to originate from my office. I dialed the number as instructed and waited.

"Hi Shanagh. John Costa."

"Mister Costa... I don't know what to say."

"Me neither. I'm going to get good and drunk again here in a few minutes. So damn cold out there I don't feel like going out. I wanted to call and say that I'm sorry. Sorry for how things worked out — I feel like I've let you down; I've let everybody down."

"I'm a little confused myself, to be honest. I've heard some things on the news — they say she's going to confess? How can that be?"

"I don't really know. I went to see her for our strategy meeting before her preliminary hearing and she fired me. She told me goodbye and walked away. I can't even go see her; she took me off her visitor list."

"She did the same thing to me — told me to stay here and let things take their course. I spent an entire day at the doctor's office as the result of the stress!"

"I'm at a bit of a loss as to what to do. My heart tells me she's innocent, but some of the evidence we've turned up makes me uncertain."

"Are you saying there's a chance that she did it? I can't believe it! She has an iron-clad alibi, doesn't she?"

"I'm saying that I've found some evidence that calls a lot of things into question. It doesn't help that I feel like a damned fool, too. I thought that maybe things would somehow work out; that Angie and I would end up together. I should have known; the age difference, we have so little in common... I'm torn, Shanagh. The right thing to do is to share the evidence, especially since I technically no longer have any standing, but I'm not sure I can bring myself to do it."

"You've got to do the right thing, John. Only you can answer what that is. I trust you'll do the right thing."

"Sorry it came to this. I've enjoyed getting to know you. Look me up if you're ever in the States."

* * *

The cool air of County Tyrone passed through my car as I drove north. Several turns took me to my destination east of Derry. The builder's showcase home sat on a small lot, a row of trees and a gentle rise obscuring what was beyond. I didn't need to see to know what was there. A steady flow of cement trucks coming and going from an access road east of the property revealed the secret.

Derry Construction Group operated several subsidiary businesses under one corporate umbrella, including the nearby cement company. I parked my car and walked through the front door. As expected, the house was immaculate, constructed carefully to show off the company's attention to quality and detail. I had barely closed the front door when a voice called out to me from one of the rooms toward the back of the house.

"I'll be there in a moment. Please feel free to take one of our brochures and look around."

I pulled a brochure from a nearby stack, glancing through its contents. Shortly, a woman appeared from the kitchen beyond, smiling. "Good afternoon and welcome." She handed me a business card and launched into a brief sales-pitch. I listened patiently. Finally, I was given an opportunity to speak.

"Actually, I called a few months back in inquire about building a single-floor home for my father. You were quite busy at the time. I happened to be here on business and wanted to review your offerings. I'm not in a rush, but while I'm in the area, it seemed worthwhile to stop by. My name is John Baxter."

She smiled. "Oh yes, the gentleman from the United States; I actually remember your call."

I allowed her to go through the requisite explanation of their quality, their options, and the myriad of reasons I should consider using their services. Finally, we looked at floor plans. "You know, I do like some of these, but are you able to do custom work? My father is rather particular about certain things."

"Certainly we can do custom work. It takes a bit longer and typically costs more since we have to engage an architect, but we can build anything you would like." She started taking notes on her computer, typing vigorously.

"I've taken a few pictures while driving around, some houses that caught my eye — things that he might like. Care to take a look?"

"It would be my pleasure."

I opened my laptop, navigating to a collection of images I had prepared specifically for this visit. I made idle chatter while clicking through some of the pictures, observing her expression as each appeared. Her smile briefly faded on one particular picture. "I think this is a bit much for Dad, but I know he'd like that sort of general layout. Do you offer anything like this?"

"Where is that picture from?"

"I think this one was south of here, in County Tyrone if my memory serves me correctly. I made a wrong turn somewhere and ended up passing by this house on my way back to the main road. I had to take a picture to show my father later on."

"We don't do as much in County Tyrone as we once did," she said, looking slightly uncomfortable, "the costs of transport have gone up significantly."

"But could you build this if he likes it?"

Her composure returned. "I don't see why not."

We looked through the remaining images, none of which solicited any reaction. I returned to the image of Tully Smith's house a few times for good measure, each time pointing out a feature that might be desirable. If there was a bear to poke, I wanted to make sure that I was using a sufficiently heavy stick. Her typing continued well after answering my last question.

"Thank you for your time today. I'll be certain to share our discussion with my father; he'll be quite interested I'm sure."

"Have a lovely day, Mister Baxter"

* * *

I sat in my car, looking through the front window while she made a call. My mind otherwise occupied, I almost turned onto the wrong side of the road as I pulled out of their parking lot. I corrected my mistake quickly and, fortunately, without incident. A couple more turns, this time properly handled, had me on the A6 heading east. My next meeting would be with Charlie Hannon. Not wanting to risk the chance of being recognized in Belfast, we opted to meet in Antrim at a pub he recommended.

My mind had briefly drifted elsewhere when I became aware of a cement truck closing on my back bumper at an alarming rate. I tried to hit the gas pedal, but my car was underpowered and he had momentum. Approaching traffic gave me no exit to the right, so I had little choice in the matter: go left or be hit.

I turned the wheel to the left, sending my car off the road. The cement truck missed my bumper by what seemed to be inches. Its horn sounded ominously as it roared past. Fortunately, the terrain was flat where I left the road. Sadly, it was quite soft and my car kicked up massive chunks of dirt, grass, and several bushes before coming to rest in a pasture. I was lucky to be alive; a few feet past where I exited the road a stone wall began.

I got out of my car, assessing the damage. It was mostly cosmetic, a few dents and scratches. The bigger problem was the car's immobility. In skidding, the front tires had burrowed fairly deeply into the dirt and could get no traction whatsoever and attempts to push the car were futile.

I started a lonely walk to the nearby house. The owner must have seen my predicament. He hopped on his tractor and came out to meet me, offering to pull my car out.

"John Baxter," I said, offering him my hand. "A cement truck ran me off the road. I figure he lost his brakes or something, because he didn't leave me anywhere to go. Sorry about all this. I'll be more than happy to compensate you for your damages."

He smiled, shaking my hand. "An American. Sure you weren't on the wrong side of the road?" He winked at me, connecting a tow strap to the rear of my car.

I laughed. "No. I almost made that mistake earlier, but not this time."

The tractor belched a puff of dark exhaust as it tugged my car out of its morass. Examination revealed nothing broken, and the engine started immediately. I tried to pay him for the damages, but he refused.

"Happy I could help," he said. "You know, some of those trucks roll past here pretty quickly. They're dangerous as hell if you ask me, especially as heavy as they are. You're lucky, Mister Baxter. Damn lucky."

CHAPTER TWENTY-EIGHT

Charlie Hannon looked at my car, a smirk appearing on his face. "What the hell did you do to that car, plow a god damn field?"

"I poked the bear, Charlie, and the bear answered. Either that or my sense of coincidence is slipping."

Charlie offered me his hand. He was short and slender, his hair rapidly going gray, but lean and powerful. "I know the man that runs this pub," he said, holding the door for me. "He'll make sure nobody bothers us."

The pub had a small, private room tucked behind the kitchen. Pints appeared shortly after we were seated.

"My assistant has been poking around Mullingar a bit more, especially since you told me about that house that Angela remembers visiting. Talked to a few neighbors and finally one remembered the man that lived in the side opposite the widow. His name was Seamus Milligan. Took quite a bit to turn up information on him — seems he covered his tracks pretty well and with good reason. He was mixed up in a variety of republican causes. The Constabulary had a file on him a foot thick if you count the various aliases he used."

I took a sip of my beer, finally relaxing a bit. "What kind of republican causes?"

"The violent kind, John. He was a serious man by all indications. I'll give you one guess who he worked for…"

"David A. Brennan is what comes to mind…"

"And you would be correct. His immediate supervisor was none other than Connla O'Grady."

"Connla ran in some interesting circles! Makes me wonder, really wonder, what they were talking about that day and why Shanagh was along."

"A fair question. Milligan was implicated in at least two bombings, 1982 and 1988, but nothing ever stuck. The smart money says there were probably more. This one in 1980 and this in 1993 seem to be his style." Charlie passed me copies of several newspaper articles, pausing to drink while I parsed them.

"Interesting. There seems to be a subtle change in tactics. The earliest one seems to be targeting law enforcement or military target. The later three seem to be indiscriminate in their targeting, maybe even favoring civilian casualties. Why do they think that all of these are the work of Seamus Milligan?"

"Circumstances, mostly. He was in the general area of all of them, working various construction jobs. The real clincher is the detonation mechanism. You know anything about explosives?"

"Not much beyond what I've learned on this case."

"All of them were triggered using a mechanical timer; fairly reliable if properly done and almost impossible to trace. Downside is that they can be a little imprecise on when they go off; a few minutes here or there, depending on the quality of the mechanism."

"An hour?"

"Not likely unless things went horribly wrong. Why?"

"Jim Finnegan told me that if the Strabane bomb had gone off an hour later there could have been a hundred casualties, maybe more. I was thinking aloud. Sorry."

"I can see where you're going with that, but the trigger used in

Strabane was electronic and fairly sophisticated from what I've been able to turn up on the case; not Seamus Milligan's style at all."

"I've not seen anything detailed on Strabane beyond what was released to the public and the tidbits we've turned up."

"I may be able to help with a few things in that regard if you fancy risking a trip into Belfast to meet someone. You're pretty hard to recognize with that scruffy beard — we should be safe."

"I think we can probably risk it if you think it is worth it. Who is this guy, anyway?"

"He's an old Constabulary man, retired now, but still with connections and access, legitimately or otherwise; I truly can't be certain which. He worked what amounts to counter-terrorism back in the day. He's a wily old bastard, to be sure. Hell, truth be told, I don't even know if he'll see us. It took me a month to pry his name out of Gregory Finnegan's old partner, so it could easily be a wild goose chase."

"Well, I don't mind giving it a try. I guess chasing geese is better than getting chased by a cement truck."

* * *

Charlie took a circuitous route into Belfast. I wasn't entirely sure where we were, but it didn't seem to be the best neighborhood. The man we were waiting to see had a second floor flat above what was once a shop of some sort. The lower floor looked to have not had a tenant for several years; a small sign quietly advertised its rental availability.

We trudged to the top of a narrow staircase that led to an upper hallway off which were two doors. We turned toward the door on our left. Charlie tapped on the door a few times. It opened slightly and a man peered out as us, suspiciously.

"Charlie," he said, unemotionally. "Who's this with you, and why did you bring him."

Charlie turned to me and whispered, "wait out here a moment." The two of them disappeared behind the door. I could hear sounds of a quiet but energetic conversation, although I couldn't make out any words clearly. It went on for several minutes before the door opened again, a hand extending outward motioned me in.

The man apparently favored function over style. Were it not for several modern appliances and a flat-screen television, the flat could easily have passed for fifty years prior. He said nothing, guiding us toward a hallway that led to what I presumed to be bedrooms. He opened the first door on the right, inviting us to follow. It was anything but what I expected. The room, once a bedroom, had been converted into an office. More importantly, half a dozen monitors and computers ringed the main desk. Mack would be happy here!

"Tom Preston," he said, shaking my hand. "I didn't recognize you at first, Mister Costa."

I smiled, "thank you for inviting us in."

"Normally, I wouldn't talk to the man trying to defend the mastermind of the Strabane bombing, but I owe Charlie a favor. For that reason, I'll hear you out. But I won't promise you my help."

"I understand. Officially, I'm not involved with the case. My investigation is, at this point, private and off the record."

"Understood," Preston interjected. "You're taking a hell of a gamble. I expected there would be a hell of a fight over her extradition. She could be flying back to face a full life sentence, you know."

"It was an emergency contingency we planned but hoped never to use. Threats against my team, her friends, and family forced us to continue our investigation undercover."

"Charlie tells me you had a run-in earlier today."

"I did, with a cement mixer care of Derry Construction Group. Like I told Charlie, I was poking the bear and it is still sensitive when Tully Smith is mentioned. All I did was show them the picture of his place a few times."

Preston laughed, quietly. "You've got balls, I'll give you that. I wouldn't have figured you for the type looking at your file."

"Yeah, I wouldn't have either. Things just sort of worked out that way."

"Tully still has a few friends that probably didn't like you poking around. So how can I help you?"

I opened the report on Sean Grady, turning the laptop screen around where Preston could see it. "We turned up this document, but we don't know exactly what all these things mean. Perhaps you could explain it to us."

"Where did this come from?" He glanced at me, then at Charlie.

"It came from an anonymous source," I said.

"What you're looking at is a Constabulary Indexed Reference document. They're rare and almost never seen. When someone volunteered or was under consideration for an assignment, we used a form like this. During the troubles, we would approach certain individuals from time to time to see if they would find things out for us, do things, and so forth."

"So you're saying that Sean volunteered or was approached by the Constabulary?"

"Possibly. What is missing from this document, though, are the pages that show and describe the details of what his role might have been. This portion of the file is our background check."

"What do all the numbers after each name mean?"

"That is what is so damned interesting about this document. That particular numbering scheme was used exclusively by one of our watchdog groups. They tracked organized republicanism using every means available. You've probably guessed that the first digits represent the year. The others represent the file number for that year where the subject is mentioned."

"The asterisk?"

"Unsolved. I'll tell you, if I was asked to evaluate Sean Grady based on this file, I'd not use him. There are sixteen unsolved cases surrounding his father, another half-dozen around his wife, two around his daughter; no thank you!"

"I bet you know what I'm going to ask you, don't you?"

"You're about to ask me if I can get some of those other files and figure out what the linked cases are, am I right?"

"That and the other pages of the Sean Grady report."

"I'd be pressing the limits of my access to do it, and you've really not explained to me why I should," Preston looked uncomfortable. "I've read about you, Costa. You wouldn't think twice about using every dirty trick in the book to get your lady acquitted. I don't think I can help you."

"I think you meant to say that you won't help me, not that you can't. Yeah, that was me: the lawyer everyone hated but always called when things got rough. Did you read about how I drank myself out of a such a promising career? How many times did the word *disappointment* show up when my so-called friends were interviewed?"

Charlie tried to intercede, but I brushed him aside.

"I drank because it was the only way I could sleep at night. I left that world because I couldn't stand to look at myself in the mirror and I've been making mad, passionate love to indifference and mediocrity ever since. Come on, Charlie, we're wasting our time. I'll put a copy of this document out on a the internet. I'm sure I can find someone who, for a few dollars, will help rat-out the Constabulary and maybe turn up the real Siobhan O'Connor in the process."

"I wouldn't recommend that." Preston's voice betrayed urgency. "You already seem to have garnered some undesired attention. That would only make it worse. You've already got Tully's friends all up and about, it is reasonable to assume that Siobhan O'Connor had some connections that might not appreciate being made public. Siobhan herself might not be too happy with you, either."

I was frustrated, exhausted, and a good opportunity to learn critical information was slipping away. "I believe Angela Grady is innocent. She's being set up to take the fall in place of the real Siobhan O'Connor. If she's guilty and the outcome isn't in doubt, then what will it hurt to give me a moment of your time? I've no standing in this case, Mister Preston. I'm only here to find the truth regardless of what it might be."

He studied me for a moment, my face undoubtedly flushed and angry. "All right, I'll hear you out if for no other reason than to square things with Charlie."

I returned to my chair, pausing briefly to reconnect my computer. I opened one of Mack's charts. "Can we look at this on one of those big monitors?"

Preston handed me a cable, and soon the complex diagram was visible in glorious detail. "This is David A. Brennan's masterpiece, a fair amount of which was architected by Connla O'Grady, Angela's grandfather. Construction, cement, lumber, imports, connections all over North Africa, operations here and in the Republic. This innocuous little box over here was A&C Construction. They've since changed, merged, morphed, if you will, into Derry Construction Group. That is the firm that built Tully's house for little more than cost, and the part of the bear I poked today."

He looked at me, his face making no effort to hide his surprise. "You've gone from nothing to this in what, around a year? Impressive."

"Thanks." I switched to a picture of Maggie Albin. "Maggie Albin, she died in a car accident in County Tyrone. Tully ruled it drunk driving and death by blunt force trauma. I've not the time to go over the myriad of problems with that ruling — even Jim Finnegan found it unpalatable. Now — Tully was a sleaze bag, no doubt of it but why would he bother to cover up her death?" I changed to a view of the ledger, partially decoded by Mack. "Because he was paid to do it. We know the amount but not the source — not yet, at least." I switched the view to the original ledger. "This is the original; he encrypted it, but not well enough to fool my researcher."

"Who was Maggie Albin?"

"Angela Grady's best friend; the person she was visiting the morning of the explosion. There were three payments in quick succession all around the time of her death and the official ruling; hard to call that coincidence. Now you see part of the reason why I'm here, Tom. I think the two pieces are related, and somehow Maggie holds the key. The other piece is the organization that Angela's grandfather helped build. Some of the answers might be in those files."

Tom Preston sat silently for a moment. When he spoke, it was quiet and deliberately paced. "I don't know what's in those files. There's a chance that you might not like what you read. Have you considered the chance that you're being played?"

"On more than a few occasions, to be honest."

He stared at the computer screen, slowly returning his attention to me. "I'll see what I can do. Have a good evening."

CHAPTER TWENTY-NINE

The trip back to County Tyrone was uneventful and mercifully free of wayward cement mixers. Charlie was busily pursuing an unspecified lead, so I spent a quiet afternoon at the Albins reviewing some new material that Mack had sent. I offered to help Frank with his chores, but he'd hear nothing of it.

I caught myself staring out the window, locked in a pleasant daydream when my satellite phone chirped with a message. Almost simultaneously, I heard Margery Albin walk quickly into the room. "Come look at the telly; they're moving her."

The story was, predictably, on most of the available local stations as well as various news outlets. A scrolling message ran continuously at the bottom of the picture:

Alleged 1998 Strabane bombing mastermind Angela Grady formally extradited to Northern Ireland for trial...

The split screen featured the news anchor narrating what amounted to a collection of shaky, often poorly focused cell phone videos mixed with older clips and stills of Angela. The two new videos upset Margery Albin deeply, causing her to cry. They showed Angela, chained, wearing a bulletproof vest and surrounded by armed Marshals being hustled from a black van into a door somewhere on the grounds of an airport. A second showed a similar scene inside the airport as she was whisked onto a waiting plane.

Other videos, from different angles but of equally poor quality, ran on other stations. I searched them intently looking for any hints I could get of Angela's mental state. Finally, a glimpse revealed what I hoped to see: Angela had not given up. Although she looked tired and scared, her eyes still revealed determination and her head was held high. Margery noticed it, too, calming noticeably when the image crossed the screen.

My phone rang with a call from Mack. "I called Solicitor Molloy to let them know her status. They are aware of the procedures to contact you should the need arise."

"Any word on the trial date?"

"They'll go through the normal pretrial stuff in a few days, I'm sure, but until we hear from Molloy we won't know with certainty. The bad news is the clock is ticking."

"Dammit. We need more time."

"I do have some good news, on the off chance that you're interested."

"Mack!"

"I take it that you're interested in hearing good news. By the way, Charlie says that your beard looks deadly. I'm not sure if that's good or bad."

"Mack!!"

"Okay, okay! I've decoded some of the payments from Tully's journal, and it is damned interesting reading. I'm going to send it over to you right away. One thing is certain: Tully was getting money from O'Hegerty and Padraig Brennan."

"Outstanding work! Share it with Molloy as soon as he's ready to start."

"Done. The payments he received right around the time Maggie was killed and the investigation was completed came directly from Padraig Brennan. He kept half for himself. The other half went to a C. Alexander. I've not been able to find anyone associated with Tully or

Padraig that has a name anything like that."

"I don't suppose the reasons for the payments are included."

"That, my optimistic friend, would be asking too much. I'll keep working on it. There are some more entries that I've still not figured out."

"And the other thing?"

"Patience, oh urgent one! Another day or two…"

* * *

The payments were an important discovery. For the first time, we had a connection between David A. Brennan's collection of companies and Tully Smith. Sadly, we did not have the smoking gun that revealed what Brennan's money was buying. Sensing that we were, for the moment, at a dead-end on that line of inquiry, Frank and I took an afternoon to drive into Strabane. The site of the explosion was easily identifiable. Most of the original buildings were still there, although their facades had been repaired and modernized. After lingering briefly to look around, we found our way to a nearby pub.

Our arrival and selection of establishment was anything but accidental. Charlie had turned up a rumor of a patron who claimed to be a survivor. With only a description to go on it was a long shot at best, but with the clock ticking, I decided to play Charlie's hunch.

We found a small corner table from where I could quietly observe the comings and goings. An apparently regular clientele worked their way in as we slowly finished our first round and ordered food. Not wanting attention as an American, I used my Cork accent, lovingly learned from grandmother but long unused. It was apparently passable; nobody commented on it.

The bar grew quickly silent as Angela's face appeared on the screen. I rose, working my way toward the bar so that I could hear the television. Angela, who had arrived amid great secrecy, would have a preliminary hearing on the following Monday. Bail, the denial of which was already a foregone conclusion, would be the subject.

An older, white-haired man matching Charlie's description took interest in my fervent gaze at the television. "You seem rather interested in this whole thing." It took me a moment to shake my attention from the newscast.

"That I am."

"You're not from around here, I'd say. What brings you to this area?"

"I'm looking around for a nice place for my father to retire. He's always been partial to County Tyrone, although he liked a couple of places up in Derry."

"What do you think of all this?" He tilted his head toward the television.

"I can't seem to stop myself from watching it, but I don't know what to think, to be honest. And you?"

He looked at me briefly, returning his gaze to the screen. "I was there that day, and I don't have any answers either."

"You were there?" I stared at him, studying his expressions carefully.

The man rolled up his sleeve showing a heavily scarred arm. "I caught some of the shrapnel right here. A bit in my gut, too, but this got the worst of it."

"John Baxter," I offered him my hand, which he accepted.

"Angus McClintock."

"Nice to meet you. Can I buy you a pint?"

"Thank you!"

Frank introduced himself while I quietly sent a message to Mack. I needed to know if Angus McClintock was officially listed as injured in the bombing. Small talk, mostly from Frank, dominated the next few minutes. A quiet buzz drew my attention back to the phone's screen. Mack replied with a single word: yes.

"Angus, would you like a bite to eat while we're talking? My treat."

He nodded, saying nothing. His clothes were in fair condition, but his shoes betrayed what likely were economic rough times. Angus had been lucky but at the expense of another person that happened to pass in front of him at exactly the right moment. His wounds healed, but the scars served as a constant reminder and refreshed what was obviously deep survivor's guilt.

He stopped eating to add a stunning sentence to his narrative. "I saw her, you know."

My eyes narrowed. "You saw the woman that parked the car?"

"That I did, but never made it into the official record."

"Why is that?"

"Well, most of us knew better than to get involved. A couple of lads I knew gave a statement that never made it to the right people. It was like someone was telling us to stay quiet, so we did."

Frank subtly mouthed "Tully Smith" to me from across the table.

"Angus," I said, putting my beer down, "do you think they've got the right woman? You saw her. You should know as well as anyone."

He finished his second beer placing the glass carefully on the table. His smile told me he'd like another, which I ordered immediately. "I might be curious to know why it matters so much to you, Mister Baxter. What does a man from Cork care about our problems up here, anyway?"

I sighed. "I guess I'm guilty of a strange morbid obsession about this whole sad thing. Since I was in the area I wanted to see where it happened. I had no idea I'd actually run in to someone who was there. I hope you're not offended by me, Angus, but I can't get it out of my mind."

He nodded, his eyes carefully regarding my face. "We get a few people who come by for a look. Some want to hear about what happened. But you're different. I can see it in your eyes now; I could see it when that woman came on the telly. Did you lose someone on that day, family perhaps?"

"I don't know. I'm still trying to sort it all out."

I wasn't sure he would understand my answer, but I wasn't giving him the credit due. "Aye. That I can see. I tell a few people from time to time that I might have caught a glimpse of her. What I'm about to tell you, I've not shared since the day the bomb went off: I saw her *twice*."

I pushed my beer to the side, my focus solely on Angus McClintock. "Twice?"

"God's truth. First was a short look as she left the car. It was from a distance, but I got a decent look at her. Didn't think anything of it at the time — just a pretty woman here to sell at the market. If you asked me based on that, I'd have to say that they've got the right woman."

My heart sank. I tried to maintain an indifferent appearance, but I don't know how successful I was. Angus didn't seem to care. His eyes were looking at me, but he was elsewhere.

"But if you ask me based on the second time I saw her, I'd not be so certain."

"I don't understand…"

"I got a real good look at her a few minutes after the first. She was driving a different car; a small white coup that happened to round the corner and head back toward the main road. Closer like that, she looked a touch older and her hair was darker and shorter, but it was her — no doubt about it. But not the woman they've got in custody now."

"Why didn't you tell this to anyone?"

"The bigger question is why I didn't add it up back then. Why would she park one car and then leave, her appearance changed, in another? I wasn't thinking fast enough that day, I guess. I could have made a damn difference, maybe even stopped it. Well, as it stood I ended up with a torn up arm and a few scrapes from getting knocked down. I told what I'd seen to the policeman who was helping me, but he told me that I must've been mistaken. He said they were looking for a blonde woman. With all that was going on, I accepted what he told me. All these years later I keep asking myself, how could he have known who they were looking for so soon after the explosion? In the heat of the moment, everything happened so damn quickly and I couldn't think. Of course, now nobody believes me because I'm just a crazy old man. But there you have it."

"Tell me something. Of all the people that have walked in to this pub, why are you sharing this with me?"

"Because you looked like a man that needed to know; that and you treated me decent — not like the worn-out old man that I've become."

"Is there anything I can do for you? Do you have a place to go that is warm and dry? Can I get you anything?"

"Thank you, but you've been more than kind in listening to me. Sometimes that means more than anything." It sure would be nice to know who and why all this had to happen, I don't suppose you've got that miracle up your sleeve." His eyes narrowed, studying my face carefully. "Or do you?"

"Hard to know where miracles come from, isn't it?" I said, hinting at a smile. "Keep an eye on the telly and if anybody asks I'm merely a man from Cork passing through the area. That's important, Angus. Can you do that for me?"

"I can, Mister Baxter." He arose, shaking my hand briefly before departing in silence.

Frank and I regarded each other in silence. After a few shallow sips of beer he spoke. "What just happened here?"

I looked at him, vacantly. "I hope I'm wrong. I hope to God I'm wrong, Frank."

"John, what on earth is it?"

"It is probably safer for all involved if I don't say any more. Let's get the hell out of here."

* * *

"Mack," I said, my voice barely above a whisper, "Charlie's tip was spot-on. We met the man he was talking about — a victim and an eyewitness. Good information, but the poor guy would probably get shredded in court. I doubt Molloy would risk putting him on the stand to be honest."

"What did he tell you?"

"I think the real Siobhan O'Connor wore a wig so that she'd look like Angela. She set the bomb and drove away in a different car without the wig. It just so happened that Angus McClintock got a good enough look that he recognized her face. But get this: when he told the police, moments after the explosion, they already knew they were looking for a blonde woman. How could they have possibly known so quickly?"

"They couldn't have known unless..."

"Unless they had advance knowledge. Were any other police officers killed that day?"

"Amazingly, no. Only Gregory Finnegan."

"Get me the names of all the officers that were on duty that morning and dig up everything you can on them. Unfortunately, I still need the other thing. I wanted desperately to be wrong, but I don't think I am."

"I've got it, and you're probably not going to like it. I'm sending it now..."

"Excellent. If you find yourself lacking things to do, see if a white or tan car happened to belong to any of the people you're looking in to."

"I like how you never ask much of me..."

"I like how you always come through. In case I haven't said it recently, thank you. Thank you for everything."

* * *

The morning's plans were quickly derailed by television coverage of Angela's preliminary hearing. Greatly hyped and heavily covered, it proved to be disappointing. She appeared by video from an undisclosed location and offered nothing but a not guilty plea. The magistrate's court, as expected, denied bail and referred the case on to the Crown Court at Laganside. A new flurry of press-fueled speculation ensued. Even the bookies chimed in, offering odds on a variety of outcomes and events.

It would be a Diplock court, Angela's fate resting in the hands of a single judge. The procedure, implemented during the height of the Troubles, sought to eliminate the impossibility of finding an unbiased jury. The use had been relegated to exceptional cases in recent times, terrorism in particular. Angela's case qualified in all regards.

Morton Molloy, the head of our legal team, would argue the case. Mack had faithfully shared our progress, and I spent the afternoon filling in the gaps and sharing recent developments. We agreed to reconvene once the discovery process was underway. Molloy expected some resistance from the prosecution in this area and already had his staff researching precedents and working on various contingencies. The team I had assembled, expensive as hell, suddenly seemed well worth it.

"Mister Costa," he said, "based on what you've turned up so far, we can instill enough doubt to offset the physical evidence and the facial recognition. Unless they've got something completely damning, I feel pretty good about our chances."

"I'm worried more about the safety of Angela and our witnesses than I am about unexpected evidence. Have you taken all the recommended precautions?"

"We have, and then some. Julia Rohnan is out of the country on holiday, but we've located her. She'll return when the time comes. In the mean time, we've hired some protection for her. I hope that is alright — it didn't come cheaply."

"A wise precaution and well worth it."

"Angela's accommodations are anything but pleasant, but she seems to be holding up well enough. She's strong, I'll give her that. At some point, we need to have a conversation about whether she will take the stand."

"It is your decision, Morton; I trust your judgment. With any luck, it will become a moot point."

"Here's to good luck, then!"

CHAPTER THIRTY

A call arrived from an unexpected but welcome source. I was not certain if Tom Preston had really considered my request or if he had merely been polite. His call tantalized me, as he refused to offer any details over the phone beyond repeatedly using the word *interesting*. Instead, he wanted to meet at his flat, the sooner the better.

* * *

Preston was far more talkative and accommodating than on my previous visit. "You don't mess around, do you?" He raised a single eyebrow while handing me a cup of tea. "I ran in to half a dozen or more case files that are still classified." He ushered me in to his office, carefully locking the door behind us. "Sorry to drag you all the way over here, but as you will see, I couldn't discuss some of these on the phone."

"I understand," I said, accepting the tea and settling into a chair. "I appreciate your willingness to look into this."

"I wasn't sure I would do this, but you were so passionate in your beliefs that I decided to take a look. Curiosity took over after that. Now, understand, some of this can't leave the room. You'll never be able to use it in court, and you'll get in a spot of trouble were you to try to do so. I won't testify, Mister Costa, but if a few of these things point you toward the truth, you should be able to handle the rest on your own. Are we clear on that? If not, I'll bid you a good day right now."

"Completely clear."

"We had a lot of this information, but it was spread across various agencies that never talked without the good lord himself intervening. To compound the problem, some of this happened in the Republic, making it all the more difficult for us. Various bits of Brennan's conglomeration were investigated for any number of things; mostly minor, but enough to show a pattern if you look at the whole picture."

"Such as?"

"Little accounting irregularities, some regulatory shenanigans that resulted in small fines, a few bids that looked a bit iffy. The genius of the whole thing is that at any given time, only a handful of his many wee companies would be under the microscope. They'd clean up their act for a few years and our attention would go elsewhere. The offenses were never serious, so we never considered the myriad of holding companies and the organization as a whole. Overall, there was quite a bit going on. A lot of money went *somewhere*, but we're not entirely sure where."

"Funding corruption, payoffs, perhaps?"

"Among other things… Here is an interesting bit, though, and I got this from a couple of friends in the Republic. There were several investigations into Brennan's import business, specifically dealing with some questionable deals in North Africa. They dragged on for a couple of years before ending for lack of evidence. Seems a few key witnesses ended up floating in Lough Allen and the case lost its momentum. Brennan's import branch here in the UK had a few similar."

"Let me guess… explosives, weapons, all from Libya."

"That was the working theory on several investigations but as always, they went nowhere. It was also cause for at least four of Connla O'Grady's case references, none of which were ever solved or closed. He was a person of interest in no fewer than twelve other case files. What has Angela told you about him, if I may ask?"

"Her memories are those of a loving grandfather from everything she's told me. She tells of music sessions in Mullingar, his mixed-up stories of being a rebel. According to her, nobody took him seriously."

"A man with rebel parentage and extensive connections in North

Africa and the Middle East? We sure as hell took him seriously, doubly so after the death of his wife. Between him and his buddy Brennan, there was enough to keep our eyes focused on him. In spite of our efforts, we could never find anything definitive. Those twelve cases include bombings, assassinations, sabotage, attacks against British soldiers, you name it — and all of them unsolved to this day. The only file we have certainty on is that the old bastard finally died."

"What was the cause of death according to your records?"

"Cancer, why?"

"There is an interesting disconnect between Angela and her mother on that subject. I've not broached it, but Shanagh insists that Connor was senile in his final years."

"There's nothing to suggest that. The old boy slowed down a bit in his final years, but there were at least several unsolved case references during that time; one less than a year before he passed."

"How much can you tell me about the cases where Connla was a person of interest?"

He looked uncomfortable with the question, pausing briefly to sip tea. "I can't share the files, as much as I'd like to. But if I were to accidentally leave this flash drive sitting around, and you were to accidentally take it with you, you might find a few helpful details that will point you in the right direction."

I slipped the drive into my pocket. "I have to ask about the files related to Angela and Shanagh. What can you tell me?"

"There are only three related to Miss Grady. One is related to the explosion in which she was injured. It was marked unsolved at the time the file you have was created, but it was closed in 1999. The second was a report on her injuries and subsequent recovery — a follow-up to the original entry. Nothing there."

"And the third?"

"That is reference 96-0096, and appears on her list as well as Shanagh's. I had to call in several favors to get that one. Apparently, it is still considered sensitive. I can't let you keep it, but I'll let you review it while you're here. I wasn't able to find any active investigations but that doesn't mean there aren't any."

I spent a few moments silently reviewing the case file. An explosion in 1996 destroyed several Constabulary paramilitary vehicles. The crime produced several injuries and one by-stander fatality. When viewed through the looking glass of hindsight, it bore disturbing similarities to Strabane. The explosive used was the same; the detonation method and timer were eerily similar, too. I turned the page, sinking into my chair as familiar names appeared as *persons of interest*: Shanagh and Angela Grady.

The connection to Shanagh came through a series of notes on Connla and his immediate associates and numerical references to case files, most of which looked to match those we already had. Angela appeared as part of a curious and worrisome note added to the report:

Several witnesses saw a man accompanied by two women in the vicinity before the explosion. The women were described as young, slender, and possibly sisters. One of the women was said to have shoulder-length light brown hair while the other was said to be blonde with longer hair. The witnesses did not recall seeing any of the people prior or since the event. Description of woman given by witness is generally consistent with Shanagh Grady. Her daughter, Angela, meets witness descriptions of the blonde woman. The man could not be identified from witness descriptions.

1. A witness [redacted] reported that a man and a woman were seen lingering in the vicinity of the Constabulary vehicles. The woman was described as young-looking with medium length light brown hair.

2. A second witness [redacted] saw a slender blonde woman lurking near the corner for ten to fifteen minutes before being picked up by two others. Apart from this, there was nothing unusual noticed until the explosion

occurred some ninety minutes later.

3. A third witness [redacted] stated that
the blonde woman exited a small, light-
coloured (white or tan) automobile and
proceeded to a nearby shop. The man and other
woman parked and walked together around the
corner to where they could no longer be seen.
Their general direction of travel was toward
the parked Constabulary vehicles. The blonde
woman emerged from a shop approximately twenty
minutes later. She waited outside the shop,
positioned in such a way as to be able to see
the road in many directions, another ten
minutes until the others returned and departed
in the car.

I looked up at Tom who seemed intently interested in whatever expressions my face had formed while reading the file. "A rehearsal for Strabane?"

"That seems like a plausible theory. Of course, the current case files are off limits, so the only people who know for sure are the prosecution team and Jim Finnegan's department. This document is a snapshot of what they knew and were working on in 1997. He could have built many more connections since then."

"And with a fatality involved, those connections could explain why Finnegan's so supremely confident. All that we've done could be irrelevant if he's connected the dots on another incident and plans to amend the charges to include this."

"That might explain why this file was locked-down the way it was, too. Jim Finnegan is damn good; one of the best."

* * *

I left Tom Preston's flat feeling that Finnegan's next aplomb would come at Angela's expense, no thanks to my efforts. Ready to drive my fist into the dashboard of my car, I pulled over at a small coffee shop to regroup. It turned out to be a good decision. A single patron sat silently near the front window and a friendly woman with reddish-brown hair busied herself with various chores. Traditional Irish tunes played quietly in the background interspersed with an occasional song. I found a corner table and briefly let myself drift into the music, my fingers wrapped around the warm mug of tea.

Had I been masterfully played by Jim Finnegan? My mind drifted into undesirable territory, longing for that good, pointless feeling that a bottle of Irish whiskey could bring. A pub awaited; simply crossing the street would leave me with several options from where I could imbibe momentary forgetfulness.

Sanity, however, won the day and I flipped my computer open. Quickly, I typed all the relevant details from the file that Tom Preston had shown me. I had committed as much of it to memory as possible in the limited amount of time I had to view it, hoping that I had correctly captured the most vital details. My frenetic typing earned a brief glance and smile from the woman working there. I quickly sketched the diagrams that accompanied the 96-0096 case file, photographed them, and sent the entire collection to Mack along with a simple note: call me.

I had only been on the road for a few moments before my phone alerted me to an incoming call. "Hi Mack, thanks for calling me so quickly."

My emotions must have leaked in to my words because she immediately knew… "What on earth is wrong?"

"That obvious, huh?"

"That obvious. John, tell me."

"Mack, I'm not sure, but there's a chance we're being played. Strabane might not be Finnegan's end game. We may have spent all this time investigating the wrong case! The real case might be 96-0096. I got a short look at the file earlier today and wrote down what I could remember. It is all within what I sent you including what I was able to get on Connla and Shanagh."

"I saw it come in — there's a lot there. I'll get through it as quickly as I can."

"Call Jerry if you need help looking at it. I'm sure he knows someone who knows someone. Long and short, Finnegan's play might be to get her over here on the Strabane evidence then convict her on the

1996 case. One person died, Mack, and it was a terrorism-class crime. If he has a way to tie Angela to it, she's going away for life. We've not got a shred of anything to defend her with if that is his intention."

"Is there anything that makes you think this might be happening?"

"The 96-0096 file was locked-down to the point where my contact had to call in a few favors to get it. That could mean that there is an active investigation going on."

I could hear the rapid chatter of Mack's keyboard in the background. "A lot of stuff you noted as redacted. It could also be classified because it contains names that are best left as a secret."

"That's true, I guess. What I'd really like to do is ask Angela what she was doing that day and who was with her."

"And who owned the car... Angus said he saw Siobhan O'Connor driving a small white car."

"Any record of any of the Grady clan owning a car like that?"

"No."

I sighed heavily. "If I contact Angela, the gig is up. See what you can do with those files and get back to me. I'm going to spend the next couple of days nosing around Angela's old neighborhood."

CHAPTER THIRTY-ONE

The morning was crisp but clear as a cold front settled in. My room came with a complimentary Irish breakfast into which I tore with zeal. My concentration the previous evening had caused me to skip dinner, an omission I noticed only now. I returned to my room for a brief conversation with Mack before heading out.

"Good morning, Mack. Is there anything new that I should know about before I head into Belfast this morning?"

"Nothing worth mentioning. Have you done your homework, or are you going to randomly poke the bear?"

"I've done my homework, enough so that I forgot to eat dinner last night. But I made up for it at breakfast this morning."

"You're going to gain back all that weight that you lost trying to keep up with Angela!"

"Have no fear! My morning started with a bike ride. Granted, it was on a stationary bike, but it was better than nothing."

"Keep this up and you might live past fifty."

"That isn't all that far away."

"Until Angela came into your life, I honestly wasn't sure you'd make it as far as you have, yet I can tell in your voice you've not shaken all your doubts."

"Sometimes I wish my brain would be quiet but it never listens."

* * *

Mack had provided me a list of names, people that Shanagh and Angela had mentioned in various interviews that still lived in the area. Armed with freshly printed business cards: John O'Brien from a Cork-based internet news outlet. I made the final turn onto the street where Angela grew up.

The houses were modest but looked comfortable. I eased my car into an available spot; eerily, it was in front of the former Grady home. I took a deep breath and steadied my nerve. There was no answer at the first door. My nerves raced. The next two stops, however, quickly dispelled my fears; I was treated quite kindly. Sadly, I learned nothing new from either interview.

I knocked on the door of Alice Sheehan, the woman with whom Shanagh spent the morning of the Strabane bombing. The two houses faced back-to-back, sharing a small backyard separated by a narrow hedge. She appeared unwilling to talk initially but warmed to the idea as I explained the purpose of my visit.

"Angela was a sweet kid when she wanted to be," she said, offering me a scone, "but certainly not an angel by any sense of the imagination. A bit of a temper, that one, and a headstrong streak to be sure. You'd think she never said a cross word in her life if you believe some of her friends on the telly."

"Did she get the temper from her mum, do you think?"

"The only reason people say Shanagh has a temper," Alice said, curtly, "is because one of them had to be a parent. Sean would have let Angela get away with murder, Mister O'Brien. Someone had to set some ground rules."

"Sounds like Sean wasn't willing to do that."

"Sean, God rest him, wasn't *able* to do that. He wasn't one for conflict of any sort, nor discipline. And we see where that has gotten us, haven't we?"

"Sounds to me like you're not surprised that Angela is in trouble. Honestly, you're the first person who has said this to me."

"Looking back on it all, it seems less surprising. I should have known something was up when she went running off to America with her friend Karen. Those two were always trouble!"

"What kind of things?"

"They were always talking, giggling, hushing up if someone came near. It wouldn't surprise me to see Karen Boyle on the news one of these days, either; likely on her way to prison!"

I was briefly caught off guard by Alice's stinging indictments. Uncertain if she was merely a bitter person or the one voice of reality in a sea of delusion, I decided to press. "Sounds like Shanagh had her hands full. I've not been able to interview her, but I'm sure all of this has to be weighing on her."

"I can't imagine what this is doing to her!"

I shook my head, pretending my best to empathize. My eye caught a glimpse of a framed photograph on the nearby mantle. "That picture," I said, pointing to it, "that is you, Shanagh, and Angela, isn't it? My goodness, Angela looks like her mother."

"It is," she said, smiling and reaching for the picture, handing it to me.

"Who is the gentleman?"

"Oh, that is Connla Grady, Angela's grandfather. She loved him so. He was such a good influence. A girl needs a strong father figure, you know. In her case, it had to be Conn because his son certainly wasn't up to the task."

I stared at the picture, likely from a year or two before his passing given Angela's age. While I took reasonable interest in the subjects of the photograph, the small white car parked in the drive caught my attention. "Thank you for sharing that. If it isn't too much trouble, could I bother you for another spot of tea, please?"

She rose and headed into the kitchen. I quickly used my phone to take several images of the picture before she returned. I returned it to its place before accepting my tea.

"Have you interviewed Angela yet?" She said, returning to her chair.

"I've not. They won't even say where she is incarcerated or who to call to arrange visits. I'll keep trying, though. May I ask you another question?"

"Certainly."

"Is that your son?" pointing to a prominent picture, one of several of the same young man.

"It is," she said, her face brightening. "You know, he had quite a fancy for Angela when he was younger, and he wasn't alone, of course. She'd flash that pretty smile of hers and get whatever she'd want from people. She can be sweet when she wants to be, doubly so if you have something she wants. I think she learned how to manipulate people pretty well. You'll understand when you meet her. If she thinks your article will help her, she'll be your best friend. If not, you'll be lucky to hear from her."

I could tell there was some lingering resentment in the tone of her voice. I pressed the issue. "What happened between her and your son? Did they ever go on a date?"

"Oh, they did," she scoffed. "They went to a dance together, and she spent the entire evening dancing with her friends; couldn't be bothered with my Bradley to save her life!"

"Maybe things didn't click between them."

"I thought that, too, but sure enough, when she found out that he had tickets to a show she wanted to see, there she was! She played him like a master. She knew exactly what to say to keep his hopes lingering, too. I thought maybe it was a teenage thing, something she'd outgrow, but when I heard about Strabane and some of the details, it seemed I was wrong."

"Why do you say that?"

"If you read the official report, which I did, it is obvious that someone skillfully manipulated those people. I'm sorry to say it, but

Angela Grady has it in her to do that. Please don't print that comment. I don't want to hurt Shanagh."

"I'd not thought to ask this until someone else brought it up, but do you think there is a chance that somehow Shanagh is involved."

"Shanagh was with me all morning, Mister O'Brien."

"I know it," sighing. "I'm tasked with exploring alternatives to the case in the off chance that Angela is acquitted."

"I really don't expect that to be something you need to worry about. Now, if you've no more questions for me, I've a few things to attend to."

I rose, thanking Alice Sheehan for her time.

* * *

Eva Donneley, a woman I recognized from some pictures Angela had shared with me, answered the door. Her hair had turned mostly gray since the photograph, but nothing else about her revealed any signs of aging. Her husband, mostly bald except for a ring of gray hair, stopped working on his crossword puzzle and rose to greet me.

"Evie, get the gentleman a cup of tea, will you, please?" he said, shaking my hand.

"Thank you for being willing to talk to me," I said, accepting a cup from Mrs. Donneley. "I hope I'm not keeping you from anything."

"Oh, you're fine Mister O'Brien," she said, sitting down, eagerly. "I confess to being a bit intrigued by all of this, and you're the first reporter to actually come around. A few have called, but they're all looking for the same thing: a short, sensational reaction."

"She wants to get her name on the Internet," said her husband, smiling as he returned to his puzzle.

"Hush, you!"

I smiled, their exchange calming my nerves. "I'm more interested in the background; things that led up to what happened, family and all. I'm not going to write an article that presupposes an outcome."

"That's a bit refreshing to hear. If you listen to all the folks on the telly talking away, the result isn't in doubt. I hear they have her picture at the scene; hard to believe."

"I've heard that from others. Can you walk me through the events as you recall them?"

"I was home that evening. I recall it as a pleasant night. I had settled in with a book when I saw the lights from a police car. I didn't think much of it. There's a pub nearby and occasionally some poor soul that's had a bit much would stagger into our street. It dead-ends a bit up that way," motioning to her right, "and that seems to get them confused. The police take them away to sleep it off. It happens every year or two, so that was my first thought." She paused, sipping her tea. "But I quickly realized that this wasn't the case."

"Why is that?"

"There was too much commotion for a simple drunk. I peered out the front window and there were three cars sitting out there." She motioned directly in front of her house. "They had one of those military-looking vehicles blocking the street and another one near the police cars. Whatever the fuss was, it was centered on the Grady house and damned serious. The police had their guns out, chasing everyone off the street. One of them yelled at me to get back when they saw me at the window, but I watched anyway. Not every day you see something like that!"

"At that moment, do you recall what you were thinking?"

"I had no idea what might be going on. I think I hoped that the Grady family was safe - Sean and Angela were always so nice to me."

"And Shanagh?"

"Oh, her too, but not like Sean and Angie. They'd go out of their way to say hello, ask how I was doing, or if we needed anything. Shanagh would smile, but she didn't make a concerted effort to be friendly."

I could tell she was choosing her words carefully, so I moved off the subject. "So what did you see?"

"Nothing happened for quite a while until they emerged. I

couldn't believe what I was seeing, them hustling Angela into the back of their truck and speeding away. She was the last person I'd ever expect to see in that situation. As soon as they left, I went over to check on the family to see if there was anything I could do."

"You went over there because you are an insufferable busybody, Evie," her husband said, peering over his newspaper.

"And what of it? This nice gentleman would have no reason to interview me otherwise. It makes me interesting, don't you think?"

I glanced at her husband who returned a shy grin before disappearing behind his newspaper. "What happened at the Grady house, Mrs. Donneley?"

"Poor Sean was a wreck, disoriented, confused, terrified. I felt bad for the man, I truly did."

"And Shanagh?"

"Pretty much the same, in her own way, of course." I hoped she would elaborate, but Eva Donneley continued in a different direction. "Things were never quite the same after that. It hit Sean hard and the fact that the Constabulary kept coming around for Angela didn't help. He was still friendly, but his mind was elsewhere after that. I could see Shanagh and Angie drifting apart, too. Before all of this, they'd pal around like two peas in a pod. They looked so much alike back then it wasn't uncommon for people to mistake them for sisters. They acted it, too. They'd have their little squabbles; more like siblings than a parent and child. Shanagh was awfully young when Angela was born; I'm not entirely sure she was ready to be a mum, especially given her temper and all. Good thing that Sean was so steady — it helped them work through those rough spots."

"Didn't another family member live when them for a while?

"Oh yes," said Eva, the pitch and volume of her voice dropping. "Connor Grady, Sean's father. I didn't care much for him."

"Ha! An understatement," interjected her husband.

"While it loathes me to speak ill of the dead, I'll make an exception in his case. I thought he was wicked." Her nose wrinkled. "He manipulated everyone around him. Poor Sean couldn't do anything right; nothing was ever good enough. He'd start in on Sean about this and that, and Shanagh would jump right in twisting the knife a bit more."

"And Angela?"

"She stayed above the fray, and bless her heart she seemed to have a free pass with the old man. I never heard him say a cross word to her."

"Could he have been suffering from dementia? I've read that personality changes can happen."

"He wasn't senile, just bitter and damned wicked if you ask me; except when Angie was around. I didn't shed a tear when the cancer got him. I've already said enough!"

I changed the subject, moving into a chain of questions that Mrs. Donneley seemed to expect. Her answers provided little additional insight beyond what we already knew. One question, though, seemed to catch her slightly off guard. "That night when they took Angela away, you said she was the last person you'd expect to see in that situation. If they had brought out a different Grady, which one would have surprised you the least?"

She muttered something before looking at her husband who had lowered his newspaper. "That's an odd question," he said, a puzzled look on his face.

"I know," I said, trying hard to maintain my demeanor. "I'm trying to look at this from every possible angle."

Before he could say anything else, Eva blurted out, "Shanagh Grady."

Her husband added, "now don't you go printing that, Mister O'Brien, and getting us sued! Shanagh's the type that would, too, if she got her hackles up. Poor Sean's corpse was barely cold before she collected his money and moved to greener pastures. We were neighbors and friends, supposedly, for all those years. You'd think we'd hear from her now and then, but she's not said a single word to us in all that time."

Eva quickly interjected, "We hear from Angela every Christmas without fail. Even this year, in spite of all her troubles, she dispatched a lovely card to us."

"I'll not print a word of it," I reassured, "but you're not the first that I've interviewed that has said something along those lines."

Eva continued, unperturbed, "I'm not saying that I believe any of them would be involved in such a thing, but you asked the question and I answered it."

* * *

Visits to additional neighbors added no clarity. One echoed the sentiments of Eva Donneley while another agreed wholeheartedly with Alice Sheehan's assessment.

As I walked toward the main street, a man exited a nearby house. We briefly regarded each other, silently, before I returned my attention to where I was going. Shortly, two additional men rounded the corner, walking toward me. I paid it little heed until it became obvious that I was the subject of their attention. I casually crossed the street. Ominously, they followed suit.

My thoughts quickly turned to escaping as I heard footsteps behind me, closing quickly. The men in front also started running toward me. I was in deep trouble.

Waiting until the last possible moment, I darted quickly to the side moving more quickly than my attacker expected and he tumbled over my intentionally outstretched leg. It improved my odds only momentarily. The men were younger and quicker making an outright escape unlikely. Still, my best chance was to get to the main road where perhaps my unpleasant situation would be noticed and a passer-by might assist.

Quickly reaching full sprint, I ran toward the road. My assailants blocked my path, forcing me to plow into one. My momentum sent him tumbling, but also sent me to the ground. He was stunned long enough for me to get up and land several solid punches to his face that sent him sprawling before he regained his footing. I tried to escape, but slipped as my foot lost traction. The delay was enough to allow his companion to catch up to me. The man dove at me and I stumbled backwards, a violent scuffle erupting. I had no time to regain my composure; their numbers allowed a nearly non-stop attack.

A fist from an unseen direction landed squarely in my gut driving the wind from me. Gasping, I staggered briefly while other blows sent pain ripping through me. A fist met my jaw, powerfully. The pavement rose to greet me as darkness set in.

CHAPTER THIRTY-TWO

The monotonous beeping of a hospital monitor stirred me from an uncomfortable slumber. Slowly, my eyes gained their focus. I was alone except for the myriad of machines to which I was connected. I tried to assess my situation, gently stirring each limb. They all seemed to be there and more-or-less working.

A nurse, strong looking and widely built, popped her head into my curtain-lined enclosure. "Ah, you're back with us, I see."

I grunted something, an attempt at agreement, but it was utterly unintelligible. She came over to the bed, raising the back to the point where my position was more vertical. I was offered a small cup of water that I drank eagerly. "Better," I rasped. "Thank you."

She smiled, briefly exiting only to return a short time later with a guest. Jim Finnegan greeted me. "Your bake looks like the grill of a street racer, Costa."

I laughed as best I could but everything hurt. "Good to see you, too, Jim. How long have I been here?"

"A few days. You can thank Tom Preston for your life. He told me you were swimming around in shark-infested waters, so we had someone keep an eye on you. Lucky we got there when we did or it might have ended up worse for you."

I took another sip of water. "Your lads must've gotten there quickly; I've felt worse after a good bender."

"That's the painkillers, John. For being outnumbered, you handled yourself pretty well. You broke the one bloke's nose, and the other has a couple of broken ribs for his trouble."

"I might've done a bit better had my damn foot not slipped. So, what's the damage?"

"They want to keep you for a couple more days to be certain you're going to be okay. You've a mild concussion and a lot of bruises. Probably a tooth or two that are going to need some cosmetic repairs some point down the line. The big lad kicked you in the gut a few times, so they're worried that there might be some internal problems."

"I've had internal problems for years, all between my ears. I need my laptop and my phone. The phone was with me and the laptop is locked in the boot of my car."

"Boot? We're rubbing off on you; there's hope for you yet! I took the liberty of having your car towed back to your hotel, and I extended your stay for a week." He slipped a small key into my hand. "They'll be taking you to your room in a few minutes. You'll find your equipment there. I'll come back and see you in a few hours; there are a few things I want to share with you."

"Well, I doubt that it matters — my cover is blown."

"How so? Some reporter from Cork went missing earlier today, and we found his body in the Lagan River. The story even made it into the news."

"And the bastards that attacked me?"

"I'll tell you about them later. Rest up, Mister Baxter, O'Brien, or whatever you're going to call yourself next."

I smiled, or at least I tried to. "Jim. Thank you."

* * *

As much as I wanted to stay awake, shortly after the doctors were done talking to me and wheeled me upstairs I fell asleep. It wasn't until sometime later that I was awakened by the arrival of Jim Finnegan. He made small-talk until the nurse attending to me was done with her routine. He locked the door behind her, pulling a chair next to my bed.

"The men that attacked you scattered when we showed up, but we've managed to track all of them down. We've kept them separated plus they think they're looking at a murder charge."

"Ah yes," yawning, "prisoner's dilemma. First one that talks gets the mythical deal. But they're going to know that they didn't throw a body in the river."

"That story's not for their benefit; it was to try to keep your stupid ass alive. They think you died of a brain injury."

"Well, I appreciate you giving me credit for having a brain."

"You'd get credit for a bigger one if you hopped on a plane back to the States as soon as you're fit to travel. I know full well you'll not, but I had to try, didn't I?"

"I'm close, Jim; close to the truth."

"You're close to getting yourself killed. Siobhan O'Connor's organization is like an injured wild animal at this point: desperate, angry, and deadly. We've got their leader dead to rights and they're in a panic."

"I agree with you. They're definitely reacting, but not for the reasons you think."

"Oh?"

"If you're expecting more, you've come to the wrong place; until you come around to the fact that you've got the wrong person in custody, that is."

Finnegan sat down, his eyes studying me relentlessly. "You seriously think I'd go to all the trouble of extradition, a trial, almost fifteen years of hard work if I wasn't certain."

"96-0096? Are you really going to rely on a bait and switch? I'd expect better from a chess master than to attempt a fool's mate." It was a risky bluff, but I needed to see his reaction.

Finnegan's eyebrow twitched briefly. "You are a devious bastard, I'll give you that," he said, his lips curling into a smile. "Our interest in 96-0096 was elsewhere."

"Is that to say that your interest is in someone other than Angela Grady?"

He paused, his eyes drifting back to the window. "We could never prove that the women mentioned in the report were from the Grady clan. We turned our attention to the man that was also mentioned, exploring the possibility it was Donny Cassidy. That doesn't change the heart of the matter. Rest up, my friend, and think about taking that flight, will you?"

"If you get me my laptop and phone, I'll think it over. Something for you to think over: Those thugs didn't show up out of the blue. Someone called them and gave the orders. Trace those calls. Let me know what you find, and I'll let you know who Siobhan O'Connor really is."

He stared at me, an incredulous look crossing his face. Surprisingly, though, he nodded before leaving.

* * *

"Where the hell have you been?"

"Good to hear from you, too, Mack. I've been a bit out of it for the past couple of days. A couple of thugs decided to use me as their personal punching bag. At least we can compare battle scars when I get back."

"Oh my god! Are you okay?"

"I'll know better when these damn painkillers wear off. Everything is still attached and seems to work, more or less. Hurts like hell, though."

"I guess you poked the bear in a sore spot. Question is which spots were you poking?"

"Unfortunately, it's hard to say. I talked to about half a dozen people and came away with two separate stories about the Grady clan. I figure one of them made a call but I don't know which. I'm going to send you a picture. I surreptitiously photographed it while I was at Alice Sheehan's home. Might be worth exploring if any Grady family friends had a white or tan car around the time of Strabane."

"Are you thinking it might be the car Angus saw?"

"A long shot, I know."

"I'll look into it. There's more to follow once I get it all sorted out, and it should lift your spirits a bit. Now, get some rest, will you?"

"You're really going to tease me like that, Mack, especially given the condition I'm in?"

"Just providing you some incentive to rest and recover."

"Okay. I'm too tired to argue."

* * *

The painkillers were fading, obviously, as my mind cleared and soreness flooded over me. Dammit. I owed Jim Finnegan a serious favor. The places where I hurt — and hurt badly — grossly outnumbered those that were pain free. I owed my life to the timely arrival of the Police Service. I took a deep breath, or as close of an approximation as my sore body allowed, and turned on my computer.

The first handful of awaiting messages was Mack chiding me for not responding. A series of apologies ensued, none of which were necessary. A missive from Charlie Hannon caught my eye.

Costa,

I've a solid lead on Fergus Clarke. He dropped out of sight not long after the Maggie Albin investigation finished, but I think I know where he turned up. The lad I've working on it started running down some of Brennan's companies in the area. Given Clarke's background, we could eliminate a few of them straight away. Several caught his eye, though, and he started digging a bit deeper. One in

particular, a company that deals in building
demolition, haul-away, and earth moving has
the best candidate: a certain Mister Alexander
that seems to lack any sort of documentation
prior to about 1999. I'll send you and
MacDonald the particulars as soon as we know
more.

CH

Building demolition — sounded like exactly what the Clarke boys
would be good at. But why disappear after killing Maggie Albin?

It almost felt sinful to interrupt the blissful silence of my room,
but I needed the share my thoughts. "Mack! Tell me something: does
Maggie's murder strike you as well-planned and carefully executed?"

"Hardly. It was brutal, sloppy, likely done in haste."

"Precisely! So much so that it had to be covered up."

"Even the cover-up was clumsy. Where are you going with this?"

"Throughout this entire mess, people who have ended up getting
in the spotlight, even briefly, end up dead."

"You have a point there…" I could hear the wheels turning.

"All but one, Mack. Fergus Clarke. He was one of Tully's boys and
he talked to the cops. And not to just any cop; he talked to *the* cop: Jim
Finnegan. I would expect that to make him undesirable."

"Are you thinking that all this time, Fergus Clarke has been the
person pulling the strings?"

"That occurred to me, but the Clarke boys are muscle, not brains.
No — he's not in charge. He's an expendable pawn in Siobhan's game,
yet he's likely still alive. If Charlie is right, he's hiding within one of
Brennan's companies. Hardly the place to go to get away."

"True that. Oh! I see where you're going. He's got himself an
insurance policy!"

"Bingo. Siobhan can't kill him because he's got something on her. And I think I know what it is, too."

"The notebook! Why else take it?"

"Double-bingo. Maggie's notebook."

"John," she hesitated briefly before speaking. "If Maggie's notebook is Clarke's safety net against Siobhan, it can only mean a couple of things. It isn't as if Maggie was involved in international intrigue; her only connection to this mess was Angela. Unless…"

"Maggie was working for Siobhan?"

"Yeah or somehow knew Siobhan's identity."

"Well, we're not going to know until we find it, if it exists at all. We could be totally off base."

* * *

A call to Charlie Hannon followed. He was concerned that he had not heard from his assistant for several days.

"I hope the lad is alright," Charlie said. "It isn't like him to not check in. He's eager, you know, wants to do a good job. The bastard was filling up my e-mail every day until I told him to ease up a bit. Like I need to know what the son of a bitch is shoving in his gob every day for breakfast!"

"Is he savvy enough to realize who and what he's dealing with?"

"I hope so. He's done alright for himself so far."

"If we do find Fergus Clarke, we need to keep our options open. Not much is off the table right now. It would be good to hear his story, but what we really need is that damn notebook. I'll pay what it is worth, if you follow me."

"I do, to be sure."

"It might be worth your time to let him know that we have Declan. Maybe even intimate that he's talking — you know the game."

I had more to say but the nurse had run to the end of her patience.

When she threatened to take the phone and laptop away, I quickly excused myself from the call. Fatigue called but restfulness did not answer; my racing mind made sleep a fleeting visitor.

* * *

Against the wishes of my doctor and my own better judgment, I checked myself out of the hospital mid-morning. They wanted to run more tests, another ultrasound, and re-evaluate me in another day or two. I, on the other hand, wanted peace and quiet and had no desire to be poked and prodded further. Reluctantly, they sent me off with a bottle of painkillers and explicit instructions should things take a turn for the worse.

The ride to Lisburn seemed unusually bumpy. Every jolt, and there were plenty, seemed amplified. I arrived sore but intact. My room's bed looked inviting, but work beckoned.

Mack had flooded me with bits and pieces of information she had collected on her various explorations. The first to catch my eye was a brief note confirming a suspicion I had harbored since meeting with Angus:

John,

There were four police officers assigned to the market day in Strabane. One was Gregory Finnegan. The remaining three were local to the area and were definitely tied to Tully Smith. One was the responding officer to the scene of Maggie Albin's crash.

Here's the interesting part: All three of them happened to be conveniently elsewhere when the explosion occurred and far enough away so that they emerged mostly unscathed. The scene erupted into chaos and most people lauded them for helping. As far as I can tell nobody ever asked how they avoided injury. Tough to write that off as coincidence. You ask me, they knew.

304

Of course, asking them is going to prove to be a bit difficult since I've not found any record of them in the last two years.

Don't do something stupid like leaving before the doctors say you're able.

Mack

John,

O'Neil accidentally let it slip that the calls to and from Declan's phone were to the Derry area. If they have more details, they're not telling.

Declan still isn't saying much of anything. I took it upon myself to tell O'Neil that we have Fergus. Maybe that will loosen Declan's tongue a bit. I hope you're not mad at me, but it seemed like the best play at the time.

Rest, Sir Aches-a-lot!

Oh Mack, you're a genius!

CHAPTER THIRTY-THREE

An unexpected knock that grew more insistent by the second interrupted my nap. Dammit. I had slept into the early afternoon, far longer than planned. I eased myself out of bed, trying to avoid the nearly countless areas of soreness. Jim Finnegan looked upset.

"Jim, what's wrong," I said, inviting him in.

He said nothing as he closed the door behind him, pulling a chair up to the small table that doubled as my desk. He handed me a picture, the subject of which was obviously deceased. "Do you know this poor fellow?"

"No."

"Does this help?" he said, handing me a copy of the man's driving license.

I recognized the name and was instantly sick to my stomach. "Oh no. What the hell happened?"

"He was found along the River Foyle. Had a wee bit much to drink, it seems, and decided to take a walk along the river. Must've fallen, hit his head, and drowned.

I looked at him, my eyes narrowing. "So what really happened?"

"For now, that is the official word. Problem is a couple of his injuries are inconsistent with that finding. He had gypsum on his shoes and pant legs. That isn't something one would pick up walking along with river. But one would find it here." He handed me an aerial picture.

"What am I looking at?"

"The headquarters of a Londonderry company that specializes in tearing down buildings, earthmoving, and the like. They're the only ones in the area that is in the midst of an active project where they're dealing with large amounts of drywall. That stuff is nasty, you know. The dust gets everywhere. Strange how there wasn't a bit of it in his car or in his hotel room. Only on his shoes and pant legs."

"What are you getting at?"

"I think you know precisely what I'm getting at! This poor fellow was working for Charlie Hannon who is working for you, and it doesn't take a big stretch of the imagination to guess what case he might have been working on. I've let you have a lot of latitude on this, but now we have a dead body on our hands, and I need some answers. I've got two men waiting outside to take you in for interfering with a murder investigation if you don't start talking to me."

"Oh, don't pull that crap on me, Finnegan! We both know Molloy would have me out in less than two hours, and that would be only the beginning of your problems. If you pull a stunt like that, I go public with everything, get the embassy involved, make it ugly for as many people as I possibly can. Angela Grady will go free, you'll come off looking like a first-class buffoon, and the real Siobhan O'Connor will slip unseen into the night. Neither of us wants that and you goddamn know it." It hurt being angry, but I didn't care.

"I can't go back empty-handed, Costa. I either bring back something to go on or I bring you back."

I sighed. "Hell, it may not matter anymore. As far as I know, we may already be too late."

"Too late for what?"

"Too late to find Fergus Clarke. The man you found in the River

Foyle was following a lead on his whereabouts."

Finnegan looked at me blankly as if momentarily uncertain as to what to say. "Clarke is a prosecution witness. He can't possibly help your case; what do you want with him?"

"I think he killed Maggie Albin."

Finnegan raised his eyebrows. "That would be an interesting turn of events, to be sure, but I'm not sure why that helps you."

"It helps me because Fergus Clarke was receiving payments from Tully Smith, conveniently right around the time that Maggie met her unfortunate end. Tully, in turn, was in bed with Paddy Brennan — a man you might know as Padraig Bannion. Yes, the same Brennan family as David A. Brennan, Connla Grady's old business partner. We deciphered Smith's journal — the one you thoughtfully included in Maggie's case file. It ties all of the players together; payments, amounts, dates, everything except what was being paid for. Paddy and Brian O'Hegerty have business interests all over Ulster. One was the construction company that built Tully's house. It has long since gone out of business, replaced with a new facade under a fresh holding company, but with the same players at the helm. I investigated and ended up tangling with a cement truck. Among their other interests is a demolition company in Derry…"

Finnegan showed me an official-looking paper. "This one, by chance?" he said, pointing to a name.

"Yep. Mack has all of it: the companies, holding companies, shell corporations. Your brother was investigating these people. If I can find one person that is willing to talk, I might be able to find the truth."

"And if the truth tells you that Angela is guilty, what then?"

"I believe in her, but if the truth tells me otherwise, you'll be the first to know. I'm not her lawyer anymore, remember? I have no standing over here, no code of behavior to follow, no propriety to uphold. But I know one thing: for the first time in years I'm happy with the person that stares back at me from a mirror and I plan to keep it that way."

He rose, staring out the window of my room. "You remind me so damn much of him, Johnny. That's probably why I've done things I normally wouldn't even think of doing to help you. Nothing could sway him from his pursuit of the truth. It cost him his life; it has almost killed you twice. When is it enough?"

"When is it enough for you, my friend? You've got the same fire burning — I can see it in your eyes."

"Aye, so I do, and there are plenty of times when I wish I didn't." I cast Finnegan a puzzled expression. "Gregory always wanted to be like me, ever since he was a kid. Maybe if I had set a better example he'd still be here."

"That's a dangerous road to travel. From where I stand, your brother had the best possible example; a man with principles; a man I'm proud to call my friend. Your brother died trying to make the world a better place. Honor his memory and sleep well at night."

"I don't think that will be possible until I know who killed him and why."

"Then help me! I'm close to knowing both of those answers; I just need proof."

"It's always that way with this case. Another damn clue, another riddle, another connection that goes nowhere. I finally got what I thought I wanted when we got the picture and the fingerprint."

"And in spite of that, you still couldn't sleep at night without whiskey and beer, could you?" I said, interrupting.

Finnegan returned to his chair, heavily. "It looks so good on paper; clean and simple like my superiors prefer. Method, motive, opportunity, physical evidence; even with your high-priced legal team, we stand a good chance of getting a conviction. But god damn, it doesn't *feel* right. But my superiors and the prosecutors don't operate on my feelings and hunches, Johnny. Her trial is moving forward, and soon. And we still have that unpleasant matter of the dead body…"

"I need time; a few days, maybe a week, before your boys start tromping around. And I need some assurance that we could get some sort of a deal on the table for Fergus Clarke if he's willing to speak to us, assuming he's not already dead."

"I'll see what I can do, and be careful you stubborn son of a bitch."

* * *

I spent more than a moment staring off into space after Finnegan's departure wondering if I'd done the right thing. I'd shared a lot, more than I hoped would be necessary, and in so doing might have jeopardized Angela's defense. Going with my gut felt right at the time, but it wouldn't help make her long, hopeless prison nights pass any easier should my gambit fail.

It wasn't long before I had my answer. I had only made it through a small portion of a deluge of notes from Mack before my e-mail chirped with a message from Jim Finnegan:

```
Costa,

The dead man's cell phone had a message
queued to send that never made it. It was
meant for Charlie Hannon, but you do with it
as you see fit. Perhaps it will help — God
Speed.
```

The message was simple, but deadly confusing:

```
The MAN is chilling in 314
```

Dammit. What did it mean? Slowly, I made my way to my car, feeling every step. I forwarded the cryptic message to Mack with a brief explanation then dialed Charlie Hannon. It was a call I didn't want to make, but he needed to know, and know quickly.

The first part of the conversation was met with silence followed by an expletive-laced, seething tirade. I was north of Belfast before he had calmed down enough to speak rationally. "Charlie, we need to do this together and with some caution. Where are you?"

"I was headed to Derry anyway to check on the poor fellow. I'm a few minutes to Dungiven."

"Find someplace and wait for me — I'm an hour back. If we go in there guns blazing we're not going to stand a chance."

"Here's a wee coffee shop right on the main street. I'm parking now. I'll wait for you here."

* * *

The official announcement of Angela's trial quickly dominated the news. Even the small coffee shop where I met Charlie had it on the television, several patrons and workers gathered around. The pictures shown and the short-on-fact conjecture were no different; only the immediacy of the event had changed.

Charlie had, as promised, waited but from the expression on his face it was clear that it was hardly done patiently. He wanted revenge, and made little effort to hide it.

"I want the bastards, Costa; I want them dead." The muscles in his neck tensed with each word.

"We have a chance to get them Charlie, but we've got to keep our cool, my friend. What do you think your investigator meant by his message?"

"My guess is that he's got Fergus stashed in a hotel room somewhere."

"That was my guess, too. We should start with where he was staying."

"I've got the address, but it doesn't have a third floor. He was smart enough, I hope, to hide Fergus elsewhere and under an alias. We're going to have to do this the old-fashioned way, knock on doors and ask questions. Are you feeling up to it? You've looked better."

"I don't have much choice, although I don't think I'm up for another scrap any time soon."

* * *

311

The drive took us from Dungiven to the hotel rented by Stephen Walsh, our investigator. Charlie made no attempt to obtain a key from the reception area, opting to go directly to the room.

"No point in wasting our time and drawing unwanted attention," he said, pulling a small device out of his pocket. The lock offered little resistance against his skill.

"One of these days, I need to learn how to do that," I whispered as he pushed the door open.

Someone had gotten to the room before us. Everything, except the contents of the room's small refrigerator, was tossed haphazardly around the room. Apart from the room's overt disorder, there were no signs of a struggle.

"I don't think they found whatever it was they were looking for," whispered Charlie. "Let's get the hell out of here."

I wasn't sure exactly how he could tell, but he seemed certain enough that I didn't question his judgment. We closed the door and quietly left. The better part of the day behind us, we found a nice hotel on the outskirts of Derry and took rooms. We could restart in the morning and I could use the evening catching up with Mack's progress.

* * *

My first order of business was reviewing Mack's analysis of the cases Tom Preston enumerated for us. He had given us only the dates, times, and a few sparse details. Mack had done the rest, correlating various sources into a consolidated report. It lacked, of course, the official findings but was otherwise surprisingly thorough.

I was confused within a few glances. My tacit assumption was that Connla Grady and David A. Brennan were operating or supporting some sort of IRA faction, but the case reports told a starkly different tale. The incidents, common by their violent and sometimes deadly nature, were more-or-less evenly distributed between loyalist and republican targets. A stark commonality throughout was no claim of responsibility, regardless of the target. Similarly, even though some produced fatalities, compared to larger events throughout Northern Ireland, they were minor, isolated events. The end of Mack's report included a timeline highlighting Preston's cases against other events throughout The Troubles. They fit with astonishing elegance into the lulls in the violence.

Stunned, I flopped the report onto the bed and turned on the television. Inevitably, Angela's picture appeared repeatedly on several stations. The words from the reporters blurred into an unintelligible cacophony, a distant background to my own thoughts. I missed her, worse than I ever imagined possible. The pain of longing, arriving quickly and unexpectedly, hurt worse than any wound my attackers had inflicted.

Tears followed, in torrential proportions. I grabbed a pillow, clutching it as tightly as my arms would allow, willing it with all my might to somehow become Angela Grady. The abject foolishness of such fantasies oblivious to me, I chided myself harshly for yet another failure. The cycle only deepened as conversations on the television, all discussing the inevitability of a conviction, broke like waves against the walls of my consciousness.

Solace lurked, I hoped, at the hotel's small, but well-stocked bar. The bartender asked no questions about my obvious angst, complying silently with my request for a double-shot of Irish whiskey. My fingers lingered on the glass briefly before bringing the elixir to my lips.

I had amassed a respectable line of empty shot glasses before the steady hand of Charlie Hannon prevented my request for another. Silently, he guided me back to my room where sleep quickly overtook me.

* * *

I met the morning with regrets and a terrible hangover, exacerbated by the relentless chiding of Charlie. "Get the hell up, you drunken bastard!" thundered in my ears as he stomped around the room, impatiently. He made no pretense to his frustration. "We've already wasted nearly half the goddamned day because you decided to be a lousy drunk. I should throw your ass into the ocean. What the hell got into you, anyway?"

"I don't know. Suddenly, it all got to be too much."

"It got to be too much? For you!? You selfish git! You're not the one rotting away in some secret PSNI hellhole facing what might as well be a death sentence. You're in love with this girl, right?"

It was the first time that anyone had said it in such unveiled, simple terms. "Yes, Charlie, I am. God help me, I am."

"Then get your sorry ass up and about! You're all she's got, mate. And if you don't, I've half a mind to finish what Siobhan O'Connor's thugs started!"

CHAPTER THIRTY-FOUR

I had cost us half a day with my ill-conceived bender. Fortunately, as Charlie quickly pointed out, Derry had a limited number of hotels with three floors. Sadly, by the end of the day we had checked most of them without the slightest hint of success. Our failure was complete by noon on the following day.

Hunger calling loudly, we stopped at a small pub that Charlie recommended. The handful of patrons scattered throughout took no notice of us as we quietly settled into a corner table.

"Any ideas?" I said, sipping my water and regarding the menu.

"The fish is good..." I'd let Charlie ponder the situation in whatever method he preferred, which, for the moment, appeared to be in silence.

Our meal cured our appetite, but did little to satisfy. Reluctantly, I called Mack hoping that perhaps she had discovered something. Her voice quickly deflated me.

"Hi, John." She sounded tired and I was robbing her of much needed rest.

"I'm sorry to call so early, but we're a bit stuck for ideas at this point." I quickly explained our situation.

"You've already done what I was going to suggest. A hotel room was the first thing that came to mind, then perhaps an apartment. I'm a bit bothered by the capitalization of MAN, but I expect he did it to emphasize the importance of whoever he was referring to."

"I suppose we could knock on a few doors, but there could be dozens of three-fourteens in and around Derry. If the wrong people get word that we're nosing around, the game is up. Hang on…" Something had finally broken Charlie out of his doldrums, but it was not what I expected. A lively discussion with our server about dessert had erupted.

"Sorry; didn't mean to stop there. Charlie is trying to decide what kind of dessert he wants. I can't imagine he eats it often, given how trim he is. Maybe he's one of those people who can eat everything in sight and not gain an ounce."

"Are you going to have something?"

"I'm not. After that shepherd's pie, I don't have room!"

Mack chuckled quietly, a yawn cutting off its end. "Shepherd's pie — doesn't sound too appealing in the morning. Oh — it's lunch time there, isn't it? I'm so tired I've forgotten the time difference. Of course, I'm such a closet nerd that I can't help but think of the other pie."

"Like apple pie?"

"No. Pi. You know… the ratio of circumference to diameter of a circle." She probably knew it to five hundred digits, but another yawn interrupted her.

"Mack! You may be on to something…"

"Yeah, like needing more sleep, but *somebody* interrupted me."

"No. What if he meant Pi and not a room number?"

"That would be a bit nerdy, even for me. I think you might need some sleep, too."

"Charlie," I said, my voice slightly raised to garner his attention, "what did Stephen study in school?"

"What the hell do you care? Are you getting dessert or not?"

"Seriously; what did he study?"

"He studied math and computers. He fell in with the wrong crowd and ended up spending a couple years enjoying the Queen's hospitality. He was a good kid and needed help getting back on his feet, but nobody would hire him."

I returned my attention to the phone call. "What would it tell you if the person who created the message studied math and computers?"

"Well, you've got my attention," she said, fighting off another yawn. "I'd say that if 314 means pi that all the other bits likely mean something as well. Like MAN — probably stands for something rather than someone. Computer people toss terms like that around all the time. Metropolitan Area Network - MAN. Storage Area Network - SAN. You get it, right?"

"I think so, but…"

"It is a bit of our own language really. Like when you're having computer issues, I'm likely to refer to it as PEBCAK."

"I'm half afraid to ask…"

"Problem Exists Between Chair And Keyboard. See how it works?"

"Remind me to fire you unceremoniously when I return…" My voice drifted off, as the sounds around me faded into the background. Suddenly, I understood! "But that'll have to wait until after I tell you how much I love you, Mack! You've done it!"

"Done what?"

"If I'm right, MAN stands for Maggie Albin's Notebook. He found it! The son of a bitch found it!" My voice was apparently loud enough that Charlie's attention turned to me, undivided. "Dammit, Charlie, get a box for that. We've got to get back to Stephen's hotel room."

* * *

We drove, with haste, to the hotel where Charlie's investigator had stayed. I didn't even wait for Charlie to open the lock; an adrenalinfueled kick was sufficient. I'd probably regret it later, but it seemed like a good idea in the heat of battle. The room had been cleaned. I rushed to the refrigerator, throwing it open. It was empty. Dammit.

The manager arrived, furious to find us there. He was full of bluster and threats until Charlie managed to calm him down. I had no such patience.

"When was this room cleaned?" I growled.

"This morning. They said it was an awful mess, like someone had tossed everything around here and there."

"And what of the contents of the refrigerator?" My words were hurried, impatient, pressing.

"Thrown away, I'm sure."

"Has the garbage been hauled away?"

"No, won't be until tomorrow."

"Where are your dumpsters?"

"Around back, but sir, what about the door?"

"I'll pay you a thousand quid for the damned door and another thousand if you let me rummage through the dumpsters. Seriously — it's a matter of life and death."

His eyes widened. "I'll help you go through it myself. What are we looking for?"

"I'm not entirely sure, but I expect it will be round..."

* * *

The work was disgusting and took the entire afternoon. Frustratingly, it produced nothing. We left, exhausted, poorer, and smelling decidedly awful. A shower followed by a change of clothes was a dramatic improvement.

"Dammit, Charlie, I was sure we were going to find it," I said, taking a drink of water and surveying my dinner.

He nodded. "It sure sounded like something Stephen would do. I'd get notes like that from him from time to time. It was a bit of a game we played when times were slow. I'm a bit surprised that he used it for something important, though."

"If we're right, it was clever as hell of him. If the wrong person got a hold of it, they'd make the same mistake we made. Can you think of anywhere else he might have hidden something important?"

"I suppose he could have tucked it away somewhere at his flat in Ballymena. I had him stay here so that he wouldn't waste half his time driving. Besides, you were paying for it." Charlie smiled at me, sheepishly.

"Any chance you can get me in there tonight?"

"Not tonight, but I'll get in touch with his landlord in the morning. He'll let you in."

"You're sure?"

"Absolutely. The landlord's my brother and the place used to belong to my mum. You're god damned right he'll let you in. But not tonight; its session night, and nothing will pull him away from his music."

"What does he play? I might want to go."

"Accordion."

"Oh, Jesus... I can wait."

* * *

I had the best of intentions for an early start to my day but was quickly drawn in to the unfolding story that was the opening day of Angela's trial. The press was everywhere, swarming the Laganside court from every imaginable angle. They all tried to apply their special spin to the story, but the truth was evident: they were all hoping to catch a glimpse of the nefarious Angela Grady.

They were all destined to be disappointed. Angela arrived in secrecy. Their attention quickly focused on the trial's principles, each earning their brief period in the spotlight. Molloy and team arrived, followed shortly by the prosecution team. Neither offered a word to the press, nor did Shanagh who arrived much later but to no less fanfare. She looked strangely calm and unfazed by the events swirling around her. I caught a brief glimpse of Jim Finnegan, looking stern.

It wasn't until Charlie knocked insistently on my door did the spell of the television lose its magic. Breakfast was quick, the conversation sparse but efficient. We agreed that Charlie would remain in Derry to continue searching for Fergus Clarke. If our interpretation of the investigator's note was accurate, Clarke's life expectancy was undoubtedly short.

* * *

Stephen's flat was, in reality, a small cottage nestled on a quiet street. I drove by, hopefully inconspicuously, scouting the property. At Charlie's recommendation, I parked on the adjacent street, selecting a location easily accessible from the cottage's back door.

Joseph Hannon, Stephen's landlord and Charlie's younger brother, lived next door. We walked quietly to the cottage.

"Stephen was a good egg," he said, quietly opening the door. "He always paid his rent on-time; no issues with him. You'd never guess his past legal issues from his behavior."

"Charlie told me a bit about him. A bit of a math and computer whiz from what I've heard."

"He was the person all of us went to with our technical problems," Joseph said, laughing. "He never grew tired of us, in spite of our collective ineptitude."

"I'm blessed with a similar friend. Too bad they'll never get the chance to meet."

"Aye, sad it is. You take your time, as much as you need. Lock the place behind you, and if I'm not at home when you're done, tuck the key under the mat."

Joseph departed, leaving me alone in the cottage. A small front room served as the living room, complete with a modest television, radio, and furniture that looked lightly used. The kitchen, small and cramped by American standards, was simple and functional. A quick glance in the refrigerator confirmed Stephen's bachelorhood. It was sparsely populated, several of the items long past their expiration date. The freezer held several frozen meals but nothing within held any promise as the notebook's possible hiding spot. The rear room served as both a library and study. Several bookcases were filled with books, mostly on computer-related subjects.

Off the rear room, a narrow staircase ascended to the floor above. It was obvious that most of Stephen's work took place here. Several computers, each with multiple large monitors, sat on a long table. The room doubled as a bedroom, his sleeping area tucked efficiently at the far end of the room.

On the opposite wall, a door revealed a closet and access into a small storage space created behind where the wall met the pitch of the roof. I was about to start a more thorough search when I heard the front door open. Footsteps on the ground floor confirmed that I was no longer alone. Strangely and suddenly aware of the silence around me, I could hear the front door latch closed. I almost called to out Joseph to let him know I was upstairs, but my intuition stopped me.

Quietly, I turned off the upstairs light and retreated into the closet as slowly and quietly as possible hoping that my steps would not cause creaking. I entered the closet, sliding clothes out of the way to make room. I pulled the door closed, but the latch refused to catch. Try as I might, I could not get the door to stay shut. A gap remained, allowing a narrow view into the door beyond. Cautiously, I rearranged the clothes in a way that would hopefully obscure my presence.

The movement from below me continued, growing steadily closer. I could hear the drawers in the study opening, the rustling of papers and other objects followed. The sound of footsteps slowly climbing the stairs caused me to become painfully conscious of every breath as I attempted to be utterly silent.

The steps continued, unabated, slowly reaching the top of the stairs. The light turned on as someone slowly entered the room. Motionless, I peered out from behind the clothes, straining to see who was there. I could see a single, gloved hand reach toward the table, grasping a small notebook, only to return it moments later. My breathing suddenly sounded deafening regardless of my best efforts to control its depth and pace. Surely he could hear me!

Finally, the visitor came into view but only in silhouette. He was tall and slender. His left hand held a long handgun, its length artificially increased with the addition of a suppressor. His attention seemed focused elsewhere until suddenly he turned toward the closet, gun raised and pointed in my general direction. He took a few steps before a noise from below startled him.

Joseph! Oh no — you're walking in to a trap!

The man, gun still in-hand and ready, walked quietly down the stairs, his steps fading to near silence. The brief peace was interrupted by a solid thump. It was heavy, like a body had collapsed on the floor at the base of the stairs.

Frantically, I evaluated escape plans. The upstairs had several small windows, but they offered no viable means of exit. Perhaps if I could remain hidden until he returned to the front room, I could slip down the staircase and out the back door. If I could cross the small back yard and get to my car without catching a bullet in the back, I might be okay.

Before I could conjecture further, I heard the call of a familiar voice. "Costa!" shouted Joseph, "are you okay?" Relief rushed through me at the sound of his voice.

I scrambled out of the closet. "What the hell happened down there?"

"Charlie told me to keep an eye out for unwelcome visitors. This fellow's head got an opportunity to meet my shovel."

"Get something to tie him up. I need a bit more time to see if what I'm looking for is here. If it is, I can't be here with it when you call the Police Service. The lives of several people depend on this, and the last thing I want is for it to end up stuck in an evidence room."

Joseph ran to his shed for suitable rope while I guarded the man. He was younger, likely somewhere around Angela's age. Not surprisingly, he wasn't carrying any form of identification nor did I recognize him from any pictures. After we secured him, I resumed my search for the notebook.

Stephen had obviously spent many hours in his upstairs bedroom, enough so that it included a small refrigerator tucked neatly into the gap

322

between his table and the far corner. I opened it, finding the typical assortment of beverages and snacks. Slightly wider and deeper than the typical hotel room model, the refrigerator had a larger-than expected freezer section. I smiled as I removed the contents, hurrying down the stairs carrying several boxes.

"I'm going to open these up in the kitchen. We'll need to clean up before you call the Police Service; we don't need to be answering questions about why we were digging through frozen pies."

He grunted his acknowledgment, never taking his eyes of the unconscious man.

I started with the smaller boxes and met with the expected disappointment. The setback didn't bother me too much; my hopes fell onto two larger boxes that held full-size steak pies. Not only were the boxes large enough to accommodate a notebook, they seemed out of place. A bachelor rarely needs anything above a single serving, yet these pies could easily feed four.

On each, the seals looked intact and undisturbed. Carefully, I eased them open. My heart sank as I looked within. Steak pies. Dammit! I slid them onto the counter, tossing the boxes to the side. So much for my cleverness! I came within a breath of sweeping them off the table in frustration when I noticed a slight difference in one. A small gap between the tray and the clear sheet that covered the pie caught my eye.

On closer examination, I observed that the covering had been removed and painstakingly glued back into place. My heart nearly leapt from its chest at the discovery. I took a deep breath and carefully removed the cover. Nothing about the pie seemed out of the ordinary until I began to remove it from its container.

Stephen had carefully bisected the pie laterally, making his cut low enough that it was only noticeable when the pie was fully exposed. The center had mostly been removed, the missing volume replaced with a small notebook. He had loving wrapped it in numerous layers of plastic wrap then enclosed it within several tightly sealed freezer bags. I discarded the outer bag, slipping what remained into my jacket's inner pocket.

Quickly, we cleaned up what little mess I had created, all the time keeping a close eye on our uninvited and still unconscious guest. "Give me fifteen minutes and then call the Police Service." I grabbed a sheet of paper and wrote down several numbers, handing it to him. "Have them call this number. It rings to a detective in Belfast who can explain everything to them. This is a case number for them to look up in case they're being obtuse. Until they talk to Belfast, your story is that you found an armed man snooping around. Nothing else. If they press you, tell them you want a solicitor. That is the third number on the paper. And for the love of God, don't mention the notebook to anyone. Not even Charlie. Got it?"

"Aye. Best luck to you!"

CHAPTER THIRTY-FIVE

The contents of my pocket suddenly made me feel like the most endangered man in Ulster. I walked to my car, hoping that I was being inconspicuous. In truth, I was thinking about the nuance of each step I took. I was so focused that I almost hopped into the passenger side, but I veered in the correct direction at the last moment. As I heard my door close, the locks click closed, and the motor spin to life, I took what felt like my first breath.

I felt safer with the car moving, but I knew I needed to discover what was really in my pocket. I drove aimlessly for a bit, as much to see if I was being followed as to collect my thoughts. Every car looked suspicious at first, but as my mind finally cleared, the fear diminished.

I stopped briefly for petrol and sent Mack a quick note:

The man is with me, but he's not said anything yet.

As much as I loathed bringing danger to their doorstep, the Albins deserved to be the first to know and were uniquely qualified to verify the notebook's authenticity. I pointed my car toward Drumquin as a gentle misting rain settled over the countryside.

Charlie's voice sounded rough as he answered the phone. "Costa!

325

What that hell?"

His response, a prearranged code, told me he was safe. "The man's with me but quiet at the moment. We're off the see the relatives."

"Good enough. Rainy, dull day here. I'll let you know if anything changes."

* * *

The gentle rain that had been my companion from Ballymena finally lifted, giving way to cool temperatures and a bright, blue sky. Margery Albin came out to greet me as I eased my car into its previous hiding spot.

"I heard you got hurt in Belfast," she said, giving me a brief embrace before inviting me in. "Frank will be here shortly. We're both eager to hear what you've learned." She offered me tea that I gladly accepted. I had been so lost in thought that I'd forgotten to turn on my car's heater.

It was about fifteen minutes before Frank joined us. "I expect you have something to tell us," he said, shaking my hand.

"I might," I said, "but I need your help with something."

"Of course; what can we do?" said Margery, pouring me more tea.

"I may have the notebook." My words made Margery gasp. She abruptly sat down, her expression distant. "Unfortunately, I can't let you have it until after the trial is over. I need you to validate that what I have is the real thing. If it is, we'll need to get a statement and possibly testimony."

"You'll get it, Solicitor." Frank's voice quivered.

"Margery," I said, hesitating before producing the notebook, "are you in agreement?"

"I am," Margery said, shaking.

I reached into my pocket and placed the notebook, still wrapped in several protective layers, onto the table. Frank leaned forward, his eyes narrowing. Margery started crying at her first glance. Carefully, I removed the outer zipped plastic bag, then the inner cellophane wrap.

I snapped pictures every step of the way, meticulously sending each one to Mack with a description. Finally, I gently flipped the cover open exposing the first words within:

```
Property of Maggie Albin
If found, please return at once.
```

Frank needed to look no farther to offer his prognosis. "You've got it," he said, choking back tears. Margery nodded, unable to speak.

The pages were neat and organized; Maggie's handwriting was small and precise yet showed signs of being penned quickly and with purpose. I carefully eased my way through the notebook until I neared the days preceding her death. A surprise awaited us on the last page. The left hand page showed a series of entries written in quick succession. Stapled to the right-hand page was a small, yellow receipt, carefully folded to fit inconspicuously within the pages. Carefully, I unfolded it as Frank watched intently over my shoulder.

The meaning slowly unfolded to me as I frantically snapped pictures of it. "Who is Michael Kinney?" I asked, looking at Frank.

"He delivers our fuel. He's supposed to come round on the third Friday of each month, but occasionally spends the afternoon in the pub instead. He's a good man, always makes up for it by bringing it first thing Saturday morning instead."

"Is he still around?"

"He is. We shouldn't have any trouble finding him. We can do it now if you'd like."

"Not yet, Frank. It is safer for all involved if his role stays our little secret."

* * *

The waiting grew intensely painful as the days stretched on. Reports rolling in from the trial only made things worse. The prosecution had attacked swiftly and viciously, offering the theory that a young, angry Angela had set the bomb as revenge for her injuries. It was a dangerously plausible theory that set the press buzzing. It became incendiary when her entries, angry vengeful rants, were read in open court; worse still when theories about radicalization at the hands of Connla Grady were offered.

Molloy was fighting the good fight, objecting to anything and everything where the opportunity presented itself. He was buying me precious time, but the price was likely to be dear; reports of Angela's flagging spirits became constant. I knew that I couldn't delay much longer before a change in strategy would be required. Fortunately, on a clear and surprisingly pleasant evening I received the call that I had been waiting for.

"Costa," Charlie said, "I have someone who wants to talk to you."

Those were the words I had been desperately wanting and hoping to hear. I made my way to a small restaurant in Omagh, our appointed meeting spot. Charlie and his guest were waiting at an isolated, corner table.

"This is my cousin's place," Charlie said, shaking my hand. "We'll be safe here."

"Thank you." My attention turned to our guest. "Mister Clarke, I presume," I said quietly.

He nodded. "I go by Curtis Alexander these days."

"Very well," returning to my seat, "what is it that you want to talk about, Mister Alexander?"

He pulled a picture out of his wallet. With him in the picture were a smiling, brown-haired woman and a young girl. "That is Eilidh," he said, "and Aiofe, her daughter. We met when Aiofe was a wee one and as you can see, we've grown quite fond of one another." He paused, ostensibly expecting a comment, but I offered none. "It doesn't seem right that they are in danger over something a foolish kid did almost fifteen years ago. Up until recently, I could protect them, but this situation has changed. And that's why I want to talk to you."

"I'm here and I'm listening. Speak your mind."

"I want a deal."

"I'm not in a position to offer a deal to you, but I can broker the discussion and keep you safe."

His jaw tensed. He started to speak but caught himself before anything came out. "I don't want Aiofe growing up in the world that I did. Damn, I never thought I'd hear myself say those words." He laughed nervously, lightly sipping his drink. "Working for Tully was so easy. I'd rough a few people up, collect some money, and do it all over again. I knew there were people behind the scenes pulling Tully's strings but I had no idea how serious it was until Brian asked me to work security for a meeting."

"Brian O'Hegerty?"

"Aye. I didn't know who or what I had fallen in with until Paddy Bannion and a woman showed up. Brian told me she was Siobhan O'Connor. Not many people intimidate me, but she did; chills right to the bone, if you know what I mean."

I showed him a photograph. "One of these women, by chance?"

"Right there," he said, tapping on the picture. "That's her, no doubt about it." I looked at Charlie; his sad expression acknowledged what I was feeling inside. "They all treated her like she was the damn queen and with good reason. She could make or break you with a single word. You screwed up, you were dead; it was that simple. So I did my jobs and did them well."

"Then why do it? Why get involved with such people?"

"I was a stupid kid in too deep before I knew what I was into."

"So tell me about Maggie Albin."

"When Siobhan O'Connor called me that afternoon I was so nervous I think I threw up a dozen times. I'd never killed anyone before and, God's truth, I've never since." Fergus Clarke related the horrible details around the death of Maggie Albin, including specifics never released to the public. "I knew I'd messed up pretty badly. It didn't go how Siobhan wanted, so I figured that I was a dead man. Once I figured out what was in the notebook, I kept it as insurance. Tully had to cover-up the mess I made and her parents and that damned reporter wouldn't let it go. That was when I knew it was time to disappear. I changed my name, slipped into the Republic for a bit, then to Scotland but came back because I needed work. It kept things in balance until your man pinched the damn notebook. Now you've got all the cards."

I pressed him for more and he told what he could. His knowledge of Strabane was tangential and more around the aftermath. Similarly, his knowledge of the larger organization was limited. "What are you prepared to say in court?"

"That depends entirely on the deal that I get, but anything and everything you heard today is for sale, so to speak."

"I've taken the liberty to arrange a solicitor for you that can get you the best deal the Crown is willing to offer. There are a couple of men outside who can and will keep you safe until we have an arrangement. Is your family safe or do you need my help there, too?"

"They're in highlands of Scotland with some of her distant relatives. I don't expect they'll have any trouble."

"If you change your mind about that, we can help."

* * *

Our meeting had run into the wee hours of the morning, but that didn't stop me from making a necessary and sadly overdue call.

His voice sounded tired. "Finnegan here."

"Jim," I said, "Sorry to be calling so late."

"Costa, it is three in the morning, and I have court in a few hours. This had better be damned important."

"Life and death. I found the notebook and I'm working on an unexpected bonus. It's time to start talking deals."

I could hear him sit up, abruptly. "You have it?"

"My security team delivered it to Molloy a few days ago. I just met with the person that took it from Maggie."

"And was it as you expected?"

"Mostly. Molloy will reach out to you and the prosecution team in a day or two. If I'm not there in two days send the cavalry to Derry, but

I expect it won't do much good."

"What the hell are you up to, now?"

"I want it all and I think I've got a chance at it. If I've misread the situation, though, I'm a dead man. Molloy will have everything necessary to finish the case should that happen."

"Isn't it time you put those cast-iron balls of yours on the shelf and let us handle things?"

"Probably, but I'm not going to. See you in two days."

* * *

Brian O'Hegerty maintained an office in a small complex of buildings northwest of Derry. It reminded me more of the low-rent space Karen optimistically rented than the headquarters of a conglomerate holding company. I was trying one final gambit, and the possibility that I was seriously overreaching weighed heavily on me.

Under the watchful eye of several security cameras, I walked into the building. It was much the same on the inside as on the out — simple, functional, and understated. A disinterested receptionist with striking, but likely dyed, blonde hair regarded me.

"I'm here to see Mister O'Hegerty," I said, trying to sound confident. "He should be expecting me."

She looked at her screen, giving it the same blank stare I had received moments earlier. "I don't see anything on here."

"Tell him his cousin from Cork is here to see him. He'll see me."

A hushed phone conversation followed, her look of confusion remained unchanged. She put the phone down, continuing to stare first at me, then at her screen, then back again.

"It's alright, Molly," a voice said, "my cousin is paying me a surprise visit. Come on in, John."

Her look of understanding bore little difference from her look of confusion. I smiled at her before entering the office.

"I admit that I was surprised to see your face appear on my

cameras," he said, closing the door behind us and offering me a chair. "You are far more devious and resilient than I gave you credit for. After all the warnings I've sent, you still have the audacity to stroll in here, especially since it is unlikely that you'll be leaving here alive. Seems decidedly out of character and, dare I say, foolish."

"Actually, I'm giving *you* the opportunity to leave here alive. You should consider being a bit more gracious and welcoming to someone who is trying to save your life. You see," I said, pulling a file from my case and opening it slowly, "I've all the cards in our little game, my friend."

"A bullet through your thick skull might improve your understanding of the kind of card games *we* play."

"No, it wouldn't. It would end the game for us both. If I don't return there will be no chance for you to save your own skin. As I see it, we go two ways from here. I leave and the Police Service rolls in. You, Paddy, and everyone associated with this foul venture, right down to that confused little blonde you've got working the front desk, goes to prison forever. You'll probably not live to see trial, though. We all know how Siobhan deals with failure."

"Or?"

"We have a conversation and you decide from there where your loyalties should be."

He sat down, looking at me with a disconcerting air of confidence. "Go on."

"We have the notebook, we have Fergus, and he's singing like a thrush in a hawthorn bush even as we speak. We have the connections to Tully, the payments, the holding companies, all of it. We even have Declan Clarke, and he's talking. We even have the bloke that killed our investigator."

"If you've all that," he said, "why are we having this conversation instead of visit from the Police Service?"

"Because I want Siobhan O'Connor convicted and I need you to help me."

"Why on earth would you think that I would ever do something like that?"

"There is a chance your life has been built largely on false pretense. Do you know how your father died?"

His face betrayed his surprise at my words, curling into a confused frown. "Of course I do. He was killed in an accident where he worked. It was thoroughly investigated; I've read the reports."

"Sure you have. But I'm betting you've never read this." I handed him a document. "That is the unsolved case file about your father's murder. Yes, I *did* say murder. He worked for David A. Brennan and Connla O'Grady running some of their shipping interests. That's an important role if one of the things you are bringing in to the country is contraband; Semtex via Libya, in particular, comes to mind. Your father got a bit careless which led to several investigations. Connla and D.A. decided to cut their losses and arranged for your father to have a convenient accident. It was ruled as such because as you will see when you reach the fourth page of that report, Connla had another man with the scruples of Tully Smith on his payroll."

I allowed him to make the rest of his discovery in silence. When he had finished the report, he lowered it, quietly. "Why? Why are you telling me this?"

"I'm not sure. Something Fergus said gave the impression that maybe there was a shred of humanity left in you somewhere. Hell, maybe it was to offer you an opportunity for revenge. Tell me — why did you help Fergus?"

He rose, quietly opened a cabinet and poured two drinks, handing me one. "Eilidh is the only decent thing I've done in my life." He took a deep breath before speaking further. "She's my daughter. I was in Scotland for business, met a girl, one thing led to another and… you get the idea." He drank his first drink quickly, pouring himself a second without hesitation. "It was pure chance that she met Fergus! To his credit, he treated her wonderfully and little Aiofe like a princess. I helped him get a new identity and gave him a job, all of it behind Paddy and Siobhan's back. Unlike her, I can't arbitrarily sacrifice my family."

"I'm giving you the chance to save them. Lord knows, you don't deserve it, but they're blameless in all of this, and I'm not prepared to add any more innocent victims."

He stared out the window. "So what do you propose?"

"I'm going to Belfast to meet with the people that can offer deals. You come back with me, and you get a chance to make things right. If I leave this building alone, you better hope the Police Service gets here before Paddy or Siobhan figures out what's going on."

He poured a third and final drink, consuming it in one decisive motion. "You are truly a devious bastard, John Costa. You would have made a powerful ally for us had circumstances been different."

CHAPTER THIRTY-SIX

The weather in Belfast was unexpectedly pleasant, but we were able to enjoy only fleeting glimpses of it. Finnegan had arranged a safe location for us to meet, collect statements, arrange deals, and develop our strategy. The work was non-stop, our schedules routinely taking us into the early morning. The cycle would relentlessly resume after only a few hours of sleep.

Meanwhile, the trial pressed onward. Finally, as the prosecution's case roared to its conclusion, the physical evidence was introduced. Relentless and meticulous in his delivery, the prosecutor used the photograph as his final evidence. To his credit, his approach was masterful. The shreds of doubt left in the eye of the public faded. News articles proclaimed that conviction was merely a formality; one analyst even suggested that the defense should summarily rest in the interest of taxpayer saving and public safety. Throughout it all, Molloy was unflappable; his comments, unfailingly vague but optimistic, reminded everyone that they had only heard half of the story.

Even as it fell to the defense to present its case, we were still making the final arrangements for what was an ambitious, nearly theatrical, plan. Mercifully, Molloy was able to convince the judge to grant a two-day recess, citing the defendant's growing exhaustion. Finnegan confirmed that this was not merely a defense ploy.

"We're going to have a physician take a look at her, John. She's clearly not sleeping well, and I think she's losing weight."

"Do you think it would be possible for me to see her? Any uptick in her demeanor could be explained by the recess."

"It would ruin the illusion we've worked so hard to create. We've done our best to check the background of everyone involved in her situation; most if not all of them are people I've worked with for over twenty years. What I can't vouch for is everyone that might get a glimpse of you. We'd like to think there is no corruption in what amounts to our inner circle, but we can't ignore the possibility."

I sighed, resting my head in my hands. "You're right, Jim. That was my heart talking, not my brain. Will things be ready?"

"They will. The recess bought us the time we needed."

Morton Molloy, who had remained silent up until this point added, "I have several days of rebuttal witnesses that will help, too. Besides, it is in the long-term interests of my client to undo the damage done by the prosecution. Alice Sheehan was little more than a character assassin. The repeated message of radicalization needs to be answered, too. People will remember that, long after they've forgotten that she was acquitted. After that, it's the John Costa show. Don't screw up, buddy!"

Jim Finnegan slapped my shoulder, squeezing it confidently. "No worries about that."

I wished that I shared his confidence. "Where do we stand with the judge and the prosecutor?"

Our representative from the Prosecution Service joined the conversation. "The lead prosecutor knows that something is happening behind the scenes, but not the specific details. I've instructed him to give you full latitude. It is more than a bit irregular and he knows it, but he's a good soldier and will follow the directives given. When we get our signal from Solicitor Molloy, he will ask for a brief recess. I will facilitate a meeting with the judge at that point."

"He'll already have given his admonishment to the people on my witness list to be available," added Molloy, "and I've included everyone you requested on that list. Jim's men are keeping a close eye on all of them."

"What if the judge isn't receptive?" I asked, looking around the room.

"Then we go to plan B," said Finnegan without hesitation. "It isn't ideal, but it gets us mostly to the same place."

"It is the *mostly* part that bothers me," I said, running my hands through my hair. "Just thinking of the long-term safety of all involved."

"With an allied front from the Prosecution Service, the Police Service, and the Defense, it is hard to imagine that he will have issues," said Molloy. "We've done all we can here. Let's all get some rest."

* * *

Morton Molloy's defense opened vigorously, attacking the prosecution's case as largely circumstantial. Alice Sheehan's stinging indictments faded as defense character witnesses testified, all painting a favorable and consistent picture of Angela Grady. Cleverly, Molloy had arranged them chronologically so that Frank and Margery Albin were last. Their testimony was powerful, moving, and initiated another shift in public sentiment. Pundits were, once again, questioning the outcome of the case and debate resumed.

A short text from Jim Finnegan arrived shortly after lunch:

`Fiat justitia ruat caelum.`

Leave it to Jim Finnegan to offer one final dramatic moment delivered by text message! I smiled, walking for the first time onto the balcony of my hotel room. For over a week, I had lived in luxury but confined to the life of a hermit. According to Finnegan, it was a matter of safety and maintaining the illusion of my absence. Today, though, I could enjoy the cool air and crisp sunshine, albeit only briefly. I quickly returned inside to prepare for my court appearance.

A car, nondescript but undoubtedly armored, took us confidently through Belfast traffic. We passed through an armored gate and several checkpoints before arriving at our destination, the Musgrave Road police station. Several additional checkpoints awaited us before we proceeded deep into the building.

The elevator took special keys to operate and delivered us to a subterranean level where a tunnel, presumably to the courthouse, awaited. A small electric vehicle ferried us quickly to our destination. Another elevator ride, checkpoints, and a labyrinth of hallways and turns took me to a small room where Morton Molloy awaited.

"Shanagh just finished," he said, shaking my hand, "and we met with the judge. He used the word *unprecedented* more than once and frowned a lot but ultimately agreed with our plan."

"How did Shanagh do on the stand?"

"I kept her on the facts of the case for the most part. She has a tendency to drift into other areas. I'm sure the judge isn't interested in the stress and ailments all this is causing *her*."

"Do you think she was convincing?"

"She didn't hurt us if that's what you mean. Julia's going next, and then you're up."

Molloy disappeared quickly into the courtroom. It was over an hour before I was finally called. My anxiety worsened as I entered the courtroom. A short buzz spread throughout, commencing with the announcement of my name and swelled as I made my way to the witness stand. It meant nothing to me. My eyes met Angela's and, for that fleeting moment, it was like the first time I'd seen her walk through the office. She looked tired and her hair lacked its normal style and luster but her eyes had not changed. They sparkled with all the warmth and life that I remembered. My resolve returned.

Molloy opened with a series of short questions that served to establish my identity and my role as an independent investigator. My answers produced only passing interest from the audience. That would change quickly as we moved into our analysis of the physical evidence.

With a brilliantly orchestrated presentation from Mack, we attacked the photographic evidence. Our contention that lighting, focus, grain, distance, and angles made for weak facial recognition results seemed to be scoring points with the press. They diligently took notes as my testimony plodded slowly through the details. Hopefully, the judge would be equally impressed.

The nods and whispers became more intense as I moved into the second part of our analysis. With the help of several photographers and film experts, we had painstakingly recreated the original photograph. Professional models, each selected for their general resemblance to Angela, were photographed and the results analyzed with the same software as used by the Police Service lab.

The result of our re-enactment was the first of what I hoped would be many blockbusters. The models were within a few percentage points of Angela Grady's facial recognition score.

My next salvo was directed at the physical evidence. The initial testimony centered on the unlikely survival of the hat and the improbable fingerprint retrieved from it using modern technology. Repeatedly, I emphasized that the existence of the hat and the fingerprint did not necessarily link it with the car. My claim was strengthened by a simulation Mack created showing the most likely spot for fabric to survive a Semtex explosion was the engine compartment.

I directed my subsequent attack at the chain of custody.

"The only viable place where a hat such as this one could reasonably survive an explosion of the magnitude of the Strabane bomb," I said in response to one of Molloy's questions, "was in the engine compartment. Not a place where one normally stores a hat! And strangely, the hat didn't enter any evidence reports until three days after the explosion."

The lynch pin of our hypothesis, and subject of what would be the second blockbuster, was a constabulary policeman named J.A. Sinclair. The mere mention of an unfamiliar name sent the journalists' pens in motion. Mack had meticulously tied the discovery of the hat to him. More telling, however, was Sinclair's appearance on Tully Smith's journal as the recipient of payments corresponding to the happenings in Strabane.

Molloy peppered me with a series of short questions about Tully Smith, leading inevitably to the case of Maggie Albin and our theory linking her murder to the Strabane explosion. Citing the length of the impending testimony, Molloy moved for an evening recess. I returned to my hotel, exhausted but confident.

* * *

Restfulness, however, was not in the cards. My computer chirped, uncharacteristically, with a request for a video chat with Mack. She routinely eschewed the technology, claiming it was fundamentally insecure. Whatever was on her mind apparently didn't warrant her normal level of secrecy.

One look explained so much. Even with the occasionally choppy, distorted video, her puffy red eyes and disheveled look betrayed her. It took her several tries before a full sentence emerged.

"I've spent the last two days agonizing over whether to send this to you." Her words gave way to sobbing as she half-heartedly held a paper in front of the camera. Between her shaking and the resolution of the camera, I couldn't make anything of it. "I've finally decided to send it because I don't think I'd be able to live with myself otherwise."

My brow wrinkled, my left eyebrow lifting in response. "Mack, I trust you to do the right thing. If it is something I need to see, then I want you to send it and feel good about it."

"I'm not so sure about that," she blubbered, "but here goes."

It was probably for the best that the quality of our video was mediocre. I didn't want the color draining from my face to be too noticeable. I don't know how long I stared at my screen. It was only interrupted by a timid squeak from Mack.

"John," she said, her voice trembling.

The tone of her voice caused my focus to instantly return. "Sorry, Mack."

"You're still speaking to me, at least."

"Mack, you're my friend and I love you. Nothing will ever change that. Sleep well tonight, my friend; you did the right thing."

"Are you going to be okay?" she whispered.

"Yeah, Mack, I am."

"What are you going to do?"

"I'm not entirely sure."

* * *

I poured one glass of Irish whiskey before sending the bottle's remaining elixir down the drain. The air on the balcony was crisp, the breeze swirling enough to make its direction unknown. The warmth the whiskey produced chased away any thoughts of needing a jacket. I took the final sip from the glass and peered over the railing. The ground, many stories down, was peaceful, quiet, and inviting. Staring resolutely into space, I made one final call on my cell phone.

CHAPTER THIRTY-SEVEN

It was all I could do to summon the energy or motivation to take the stand. Angela's eyes searched my face, then the courtroom. She found solace in neither, her expression growing more concerned and confused by the minute.

Molloy noticed immediately that something was wrong, but I motioned for him to continue. I needed to finish. I *had* to. My voice dropped to a quiet monotone as I responded to questions about Tully Smith.

My testimony traveled far-afield, spinning through the sordid details of Tully Smith's blatant corruption. Most of the court, including the judge, was mesmerized but I knew that my window of opportunity was closing quickly. I needed to show the relevance of my testimony and the complex interconnection of the events.

I was afforded a much needed break as Fergus Clarke was called to deliver the day's first earth-shaking evidence. His agreement, one that I found unexpectedly generous, was predicated by full disclosure as a witness. He did not disappoint.

His story meticulously stepped through his early days as hired muscle working for Tully Smith up to when his cousin, Declan, ensnared him in Siobhan O'Connor's world. It inevitably led to the gruesome details of Maggie Albin's murder.

"Siobhan called me around four with a job that needed to be done right away," Fergus testified. "If you work for Siobhan, you get things done and done right, or you're dead. So I did what I had to do. I waited for her to leave her house and followed her. When we got out into the countryside a bit, I overtook her and got well ahead. I made it look like I was having car problems and she pulled over to help me."

Fergus paused to collect himself. Frank and Margery looked on, stoically.

"It was the first and only time I've ever killed anyone, and it didn't go very well. She put up more of a fight than I expected. I had to rough her up pretty good to get the alcohol in her. I rigged the crash to cover it up, but even that didn't work out. Tully had to step in and make sure things looked like an accident. It was all sloppy as hell, but I had an insurance policy: Maggie's notebook. It tied the whole mess back to Siobhan O'Connor."

Molloy asked the question that surely hung on the lips of everyone in the utterly silent courtroom:

"Mister Clarke, is Angela Grady, the defendant on trial, the woman you know to be Siobhan O'Connor?"

"There is a strong resemblance, but it is not her."

A smile crossed Angela's lips as the courtroom was again rife with whispers, enough so that the judge had to restore order. I had to summon one final measure of resolve to complete my testimony. The last full page of Maggie's notebook appeared on the monitors throughout the courtroom.

```
    3:07pm: Sorting receipts and categorised.
    3:28pm: Found fuel receipt!!! Proves Angie
was here at 7:30!!!
    3:30pm: Rang Angie. No Answer.
    3:35pm: Rang Angie. No Answer.
    3:40pm: Rang Angie. No Answer.
    3:45pm: Rang Angie. Spoke to her mum. Mrs.
Grady advised that I take it to the Strabane
Constabulary station as they are handling the
local portion of the investigation. She told
me not to leave until my parents get home so
they won't worry about me.
```

A receipt, signed by delivery driver Michael Kinney and Angela Grady appeared next to the diary page. The meaning of the page slowly dawned; it revealed Angela's innocence and the true identity of Siobhan O'Connor: Shanagh Grady.

My voice struggled to exceed a whisper as my testimony neared its end. "After court yesterday, Shanagh Grady was taken into custody without incident. Her arrest was part of a coordinated police operation here, in the Republic, and in North America. Many key members of what we believe to be the organization behind the Strabane explosion and several other events during The Troubles were arrested. With the court's indulgence, I would like to describe what really happened that morning in Strabane."

The judge nodded silently, motioning with his hand for me to continue.

"The target of the bomb was a bright young Constabulary officer named Gregory Finnegan. He was in County Tyrone to investigate political corruption when he turned up evidence of a larger organization, ostensibly republican, powerful, and violent, operating behind the scenes. We will likely never know the extent of his knowledge, but it was enough to get him killed and enough to make the lives of over thirty innocent people expendable in the eyes of the group's leader, Siobhan O'Connor; Or as we know her, Shanagh Grady."

I paused, glancing at Jim Finnegan. He appeared lost in thought, but content.

"Unthinkably, the plan was to place the blame on her daughter. Angela was an easy target. Collecting something with her fingerprints was easy. Angela's anger from the explosion that injured her as a teen, all conveniently written down, provided ready-made motive. They even had Fergus Clarke ready to testify that Angela was Siobhan. It was a devious and brilliant frame. It failed thanks to a malfunctioning petrol gauge and a fortuitous alibi."

I paused, taking a drink of water, clearing my throat. My voice had weakened to the point where the microphone struggled to pick it up without feedback.

"Then poor Maggie discovered the receipt. Angela signed in haste the morning she left and simply forgot about it. Maggie knew she held the evidence that would end her best friend's nightmare. Unfortunately, she told Shanagh, someone she thought she could trust. That left Shanagh no recourse but to have Maggie killed in order for the real events of the day of the bombing to remain hazy."

"However, the haze has parted and we know what happened. Shanagh, wearing a blonde wig, drove to Strabane using Alice Sheehan's car. She set the bomb and left. A few people caught glimpses of her and they remembered the distinct, blonde hair; exactly the result she intended. The policemen, all but Gregory Finnegan on Tully Smith's payroll, quickly propagated the 'blonde woman' story. Mary Delane's sketch, created from her memories of Shanagh wearing the blonde wig, completed the frame."

"The proof comes in three parts. My assistant repeated this process with a 1998 picture of Shanagh Grady. It produced a match with 85% confidence, easily the best match achieved. Additionally, the police have sworn statements from a high-ranking member of her organization verifying our theory. Lastly, I was attacked and injured while investigating this case. The police were watching me and captured the men responsible for the attack. Shortly beforehand, Alice Sheehan called Shanagh Grady who, in turn, dispatched her thugs from what she incorrectly assumed was a secure, untraceable cell phone. The appropriate authorities have the evidence we collected throughout the investigation and will act on it accordingly. A future trial will decide Shanagh's fate. Today's decision, though, is not in doubt. Angela Grady is innocent of the charges brought against her."

I slumped, resting my head in my hands. I drew a deep breath and nodded weakly at the judge. He said nothing as he turned to the prosecutor, raising his eyebrows expectantly.

The prosecutor rose slowly and withdrew all charges against Angela Grady. The judge, without hesitation, announced Angela's freedom. She smiled faintly as a police officer freed her from the dock.

* * *

The courtroom was a flurry of activity, and we were hustled to a waiting car that took us to my hotel room. Angela's first interest when arriving at our room was a shower. I sat quietly, completely ignoring the appetizers and Champagne that the hotel had provided.

She emerged sometime later, fussing with her hair and examining the food. Eventually, her eyes found me. Her expression changed immediately.

"Get dressed," I grunted.

"I only have what I was wearing in court," she protested. "Besides, I'm interested in doing things that don't involve clothing."

The smile on her face faded abruptly as I jumped out of my seat and moved away from her.

"What on earth is wrong with you?"

"Get dressed, then we'll talk."

She shrugged, returning a few moments later wearing the outfit she had worn in court. "Okay, I'm dressed. Now — tell me what on earth is going on?"

"The constabulary had three files on you prior to 1997. Two of them were related to the explosion in which you were injured. The third involved a trip where your mother dropped you at a store and picked you up some twenty-odd minutes later."

Her brow wrinkled. "I don't understand."

"About an hour later, an explosion destroyed some Constabulary vehicles and killed an innocent bystander. Now do you remember?"

"I think so. My mother needed me to pick something up from one of the stores, so I did. John — you're scaring me. What exactly are you saying?"

"What store did you go to, and what did you get for your mother?"

"It was a fabric store, I think. She had an order waiting. I picked it up while she ran an errand and waited for her."

"Are you sure about that?"

"What are you hinting at? After all this time, I would think that you would believe me. I love you, John. That is all that matters."

"The only thing you love is what looks back at you from the mirror."

Tears welled in her eyes. "How can you say that? I thought you loved me, Johnny."

"I loved who I thought you were, or maybe it was that I loved who I hoped you could be. But that is only an illusion, isn't it? Care to try again at answering the question?"

She hesitated, almost imperceptibly, and with it my heart shattered. "It was Wyatt's Fabrics."

I closed my eyes, shaking my head sadly. "No, Angela, it wasn't. The file was from 1996; Wyatt's didn't open until late 1997. You went to a wig shop; you picked up the wig your mother wore in Strabane. The wig you modeled for under the pretense of upcoming chemotherapy. We have all the receipts, your signature, and even the pictures they took of you to create the wig.

She exhaled heavily, casting her eyes downward. I continued before she could comment.

"The shenanigans you and your mother pulled almost got me killed. What is worse, though, is that you hurt Mack."

"You have to believe me," she cried, "that I had nothing to do with either. That was my mother's doing."

"I don't know what disgusts me more: You, your mother, or the fleeting thought that had you been even remotely honest with me, I could have somehow excused your actions."

Her voice grew quiet, becoming almost inaudible. "Isn't there anything I can say or do to earn your forgiveness?" She forced a warm smile as she moved toward me. "I was wrong to not tell you, and I'm deeply sorry. Can we somehow put this behind us and see where the universe takes us? Please? It will be grand, I promise!"

"You picked the wrong lovesick fool, Miss Grady, if you think your guiles, lovely as they are, can make me forget who and what you really are. I don't know where the universe is going to take me, but I've got a pretty good idea of what awaits you."

She stared at me, dumbfounded. I opened the door, inviting Jim Finnegan and three other Police Service officers into our room. Quietly and without pomp, he arrested Angela Grady on a fresh collection of charges. He looked somber, but I noticed the briefest glint of a smile as he cuffed her hands behind her back.

"For what it's worth," she said to me as they led her out, "I never lied about loving you. I still do and I always will."

What it was worth was nothing. My only reply was to turn away. There I stayed, staring blankly into space before sinking to my knees and sobbing uncontrollably.

CHAPTER THIRTY-EIGHT

I returned to our table with two fresh pints of Guinness. "Thank you, Jim," I said, handing him a glass, "for believing in me and saving me from a world of suffering. And I'll say it: you were right."

He smiled faintly, drawing his fingers across his beard. "Her big mistake was underestimating you. She assumed that you were so blinded that you would ignore the connection or that she could explain it away. I knew better, or at least I hoped as much."

His phone rang, calling him away before I could reply. He returned after a brief, hushed conversation. "Perhaps you had more influence on her than you thought." I raised my left eyebrow and sipped on my Guinness, quietly. "Angela Grady is talking to us, telling us what she knows. She signed a confession this morning. It isn't as sweeping as we'd hoped, but it's better than nothing. She seems contrite, but with her it could easily be an act. In my opinion, her regrets seem limited to Maggie's death and losing you. She asks about you every time I see her."

Perhaps a few droplets of the poison that lurked in the core of the beautiful apple that was Angela Grady had kissed my lips; perhaps it was my grandmother O'Brien's endless lectures about forgiveness on the way home from mass. Whatever it was, I found my response unexpected but oddly cathartic. "Tell her I'm well, and that I hope, somehow, she finds some peace."

"That was not what I expected to hear."

"Silence is the harshest form of rejection. She's finally admitted her transgressions and will pay dearly for them. I've said my piece; nothing is gained if I scourge her further."

He nodded, drinking deeply from his glass. "I'll pass that along. You're far kinder than I would be were the situation reversed, I think."

"Funny," I said, staring off into space, "Had she admitted to the wig purchase from the beginning I could have explained it away, found a way to get it excluded. She could have walked away with a slap on the wrist, if not complete exoneration as an unfortunate victim. What bothers me is that I *would* have done that and probably patted myself on the back for my cleverness."

"I doubt that," he said, returning his pint glass to the table. "You've grown much too fond of being the honest, principled man you really are."

"Don't say that too loudly, Jim, I've got a reputation to maintain."

"I promise," he chuckled, "to keep it to myself — and anyone and everyone who asks me about Johnny Costa." He motioned for two more pints. "What are you going to do with yourself, now?"

"Well," I sighed, "I have a few loose ends to wrap up and a small project that Mack suggested to me. After that, I might just roam for a while."

"You know, we still don't know much about all of the things Connla O'Grady and subsequently Shanagh had their fingers in. I can't promise that you'll be safe wandering around the countryside."

"Tomorrow isn't a promise that is ours to make, my friend. I don't know exactly what Shanagh's plans were, but my suspicions are that the peace process wasn't something her ilk liked. If I skulk off with my tail between my legs, it goes against fifteen years of progress. I look around Belfast and I see the results; businesses locating here, construction, flourishing commerce, and tourists. Things aren't perfect, of course, but it's grand to see this lovely old city finally getting rediscovered."

"Well, if you ever decide that you've had enough roaming, there's a job waiting for you as an independent consultant to the Police Service

350

— wee Jillian, too. I know you don't need the money, but you might find the challenge of tracking down Shanagh's compatriots exhilarating. No need to answer now, but think it over, will you?"

I smiled, nodding.

"And if your travels happen to take you near Galway, here is someone you should look up when you're there." He handed me his card, but on the back was written a name, phone number, and address.

"Who is Shannon McLeod?"

"She's my cousin and I've told her all about you. In spite of that, she's still eager to meet you; unless, of course, you're not interested in meeting a fine Irish lady…"

* * *

I arose early, shortly after sunrise. Frank and Margery Albin were already awake and preparing breakfast. I protested that they needn't have gone to the trouble, but my words fell on deaf ears.

"It is the least we can do," said Margery, piling food onto my plate. "Knowing you, it is entirely possibly you'll get busy with something and forget to eat."

I rolled my eyes in tacit acknowledgment.

"We both don't know quite what to say," she said, abruptly changing subjects. "We're terribly nervous about the prospect of speaking in public, though."

"Well, you've got a few months to prepare. I'm sure Mack can help find you a coach if you're really worried about it. But if you want my advice, when the time comes, speak from your heart. The right words will be there."

"We appreciate the memorial to Maggie," added Frank, "but the perpetual scholarship you've established in her name is something I know she would appreciate. She was always so eager to help others."

"It was Mack's idea, and I've learned not to argue with her when she sets her mind to something. Especially when she's right, which seems like bloody always!"

"They have that way about them," he said, coyly glancing at Margery. "How is poor Karen getting along? We're struggling with our own doubts and confusion; hard to imagine what she's going through."

"She's having a rough time of it, as can be expected. We talk occasionally and Mack has been spending a lot of time with her. They've gotten to be pretty good friends from all accounts."

Frank shook my hand as we walked to my car. "I don't know where you're headed, but you're welcome here any time. Safe travels to you." He cast me a knowing look. "I hear Galway is quite lovely this time of the year," he said, turning toward his house.

* * *

Jim said I would know quickly if Shannon McLeod was home, and I did. Traditional tunes, played skillfully on a flute, greeted me as I neared her front door. I hesitated before knocking, waiting for a natural pause in the music.

A warm smile crossed her face as she opened the door.

"Mister Costa," she said, twirling a lock of hair with her left hand as she shook my right hand. "Jim said you might be visiting the area. Would you like to come in for some tea?"

"That would be nice," I said, completely lost in her blue eyes. "I heard you playing as I walked to your door. Lovely music — I felt bad interrupting."

"Oh, no bother! Perhaps after tea we can play a few tunes together if you're feeling up to it. Jim tells me that you're a musician."

"Among other things," I said, oblivious to my surroundings.

"Perfect!" she said, pouring my tea. "Galway is a lovely city; lots of music and fine culture. I'd be delighted to show it to you if you're going to be in the area."

"That sounds fun," I said, trying not to sound too eager, "but I don't want to be an inconvenience, especially after showing up unannounced."

"No worries! We'll have a grand time!" She looked at me, intently studying my face, "Jim's told me a fair bit about you. Maybe that's why you seem so familiar to me, but somehow I feel like I've known you for a long time... Oh listen to me! Would you like to play some tunes?"

"Certainly," I said as she handed me an aging violin. A few notes confirmed that time had only served to sweeten its tune.

"What do you want to play?"

"Anything, really. It will be good just to play again. Surprise me."

She picked up her flute and smiled knowingly at me before starting. The tune was her namesake and my favorite: Miss McLeod's reel.

Dammit. I love surprises!